THE TROUBLE WITH HUGUENOTS

Virginia DeMarce

Cover designed by Laura Givens

Printed in the United States of America

First Printing: Dec 2019
1623, Inc. and Eric Flint's Ring of Fire Press

ebook ISBN-13 978-1-948818-62-9
Trade Paperback ISBN-13 978-1-948818-63-6

Dedication

To my brother,

Alan Edward Easley,

who writes books and stories that are much funnier than mine.

Acknowledgments

The major acknowledgment, of course, is to Eric Flint for writing *1632*, which spawned this fictional universe, and for inviting me to be a part of it.

I gathered suggestions from participants in the 1632 Tech forum on Baen's Bar in regard to choreographing the hand-to-hand combat scene. Thanks go to those who responded for even the suggestions I could not use and specifically to Thomas Scott for adopted suggestions regarding chain mail underwear and triangular stilettos.

I am grateful to all the historians and researchers who spend time in early modern European archives and publish their results.

Many thanks to Walt Boyes, the editor in chief of the Ring of Fire Press, for struggling with my manuscripts, and to Gorg Huff for turning them into something that is e-book friendly.

CONTENTS

FOREWORD

The purpose of this foreword is to provide a little orientation for readers of the series as to how this book fits into the timeline.

The beginning of the story derives from the decision made by Henri, duc de Rohan, in Eric Flint and Virginia DeMarce, *1635: The Dreeson Incident* (Baen: 2008) to send his younger brother, Benjamin duc de Soubise, to England to deal with Michel Ducos and his cadre of fanatical Huguenot assassins.

In the ten-plus years since that book came out, Eric developed another idea he wanted to use for dealing with Ducos and his people in the British Isles, which left the authorial team with the literary challenge of extricating Soubise from England in a plausible manner, so as to prevent his presence from interfering in the . . . well . . . what Eric is going to write about it. Tum-te-tum-tum, snerk collar, and all that.

That challenge led to my writing *The Red Headed League*, which came out in the *Ring of Fire IV* anthology (Baen: 2016), portions of which have been incorporated into *The Trouble with Huguenots* by gracious permission of Baen editor Toni Weisskopf. That reworked material makes up about a third of *The Trouble with Huguenots*. Another part has been adapted from the story "Les Futuriens," which ran in the *Grantville Gazette*, Numbers 65 (May 2016) and 66 (June 2016). The sections of those publications not included in the book have not been thereby excluded from the 1632-verse canon; they just weren't pertinent to this narrative. Approximately half of the material in the book is new.

* * *

The Trouble with Huguenots runs chronologically parallel to *The Legions of Pestilence* (Ring of Fire Press: 2019). It involves a number of the same characters and locations, especially Besançon, the capital chosen for his new country by Bernhard of Saxe-Weimar, Grand Duke of the Free County of Burgundy. However, aside from the high politics that float along in the background of both books, there is little duplication of events. Every major player on the European stage was trying to keep several balls in the air and a wary eye on several more which were, for the time being, lying placidly in a groove, but any one of which might suddenly spring into the midst of the active ones.

For example, Henri de Ruvigny and his friend August von Bismarck play significant roles in the first half of this book. Then they disappear for much of the second half, because they are employees of Grand Duke Bernhard and in *The Legions of Pestilence* he pulls them back from being on loan to Henri de Rohan and sends them off to do two other sets of errands for himself.

Please do not be distressed, dear reader. It will all make sense in the end.

CAST LIST

This is alphabetized according to the name by which the character is most often called in the stories; e.g. "Bernhard" rather than "Burgundy, Bernhard, Grand Duke of the Free County of." The cast list does not include minor characters, whether up-timers or down-timers, whose brief cameo appearances are self-explanatory.

For some important people who are mentioned but who don't appear in person in the book, see the second list at the end.

Allegretti, Susanna (fi d-t), court seamstress, fiancée of Marc Cavriani

Amalie Elisabeth [nee countess of Hanau-Münzenberg], landgravine-regent of Hesse-Kassel (hi d-t), Calvinist; regent for her son after the death of Landgrave Wilhelm V in November 1635; Crown Loyalist USE political leader; children Wilhelm, Charlotte, Philipp, and Karl mentioned (she has others)

Anne, Mademoiselle.   See: Rohan, Anne de.

Bell, Dominique (fi u-t), lady-in-waiting for Marguerite Rohan; daughter of Carey Calagna

Benserade, Isaac de (hi d-t), event planner and choreographer in Paris

Bernhard, Grand Duke of the Free County of Burgundy (hi d-t), formerly Bernhard, duke of Saxe-Weimar; brother of

Virginia DeMarce

Wilhelm Wettin, Albrecht, and Ernst; husband of Claudia de' Medici

Béthune-Sully, Marguerite de, *duchesse de* Rohan (hi d-t), daughter of Maximilien *duc de* Sully; wife of Henri *duc de* Rohan, currently mistress of the *comte de* Candale

Bismarck, August von (hi d-t), military officer, captain in the service of Grand Duke Bernhard

Burgundy, Grand Duke of.   See Bernhard.

Calagna, Carey (fi u-t), employed by Grand Duke Bernhard; former clerk of the Probate Court in Grantville, friend of Kamala Dunn; divorced from Norman Bell; children Dominique, Ashlyn, and Joe

Candale, Henri de Nogaret de la Valette *comte de* (hi d-t), current and former lover of Marguerite de Béthune-Sully *duchesse de* Rohan

Cavriani, Alis [nee t'ser Haag] (fi d-t), Calvinist, widow of Leopold Cavriani's younger brother, manager of a branch of Cavriani Frères, bankers, formerly in Rotterdam, now Brussels

Cavriani, Idelette (fi d-t), daughter of Leopold Cavriani, business student in Grantville

Cavriani, Leopold (fi d-t), Calvinist from Geneva; general free-lance fixer

Cavriani, Marc (fi d-t), son of Leopold Cavriani, fixer-in-training

Cavriani, Potentiana [nee Turettini] (fi d-t), Italian Calvinist in Geneva, wife of Leopold Cavriani; mother of Marc Cavriani

Chabot, Henri, seigneur de Saint-Aulaye (hi d-t), minor French nobleman who, in the original timeline, became the husband of Marguerite de Rohan

Cinq-Mars, Henri Coiffier marquis de (hi d-t), very young nobleman and intriguer at the French court

Claudia de' Medici (hi d-t), widow of Leopold von Habsburg, count of Tyrol; regent of Tyrol for her sons; wife of Bernhard, Grand Duke of Burgundy

Dunn, Kamala (fi u-t), employed by Grand Duke Bernhard; nurse prominent in Burgundy's plague-fighting efforts; widow of Johnny Lee Horton; children Shae and Shaun

4

Durand, Thierry (fi d-t), miller in a village near Villebon, France; wife Babette; adult sons, Jean, Renaud, Claude, Pierre and Paul; adult daughter Madeleine

Gage, Henry (hi d-t), English Catholic exile, free-lancing as soldier and diplomat on the continent, currently employed by Bernhard

Gardiner, Lion (hi d-t), English Puritan exile, free-lancing as soldier and diplomat on the continent, currently employed by Bernhard

Hamilton, James (hi d-t), Calvinist; young Scotch-Irish nobleman, heir of Lord Clanboye

Hanau-Münzenberg, Philipp Moritz, count of (hi d-t), Calvinist; oldest brother of Amalie Elisabeth and Katharina Juliana

Hesse-Kassel, Wilhelm V, landgrave of (hi d-t), German territorial ruler, kia November 1635

Horton, Shae (fi u-t), lady-in-waiting to Marguerite de Rohan; daughter of Kamala Dunn

Johnson, Gladys [nee O'Donnell] (fi u-t), Grantville, owner of a part-Siamese cat; died in 1635 at the age of 95

Jones, Marsha (fi u-t), granddaughter of a deceased Siamese cat owner, Grantville; teenaged daughter Miranda

Katharina Juliana [nee countess of Hanau-Münzenberg] (hi d-t), Calvinist; younger sister of Amalie Elisabeth; wife of Count Albert Otto II of Solms-Laubach; "Käthe"

Lambert, Gary (fi u-t), manager of the Leahy Medical Center, Grantville

Le Bon, Tancrède (hi d-t), illegitimate son of Marguerite de Béthune-Sully who is the wife of Henri de Rohan

Lemercier, Denis (fi d-t); young member of the immense extended family of builders and stonemasons related to Jacques Lemercier (hi d-t), the architect of the Palais-Cardinal

Lund, Lisa (fi u-t), employed in mechanical support by Grand Duke Bernhard; married to Thomas Wedekind (fi d-t)

Mirepoix, Alexandre de Lévis *marquis de* (hi d-t), widower of Sully's younger daughter Louise

O'Neill, Con Oge [aka Constantine] (hi d-t), Irish nobleman, reared in England as hostage; officer in service to Fredrik Hendrik in the Netherlands

O'Neill, Daniel (hi d-t), Irish nobleman, reared in England as hostage; officer in service to Fredrik Hendrik in the Netherlands

Orval, François de Béthune *duc d'* (hi d-t), son of Sully by his second marriage, full brother of Marguerite *duchesse* de Rohan

Partow, Gordon (fi u-t), Grantville Presbyterian studying for the ministry in Geneva

Patton, Hazel (fi u-t), elderly Siamese cat breeder, Grantville

Raudegen [assumed military alias; he was born as Josef Kempinger] (fi d-t), colonel in the army of Grand Duke Bernhard

Rohan, Anne de (hi d-t), sister of Henri *duc de* Rohan and Benjamin *duc de* Soubise; intransigent Huguenot and avid matchmaker; "Mademoiselle Anne"

Rohan, Henri *duc de* (hi d-t), leader of the French Huguenots; brother of Soubise

Rohan, Marguerite *duchesse de*. See Béthune-Sully

Rohan, Marguerite de (hi d-t), only surviving child and heiress of Henri de Rohan

Rosny, Maximilien II de Béthune, marquis de (hi d-t), only surviving son of Sully by his first marriage, half-brother of Marguerite *duchesse de* Rohan

Ruvigny, Henri de Massué *seigneur de* (hi d-t), military officer and burgeoning diplomat in the service of Grand Duke Bernhard

Sandrart, Joachim (hi d-t), artist from Frankfurt am Main, occasional employee of the Rohan family

Solms-Laubach, Albert Otto II, count of (hi d-t), husband of Katharina Juliana von Hanau-Münzenberg

Soubise, Benjamin de Rohan *duc de* (hi d-t), brother of Henri, duc de Rohan

Stone, Gerry (fi u-t), son of Tom, brother of Ron of the Lothlorien Pharmaceuticals company, would-be Lutheran pastor constantly diverted from his studies by family business

Sully, Maximilian I de Béthune, *duc de* (hi d-t); Calvinist, former first minister of France under King Henri IV; married to Rachel de Cochefilet; father-in-law of Henri duc de Rohan

Traill, James (hi d-t), Presbyterian clergyman; tutor to James Hamilton

THE TROUBLE WITH HUGUENOTS

Offstage characters with significant mentions, for fast reference

Christian IV (hi d-t), king of Denmark, subordinate to Gustavus II Adolphus in the revived Union of Kalmar; father of (among many others) Ulrik, Anne Cathrine, Sophia, Leonora Christina, and Waldemar

Cork, Richard Boyle, 1st earl of (hi d-t), Anglo-Irish nobleman exercising predominant influence over King Charles I of England

Fernando, Infante of Spain (hi d-t), "Don Fernando," now Fernando I, king in the Low Countries, formerly the Cardinal Infante; brother of King Philip IV of Spain

Gaston duc d'Orleans (hi d-t), Bourbon; "Monsieur Gaston," brother of King Louis XIII of France; after May 1636, self-proclaimed king of France; married to Marguerite de Lorraine, his second wife

Gustavus II Adolphus [Vasa] (hi d-t), emperor of the USE, king of Sweden, high king of the Union of Kalmar

Henri IV [Henry of Navarre] (hi d-t), Calvinist who converted to Catholicism on the grounds that "Paris is worth a mass;" deceased king of France who issued the Edict of Nantes granting toleration to the Huguenots; father of Louis XIII and Gaston

Hesse-Kassel, Wilhelm V landgrave of (hi d-t), husband of Amelie Elizabeth, kia November 1635 leaving children Wilhelm, Charlotte, Philipp, Karl, and several others

Louis XIII, king of France (hi d-t), Bourbon, assassinated May 1636

Richelieu, Armand, Cardinal (hi d-t); owner of Siamese cat from Grantville; attacked and purportedly assassinated May 1636

Stearns, Michael (fi u-t), overall hero of the 1632 series

Stone, Ron (fi u-t), older brother of Gerry Stone; pharmaceuticals executive; friendly with Rohan

Tremblay, Cardinal [aka Pere Joseph] (hi d-t), last heard of as imprisoned and beaten near to death by thugs of Marie de' Medici, August 1636

Turenne, Henri de la Tour d'Auvergne vicomte de –(hi d-t), Huguenot; French general under Louis XIII and Gaston

Urban VIII (hi d-t), pope, birth name Maffeo Barberini, assassinated May 1636

SECTION I

June 1635-January 1636
Roi ne puis, prince ne daigne, Rohan suis[1]

---

[1]There have been many tries at making snappy English translations of this motto of the Rohan family, none of them very successful, partly because of the disparate meanings of the word 'prince' in French and English and partly because the English word 'deign' is obsolete but has no other one-syllable equivalent. The meaning, if not the pithiness, is conveyed by: I can't be king; I don't condescend to be a feudal subordinate; I am Rohan.

Virginia DeMarce

PROLOGUE

Grantville
June 1635

"All Huguenots are Calvinists, but that does not signify that all Calvinists are Huguenots. For which we may sincerely thank the Lord our God."

Gary Lambert raised his eyebrows at Leopold Cavriani. "The duke of Rohan is a Huguenot, though. Do I have that right?"

"Not only a Huguenot, but the titular leader, certainly the most important lay figure, of that party in France."

"Then why is he working for Bernhard of Saxe-Weimar, who is Lutheran? I saw him when I went to Besançon in February for the installation of Bernhard as Grand Duke of the County of Burgundy. For that matter, if he's that important a nobleman, why is he working for anybody? Why isn't he rich?"

"He's in exile and has been for years. He and his brother. Soubise is a secondary title that the brother uses; he's a Rohan also. They simply led more rebellions than the French crown was ultimately willing to tolerate. Exile doesn't mean that he no longer feels that it's his responsibility to deal with fanatical criminals like Ducos and his men, given that they proclaim themselves to be representatives of the Huguenot cause."

Gary picked up his beer. "They're equal opportunity assassins, at least. First trying to off the pope last year, now gossip that they were behind the attack on Henry Dreeson and Enoch Wiley in March. Two of their own. Two Presbyterians. Calvinists. Enoch a preacher. That's what I don't understand. If they're all Calvinists . . ."

"Huguenots excel at internecine conflict." Leopold slowly turned his wine glass around and around, watching the trail of light that reflected through the fluted stem onto the varnished table top at Tyler's Family Restaurant. "Rohan regards Bernhard as a friend, I believe, as well as an employer. There was talk of a possible marriage between Bernhard and Rohan's heiress, but it didn't come to anything, and then the Grand Duke married Claudia de' Medici a couple of months ago, so that possibility is off the board."

CHAPTER 1

Besançon
July 1635

"**M**ay I remind you that I was *already* in England." Benjamin de Soubise sat down on a high stool that was usually used by one of Henri de Rohan's clerks. "You're the one who sent me a rather peremptory summons to come to Frankfurt am Main to deal with Ducos' men. Now you've hauled me here and say you want me to go *back* to England. I'm not as young as I used to be."

"You're young enough," his brother said. "Moreover, in spite of your allegedly advanced age, you keep yourself in good condition. I have intelligence that Ducos and his followers will be moving to England next. Not great intelligence, but better than nothing."

"It's not just Ducos, you know."

"I can keep an eye on the rest of it from here. Two eyes. One on the Netherlands. One on the USE. I don't have a third eye that I can focus on England."

"What do you want me to do with Sandrart? He was useful in Frankfurt."

"Keep him on retainer; a modest retainer, nothing extravagant. Otherwise dismiss him to go do his artistic things. He was useful in Frankfurt am Main, since he has family connections there. That won't be the case elsewhere. If he should overhear anything important in the households where he receives his commissions, I'll be glad to have the information and will see to it that he's recompensed. Right now, though, I don't see any real reason to keep him on my staff. Nor on yours. The great noble houses of England are in Van Dyke mode; staged poses and yards of satin draperies all over the place. Sandrart wouldn't be popular there if you took him along; his canvases aren't in that mode at all. So having him with you would not help us gain entry at the level where you would need it to monitor King Charles' unsteady policies and Cork's machinations, either."

Laubach, County of Solms-Laubach August 1635

Countess Katharina Juliana—Käthe to her own family—once upon a time she had been their "little Katie"—sucked on the top of her new pen. It had been a bit of an adjustment to learn to use it, since she had grown up with quills, but made the whole process of writing much less messy. With a reasonable amount of practice, not excessive, the calligraphy that resulted was as attractive. Not to mention that she could rub her tongue over it when in doubt, rather than chewing on her fingernails.

Amalie Elisabeth had sent it as a gift when Elisabeth Albertine—they called her Berta—was born in March.

A nice and thoughtful gift.

Amalie Elisabeth was a good sister. A somewhat overwhelming personality, perhaps, but a good sister. Who had produced another living, apparently healthy, son.

Young Wilhelm had come as such a relief to the family, after her sister's ten years of marriage and the early deaths of the first four children she had borne. Then Philipp for a spare the next year; and Adolf for good measure the year after that. A fourth was almost too much of a good thing, not to mention the three now-living girls. As her brother-in-law knew, a mass of younger siblings got expensive for a territorial ruler with limited resources. If Amalie Elisabeth didn't stop this reproductive surge soon . . . No, children were divine blessings. The Bible said so.

If she examined her conscience, she would have to admit that she had trouble working up much interest in the three she had produced. Not that she wasn't grateful for them and for the Lord's mercy in permitting her to fulfil her duty to Albert Otto, but they were so messy. There was nothing to be done about diapers and drool. No equivalent to replacing a quill with a pretty glass pen.

Well, there were wet nurses and nursemaids, thanks be to God!

Congratulations were in order, along with a nice christening present.

In Magdeburg, Amalie Elisabeth had easy access to all the new technology. It would not have been a challenge for her to send a servant to buy a modern pen to celebrate the birth of a niece.

What on earth was there in beyond-the-backwoods Laubach, on the far southwestern border of Hesse, that would stand out among the dozens of gifts that little Karl would be receiving?

Virginia DeMarce

CHAPTER 2

Besançon
September 1635

"**I** can read an encyclopedia as well as anyone else." Henri, *duc de Rohan,* continued to pace around the room. "In less than three years, I will be dead."

"You were killed in a battle we fought at Rheinfelden," Grand Duke Bernhard countered. "which is an encounter I see no need to fight in this world. You're pushing paper rather than commanding cavalry. How old are you? Fifty-five or so? You could live another thirty years."

"Fifty-seven. I could be thrown off my horse while I'm going up to the Citadelle on routine business and be dead next month. The Word of God admonishes that we should not seek to know our times. However, I have read the encyclopedias and I am determined to see my daughter married to a Protestant while I am still alive."

"To about any Protestant in your more frantic moments. To a suitable French noble of the Reformed persuasion in your more rational ones. If not that, then to a foreign Protestant prince, preferably Calvinist. Or . . ." Bernhard rotated his shoulders. "Are there Protestant space aliens in this up-time 'science fiction' you have been reading these past few months? One of them might be the best choice."

"I am *not* in a mood for raillery," Rohan grumped. "Even if my young friend Ron Stone claims that I am 'fixated,' I *died* and the French crown controlled her. For years, they did not let her marry at all. Then they gave her a list of Catholic nonentities acceptable to them and she picked one because 'at least he's handsome and a good dancer.' That is not a potential son-in-law acceptable to *me*. Neither are grandchildren who will be reared Catholic as a condition of the king's permitting my daughter to marry at all. So . . ."

"So what do you plan to do about it."

"With *your* permission, O Sovereign Lord of the Free County of Burgundy, I will bring my wife and daughter to join me here in Besançon. Or, if you prefer, I can return to Berne and have them join me there."

"You're not going anywhere," the grand duke answered, clasping his hands behind his back as he took his turn with pacing. "Berne does not need you. You have accepted duties to Burgundy. Think of the piles of paper on your desk. Think of the hordes of petitioners who will be devastated if you do not hold personal meetings with them." His smile turned feral. "Think of the committee meetings that you are scheduled to chair, which will spare me or Erlach from chairing them. In the best of circumstances, it will take some time to get your ladies here. You can borrow a couple of my better officers for such a mission."

Rohan leaned on his standing desk and steepled his fingers. "Ruvigny, then."

"What?" Bernhard raised his eyebrows at this apparent *non sequitur*.

"Ruvigny. He's an officer in your service and I know him well."

"The redhead? The one with the remarkable nose?"

Rohan nodded. "And freckles. Don't forget the freckles. Yes, that's Henri de Massué de Ruvigny."

"Why him?"

"His family are clients of my father-in-law. They have been since long before Sully even became my father-in-law. Thus, they are in a way clients of my wife, so it's mostly a matter of *entré*. She will receive him at least, possibly as a welcome rather than unwelcome guest, and, perhaps, if I am fortunate, even pay some attention to the message he presents on my behalf. Maybe."

18

Bernhard unclasped his hands and fingered the little goatee he was wearing. "Not a bad choice. He's a good officer, but he'll make a better diplomat someday, if he ever has the money to support an ambassadorial career. Someone ought to find him a wife with a decent dowry. Who else do you want?"

"Ask him. He knows the younger officers better than either of us do. He'll make a good choice."

Bernhard's private secretary stuck his head around the doorpost as a signal for the meeting to break up.

"What's next on the agenda?" Rohan asked.

"Smallpox vaccinations, continued plague-fighting measures, and other aspects of public sanitation, with a special presentation by the up-time nurse *Frau* Dunn and information on what assistance can be obtained through the resources of Lothlorien Pharmaceuticals in Grantville." Bernhard appeared to be working up to one of his famous rants.

"I believe," Rohan said, backing out of the room, "that I hear the papers stacked beside my desk emitting a call as tempting as the voice of any siren singing to passing sailors."

*   *   *

Ruvigny chose August von Bismarck. Bismarck, he told the duke, was reliable and solid. Unflappable. The kind of officer a commander could depend on.

They also happened to be good friends, on first name terms, and, so far, said friend hadn't had any luck at all when it came to promotions. This kind of expedition could give August a chance to bring himself to the favorable attention of more powerful people. But there was no point in mentioning that to the duke and grand duke yet.

Whereupon Rohan wrote letters, and they begged the best horses that the regiment would let them take. Bismarck's horse turned out to be reliable and solid. The kind of horse a man could depend on. Ruvigny's horse went lame four days out, so he had to hire a far less satisfactory one.

"So," August said the next afternoon. "Did you find out anything about yourself from the famous up-time encyclopedias?"

Henri dropped his reins onto the gelding's neck and stared out toward the peasants who were still harvesting in the fields, weeks after the end of this unsatisfactory summer. "*Britannica* 1911. On what I'm paid, I asked the researcher I hired in Grantville to look up the main article for my family name, if there was one. It's not as if I can afford to pay for a thorough search. There was an article about my oldest son, who became a general for the king of England—who was a Dutchman, absurdly enough; one has to wonder what became of the Stuarts—and received an Irish title, Earl of Galway. King Louis XIV revoked the Edict of Nantes in 1685, crushing everything I attempted to achieve after I retired from the army. I served as Deputy General of the Huguenot Synods to the royal court from 1653 onwards, trying to maintain our rights. I failed, so I went into exile and died in England. Not one of my three sons married. No descendants, male or female. The French crown confiscated our estates. The Teacher had it right, I guess. 'Useless, useless; everything is useless.' Or, maybe, 'Futile, futile, everything is futile.'" He picked up the reins again. "But for some reason, I keep working." He raised his eyebrows. "You?"

August grinned. "Same encyclopedia, same procedure, same reason, since I'm always broke. I got less detail but more optimism. About two hundred fifty years from now, *somebody* named von Bismarck, Otto to be specific, had worked his way up in rank from country gentleman to *Graf, Herzog, und Fürst*. He guided the multitude of small German states into becoming a united country. He wasn't nice about the nation building; Gustav Adolf and Stearns have proceeded with more tact. Whether or not he was related to me in the direct line, I have no idea, but since we were both born at Schönhausen in Brandenburg's Altmark, there's likely to be some connection. I'm going to assume that one of my brothers or cousins managed to hang onto the land, such as it is, paid off the mortgages our father loaded on it in pursuit of such luxuries as family portraits and comfortable beds, and kept begetting heirs." August sighed. "My lord father wasn't frugal. He kept trying to press additional new fees out of the peasants, the peasants kept suing him, and the courts kept deciding in their favor. He left a huge mess for my mother to deal with after he died."

Ruvigny shifted in the hired saddle. It didn't fit him right. "There are millions of people, I suppose, who wouldn't find anything at all in those books. My son received an article because he became a general."

The sun was shifting into the west. August pulled his hat down to protect the pale forehead that his receding auburn hair seemed to be enlarging with every day that passed. "Rise high in the army and qualify for the small immortality of an encyclopedia entry. At the rate I'm receiving promotions, which is not at all, it's no wonder the up-timers never heard of me. It looks like I'll die still a captain, whether it's next summer or twenty summers from now."

They plodded onwards toward Paris.

CHAPTER 3

Brussels
October 1635

From: Susanna Allegretti, Brussels
To: M. Leopold Cavriani, Geneva

Most honored patron and friend,
I regret that I must request a favor from you. Because of certain difficulties that have
arisen here in the household of the king and queen in the Netherlands, I feel that it will
not be wise for me to remain in my current situation any longer than absolutely
necessary. If it would be possible for you to arrange for me to transfer to the household of
the Stadthouder in the northern provinces, I would be sincerely grateful.
Your devoted friend and servant,

From: Susanna, in Brussels
To: Marc, wherever you may be (c/o M. Leopold Cavriani, Geneva)

My dearest heart,

I'm getting so mad about all of this that if I weren't a seamstress who can't afford snags in the lace and satin that earn me my daily bread, I'd be biting my fingernails right to the quick. Or kicking the non-gentleman colonel from Lorraine where it would hurt him the most. Which I can't, because he has "important connections." Of course, with all the excitement about the expected baby, nobody could expect the queen to have time to worry about the trials and tribulations of one of her dressmakers. Not even if she is an outstanding dressmaker, which I have become if I may be so bold as to say so.

No matter how impeccable the personal conduct of the king and queen in the Netherlands is, its impact on the court as a whole is not strong. Of course, one could say the same about decades of impeccable conduct on the part of the marvelous Archduchess, who is, alas, still old and still ill.

So. This obnoxious exile, even after the truly entertaining demise of his duke last spring, will not take no for an answer, and what's worse, most of my colleagues in haute couture don't see why I'm not willing to say yes to his demands (which are more demands in the English usage than requests in the French usage). He's offered generous terms, they say, and it's not as if I'm some petite bourgeoise, subject to the rules of German guilds. When he ended an arrangement with a generous settlement (they say, they say, they all say, or at least most of them say), not that I think that he has enough money to do that, apart from any considerations of morality, then I would have a bigger dowry than I do now and could make an even better match than expected with some other upper servant in the court than I can now aspire to.

But I don't want to do this, so I have written your father asking him to get me sent to the court of Fredrik Hendrik and his wife in The Hague.

I miss you so much.

Where are you?

CHAPTER 4

Paris
October 1635

Bismarck didn't have any idea how they would be received at the ducal residence and hadn't wanted to ask. He hadn't expected that within minutes after they presented their credentials, the *duc de* Rohan's daughter would dash into the entryway and throw herself into Ruvigny's arms with a squeal of "Henri! I haven't seen you for ages!"

"Well, if it isn't the itsy-bitsy, teeny-tiny, seed pearl, all grown up." Ruvigny responded to her enthusiasm with a brotherly hug, looking her over. "Our daisy has grown petals."

In spite of the double entendre, Bismarck knew a brotherly hug when he saw one. He had four sisters to go along with his three brothers. Before he decided that he would rather embrace a military career than continue dragging around in the genteel poverty that had been their mother's lot since the wars devastated the Altmark, shortly after his father's death, he had lived in an affectionate household. Even though she, all of her offspring in tow, had made nightmarish treks that took them to Magdeburg, Hamburg, Salzwedel, and Braunschweig in search of semi-permanent refuge from the marauding armies, in sorrow and in joy the eight of them had hugged each other all the time. Their mother, even though she prided herself on exercising *firm and serious discipline* in their upbringing, had hugged them. For that matter, they had hugged their father, before he died. He shook his head, throwing off the memories as unsuited to his present duties.

As for itsy-bitsy, Ruvigny was not teasing. The young duchess was short. Pretty enough, he supposed, in the way that it's hard for a girl to be ugly when she's 17 and healthy, with a clear complexion, but short.

Introductions followed, with the accompanying protocol, etiquette, and general necessary *politesse*, with the little duchess excusing her mother's non-appearance as hostess on the vague grounds of, "She's busy."

As they migrated from the entryway toward a side salon, Bismarck whispered, "Is there something you haven't been telling me?"

Ruvigny shrugged. "Oh. Well. About five years ago, during the Savoy campaign, La Valette sent me to Venice to recruit a regiment of light cavalry. The duke was there, then. I stayed with the Rohans."

"And he paid attention to me," the little duchess said. "I was twelve. He talked to me and teased me and told me stories about the campaigns and . . . and nobody else there ever paid any attention to me at all. Henri is my best friend ever."

Bismarck added "has sharp ears" to his mental list of what he knew about the *duc de* Rohan's daughter.

* * *

They woke up the next morning to still no senior hostess to welcome them. Ruvigny said that she probably was busy—she handled, with the assistance of business agents, of course, all of the duke's financial and administrative affairs in France and had throughout his years of exile.

There was also what seemed like a mass invasion of the *Hôtel de Sully* by the staff of every theater in Paris. An expected invasion.

"Oh, Henri, you have to stay in Paris a little bit longer," Marguerite proclaimed. "I won't let you go. What need does that upstart Bernhard have for you right at the moment? Winter's coming on. Nobody's going to fight anybody in bad weather. We're putting on a ballet for the court. Papa's house on the *Place Royale* is nice, of course, but *Grand-père* is letting us use this one, since he's still in the country on house arrest. He bought it two years ago, brand new and already furnished; it's so much bigger and nicer. We wouldn't have any place to rehearse if he hadn't. I'm dancing the lead role and everyone will be there—utterly everyone. You have to dance, too, Henri. Remember how we used to dance on the balcony of the house in Venice?"

"What I am is out of practice, little daisy," Ruvigny protested. "I've been doing other things these last few years, remember?"

"Oh, poof. You can do it. Mama got Isaac de Benserade to script it. He's the newest literary sensation this year." She grabbed his arm and towed him in the direction of the ballroom, Bismarck trailing along behind.

The little duchess turned around. "You dance, of course, don't you?"

"I would say that I'm modestly competent in a ballroom. I've never even seen a ballet."

"Well, that's disappointing. *Autres temps, autres mœurs.* I suppose that applies to other places as well as other eras. You can watch."

Three hours of strenuous rehearsal later, the little duchess, not even mildly winded, plopped herself down next to Bismarck while Benserade and the choreographer once more put the male chorus through the final routine.

"Benserade is a slave driver. Even before the cast rehearsals started, he had me in here for five straight days, just learning my own part."

"If you are as careful of your reputation and virtue as all say that you are, Mademoiselle, I am surprised that you spend all these hours in the company of a young man in his twenties, quite unaccompanied." He looked around. "Well, unaccompanied except for a company of costumers, not to say several set designers, a half-dozen carpenters, and ten or so miscellaneous servants."

Marguerite sniffed. "Benserade is no threat to my reputation. I could take him to bed and he wouldn't be a threat to my virtue. Everyone knows he's tilted. Everyone who matters, at least."

Bismarck blinked.

"A bit out of plumb, like the king. But Louis only tilts this far. "She placed her elbow on the chair arm and moved it about ten degrees to the left. ". . . and he, Louis, tilts both ways." She moved it an equal number of degrees to the right. "Isaac's all the way to the left." Her arm went down to a right angle, parallel to the floor. ". . . but that doesn't keep him from being entertaining."

"Out of plumb?"

The little duchess viewed Henri's German friend with exasperation. "Are you so naïve? I am telling you that he is out of kilter. As our Provençals would say, *gai*. Slanted. The man is not straight. He might be a threat to the reputation of my cousins, Maximilien or François, but not to mine. Don't you have a word for it in German?"

Bismarck almost strangled, but swallowed hard. "None that we use in the presence of respectable young ladies of 17 years, Your Grace."

"How odd. In any case, soon everyone will know that he's the best at planning galas and spectacular entertainments, and we will have sponsored him first. Someday he'll be in their new *Académie française*. There's hardly any doubt about that, and he's one of ours–a Huguenot, I mean–so there is also no way that *Maman* will let Richelieu and Mazarin seize the glory of having discovered him for the Catholic party. This ballet will be a real coup for the Protestant cause."

Bismarck had difficulty envisioning a ballet directed by a sodomite as a coup for the Protestant cause, but was tactful enough not to say so.

✣　✣　✣

Some hours later, the young duchess disappeared to be dressed so that she might join her still-invisible mother for a yet-unspecified mandatory social occasion.

Ruvigny and Bismarck headed off for a tavern, to meet some of Ruvigny's old friends from his first years in the Royal Guards in Paris. Who were late, of course. They ordered ales while they waited.

"I had no idea you were on such close terms with the Rohans," August said, shoving his mug around the table and leaving a wet streak.

"It's not the Rohans." Henri answered. "I don't know the duke very well and I've never presumed on any acquaintance with him for advancement in the service of Grand Duke Bernhard. It's the family of the senior duchess–that is, it's the Béthunes who are our patrons. Our families have known each other just about forever. It was through her father, the *duc de* Sully, that my father got his sinecure as lieutenant-governor of the Bastille. I was three when Papa died, so I don't remember, but *Maman* has repeated constantly to all of us, ever since, how much gratitude we owe to the Béthunes. Sully himself was godfather for my oldest brother, who died in the Royal Guards. Sully's wife and one of his sons were godparents for my sister Rachel. For my little brother Cirné, too, but he died when he was no more than an infant."

He shifted on the bench. "I'm not personally comfortable with Rohan's politics. At the siege of La Rochelle, I was with the royal forces. If the Huguenots have any hope of surviving in France, they'll be better off practicing a policy of 'respect the crown and placate the king' rather than rebelling."

"Doesn't Peter, in the Epistle, say 'honor the king' rather than 'placate the king'?"

"At the French court, it's 'placate the king.' Not that such an approach succeeded either, according to the up-time books. Nor does competence. Sully is still out of favor. Nobody loved him when he was chief minister, even though he perhaps did more for France than anyone else who served Henri IV. The Catholics hated him because he was Huguenot and the Huguenots hated him because he remained loyal to the crown after Henry of Navarre decided that Paris was worth a mass."

Bismarck nodded. "It's hard to deal rationally with fanatics. The electors of Brandenburg did better, I think, when they let their subjects remain Lutheran even though they converted to Calvinism a couple of decades ago. The principle of *cuius regio, eius religio* that has governed the Holy Roman Empire since the Peace of Augsburg doesn't require that subjects must be of the same faith of their ruler, actually—it only states that the ruler gets to decide. He can tolerate religious dissent if he wants to." He grinned. "Or if it's expedient; think how the up-timers have boxed Gustavus in on that issue."

✻ ✻ ✻

The elder duchess appeared at breakfast the next morning, not apologizing for anything, but making a fuss over Ruvigny. She wasn't bad looking, Bismarck thought, for a woman who must be past forty and who had borne ten children. But nowhere nearly as good looking as his own mother, who had borne eight. *Mutti* must be a dozen or so years older than the duchess. The last time he had seen her, which was close to ten years ago now, she would have been about the same age as the woman to whom he was making a bow in this year of 1635. She had looked a lot younger and healthier, in spite of all the troubles of the war.

Making a fuss over Ruvigny stopped the instant he carried out their mission and handed over Rohan's letter. The duchess did not respond to it with appropriate wifely compliance, much less biblical submissiveness. Her reaction was more along the lines of indignation amounting to anger. Fury, perhaps. Even the ire of the classical Furies themselves.

"No way," she screamed at Ruvigny. "So 'chaos is coming.' I am quite prepared to manipulate, to the benefit of Rohan, any political advantage that is to be attained from looming chaos, but I can only do that in Paris. So 'danger lurks.' I am not prepared to abandon the court. Nor will I agree to send away my daughter, who is at long last getting old enough to play her own part and therefore belongs at the center of the world, in Paris, and not in the boondocks of the Free County of Burgundy. Doesn't he think I am capable of protecting her from some forced Catholic marriage?"

No one of any importance, she finished, ever went to Besançon. Or ever would, in all probability. Not within her lifetime.

After which she flounced out.

"That went a lot better than I expected," Ruvigny said, "considering that the duke pointed out that in the other world, where the encyclopedia was written, she did not manage to protect Marguerite from such a marriage."

Bismark thought that the French ate breakfast too late. He had practically starved before food appeared on the table.

The breakfast, as late as it was, didn't last long because there was another rehearsal, to which he was again relegated to being a spectator and involuntary recipient of the female lead's constant chatter at those times she was not onstage. Today, she was trying to explain her mother, "because I do not want you to think poorly of her, M. von Bismarck. Henri, of course, already knows it all. He lived through a lot of it. Not when she got married, of course, because he wasn't even born yet.

"She was ten years old when the late king–Henri IV, that is–commanded that she should marry my father. Not just be betrothed to him, at that age, which would not have been so unusual, but marry him. The ceremony was in the temple at Ablon. She wore a white dress, and some joker asked, loud enough for the other guests to hear, 'And who is it that presents this child for baptism?' Papa was 25. He went back to the army and *Maman* got to live with her mother-in-law."

She stopped. "How old were you when you got married, M. von Bismarck?"

"I'm not married. I'm 25 and I can't afford to get married, any more than Ruvigny over there in the chorus line can. Maybe not ever."

"Do you have a mistress?"

"If I could afford a mistress, I could afford a wife, and I would much rather have a wife, I assure you."

"Does Henri have a mistress?"

"No, *Mademoiselle*."

"Oh, good. But then *Maman* grew up and became pretty, with those big eyes, high cheekbones, and little pixie curls fluffing around her headband. She isn't quite so pretty any more, but she is very old now. She was 41 on her last birthday. By the time she grew up, though, Henri IV was dead and the Rohans were in revolt again. *Maman* has always been fiercely loyal to Papa. She has defended the Rohan political cause tirelessly to the court; she has raised immense amounts of money for his ventures, even when she and my grandfather thought they were too risky.

"And, of course, she had to bear him children after she grew up. I am certainly legitimate," the little duchess said proudly. "That is why Papa is so concerned about my marriage and sent the letter that has irritated *Maman* so much, you understand. Uncle Soubise has no children at all, so I am the only hope for continuing Rohan. Papa can be sure that I am the legitimate heiress of all that Rohan represents. It is true that *Maman* is volatile, but she was quite conscientious about her behavior until Papa gave up begetting. She didn't take lovers until after that."

Bismarck could not think of a tactful reply. At least, not one that was relevant.

At which point, Benserade and the choreographer beckoned her back onstage.

Bismarck hoped that they would have lunch, or maybe dinner, or at least a snack, pretty soon, but was afraid that they wouldn't. It was a mystery why the dancers, whether ladies-in-waiting and courtiers or actors and ballerinas, had not been reduced to skeletons.

The next day was more of the same. A ballet in Paris appeared to involve as much in the way of logistics as a minor military campaign. The little duchess and the ladies in waiting, and the men of course, danced in the traditional style, but the ballerinas hired from the theater were doing two pieces in the modern *en pointe* style that the up-timers had introduced. Since their presentations meant that the other female dancers were offstage quite a bit, though both the courtiers and actors partnered the professionals in their display, Bismarck was subjected to more chatter.

"The night of the ballet, you will be presented to M. de Gondi. Be careful. He is *Maman*'s current lover; and prone to take offence at the slightest thing he can interpret to be a discourtesy. Also, he has a retinue of favorites who follow him around and take offense on his behalf. Henri fought some duels when he was younger, before I ever met him, but I do believe that he has outgrown it. It would not be good if either you or he got trapped into one while you are here and it would not be beyond some of the courtiers to entrap you into having to fight one, just to embarrass Papa. Don't trust anyone. That's the best. Anyone, even one you think is now your closest friend or most committed ally, may well betray you tomorrow if some advantage is to be obtained from it."

"Lover?" Bismarck had learned most of his French in a classroom and was not certain of his comprehension at times, particularly when a conversational partner spoke with excessive rapidity. Which all the French seemed to do most of the time. He wanted to be sure that he had heard clearly.

"Yes, her current lover. Everyone says that *Maman* is quite fastidious. It's not as if she's one of those women who claim to be ladies but fuck the footmen for fun. She takes one lover at a time and all of them have been influential members of the highest nobility." Marguerite sighed. "Even though in the case of the Nogarets, she chose two brothers at different times, the cardinal de La Valette and the *comte de* Candale." She wrinkled her nose. "Which is . . . not fastidious."

Bismarck's eyebrows were practically up in his receding three-point hairline.

"So what was I saying? It's not as if *Maman* has a reputation like *la Chalaise*, for whom a man published a poem in praise of her slit." She punctuated that by nodding her head firmly. "Her husband, the *comte de* Chalais, killed the *comte de* Pontguibault in a duel because of that poem. It was a big scandal at the time—that must have been about a dozen years ago. But Chalais was beheaded later on, because *la Chevreuse* seduced him into one of her conspiracies against Richelieu. She's a *very* distant cousin of Papa's, from the Rohan-Montbezon line." She paused. "You *will* remember what I told you about duels, won't you? It will cause too many complications if you or Henri fight a duel while you are staying with us."

Bismarck blinked in the face of this never-ending flood of gossip. It might be true that nobody ever paid attention to her, because when she did have a captive listener, her mouth overflowed with everything she was thinking. Much of which, under the surface frivolity, was world-weary and far more cynical than a girl her age should be, he thought. If anybody asked him, which nobody would.

33

At least, when the day of the performance arrived, he would be in the audience rather than backstage. He hoped. He hoped, but he knew that sometimes hope was in vain. He had seen the modern English translation of the Bible in the school library when he was studying at Helmstedt. Well, not the modern of the up-timers but the modern of his own day, the one sponsored by King James. The passage Henri had quoted on their ride to Paris had not employed 'useless' or 'futile.' 'Vanity,' the Teacher had written, speaking the Word of God. "Vanity, vanity, all is vanity." Solomon must have visited Paris at some stage of his career. But, then, he had been presiding over a royal court of his own. With wives in the plural, concubines by the hundreds, and troubles of his own. Monogamy had a lot to be said in its favor.

Marguerite propped her chin on the heel of her hand. "And then there's Tancrède."

"Another . . . ah . . . lover?"

The little duchess managed to convey jaded disgust with one short glance. "My half-brother."

"The duke also has affairs? An affair? His junior officers, at least during my term of service, have not been aware of any."

"My *maternal* half-brother. He's six. Trust me, M. von Bismarck. One has not lived until one has ridden, most of the time in a closed carriage, from Venice to Paris, with a pregnant, motion sick, middle aged woman who is expecting an illegitimate child and knows that it will have to be fostered out because her husband draws the line at accepting a possible male heir whom he has not fathered. After such a wonderful journey, it's hard for a girl to retain any illusions about the joyous and sacred nature of motherhood, no matter what the preachers say in their sermons. "She paused. "Candale begat the boy. He and *Maman* slept together in my own father's house. That's bad taste, don't you think?"

Bismarck nodded. Bad taste was the least of it, from the perspective of a devout man.

"But at least she converted him to Calvinism before she slept with him," Marguerite added more cheerfully. "That annoyed his brother the cardinal, not that the cardinal-archbishop of Toulouse is at all pious: he has never taken Catholic holy orders and has made his career in the army. Richelieu loathes *Maman*. He calls her *une des dames brouillonnes de la cour*, one of the mischief-making ladies of the court."

Even ballet rehearsals come to an end.

"It's true, what she said when we arrived, isn't it?" Bismarck asked that evening as he finished taking off his boots and leaned back, wiggling his toes.

"Huh?" Ruvigny was half-asleep already.

"That nobody other than you paid any attention to her when she was in Venice and twelve years old. Nobody pays any attention to her now that she's in Paris and seventeen years old, as far as I can see, other than dressing her, rehearsing her for that ballet, and parading her around to salons and court appearances. She's the greatest heiress in all of France and she's neglected. Nobody listens to her at all. Nobody even tries to provide her with some kind of . . . moral compass. Not as far as I have seen."

"Not since her grandmother Rohan died," Ruvigny answered. "That must be five years ago, now. The duchess' parents, Sully and his wife, are still alive, but Marguerite doesn't see much of them. He's in retirement in the country, which is a nice way to describe house arrest, writing his memoirs and dreaming of his 'great design' for a federation of all Christian nations."

CHAPTER 5

On the Road
November 1635

A month later, Bismarck and Ruvigny reluctantly set out from Paris. Not that they were sorry to be leaving. Reluctantly because they were returning to Rohan with his wife's refusal to either join him or send his daughter to him. The duke would not be happy.

"Why did the duchess have to delay so long? If you think about it, she gave us the same answer a month ago, the instant she read the duke's letter. She postponed, then delayed, then procrastinated, and dragged her feet about giving us her written answer. Now we're headed back to Burgundy in the middle of what looks like it could be the most miserable winter I've ever seen. Even worse than last year." August looked up at the lowering gray sky, which was drizzling tiny pebbles of sleet onto the half-frozen mud of the ungraded track that was pretending to be a road in eastern France.

"She's not the one who has to ride in this," Henri pointed out. "She may have put things off so long so she could add that she didn't want to risk the seed pearl's health by traveling in midwinter to the rest of her excuses."

"He isn't going to like it."

"*Entendu*. Maybe all the church bells ringing to celebrate the child of the royal couple in the Netherlands will distract him. Too bad it was a girl."

"But healthy, which isn't something the Habsburgs can always count on. That augurs well for the future." August hunched his shoulders against the sleet. "Sometimes it's better for the heir to come second, with a girl first to undergo the process of having her head stretch out the mother's hips for childbearing."

When he heard their report, Rohan could have used some soothing medication. He started to compile yet another list of acceptable—to him—matches for Marguerite. "It's more urgent with every day that passes," he insisted. "As Grand Duke Bernhard said, when he declined the honor of fulfilling the role of her husband himself, she needs someone who can be Rohan for her."

Laubach, County of Solms–Laubach November 1635

Condolence letters were much more difficult than letters of congratulation, but she had to produce one. Her brother-in-law, Amalie Elisabeth's husband, the landgrave of Hesse-Kassel, had been killed in action at the Battle of Warta in Poland.

That was a frequent enough end, of course, for noblemen who spent their time fighting one another. She had already written over two dozen similar letters since she became old enough to correspond and would write dozens more if she lived for a biblical span of years.

She wondered if Amalie Elisabeth would miss him. That marriage had been a family arrangement, of course. Like her own. Like those of every woman of her acquaintance. They had seemed to get along well enough. At least it meant that Amalie Elisabeth would stop burdening Hesse-Kassel with another child every year.

Instead, she would become regent for young Wilhelm. She'd be regent for quite a while, considering that young Wilhelm had just turned seven years old in May. Would the emperor appoint her as the governor of the USE's new Province of Hesse as well as regent of Hesse-Kassel itself? If so, knowing her sister, she would be gaining influence under Gustavus Adolphus.

Käthe nibbled at the tip of her pen. Her sister would be an independent actress on the imperial stage, playing a significant role.

If she herself had had the slightest idea of the impact that the Ring of Fire would have on the world, she would have held out for a better match in September of 1631. True, she had already been twenty-seven, but that wasn't so old. She hadn't been desperate. It was about the age when most women married. Only the high nobility or the rich sometimes made matches like that of Amalie Elisabeth, who had been seventeen when she married.

She had settled for Albert Otto, thinking that he was the best she was likely to get, considering that he was an only son and had therefore inherited his father's lands unpartitioned, with a sick mother who had died a week after their wedding. No mother-in-law to second-guess every decision she made. He had barely come of age when he offered. Six years younger than she was by the calendar. A dozen years younger when it came to ordinary common sense.

Thinking that he was the best option might have been a mistake, but one it was much too late to do anything about. If her marriage lacked a certain vivacity of sentiment that a woman might ideally desire when contemplating the husband God had given her, neither did it contain insuperable difficulties that would prevent her from fulfilling her duties to that husband in a satisfactory manner. She shook her head. Her reasons had been good enough. And while her husband kept the local militia in good order, he had at least never joined Gustavus' army, marched off to Poland, and died for the glory of it all.

Not that his female relatives would have let him. The three months after his father died of the wounds he had taken at Breitenbend in March of 1610 had been tense. From his posthumous birth in June to the birth of her own first son, the political survival of Solms-Laubach as an independent county had depended upon the physical survival of one thin-faced boy.

His mother had dealt with a long regency, during the last dozen years suffering the difficulties of the warring parties along the Rhine. Albert Otto had three living older sisters and five paternal aunts. He also had three paternal uncles who would have been more than happy to partition the Laubach lands into the other subdivisions of Solms if the child count had died—or been killed in action. The aunts and sisters had formed a protective phalanx around him.

All that female protective cherishing had left him with a reaction of massive impatience if anyone showed signs of hovering over him. 'Anyone' included his wife. But it was so hard not to.

Besançon
late 1635

"It's far more than I want to deal with," Rohan wrote. "I was no sooner finished speaking with Bernhard (who is far from fully recovered from his acute illness of last summer) about the impact of Wilhelm of Hesse-Kassel's death on Amalie Elisabeth—whom the grand duke has always liked a lot—than we were battered by the news of the assassination of Empress Maria Eleonora in Sweden and then Gustavus' own severe injury at Lake Bledno. If the rumors of the involvement of Ducos' fanatics in the death of the empress are true . . ." The Rohans had their own, not insignificant, intelligence network throughout the Huguenot world.

He finished his instructions to Soubise and pulled a new sheet of paper from the desk. Perhaps it was not all bad that his wife had refused to leave Paris. He would be needing a pair of sharp eyes there. Whatever else anyone had ever said of Sully's daughter, no one had ever asserted that she was not shrewd.

He laid the pen down.   He needed to talk to Leopold Cavriani.

Brussels
December 1635

From: Susanna Allegretti, Brussels
To: M. Leopold Cavriani, Geneva

Most honored patron and friend,
Not having received word from you, I conclude that your other obligations have taken
you to places that the postal service does not reach. Because of the -difficulties I mentioned
in November, I am taking prudent measures to avert what otherwise might become a
series of unfortunate events.
I will remain here in Brussels for the time being, awaiting your further advice.
Your devoted friend and servant,

The old cobbler looked up from his workbench. "Are you sure that you want these shoes altered the way you described? They will be unstable to walk in, and the points are likely to damage the floors."

"Yes, Joseph. Exactly as I described." She hopped down from the wide window sill on which she had been perching and took one of them in her hands again. "The wooden heels themselves—whittle them down from about here . . ." She pointed. "Start a quarter-inch below where they attach to the sole and keep whittling until they are very narrow when they meet the floor. They're about an inch and a half high altogether—that's what's fashionable now—so the wood shouldn't break when I put weight on them. Then stiffen the matching fabric, mold it to look like it is covering a normal shoe heel, and glue it to the unwhittled quarter-inch of the wooden heel at the top." She pointed again. "Right here. The false fabric heel should be a little off the floor—an eighth of an inch, maybe. Not enough that a casual observer will notice but enough that it won't snag."

"Every pair? This will ruin them, and shoes do not grow on trees, *petite Suzette*. You have to pay for them."

"Yes, Joseph. All five pair. I have my reasons."

From: Susanna in Brussels
To: Marc, wherever you are (c/o M. Leopold Cavriani, Geneva)

My dearest heart,
Should you hear stories that a certain overly-persistent Lorrainer colonel of my lamented acquaintance has a broken instep, do not be concerned for me. I will be fine, I promise. Wishing you were here.
With all my love,

Besançon
January 1636

Leopold Cavriani came into town with his son Marc late in the month, dusted the snow off his nose and kicked the slush off his boots, did not curse the slippery cobblestones, inquired where the *duc de* Rohan might be found, and expressed cheerful relief when informed that his quarry was not at the top of the citadel.

"It's just a little garrison up there right now, Sir," the hostler said. "I'm plenty sorry for them, too, because their teeth must be frozen, not to mention their balls, the way the wind whips across that hilltop. At least the cold kills off most of the plague during the winter season. There's some smallpox in town, but the Grand Duke's people assure us that come next summer, using measures from these up-timers in the Germanies, the smallpox will be prevented from coming back. I'm of two minds about that, myself, interfering with the will of God the way it does."

Cavriani sent Marc off to look for their mail, conferred with Rohan, and then with the assent of Grand Duke Bernhard annexed Colonel Raudegen temporarily. The contents of the mail packet proved to be unsatisfactory—either a great deal of correspondence had gone astray or some malefactor had been purloining bags from the postal system. He borrowed the use of Bernhard's radio to check with Potentiana in Geneva, by way of multiple short re-sendings, only to get the dismaying news that none of the missing mail had arrived there, either.

So on the basis of the most recent information they had, which was far from recent enough, Rohan sent Bernhard's man Raudegen, with Marc as assistant, off to stage a couple of interventions in England and the Netherlands.

"England first," Leopold counseled, when it became clear that whatever Marc's mind might be advising him, his heart was of the opinion that Susanna Allegretti had priority over anyone or anything else. "When Rohan sent Soubise back to England last summer to deal with the disgrace that Ducos and his fanatics are bringing on right-thinking Huguenots, he had no idea that the true idiots to whom Charles has now entrusted control of his policies would detain him. It was supposed to be a fast trip, digging them out of wherever they had fled in those remote islands and bringing them back where saner Calvinists could control them. But the imbeciles put Soubise under house arrest, so now we have to get him out, whether he managed to do the job he was assigned or not. Just bring him back.

"Bring him back *first*, before you go in pursuit of the idol of your eyes. You should find Susanna at The Hague, or wherever Fredrik Hendrik's court is right now. Keep an eye on the newspapers to see where he is and if his wife is with him or spending the winter more comfortably in a town house in Amsterdam. I sent the request for Susanna's transfer to the head dressmaker in Brussels back in November, but the last letter I received, she was still in Brussels. Something is wrong with our communications."

SECTION II

February 1636-May 1636

CHAPTER 6

London
February 1636

Travel conditions being what they always were in the middle of winter, especially when it came to crossing the English Channel . . .

"I hope I never see this place again," Marc said as they disembarked in London. "We've been here five minutes and that's five minutes too long. How Huygens endures it, I can't imagine. It may be preferable to being burned at the stake by the Duke of Alba during the Eighty Years War . . ." He paused and took a second look at the London docks. "But not by much."

"Early March is said not to be the most salubrious season in England," Raudegen remarked mildly.

"What is?"

"Someone told me once that it was August 23rd, if I recall correctly. But it may have been July 26th."

* * *

"I wouldn't precisely call it internment," Soubise said. "I've not been in the Tower the way Charles kept the envoys from the USE. Of course, he's on firmer ground because there is precedent on handling an errant French nobleman who is *persona non grata* in his homeland, while there was none for handling unnerving strangers from the future." He smiled. "I've been here before in the course of the vicissitudes of the relations between the Rohans and the Bourbon rulers of France. It's a nice house here on the Strand, if somewhat small for my needs, and I brought my valet and cook with me. Thanks be to God the Almighty, for otherwise I'd have been wearing English tailoring and eating English food for more than half a year."

"Your brother thinks that you have accomplished all that you can in the matter of Ducos and his fanatics."

"Not as much as I hoped I would. I wanted to chase them all the way to Scotland. But . . ."

His secretary spoke up.

"Since my master is not, in fact, under house arrest, as the English authorities keep assuring us, though they also would not let him leave London, he has proven to be an excellent envoy. He has hosted at least three formal dinners each week, this house being inadequate for dancing parties. He has established a salon which the most elite *literati* of London . . ." He cleared his throat. ". . . the most elite *literati* of London, such as they are, have attended. Thus, everyone of importance in London is aware that the House of Rohan does not in any way condone these regrettable assassinations."

"The trouble Ducos is causing is regrettable," Soubise interjected, "but I for one would not have been heartbroken if he had succeeded with the pope."

The secretary cleared his throat. "My lord de Soubise has not only regularly attended divine services at the French Protestant Church on Threadneedle Street, founded by the good offices of and under the charter issued by the late King Edward VI, but has also heard sermons here in his own house from the pastors of the other Huguenot churches in and near London."

"You would not believe how many sermons I have heard in these past months," Soubise exclaimed. "Enough to be a lifetime supply for any normal man. Biblically sound and well-delivered, but sermons nevertheless. Forgive an old sailor for saying it if either of you are of a pious bent, but there ought to be some kind of limit, some entire *statute* of limitations, on theological pontificating."

"What my master is attempting to convey," the secretary said, "is that by dint of his efforts, every French Protestant pastor in the British Isles is now aware of Ducos' perfidy. Engravings of him and of his men, made from the best descriptions that *M. le duc de* Rohan could obtain, with their names printed beneath so far as the authorities identified them, are now in wide circulation. Every pastor who came here received several copies, and each week, at the church in Threadneedle Street, all visitors from other parts of England and Scotland are invited to take copies. The pastor in the City of London has been so cooperative as to arrange a series of mid-week guest sermons, which have been delivered by the pastors from other cities, such as Bristol and . . ."

"What he means," Soubise said, is that we've placarded the whole country with wanted posters and that's all I've managed to do, because aside from the four men I brought with me and a few Huguenots I've managed to hire, I'm sure the rest of my staff are English spies. And I'm still stuck in London, because I can't get leave to return to the continent. Richelieu appears to take a certain glee in having me 'stranded' here, and the English are more than happy to oblige him."

After considering the situation, Raudegen concluded that since Soubise did have a limited ability to move about in the streets, at least on Sundays, removing him to France would not be a major challenge. Removing him along with the valet, secretary, coachman, and cook would complicate the process to the point that in his opinion, since their specific charge was to retrieve the duke, the three should be left behind to fend for themselves, which meant enduring whatever punitive consequences the English government might choose to visit upon them as retribution for their employer's transgressions.

Marc objected for humanitarian reasons.

Raudegen discussed the traditional relationship between omelettes and eggs.

"If you won't extricate them, then I'll do it myself. That's what I'll call it. An extrication, and as such, it should be made with all due delicacy. The only servants we should leave behind are the ones the English themselves planted in his household. There's no reason for us to pay to import more English spies onto the continent. There are enough there already."

*   *   *

On Thursday, Milord's cook complained about the quality of the vegetables delivered. The footman who had done the ordering countered that vegetables were always shriveled at this time of year. The cook sent him back to the market and complained again about the produce to any staff member who would listen. The footman came back, bringing no satisfaction.

Cooks did not usually lower themselves to go to the market in person, but with a dramatic screech, the temperamental Frenchman left the house, taking the unsatisfactory footman with him. He did not return when expected, but then neither did the footman, so no one raised an alarm, given that he had prepared in advance sufficient cold meats and aspics for the household's supper.

On Friday morning, the housekeeper (English) told the butler (also English) that the cook and footman had not returned the night before. As both were missing, the butler saw no reason to inform the intelligence service in any panicked manner, since they had probably fallen victim to ordinary thieves or cutthroats. The housekeeper instructed the under-cook to proceed as well as might be, while the butler sent another footman to try to pick up their trail from the market.

On Friday afternoon, the valet told the butler that there were problems with milord's tailor. Since this was a frequent occurrence, given the pickiness of the irritating little Frenchman, the butler just nodded as the valet left by the back door. Since the valet did not ordinarily join the other servants for meals, the under-cook sent up trays to his room as usual for Friday supper and Saturday breakfast. The maid who carried and retrieved the trays happened to be a Huguenot. For two mealtimes, she got to eat a lot more than she was allotted and was happy to do it.

On Saturday, the secretary gave instructions to the housekeeper that all the servants were to attend the earliest service the following day, because milord expected a dozen guests for Sunday dinner. The under-cook had hysterics, but the housekeeper managed to calm him down.

Hearing of the instructions, the butler knocked on the door of the room where milord's secretary worked and asked, "Surely not the coachman, sir? For early services?"

"No, of course not," the secretary answered. "Use your common sense, man. He will be needed to drive milord to church and will attend services at the same hour we do, as usual."

The Huguenot staff members attended the church on Threadneedle Street, of course, like their heathen Calvinist master. The English servants, in a procession headed by the butler and rearguarded by the housekeeper, attended a proper divine service at the nearest Church of England parish.

It was unusual for all the servants to be gone from the house at once, leaving only milord and his secretary there. It was not, however, unprecedented. It had occurred on a few other occasions when Milord hosted Sunday guests.

There was no precise precedent for Marc's arrival in the house and Raudegen's arrival in the rear garden.

The English servants returned before the Huguenots did. They had a much shorter walk, after all. They entered through the back door. They did not leave through the back door, or any other door, at least not for quite a while. They found all the interior exits from the back hallway, a dingy and windowless narrow passageway, barricaded, and the rear door mysteriously barred behind them.

The Huguenot servants did not return at all, having taken the words of God to heart and, per instructions, departed hence unto another place as soon as the preacher delivered the charge and the Aaronic blessing.

Milord and his secretary left the house on the Strand by the front door, of course. The coachman arrived from the stables with punctilious promptness. Milord kept a generously-sized four-person carriage, which was just as well, since it already contained four people before Milord and his secretary entered it this lovely Sabbath morning.

The coachman drove decorously toward the church on Threadneedle Street.

Then he passed it.

The coach was later found on the docks, with the missing footman who had accompanied the cook to market gagged and bound up in it. He had some explaining to do.

The next morning, a party of Dutch and Flemish businessmen took ship for The Hague with their various servants and attendants. Two had letters of passage from Constantijn Huygens who was, of course, well known, at least by name, to all English customs officials. The other four were identified by their passports as middle-level employees of the Courteen and Crommelin mercantile firms. The papers were all authentic, though they didn't belong to the men who were using them at the moment.

CHAPTER 7

The Low Countries
March–April 1636

Any given Channel crossing from England to the Netherlands was likely to be better in March than in February. Not much, but some. On the average, so to speak. Marc Cavriani said that everyone involved in Henri de Rohan's rescue mission for his brother should be grateful for that. Moreover, Soubise was out from under an admittedly rather comfortable but prolonged house arrest in London.

Soubise failed to support that cheerful perspective, but did heave a dramatic sigh of relief at being on solid ground again after the Channel crossing. Raudegen looked at him speculatively. Their charge had not shown the slightest sign of seasickness. Indeed, he had moved around the deck with considerable agility for a man of his publicly proclaimed decrepitude.

The newspapers in The Hague were still celebrating the February birth of Ernst Wilhelm, infant Grand Duke of the Free County of Burgundy, first child of Bernhard and Claudia. While it might seem premature to a rational man that the columnists were discussing the possibility that someday this infant might marry the Netherlands' own Baby Archduchess (a cutie if ever there was one!), that didn't stop the reporters.

Marc gathered up the various passports and letters of passage. He would find someone his father knew in the Dutch diplomatic service to have them returned to Huygens in England by way of a diplomatic pouch.

Soubise inquired where the *Stadthouder* was to be found, made a courtesy call, and was invited to remain for a private supper and some informal conversation, his companions included.

Over wine, Fredrik Hendrik, who of course knew the elder Cavriani, fingered the wispy blond moustache that matched his wispy blond hair and wispy blond goatee and asked Marc about his *Wanderjahr*.

"I don't have many entertaining tales to tell of my travels," Marc answered with a grin. "Alas, I am a prudent young man. Prudent to the point of stupendous dullness. It's difficult to make much of the thugs who did not beat me up in Marseilles because I didn't stay around long enough for them to locate me.

"I did mention to that bargemaster on the Rhône that there was a place in the hull that looked perilously thin, but when he ignored me, I left the boat at the last stopping point before they would have needed to pull it out to do the portage over the rapids. That particular pool was deep and tended to swirl, I had heard. It was too bad they lost the wine, though, for it was a good vintage and would have made a nice profit for the seller. I hope the shipment was insured.

"In the matter of those people in Lyon who might or might not have been Spanish spies . . . all I can say is that the aggressive pseudo-barmaid did not seduce me, because I went up to bed early and put a bar across my door." He pushed back the curl that constantly fell down into the middle of his forehead and shrugged, both palms pointing upwards. "Some of us were born to have exciting adventures and some were not. Odysseus will never need to envy me."

He paused. "If I may inquire . . ."

"Permission granted."

"I need to contact *Froken* Susanna Allegretti. Per my father's arrangement, she was to be transferred from Brussels to your wife's staff some months ago. She is a skilled dressmaker. She would be with your lady wife."

But she wasn't. Not to the best of the *Stadthouder*'s knowledge. Nor, for that matter to that of his wife Amelia, her ladies-in-waiting, the steward, or anyone else. Nobody had even heard of her, much less of any proposed assumption of her into the household. There were no letters in the files. There was no notation in regard to compensation in the ledgers. The Hague had no knowledge of her existence.

"Which means," Marc said, "that I am going to Brussels. Raudegen, you can escort Soubise directly to France if you wish, but I'm going to Brussels. Anything could have happened to Susanna since the last time Papa heard from her. Anything!"

Raudegen was more inclined to the view that one should never attribute to malice those things that could be explained by stupidity and suggested that M. Cavriani's request for her transfer might have been lost in the mail or misplaced on someone's desk, so the girl was still snug and comfortable where she had been the preceding autumn.

Marc was junior to everyone else involved in the rescue mission, both in age and rank. Nonetheless, the party proceeded toward Brussels—with ample funds, for a change, Marc having first produced the brilliant idea of drawing money on the Netherlands branch of the Cavriani Frères firm that his Aunt Alis managed and then having located a banker in The Hague who was willing to produce a substantial advance upon the *Stadhouder*'s secretary's assistant's clerk's assurances that Marc was who he claimed to be. Faced with the options of either traveling from The Hague to Paris by way of Brussels furnished with sturdy horses, comfortable inns, and good food, or going directly from The Hague to Paris under conditions of utmost discomfort and frugality . . .

Not to mention that Raudegen, having developed a sneaking fondness for the little dressmaker when he escorted her from Basel to the Netherlands eighteen months or so earlier, agreed to the Brussels option . . . The whole party was going to Brussels. Soubise would have to endure it with what little good grace he could manage.

Soubise's valet, secretary, coachman, and cook took the news with even less grace.

* * *

Soubise hadn't enjoyed their stop in The Hague any more than he had enjoyed the Channel crossing. Nevertheless, he grumbled all the way to Brussels about having to leave it in such abominable weather.

"Yes, it remains true," Raudegen commented, eyeing the dripping sky with an expression of piety. "Money cannot buy happiness."

The roads from The Hague to Brussels were mostly mud, which was natural when the calendar was turning from late March into April. If wishes had been horses, they could have cut east from The Hague and caught a new railroad line that was well under construction. When it was complete, it would go from Amsterdam to Brussels, a strange one-rail construction with a few light cars. "By June," the *Stadhouder*'s secretary said. "The contractors promise that in spite of all the difficulties, delays, cost overruns, equipment failures, unexpected engineering challenges, insufficient bridges, and the like, they will have it open by June." Marc was not prepared to spend two or three months in The Hague waiting upon an uncertain technological future when Susanna was, presumably, in Brussels.

Soubise continued to utter profound complaints in regard to the detour.

"The direct road to Paris would be just as boggy," Marc pointed out.

Boggy. Boggy with running rivulets of water. Soggy. Soggy and sticky with an astounding capacity for removing horseshoes. Squishy, creeping over the tops of their boots. Squishy mixed with manure as it crept over the tops of and into their boots, turning their socks into slimy, sliding serpents. Rutted from carts and wagons, the rivulets filling up the ruts, so it was almost impossible to detect where the deep spots were.

When Aunt Alis saw Marc standing on her front steps—her *recently scrubbed* front steps, washed by the maid whose duty it was, among other things, to keep front steps immaculate—she gave him a look that made him reach up and twirl the curl that fell into the middle of his forehead as if he were still six years old. Then she made them go around, come in through the back of the house, and strip down to their drawers before she allowed them out of the mud room. She had the servants bring a copper tub and fill it, ordering them to take baths and put on clean clothes before they set foot on the meticulously scrubbed black and white tile floor of her entryway, much less the hardwood floors, and most certainly not yet any room with a carpet.

Soubise, too. Duke or no duke. For that matter, Calvinist or not. It was possible that she might have shown more respect to him if the Rohan family had been more solvent, but Marc rather doubted it. The only ducal privilege that Aunt Alis granted was that of the First Bath. The valet got the second bath because the duke declaimed at length, with gestures, that his sitting around in the nude for hours in this weather, with no clothes and no valet and no manservant to assist him in donning the clothes, would probably be the death of him, old man that he was. Impossible! Marc laughed and deferred to the valet, but maintained precedence over the duke's other servants.

Aunt Alis also sent the scullery maid out to scrub the front steps again, which earned the guests a sour-faced glare as the woman walked around the pile of dripping, filthy, clothes they had left on the mud room floor.

Soubise's valet rummaged through the luggage and managed to find a dress suit that he deemed presentable, so the duke remained to take the noon meal with his hostess, his unhappiness much ameliorated by an excellent leg of lamb accompanied by young peas, grown in Mme. Cavriani's own little hothouse on the roof of her stables, and some outstanding wine. They agreed that Wilhelm Wettin had been a fool to let himself be drawn into Oxenstierna's manipulations and that the Crown Loyalists would suffer for it in the forthcoming USE elections. They mulled over *Monsieur* Gaston's possible responses to no longer being heir to the French throne should Anne of Austria produce a son for Louis XIII next summer. They meditated on possible outcomes for the forthcoming theological conclave to which Pope Urban had summoned the continent's theologians, this made more titillating by the presence of Soubise's brother in Besançon, where it was to be held.

Having paid due obeisance to demonstrating that they both fulfilled their obligations to remain *au courant* with European politics, they got down to the matter of the financial status of the House of Rohan, which tided the conversation over until the servants started giving them pointed looks that reminded Alis that certain someones should be permitted to clear the table and get the dishes washed before the *unexpected houseguests* for whom the cook was *not prepared* came back in their large numbers, because they would expect to be *fed.* Mme. Cavriani's domestic staff was feeling much put out.

* * *

Susanna was, as Raudegen had predicted, where she had arrived in November of 1634 and where she had been the last time Leopold Cavriani heard from her—at the Coudenberg Palace, in the service of Queen Maria Anna. She was not, however, happy to be there and voiced a litany of indignant discontent. Much of it was focused on the obnoxious Lorrainer colonel, subject of numerous annoyed letters she had sent to Marc and his father, a man who made a practice of 'dropping by' the atelier and, "although I make every effort to ensure that I am never alone there, still it seems like the mistress of the dressmakers is always sending the other women away on this or that kind of errand or they say that it is time for them to leave for the day and . . ."

To Marc's great disappointment, his beloved was not in a mood for displays of public affection. Or of private affection. He felt that this situation should be remedied as soon as possible.

"When does he 'drop by?' At any particular time?" Raudegen asked. He looked benevolently at his former charge.

"Usually just as we are finishing our work. For a few months last year, he was blessedly absent, but he survived Duke Charles' campaigns.

Unfortunately. The quality of work we need to do requires daylight, so at this time of the year, he comes about the time of vespers."

"Every day?" Raudegen asked.

"No, but too often."

After giving her a chance to put on one of her good dresses, they hired a sedan chair so she could keep the hemline clean and returned to Aunt Alis, Marc being of the opinion that she would be able to think of something. Oh, she could. Her eyes sparkled, she waved her hands as she talked, and she began to choreograph a response. Even Raudegen got caught up in the project.

The unwelcome suitor did not reappear at the palace either of the next two days, which occasioned some waiting around. Soubise was more than happy to be in a comfortable house which served outstanding meals.

On the third day, the colonel arrived somewhat earlier than customary and found that there was no obstacle to his entering the atelier. Except for Susanna, it was abandoned.

After he had waited for a few minutes, Marc stuck his head around the jamb of the storage room door and saw the sun glistening on Susanna's red-gold hair. It was a sun that should have given up the futile struggle against the thin clouds and dirty window panes, but it had wrought mightily and triumphed in order to provide a personal halo for the loveliest girl in the world. He blinked.

What he heard when he stuck his head around the doorjamb was a series of venomous and vicious threats being directed at the same loveliest girl in the world.

"M. le Colonel, you are overly persistent. If you may recall, we have conducted this discussion on previous occasions." Susanna gestured toward the cast on his foot.

"I do have contacts. You are alone. Entirely alone. If you continue to refuse me, continue to try to refuse me . . ."

Marc looked over his shoulder at Raudegen and grinned. Then he tiptoed out of the storage area, ran into the corridor, and rushed through the main door of the atelier, his arms open, crying out, "Darling! Have you found a beautiful velvet in all the shades of autumn leaves to make your wedding dress yet?"

The Lorrainer turned around. Even on crutches, he could take care of this upstart boy. Wait! Wedding dress? There was a fiancé in the picture? A fiancé might signify squadrons of interested relatives. Perhaps the little dressmaker was not as isolated and without resources in the middle of a foreign country as he had assumed. He hesitated.

There's a proverb. "He who hesitates is lost." The moment of the colonel's hesitation was the moment when Raudegen sauntered out from the storage room.

When Raudegen left, he had the Lorrainer by the back of his collar. As soon as they were out of sight, Susanna kissed Marc. Their second kiss was even better than the first had been, Marc thought. The third was delightful and the fourth verged on spectacular. It was a beautiful afternoon in Brussels.

Brussels was no more mud-free than the surrounding countryside. Leaving the happy young couple to their mutual admiration and appreciation, Raudegen located a fine, damp, well-fertilized lane behind the royal stables and left the Lorrainer to contemplate his future from a supine position. Face down.

* * *

"You're going to Vienna with us, to visit your sick mother," Raudegen said that evening. Aunt Alis' servants had cleared off the table and they were dawdling over their wine.

"Why?"

"It's the best we can do with the documentation I can scratch up here," Marc said.

Susanna leaned back against his shoulder. "But Mama isn't in Vienna. She wasn't ever in Vienna. I was working there, for Archduchess Maria Anna, and then went to Munich with her, but Mama was working at the court of Tyrol, for one of the ladies-in-waiting to the regent. I'm not supposed to go haring off to Vienna or anyplace else with you. I'm supposed to go to The Hague to work in Frederik Hendrik's court and learn to live among Calvinists."

"We're going to France, not Vienna," Raudegen said. "Nor to Tyrol, for that matter."

"Then I'm not supposed to be going to *France* with you. Brussels turned out to be no help at all for learning to live among Calvinists, at least not in the couture shop at the palace. We know that the alliance exists, of course, but for all practical purposes, this is a Catholic court and I might as well have gone back to Vienna from Basel. I'm working for the same person."

"We can't leave you here." Marc fingered the stem of his glass. "Even after Raudegen finished with the colonel this afternoon, the guy's likely to heal and come back, bringing associates."

"He isn't even seriously injured,' Raudegen said, "although he seemed to believe that I was, to use your words, overly persistent about pulling his crutches out from under him every time he tried to walk away from my voice of rational persuasion. Overly persistent from his perspective, at least. Also, there are Calvinists in France. We will be stopping at a Huguenot household."

Marc focused back on Susanna. "I can't send you up to The Hague by yourself. There's no trace of the transfer documents anywhere. We suspect the mail is being interfered with."

"The mail here was interfered with at the level of the head dressmaker," Raudegen said. "I got it out of the colonel that he bribed her to destroy the letter and not say anything to anyone. As for the mail to The Hague, I'm in no position to say. This backstairs section of the Brussels court looks to me like a nest of pro-Spanish vipers. We need to get you out of it. Our first obligation, though is to deliver our packages to France, so that's where you have to go."

"But . . ." Susanna protested. "They aren't all vipers." She grinned. "Joseph the cobbler is a sweet old man. He fixed my shoe heels to have narrow tips with metal ends, so I could break the colonel's instep when I stomped."

"Sorry," Marc said. "It's the best we can do with the documentation I've been able to procure."

He wasn't really sorry.

Susanna blinked. "Mama *isn't* sick, is she?"

"Not as far as we know, but it's a good excuse, especially since you're an only surviving child."

"I haven't heard from her for ages and I'm not even sure that she's still in Tyrol. When the regent remarried to Grand Duke Bernhard, she didn't take most of the ladies-in-waiting she had in Tyrol with her. Mama's mistress had come from Tuscany when the regent married her second husband. She may have gone back, or taken service in some other court. But if Mama isn't sick, then that's all right." She snuggled her head against his collarbone and looked up flirtatiously. "Am I your fiancée?"

"You're more than welcome to be."

"Then I need to go to The Hague and learn to live among Calvinists," she said stubbornly.

"Magdeburg," Marc suggested.

"Magdeburg is Lutheran, not Calvinist. The emperor isn't even married and when he was, he left his wife behind in Sweden for . . . how many years? . . . while he rattled around in the Germanies. She only visited him once. I'm sure he buys a few court clothes for Princess Kristina for ceremonial functions, but she's still a child and her governess-companion is an up-timer who wears simple clothing. I've seen pictures. What good would Magdeburg do me? Tell me why it would be preferable to France."

"This is not the end of the world." Raudegen was getting impatient. "We're not staying in France, even with Huguenots, after Soubise is settled in. We deliver the packages to Paris and go on. I'll stop in Burgundy and send the two of you from Besançon to Geneva. Once you get there, Marc's parents will have the pick of all the world's Calvinists for you to learn to live among."

"Oh. So that's so, I guess. Just sort of *so*. Without recourse." She looked at Marc. "Your letters were diplomatic and didn't tell me anything. Of course, with half the world reading the other half's mail, that was sensible of you, but did you learn if you could live among Catholics? Was your time in Naples as enlightening as your father predicted it would be?"

"In a lot of ways. It wasn't always comfortable, particularly after certain representatives of the inquisition became aware of my presence in the city. I spent one difficult day and most of the following night holding still in the middle of a nativity scene made up of life-sized papier-mâché figures. All of them wearing cloth costumes. I was one of the magi–the one who had his head bent down with his hood falling over his face while he made his offering to the Christ Child. It was strange, not to mention hard on my knees."

"Oh."

"I did learn, though, that not all Catholics, not even all Spanish Catholics resident in the Kingdom of the Two Sicilies, agree with the inquisition's aims, not even when they earn a living making statues of saints and such. It was my landlord, Bartolo, who sent his son to sneak me out of there through the staging area. I barely had time to get the kinks out of my legs, eat a slice of bread, and squirrel away a bottle of wine for future emergencies before I turned into a bale of denim."

"The inquisition has no interest in denim?"

"Not when the seals on the bale assured the investigators that I was being imported rather than exported. Nor was I heavy enough to be a container of forbidden books."

"Seals?"

"Well, yes. That's the whole trick, you see–or at least most of it. Be as authentic as you can be. The denim had come down the coast from Genoa. The bale happened to find itself removed to the staging area for the nativity scenes, where it was tucked into a shed, eviscerated, reinforced, filled up with me, and deposited back in its original place on the wharf before anybody noticed its side trip. I stayed on the wharf until a wheelbarrow came by and the barrow man knocked on the frame of the bale. Out I came, in he went, I pushed the wheelbarrow down the pier and across the gangplank, and the barrow's load took ship for Marseilles, which was where it was on the lading list as headed. Along with me, since I had a ticket. Under someone else's name, of course. I'd reimbursed Bartolo for the barrow in advance. The bale left the wharf again and went on its way inland, stopping in the staging area long enough to disgorge the barrow man, that was Bartolo's son again, and retrieve its original contents. Then it set out for some village in Calabria, none the worse for wear. Denim is pretty tough stuff."

Susanna nodded. "That reminds me. Before we leave, I need to pay for my new shoes. Old Joseph has ten pairs ready for me, but I'll have to borrow money from you. We had worked out an installment plan, but if I'm not coming back . . ."

Raudegen winced on behalf of the pack horse. Ten pair of shoes? Who needed ten pair of shoes all at once?

The next day they headed for Paris, assorted Huguenots in tow. Because Susanna begged, they detoured by way of the airfield. A plane was scheduled to come in. She wanted to see it. She had been in Brussels for a long time and had never seen an airplane land, because they came during the daylight, almost always, and during the daylight, she was at work. She gasped in awe. Soubise shuddered and proclaimed that nobody would ever get *him* into one of those things.

They had not expected that Louis XIII would be killed, nor that the crown would be seized by *Monsieur* Gaston. These events, news of which reached them after they had spent three more days mucking their way through mud, meant that the question "Are we there yet?" acquired some dire undertones. Gaston's people were said to be on high alert when it came to potential subversives.

They stopped at an inn—a nice one, courtesy of Aunt Alis' parting bank draft—to spend an evening considering their options. The status of Soubise was interesting. He had been exiled by Louis XIII. Was it safe to interpret that the king's death rendered the proclamation of exile invalid? Or not? If it was no longer valid, would it occur to Gaston to renew it?

"More practically," Susanna said, "*has* it occurred to the new king to renew it. We don't have any way of knowing. With everything else that's going on, sorry M. de Soubise, your status isn't front page news."

"We're miles from a radio," Marc complained. "I'm not going to get anything from Geneva. This probably explains why there weren't any letters from Papa waiting for me in The Hague or Brussels. If nothing else, Gaston has messed up the postal system for bags coming through France. We're winging it from here on."

"Don't do anything that will cause me to flee like a thief in the night," Soubise grumbled. "At my age, I'm not as nimble as I used to be."

The next day, they sank back into the mud. It appeared that the flight path to the Brussels airfield followed, more or less, the route of the road. They had seen a couple of planes going over as they mucked their way south. When the second of the craft passed over their heads, Soubise looked up at the sky, down at the brown slime caked on his horse's legs and hooves, and then muttered, "maybe they could get me into one of those things, if conditions on the ground were bad enough."

The likelihood that anyone would successfully flee the border crossing was nil. It was an approximately rectangular acre of mudhole bounded by customs booths.

The traffic, human, animal, and inanimate, was covered with mud. The border guards, mostly human as far as the eye could tell, were covered with shit-colored splatters. It never crossed their minds that someone who was in a status of "might have to flee" would even try to pass through the border that day. The best that anyone could hope to achieve was "manage to pick his feet up" out of the gluey mess.

They hit the Paris road and slogged, finally reaching the city and going to ground. Not in the Rohan household, where it would have been impossible to conceal Soubise's presence. Rather, even though it was essentially next door to the *Palais-Royal*, recently renamed by Marie de' Medici from being the *Palais-Cardinal*, they slipped into the residence of Soubise's unmarried sister Anne at the *Hôtel de Mélusine*, where she fluttered around her brother with hot poultices, soft pillows, and current gossip.

CHAPTER 8

Besançon
April 1636

"Ron Stone has notified me," Henri de Rohan said to Grand Duke Bernhard, "that your wife will be accompanied by a member of his family to serve in your vaccination campaign."

"Just as well," Bernhard grumbled. "They told me that Lambert, a decent second option since he's the administrator of the Leahy Medical Center and also has been in Burgundy before, has other commitments."

The Monster touched down with a flurry of air from its skirts. Grand Duchess Claudia emerged, followed by a nursemaid who was carrying her infant son, followed by Gerry Stone.

Bismarck whispered to Ruvigny, "The mountains were in labor and they brought forth a mouse."

"Morning, Your Grace," Gerry said to Rohan as the grand duke turned and bore his spouse and heir away. "Since you're here to meet me, I guess Ron radioed that because the Prague trip with Dad and Magda already ruined this semester anyway, he thinks I might as well be useful and come be the 'public face' for universal, or at least as universal as the grand duke can get it, smallpox vaccination in the County of Burgundy. Being as I'm a member of the Lothlorien Pharmaceuticals family and all that."

"We're delighted to have you."

"Honestly?" Gerry asked. "Do you mean it? The grand duke didn't look exactly ecstatic. This face? I'm sure some *maire* is going to be thrilled off his gourd when a kid with bright red hair and a pointy nose wanders into his village and announces, 'I'm from the government and I'm here to help you' "

"There's been a glitch," Kamala Dunn said that evening, "and nobody notified Ron. Not that I can blame the grand duke's staff for being overwhelmed, with all the high muckety-mucks in the Catholic church who are going to be arriving like a deluge. Nobody is ready to start."

"Oh, double-disgust. What a pain."

"Come on. I'll take you to dinner, at least. You can talk to some of the rest of the up-timers here and I can introduce you to a couple of local guys I know."

The food wasn't bad, and neither were the guys, even though they were a lot older, probably over 20. Not as old as Ms. Dunn, but older than Gerry.

"So," he said to August von Bismarck. "What next? There's not even a university here and I'm pretty sure my French isn't good enough to take lecture notes, even if there was one. What am I going to do now?"

"Everybody knows that the best way to learn a language . . ." Bismarck began.

* * *

The news of Louis XIII's death and Gaston's assumption of the throne reached Besançon almost immediately—rumors first and confirmation following close on their heels.

"What Rohan seemed to be saying," Gerry remarked to Bismarck, "is that his wife and daughter need to get the hell out of Dodge, and this time he's not taking 'no' for an answer. Amid all the rabid frothing at the mouth that he did."

"What's 'Dodge'?" Bismarck asked.

"Who's Ruvigny?" Gerry countered. "Dodge was a town in Kansas where a lot of wild west movies were set. A lot of the plots involved that it wasn't safe for someone to stay in Dodge, usually because a U.S. Marshal was after him."

"Ruvigny's the guy I went to Paris with last fall. He was standing next to me when you got off the Monster. He didn't come to the dinner that *Madame* Dunn held."

Ruvigny came hurrying into the room. "I'm the guy you're going to Paris with again, August. The order this time is to remove the ladies, by persuasion if possible and by skullduggery if necessary. And leave yesterday, if not the day before."

"Can I go?" Gerry asked.

"No, ye gods! Why?"

Gerry pointed his thumb at Bismarck. "He says that spending time in France is the best way for me to improve my French. There's nothing else for me to do here until Ms. Dunn and the *cordon sanitaire* folks get their act together. It's always easier to ask for forgiveness than permission. Why not?"

"We're leaving now. Right now."

"I haven't even unpacked my duffel bag."

On the Road Again
May 1636

Camped beside a poorly maintained track in eastern France, Ruvigny tapped his finger on his kneecap. "I should have given him time to unpack that cursed duffel bag, no matter how much of a hurry we were in."

"It wouldn't have done any good," Bismarck pointed out. "The infernal instrument is small and portable. He could have slipped it into his pocket."

It turned out that Gerry played the harmonica, but not well. "It's an old up-time tradition," he assured them. "People sit around a fire and some guy plays a harmonica."

Oh bury me not, on the lone prairieeeee . . .

Paris
May 1636

"I would say . . ." Soubise hoisted himself to his feet with more ease than rheumatic knee joints would normally allow a man, walked over to the sideboard, and decanted his own brandy. Among the lessons that had been dinned into him by Raudegen, by young Cavriani, even by the formidable Madame Cavriani in Brussels, over the past weeks was the infallible truth that servants had ears. He and Anne were alone. He turned and lifted his glass.

"I would say that although I haven't heard from Henri since before we left London, I doubt that he will embrace the idea of Gaston as king of France. His fits and starts caused Bernhard too much trouble in Lorraine last year."

"Is it certain that Anne of Austria is in the Low Countries with her son and that man?"

Soubise wrinkled his forehead at his sister's implication that Anne of Austria's son might not also be the son of the late Louis XIII. 'That man' would be Cardinal Mazarin.

"Yes, the dowager queen is in Brussels. Fernando and Maria Anna, and perhaps more importantly the old infanta, have taken the infant king under their protection."

"Infant king!" Mademoiselle Anne, who was hostile to Anne of Austria at the best of times, stamped her foot.

"He isn't the same child," Soubise said. "Not the one who grew up to revoke the Edict of Nantes in that other world."

"Oh, I know he isn't the same child," Anne said, slapping the table. "For one thing, he's two years older than that one was. But this baby will be brought up by the same people, a Spanish woman and an Italian churchman. He will be under the same influences, so I prophesy that he will do the same thing, or something very like it, if he mounts the throne and has an opportunity."

* * *

Marguerite pelted into the breakfast room. "Henri is back again! With M. von Bismarck and an up-timer. A genuine up-timer. I've never met one before. I saw *Madame* Mailey when she came to negotiate the treaty after the League of Ostend *débâcle*, but I never got to meet her because *Maman*," she waved at her mother, "could not decide if it was acceptable etiquette for us to be presented to her, or if she must insist that the USE's ambassador plenipotentiary, being a commoner, must be presented to us. And I saw the famous physician, too, but at a distance. He is impressive, for a barber-surgeon."

"Why," the older duchess asked, her voice like ice, "is he here?" Her well-planned morning seemed likely to descend into chaos.

"With all due respect, Your Grace," Ruvigny said as he came through the door, "you must know."

"The duke wants us to leave Paris? Still wants it? Wants it again?"

Ruvigny handed over a packet of letters.

"I would not say that he merely wants it, Your Grace. I would say that this time he requires it."

As soon as Raudegen and Marc dropped into the stables at the *Hôtel de Sully*, they encountered the emissaries from Grand Duke Bernhard. Or, to be precise, the emissaries from Henri de Rohan who happened to be employees of Grand Duke Bernhard. Complicated by the presence of Gerry Stone, the up-timer. Layers upon layers. Emissaries from Rohan who had strict orders to remove the duke's wife and daughter from the troubled situation in France whether the ladies wanted to be removed or not.

They reported back to Soubise that their group might be moving on.

"I just got here," Soubise moaned. "My muscles ache. My joints ache. I'm never moving again."

"You've been in Paris for nearly two weeks, so you should be fairly well recovered from your travels," Raudegen pointed out.

"There's no need for you to go with the duchesses when they leave," Mademoiselle Anne said. "You are always welcome to stay with me, for as long as necessary."

"I don't think his joints ache all that much," Marc commented as they walked back to the Palais Rohan. "He wasn't any worse off than the rest of us while we were riding in the mud; he was a lot better off than his valet. He may have gotten a bit soft while he was in London, but he's been in the *salle* every morning since we got to Mademoiselle Anne's."

"Where has Colonel Raudegen gone this morning?" Marguerite asked the next day.

"To start making overtures, more or less." Ruvigny cocked his head to one side. "Put out feelers at the court by way of military men who know Grand Duke Bernhard, get some sense of the mood from former associates of your *Grand-père* Sully, that sort of thing. Marc is speaking to various associates of his father–bankers, financiers, people that Gaston will need if the government is to have funds. This all has to be done before your aunt starts hinting at *salons* and *soirées* that the allegiances of the Rohans would be more likely to move in the king's favor if he revoked the exile decree. The king has a lot of popular support right now, but it's still far from universal support. If quite a few people start murmuring about how it would be desirable for your uncle to come back to France, he and his advisers may conclude that it is their own idea."

Marguerite rested her chin on the heel of one hand. "Yes, it would be harder if we were asking him to allow Papa to come, because they know that Papa is calculating and ambitious. He shows it. I suspect that Uncle is also. He just isn't obvious. But Uncle is *already* here."

"You know that," Susanna said. "I know that." She waved one hand. "Colonel Raudegen knows that; your mother and aunt know that. I don't doubt that several dozen royal spies know that. The new king does not officially know that. Right now, it will be a lot better if he and his advisers don't officially know that."

"If he reverses the edict as a 'gesture of magnanimity,' " Raudegen interrupted, "then we will wait a couple of weeks of discreet 'travel time' before your uncle 'arrives.' Otherwise, if the king won't reverse his exile, we'll have to take him on to Burgundy. But if the hints *to* the court receive favorable hints *from* the court, then your *Maman* and *Tante* can make a formal request."

"*Will* the king let Uncle Soubise stay?"

That was also a question that Soubise was discussing with Mademoiselle Anne, but not the only one. Assuming that Gaston did give permission for him to 'return' to Paris and he would be able to reside there openly, his choice of residence would have implications. Ramifications. Connotations. Public relations considerations. He would be far more comfortable if he remained with Anne. He had never liked his sister-in-law and never would. But . . .

"I think you should take up residence at the townhouse," Anne said. "Residing with the duchess and Marguerite would make you seem to be accepting charity from Sully and perhaps appear to lend substance to any rumors that we are in financial difficulties. However, occupying Rohan's townhouse on the *Place Royale* will make a statement that you are now the senior adult representative of the family in France: a member of the house by birth rather than marriage." Further discussion ensued. And ensued. And ensued.

* * *

"This is the morning that Soubise is to 'arrive'?" Susanna asked a few days later. "In public, that is, and take up residence at the townhouse?"

Marc nodded. "We 'expect' him shortly before noon. The king issued his proclamation. I—well, people I know—planted quite true reports in the Amsterdam newspapers that he had left England some time earlier this spring and met with the *Stadthouder* in The Hague. We discreetly avoided pinning down when this occurred. Vague is your friend. The Paris papers picked that up, of course. Raudegen has managed to cobble together a decent-sized retinue to 'accompany' him, since he would not be expected to travel with just a secretary, cook, coachman, and valet. He's hired several plain but good quality carriages and a half-dozen bodyguards, and rented a couple of dozen trunks. The trunks are empty, but as far as the reporters and the gawkers along the street are concerned, he'll have about as much luggage as would be expected if he were coming from the Low Countries. He'll hold a news conference, of course."

"Will Sully and his wife be coming? Not today, but eventually?"

Monsieur Gaston, not one to lose a public relations opportunity, had not only revoked Soubise's exile, but also added a *lagniappe* by ending the house arrest of his father's former first minister.

"No." It was Marguerite who replied to Susanna. "My grandfather is old; my grandmother asserts that she is not well, though she may outlive us all. In their case, it's the appearance that they are again welcome at court that matters. My grandfather is happy and grateful, but they won't return to Paris."

"Your uncle's servants that he brought from London will 'come' with him as part of his public entourage. That's obvious." Susanna turned to Marc. "Are we moving? You and I and Colonel Raudegen?"

"We're not moving as part of this morning's entourage," Marc said. "Think! Just think! In the public narrative, Soubise has no association with any of us. And shouldn't have. I rather doubt that Mademoiselle Anne has any wish to extend us her hospitality an instant longer than she must. I assume that Raudegen will find us an apartment. The rest of us will transfer to wherever it may be in a couple more days, with no fanfare whatsoever. Or, perhaps, simply go on to Burgundy."

"But I want Susanna," Marguerite squealed.

Marc quirked a smile. "I want Susanna, too, but I hardly ever get her."

"I will ask *Maman*." She looked at Marc. "If she agrees, you could ask the colonel if you could come to us. Henri and Bismarck are staying with us. There's an immense amount of space. Please come. It would be such fun to have you."

"It will also save us a significant amount of money," was Raudegen's contribution to the plan. "We are instructed by the grand duke to remain here for the time being and render all due assistance to Rohan's emissaries."

Laubach, Solms-Laubach
May 1636

Katharina Juliana opened the letter from Albert Otto's Aunt Sofie that had arrived in the mail sack, addressed to her rather than to him. The widow of Margrave Joachim Ernst von Brandenburg-Ansbach, Aunt Sofie had been regent since his death. It had been a heavy responsibility in these times of war. Friedrich would have come of age next year, but with his death last fall at Warta, in the same battle that took the life of Wilhelm of Hesse-Kassel, Sofie would continue to bear the burden until Albrecht, now sixteen, came of age. That had required another letter of condolence last November, among many others. Warta had not been merciful to Gustavus' officer corps.

She started to nibble on her right thumbnail; then pulled it out of her mouth, made a face, and pulled on a glove to remind herself not to do that.

In another world, King Louis XIV of France had revoked the Edict of Nantes that granted toleration to the French Huguenots, their fellow Calvinists. Sofie had learned that in that other world, the ruler of Ansbach had opened its borders to the refugees, bringing in large numbers of skilled workers in specialized trades that redounded to the economic advantage of the territory for centuries thereafter.

Käthe's hand came up involuntarily and she got a mouthful of fabric. Wincing, she pulled it out of her mouth.

If there should be such a revocation in this world, Aunt Sofie was making generous plans to take maximum advantage of the Huguenots' misfortune. She had also written to Amalie Elisabeth suggesting that, in case of necessity in this world, Hesse might do likewise, given its precarious economy. Pharmaceuticals would help Kassel, and the revival of the university at Marburg should attract talent, but having more resources available never hurt anyone.

It's time for Amalie Elisabeth to require Albert Otto to start representing her to the Estates or on committees of the confidential council, or something. He's old enough now. The rest of the world should see that the male members of the family support her regency.

Then maybe we could go to Magdeburg. Or at least to Kassel. And I could see my sisters.

Käthe frowned. It wouldn't hurt Solms-Laubach, either, to have an influx of skilled workers. Albert Otto rarely gave a lot of thought to remote contingencies, but she put his aunt's letter on top of the stack of correspondence his secretary had left for him and wrote a letter of her own to her sister offering their services to Hesse should they ever be needed.

Besançon
May 1636

Rohan, as Bernhard's *Statthalter* and present on the spot, learned the truth of the papal assassination 'attempt' almost at once. With the grand duke not only out of town but away in Lorraine, he had his hands full. Far too full to pay detailed attention to what his family was doing or envoys were accomplishing in Paris.

Paris
May 1636

"I'm glad Uncle Soubise will be here for quite a while," the little duchess said over a folder of fabric samples. "I hadn't seen him for ages, but I like him even though he blusters most of the time and mutters the rest of it. He doesn't really mean any of his complaints. I think he's cute."

Susanna looked up. "Should I be sitting in your presence, Your Grace? I have been concerned about this. After all, your status and mine . . ."

"You're not here as a dressmaker for me. You are here as the fiancée of M. Cavriani, whose father, if not noble, is rich and knows everyone. You are here as *Maman*'s guest, not to work for us. You will stand in my presence in the public rooms, of course, should you be called to be present. In the private rooms, you are my own guest because I invited you in. Here, I say that you may sit. Maybe you are even someone who might become my friend, if we know one another long enough. Friends can sit to look over a book of fabric swatches, can't they?"

"I guess so."

"Then that's settled. Now, about Uncle Soubise, what I wanted to say is . . ."

Susanna meditated for a moment on whether or not she was now on such terms with Marc that she ought to start practicing how to acquire intelligence data.

Yes, she was.

"Marc says that your uncle is much shrewder than he pretends to be."

"Papa thinks so, too, that Uncle Soubise is undervalued." Marguerite hesitated, as if she were about to reveal a secret sin. "I have read some of the drafts of Papa's *mémoires*. *Grand-père* Sully's also. I started because I miss them, but parts are interesting. Don't tell my mother. She loathes the *femmes savantes*, even though she owns quite a lot of books herself. More than Papa has. It's probably because *Tante* Anne is one: she reads Hebrew and writes poetry. So I wouldn't want *Maman* to think that am in danger of becoming intellectual. I don't think it's likely that I will become a *savante*, do you, even though *Grand-mère* Rohan was almost one? I don't think they had a word for it, way back then. In any case, she was a most *indomitable* woman, as shown by her actions during the year in which she and my *Tante* Anne were held captive by the Catholics after La

Rochelle surrendered. Such splendid recalcitrance in the face of persecution!" She giggled. "Richelieu said that she was *malignant to the last degree*. But, what was I talking about? Papa thinks that if the English commanders and the authorities in La Rochelle had listened to Uncle's advice during the last revolt, then things might not have gone so badly for us. I don't remember much about that time, though."

"How old were you?"

Marguerite calculated. "Ten, when it started. Eleven when it finished. I don't remember the revolt before that at all, because I was only six. For it, I know what people tell me." She closed the sample book. "They don't tell me much."

"Marc thinks . . ." Susanna began.

Marguerite's mind flitted away. "I saw Marc kiss you at breakfast this morning."

"I kissed him back," Susanna said. "It wasn't the first time, and it won't be the last time. I'll probably marry him some day, when we are old enough, if I can learn to live among Calvinists."

"I thought that you are already his fiancée."

"Our families haven't signed any contracts. His father forwards our letters to one another, though. My mother and stepfather are aware that his father, though a Calvinist, is also in a position to provide for his future very well indeed. So. Well. 'Flirt to convert' is what my stepfather said. Not that there is any prospect that he would. Anyway, M. Cavriani was there the first time we kissed each other."

"So. Well. Anyway," Marguerite mocked her. "It sounds to me as if you are indeed his fiancée, whether you know it or not. I have never kissed anyone. I never will, unless I get married. Perhaps then I will have to. Would I have to kiss a man if we were betrothed but not married yet? I hope my husband will be businesslike about begetting and not . . ." Marguerite made a little gesture that somehow reminded Susanna of worms, spiders, slugs, snails, and swarms of things that crept and crawled. ". . . not put his hands all over me or slobber all over my face. How can you stand it? How can *Maman* stand it?

"Also . . ." The little duchess assumed a facial expression that would have better suited a Scots preacher's wife with seven decades of life under her belt. "It's bad for your reputation."

Susanna raised her eyebrows. "Don't you have something more important to worry about than my reputation? You're in the middle of a country that's cheering for a usurper, and from all I hear, the usurper is on the other end of the spectrum from trustworthy. For what it's worth, Your Grace, I assure you that my *virtue* is quite intact. As for *reputation*, girls like me don't have one. Or need one, for that matter."

"Girls like you? It's women like *Maman* and the other court ladies who don't have reputations. Not, at least, good reputations. Don't you *want* a good reputation?"

Susanna's forbearance snapped. "Where would I get one? You've lived in courts all your life. You know what the morals are, and they aren't what your Calvinist preachers would like them to be. They're not even the way your ordinary provincial official or school teacher or shopkeeper or artisan manages his household. Even in the Netherlands, where both couples–the king and queen and the *Stadthouder* and his wife–are so generally well behaved most of the time, although it is said that Frederik Hendrik only married Amalia of Solms because she refused to become his mistress and his brother said he had to get married to someone, it doesn't mean that all the people who revolve around them follow their example. No one raises an eyebrow when a servant becomes a nobleman's mistress. And if, when he ends it, she comes away with a generous settlement, she has a *better* prospect for marrying some other upper servant rather than a worse one. If I had given into that Lorrainer colonel and he he'd really had as much money as he claimed to have, my dowry would have been a *lot* bigger than it is."

"Well, I will never take a lover. A husband will be more than enough." Marguerite bowed her head. "My *Tante* Catherine, one of Papa's other sisters, died before I was born, but they tell me that when Henri IV made a *galant* advance to her, she answered, 'I am too poor to be your wife and too well-born to be your mistress.' Too poor or too proud, I will never be any man's mistress. It's hard to think of virtue separate from reputation, though. Isn't reputation a mirror of a person's character?"

Then she popped her head up again, her eyes bright. "What colonel?"

Susanna tsked. "Not one you know. Just remember. Reputation is nothing but what 'they' say. A lot of what 'they' say can be malicious—rumor, insinuations, allegations. But I don't have to care. I am who I am, and Marc believes me and not anyone else's gossip. And if he damages my 'reputation' by kissing me, he'll take the greatest of care for me, for myself and not for what anybody says about me."

"It's almost worse," the little duchess concluded, "when what 'they' say is true rather than false."

CHAPTER 9

Paris
June 1636

"There's a limit to how long the duchess will be able to drag her feet," Raudegen said. "Soubise is making public appearances now and has managed to get whispers that Rohan has requested that she join him circulating around the court. If she is seen to refuse, then rumors about an unconditional breakdown of her marriage will follow in short order. As long as Rohan publicly condones her actions, her standing remains unimpeachable. Once he withdraws that toleration . . ."

Whispers did not quite cover it.

"Hell and damnation!" Soubise yelled. "You have to go. Rohan's demands, not requests, have ratcheted up to a level that not even you can ignore or refuse them. Since I'm here, I'm the one who can and will stay in Paris to advance our causes at court. Get your promiscuous little tush off to Besançon." The relations between the duchess and her brother-in-law had never been marked by familial affection.

She glared at Soubise in return. "This is absurd, you know. Within three months, you will find yourself crosswise with the king and get your head cut off."

"Perhaps so, but I am philosophical about it. Better for the family to lose a crusty old bachelor uncle than to lose its heiress."

With the senior members of the household making life rather unpleasant, the younger ones followed Marc's principle of "when in doubt, duck."

Marguerite, with Susanna as fashion consultant, went shopping. Or, more accurately, ordered certain chosen shopkeepers to bring their stock to her for examination after Susanna had gone out and scouted what was available. She purchased yards upon yards of fabric, lace, and trimming. And quite a few shoes.

Gerry went and matriculated at the University of Paris, just on general principles, in order to have his name on the register. "It's getting to be sort of like that 'Kilroy was here' cartoon," he said to Bismarck. Explanations followed. And, on the theory that he hadn't time to unpack the smaller kit from his duffel bag before he left Burgundy, he vaccinated the entire Rohan household against smallpox.

Raudegen, Ruvigny, and Marc collected rumors and avoided the salon whenever they could.

"Will you stop that? Better, you *will* stop that."

Gerry took the harmonica out of his mouth and the strains of *Your cheatin' heart* ceased to resonate through hayloft above the stables.

"Do you want something different?"

"I don't want that instrument of torture at all. Think of something else to do."

✳ ✳ ✳

"Oh grief," Marguerite said to Bismarck. "Candale's back in Paris. His only redeeming quality is that he's off serving in the army most of the time. If he's here, he'll come slithering around again, but I thought *Maman* had decided to stick with Gondi for a while longer."

"Which one is worse?"

"I don't know. I avoided Candale when he used to be around and I avoid Gondi now that he's around. 'They' say that Candale is agreeable and lively, but he's never seemed that way to me."

Marc pushed the curl back off his forehead. "What's de la Valette doing these days? Is Candale fronting for his brother?"

"Hmmn," Marguerite said. She wrinkled her forehead. "Which brother? Louis? The cardinal? He's with the army right now, I think. I haven't heard anyone say that he's up to anything in particular, though of course he'll be scrambling to ingratiate himself with the new king. Bernard was taken captive by the USE two years ago, of course, and hasn't come up with a ransom yet. Old Épernon, their father, is still alive. He's ancient, at least eighty years old. Still, he's the duke, and he holds the purse strings. As long as Bernard is rotting somewhere in Brunswick, Épernon controls his son, who's the heir after Candale since Candale is childless. Nobody likes Bernard, so his family won't pay to get him back. The politics of the Nogarets are too complicated to sort out, even for them, probably."

Gerry shook his head, He found the customs of the French nobility that allowed a father and his three sons to have four different names dizzying. Not being the kind of person who worried about saving face, he said so. "I thought I understood the German system," he said. "They use places too, but it's consistent. William, Ernst, Albrecht, and Bernhard, before he moved out of town, are all *Herzog* and all *von Sachsen-Weimar*, except for some of them changing their names to Wettin, of course. But all of them who change it use Wettin."

"The French designations aren't personal names," Ruvigny explained. "They're the names of estates or lands that the family holds. Rohan is a dukedom and the duke has its title. Soubise inherited different estates from which he takes his title from his mother."

Bismarck contributed with some disdain the opinion that the lands on which a lot of those French "*de* Somewhere" and "*sieur de* This or That" titles were based often didn't amount to more than a large farm. "Not that our estates amount to much more than a large farm," he added. "But though we may be *Niederadel*, we're also *Uradel*."

Gerry frowned. I know "lesser nobility," which is mediatized sometimes and non-titled sometimes and . . . stuff. But what's *Uradel?* Prehistoric nobility?"

"It means that when the first margrave who wandered into Brandenburg because he had been appointed to manage the territory by some Carolingian emperor hired the first man in the region who could put quill to parchment and started keeping government records, we were already there. No king or emperor or one of his minions 'raised' us to the nobility or 'created' us as nobles; they found us already in place." He frowned. "What do you know about the feudal system?"

"We had a unit on it, maybe in fourth grade. The textbook had a picture of a castle on top of a hill, another one of a knight wearing armor, and the noble in the castle had a coat of arms and was oppressing the peasants in the village at the bottom of the hill. Mrs. Jones had us make up coats of arms for our families and draw them. I drew a geodesic dome and some weed and got sent to the principal's office. Oh, and everybody held fiefs from the king."

"You were probably studying about England," Ruvigny said. "When *Guillaume de Normandie* conquered it, he denied all existing claims and rights, giving land and titles to his own followers, so England has few nobles. The king has to create a noble, there. Most of the people who would be lower nobility in France or the Germanies, Spain or Poland, are a higher class of commoners in England. They call them 'gentry'."

That evening Bismarck wrote a letter to Grand Duke Bernhard advising him to obtain a copy of one of Grantville's fourth grade social studies textbooks if possible, for it would almost certainly be of immense assistance in comprehending how the up-timers regarded the European nobility, and why.

*　*　*

Soubise also ducked, insofar as he spent most of his time, when not at court or schmoozing with friends he hadn't seen for a decade or more, with Mademoiselle Anne.

She was frowning. "Gaston is no perfect choice as a ruler, Benjamin. I'll admit that. However, any way I think about it, I believe that in the long run, the other choice would be far worse."

Soubise contemplated his feet which, clothed in beautifully embroidered but also quite comfortable felt carpet slippers, were propped up on a hassock that was just the correct height.

He could endure physical hardship. He had endured a great deal of it when he was younger and commanding soldiers and sailors. He could even put up with the necessity of constant practice to maintain his skills.

He saw no reason to endure one bit more of it than necessary.

"Mnnn?"

That was all the encouragement that she needed to embark upon an extensive diatribe that involved the current king, General Turenne, the dowager queen, Cardinal Mazarin, the current queen—which digressed into a diatribe on the perfidious ducal family of Lorraine—and, because Candale was back in town, the general undesirability of the Nogaret family.

Laubach, Solms–Laubach
June 1636

Albert Otto rustled the pages of the newspaper.

Käthe frowned. Even though the paper came from Frankfurt am Main, it was not of high quality. Or . . . Her husband claimed that the content was of high quality, but the material was not. The cheap ink was rubbing off onto his hands. From there, experience indicated, he would smear it onto his trousers, given his annoying habit of rubbing his hands against the sides of his legs to clean off anything he got on them, from goose grease to horse slobber. Why he wouldn't use a handkerchief or napkin . . .

Once he went out for his morning tour of the stables and kennels, she picked up the newspaper, pulling on a pair of washable gloves first. Another Italian man from Grantville had taken over as Gustavus' new prime minister. Piazza was his name. There was an editorial speculating about Amalie Elisabeth's growing influence as a power broker, even though she was affiliated with the Crown Loyalists rather than the Fourth of July Party.

Her sister was becoming quite well-known.

She was sitting at a breakfast table in Laubach reading about it.

She spent a lot of time reading. Thanks be to God that Albert Otto's great-grandfather had been a friend of Philip Melanchthon, who inspired him to found a Latin school in the town and establish a decent library—one that continued to purchase recent books because it had an endowment for acquisitions. A person could learn a lot by reading, but it wasn't the same thing as being there.

Albert Otto was a stick-in-the-mud. 'Homebody' would be a nicer way to put it. She had to exercise a lot of persuasion to get him to go visit relatives in the western part of Hesse, much less do a little shopping in Wetzlar, five miles away. He talked as if an occasional trip to Kassel was equivalent to some medieval pilgrimage to the Holy Land, rife with hardships and difficulties. He was not happy that Amalie Elisabeth as regent was starting to call upon him to carry out certain missions on her behalf. In his view, he was suffering from interference in his life by one more bossy, older sister. Or, in this instance, sister-in-law.

She sniffed. He rode farther on an ordinary day when he was out hunting than he had to ride when they went to Wetzlar. But, things were what they were. Getting him to Magdeburg so that she could have even a small taste of the exciting things happening at Hesse House would be far beyond her powers.

But at least they would go to Kassel next month. For a little while.

Besançon
July 1636

"It's frustrating." Henri de Rohan tugged on the queue into which he tamed the remains of his frizzy hair when he was working.

Grand Duke Bernhard murmured words of mild sympathy, words that were accompanied by a sarcastic, utterly unsympathetic, expression.

"It seemed to be a reasonable enough option for Marguerite when Captain Lefferts and Eva of Anhalt-Dessau came in to discuss the next things to be done in regard to Ducos. Her brother Georg Aribert is a reasonable age, still in his twenties. He's German *Hochadel*, Calvinist . . ."

"And, according to his sister at least, reasonably intelligent and not utterly obstreperous." Bernhard smirked.

Rohan slammed the sheaf of papers he was holding down on his work table. "Yet, which that sneaky sister glossed over, obstreperous enough that he is utterly determined to make a morganatic marriage with some insignificant lady-in-waiting, no matter what objections his older brother, as head of the family, may raise to the idea!"

"That could be a problem," Bernhard admitted, "if he's as stubborn as everyone else in the Anhalt-Dessau line. Are any other brothers on the market? Johann Kasimir is a couple of years short of my age and has been married close to fifteen years now. I don't know the younger children well."

"No others. The two boys in between Kasimir and Aribert died young. All the rest are girls."

"Cousins? I'm pretty sure there are cousins. Eva of Anhalt-Dessau wouldn't have mentioned them, of course; not when she was pitching the cause of a closer relative, but Christian of Anhalt-Bernberg had a couple of sons in the right age range, I think. Even better . . ."

Rohan raised one eyebrow. "Better?"

"Amalie Elisabeth has two unmarried younger brothers. I've . . ."

". . . always liked Amalie Elisabeth. As you have said many times. What do you know of them?"

"Heinrich Ludwig must be in his mid-twenties. He holds a canonry in Bremen—of course the city is Calvinist even though the prince-bishop is Lutheran. It's a nice sinecure that brings him a substantial income. He's on Frederik Hendrik's staff. Jakob Johann is a few years younger, a godson of the late King James of England. He was under my command for a while before . . ." Bernhard waved one hand at the view out the window. ". . . before all this came up. He opted not to join me and is serving in one of the Hessian regiments. If you asked me, I would say he's the more competent of the two.

"So don't give up yet, my friend. You may yet manage to unearth a suitable candidate for your son-in-law if you are willing to look at the German principalities. Eva's suggestion did, at least, open your mind to that possibility. The Calvinist world as a whole is much wider than that of the French Huguenot high nobility."

Rohan perched on a stool and leaned one elbow on his standing desk. "That much, at least, I have learned from our friend Cavriani."

A carefully worded inquiry directed to Amalie Elisabeth, however, elicited a courteous reply that as a result of the current delicate political problems of the United States of Europe, neither Hanau-Münzenberg nor Hesse-Kassel could envision it as a favorable time for any of the immediate members of the two families to become entangled in foreign alliances.

CHAPTER 10

Paris
July 1636

Acts of royal magnanimity such as those King Gaston had extended to Soubise and Sully rarely occurred without some expectation of *quid pro quo*. As June turned toward July, his advisers floated a suggestion to the *duchesse de* Rohan that it would be delightful if her daughter Marguerite married one of the king's close supporters.

"For supporters," the duchess snorted, "think sycophants. Favorites. Not *mignons*, at least, since he doesn't tilt that way."

"Can he make her do that?" Gerry asked Ruvigny later. "Can't her father refuse?"

"Not if the king himself is involved. French kings can make marriages for the country's important nobles, as Gaston's father did for Rohan and the duchess. Kings can unmake marriages, for that matter, just as Louis XIII refused for years to acknowledge Gaston's own marriage to the current queen. Right now, he's being tactful, but if the king decides to press the issue, our Marguerite will marry his candidate and no one else. At least, if she's still in France."

The king demanded that the two Marguerites be in near-constant attendance upon his wife or daughter. The Royal Guards placed a respectful watch on the *Hôtel de Sully*, disguised as security forces, and accompanied their carriage every time it left the mews.

"Can you do anything?" Marguerite asked Ruvigny. "*Maman* brought her little bastard Tancrède back from Normandy three years ago. At first, she secluded him there with one of her old servants. After all, what can one do with an infant but send it to the country in hopes of more healthful air? When he got old enough not to need a wet nurse or have diapers to change any more, she changed her mind. With the uncertainties that arose around the activities of the League of Ostend, she was uneasy about having him so near the coast. Since then, she goes to visit him clandestinely at the home of his foster parents. Not now and then, but regularly, dressed as an ordinary Parisian *bourgeoise*. She doesn't take the carriage with our crest on the door, but all this surveillance may uncover this and give the king another lever to use in pressuring us."

* * *

Ruvigny knocked on the door of the small home in a Parisian suburb.

The maid-of-all-work who answered wore a cap that was askew, an apron with its strings half-untied, and one shoe. She didn't appear to be dirty or a slattern. She was just disheveled.

"*Monsieur?*"

"*Madame LeBon, s'il vous plaît.*"

It appeared that *Madame*, may the Lord in Highest Heaven reward her, had taken the boy to the park.

Ruvigny raised an eyebrow.

The maid pulled her cap straight and reached behind her to secure the apron strings into a bow.

"*Madame*'s ward is a very . . . active . . . child."

"Might *Monsieur* Lebon be at home?"

"*Hélas, non.* Monsieur LeBon is at work. If he has finished speaking with the head of the new school, that is."

"New school?"

"The boy has been deemed old enough for lessons. As I said, he is . . . . active. The former school could not deal with it when he crawled under the desks, climbed up the bookshelves, or pulled the pages out of his *cahier* and folded them into air gliders."

Ruvigny nodded.

"Neither could the school before that. Or the school before that one. *Madame* will not permit the child to be caned, oh perish the thought, so . . ." She stopped talking and opened the door a little farther. "But would you like to come in? Let me see if I can find where he hid my shoe . . . he thinks it is so funny to hide things."

Ruvigny followed her. In this house, no space was devoted to a vestibule. The door opened into the room in which the family sat, ate, prayed, and slept. Because of the compact space, it didn't take the maid long to retrieve her shoe from the storage bench that provided the main seating area.

The maid rattled on. "So there is to be a new school, if one can be found that will accept him. Teachers *talk* to one another, you know." She made this sound as if it were the deepest of dangerous conspiracies.

Whereas the maid had loudly and vocally thanked the Lord in Highest Heaven for the park, Ruvigny mentally praised Him for perfect timing. Schoolmasters were inclined to ask curious questions when one of their pupils disappeared without an adequate explanation.

After some time, he asked, "When is *Madame* likely to return from the park."

"When she is about to collapse from exhaustion or the boy starts to scream that he is starving, whichever comes first."

"Perhaps, then, it would be more prudent for me to find them in the park. If you would be so kind as to direct me?"

He found *Madame* and the boy at a duck pond. The boy was soaking wet. The ducks appeared to be panicked, but not quite panicked enough to abandon the breadcrumbs that *Madame* was strewing at the edge of the water. The child was trying to catch the drake nearest to the shore and chanting, "Ducks with white feathers. Ducks with brown feathers. Ducks with gray feathers. Drab ducks, drab ducks. Jean, who has been to *L'Amérique,* says that they have ducks with blue feathers. Ducks with green feathers. Ducks with little red feathers on their heads. Feathers he says are 'iridescent.' *Madame,* what does 'iridescent' mean?" Do you think that I can ever go to *L'Amérique?* Do you think that I can ever go to the moon? If I can make paper fly through the air, why can't these big balloons that Pierre at the tailor's shop told me about—they are made of silk, he says, and cow guts—why can't they fly to the moon?"

"*Pardon, Madame*! I come on a matter of some urgency."

"In regard to the child? You must speak with my husband," she said. "Why do you assume it concerns the child?"

"Nothing else in our lives is urgent." She turned. "Tancrède, come, we must go home."

"I'm not hungry yet."

"Now." She grabbed his hand.

"*Non.*" He dug in his heels.

"Come," Ruvigny said. "I can tell you not only about silk balloons, but about machines that fly."

"Airplanes!" The child, he had to be Tancrède, pulled himself out of *Madame*'s grasp and barreled toward Ruvigny so fast that it was impossible for him to save his trousers from the dripping water. "I saw one, I saw one, I saw one. It went over the city and I saw it. Nobody can tell me how men can make them fly. How do they fly? How do birds fly? Do airplanes have bird guts inside them and feathers inside their wings? Where do they build them? Can I go see them build airplanes? I've been to the zoo but I've never seen anyone build an airplane." He stopped. "Who are you?"

The LeBons proved to be amenable to returning the boy to the care of his natural mother. Somehow, Ruvigny was not surprised.

Containing him in the rear quarters of the *Hôtel de Sully* proved to be challenging.

"What are these? Where did I find those? I found them under the bed; aren't they interesting? We didn't have a chamber pot this shape at the Lebons' house. What's it made of? I'm sorry, I didn't mean to break it. Can we go to the park? I saw horses out the window; I want to visit the horses. I don't take naps; naps are for disgusting little babies that still drool. Why can't I go see the LeBons again; they're nice to me. You're no fun! No, I won't give it back. It's interesting. I saw you kissing Marc. I drew pictures on the wall with the duchess' rouge because I couldn't find any charcoal and paper and I like to draw pictures. Why? Where did M. de Ruvigny go? When's supper? Why?"

Susanna raised her eyes to the skies. *Why me, O Lord in Highest Heaven? I'm a dressmaker, not a nursemaid.*

When she verbalized the question, Raudegen said, "Because Ruvigny can trust you. How many of the staff we can trust is an open question. Not only trust in the absolute sense, but also trust to be discreet. They aren't paid much and expect to accumulate money for their retirement by way of *pourboires*; reporters pay for stories. Christ himself said, 'Lead us not into temptation'."

* * *

La petite Rohan would be a true prize. The royal advisers agreed on that. Her husband should be Catholic and preferably an adherent of the *dévot* party. The royal advisers agreed on that. Then, of course, the question arose of who would be the best match, upon which there was far less unanimity. Each of them appeared to have a son, a nephew, a brother, a ward, a cousin, or a protégé who would benefit from marrying the Rohan estates. For every candidate, there was an objection. This one was in feeble health, so might die and leave her as a powerful widow; that one was already betrothed and the relatives of his fiancée, who had also thrown their allegiance to Gaston, would be offended if the match were broken off. Soissons was a prince of the blood and an ally (he had, in fact, been the first fiancé of the king's first wife who had given birth to little *Mademoiselle de France* before she died), but a Rohan marriage might bring him too much power.

"Does it have to be someone mature?" The question floated through the room.

"What do you mean? The king needs strong allies."

"Why not find someone the same age as *la Rohan*. He could be a trifle younger, even—someone malleable. Perhaps if we chose a royal ward who is not yet of age, it could be arranged for his guardian, our lord the king, to assume responsibility, temporary *of course*, for the Rohan estates. Her husband need not control her; the king would be in a position to control them both. That would prevent the problem of a constellation of too much power concentrated that led you to refuse Soissons."

Young. That brought a sizable flock of new candidates to the fore, but still no unanimous agreement.

"The king has been displaying his magnanimity. Why not prepare a list of, let us say, six candidates who would be acceptable to the crown and give her the liberty of choosing among them."

The other advisers looked upon this suggestion and found it to be good. The *comte de* Lafayette had two sons of acceptable age. The younger of Effiat's orphaned sons, the one who had inherited the Cinq-Mars title, was sixteen.

"Not fully orphaned," someone complained, "and his mother is a harridan."

"He's pretty, though, which might appeal to a girl. All that curly auburn hair. And he dances well."

"There's the de Bussy heir. He studied under the Jesuits."

Sheer *ennui* brought agreement on six names. The list didn't suit everyone, but compromises rarely do.

*   *   *

"No, of course I'm not happy with the idea," Soubise said.

Mademoiselle Anne was direly unhappy and letting it be known.

"I don't want to see *la petite Marguerite* married off to a Catholic any more than you do," he continued.

Mademoiselle Anne clenched her teeth. "Especially not to one who will be no more than Gaston's puppet."

"It hasn't happened yet. If we continue to maneuver to obtain Gaston's favor . . ."

"If we succeed in obtaining Gaston's favor, you mean, and can keep it once we have it."

"There are other young Catholic men in the world than those on Gaston's list, some of whom are probably more malleable."

"What?"

Soubise reached down into the small magazine caddy located next to his comfortably upholstered chair—some of the innovations brought by the up-timers were positively inspired—and extracted a piece of paper. "I've obtained this article from an up-time encyclopedia. Yes, it's true that in another world, the Louis XIV who existed there forced her into a Catholic marriage. It appears to have been happy enough, even if far from expedient for the Huguenot cause. In any case, the man she married in 1645, one . . ." He consulted the paper again. ". . . one Henri Chabot, seigneur de Saint-Aulaye, was of no particular political significance, nor does he appear to have had a strong personality."

Anne raised here eyebrows. "And?"

"My modest proposal is that we find the boy. He's scarcely more than a boy now—only a year older than our niece. Offer him as a Catholic alternative to the candidates on Gaston's list; one more acceptable to the family. If Marguerite liked him in that world, which appears to be the case, she may well like him in this one. In due time, when the fortunes of our cause rise again, he seems to have been—to be—will be obliging enough that we can convert him to Calvinism."

"In the meantime, we as her concerned aunt and uncle will have provided the heiress with a more palatable choice." Anne smiled. "It's not our best option, but it never hurts to have several different possible routes to one's goal."

CHAPTER 11

Paris
July 1636

"They can't leave from the *Hôtel de Sully*," Raudegen said. "I say that from a professional perspective. The Royal Guards have posted too many sentries. They can't disappear from the court when they are attending the queen and princess. It's not just that they are closely observed there, although they are. There are too many people milling around in random patterns. An escape party would run too much risk of encountering someone utterly unexpected."

""Maybe they could leave from the *Hôtel* if there was a party going on," Ruvigny commented. "Something like the ballet they held last summer. There would be a couple of hundred guests coming and going and a major congestion of horses, carriages, servants, caterers, etc."

"Possibly." Raudegen moved and looked down into the courtyard. "What kind of party?"

"We can check with Benserade. He'll be glad to work for us again. He's thankful now that he never succeeded in obtaining patronage from Richelieu and Mazarin."

"It would be easiest for them to leave if it's some kind of an outdoor production. Down in the courtyard there."

Benserade, when consulted, pointed out that outdoor productions were subject to the vagaries of the weather. "Even better than a ballet, hire the new *Théâtre du Marais*. It's in a remodeled tennis court on the *Vieille Rue du Temple*, right opposite the Capuchins. They renovated it two years ago, so it's all modern. It wouldn't be a good idea to use the *Hôtel de Bourgogne*, even though they've accumulated a lot of indoor sets over the years, because that theater had too many long-standing ties to Richelieu, plus the name . . . Bad association, given what Bernhard has done in Burgundy. Right now, they're probably all thinking that locating it on the *Rue Mauconseil* was prophetic—very bad advice. It might offend the king for the duchesses to sponsor a production there."

At this point, they had to take the new and better escape concept to the ladies themselves.

"Not a ballet again," the duchess said. "It would be all too *déjà vu*. We must find something different. A contemporary play will be too dangerous." Her voice was firm. "There are too many chances to offend. It will have to be a pastoral, classical theme. Comedy, not tragedy. Not a satire. Pyramus and Thisbe, perhaps?"

"Oh, *Maman*. That's so overdone."

"I want something incorporating dance and music with the dialogue," the duchess continued. "Not an opera, because Mrs. Simpson is sponsoring operas in Magdeburg. Not a musical comedy, because the queen in the Netherlands is sponsoring musical comedies in Brussels. We need something else. Something that will *not offend the king*. Perhaps even something that will placate the king."

Gerry's thoughts turned to science fiction and fantasy. "You need the development of a scion from obscurity to glory. Scions are really good, like in Terry Pratchett's *Guards! Guards!* Well, probably not just like Pratchett, considering how Carrot turns out at the end, no matter how great an author Pratchett is—was—will be—used to be—still is? Anyhow, focus on the scion. I must have read twenty books that go something like the following, by different authors. Or not so many different authors. Eddings used to write the same story over and over again. He just changed the names. Brooks did pretty much the same with the Shannara series. So to start, you've got this family living somewhere in Fantasia."

""Fantasia?"

"Well, that's an old Disney movie, but you can make it generic. There was this glorious book called *The Tough Guide to Fantasy Land* that came out a couple of years before the RoF. It was one of Diana Wynne Jones' things. We have it at home, but that's neither here nor there and you don't need it to make this play."

"Focus," Bismarck said. "Focus."

"You know what he's talking about," Ruvigny interjected. "Arcadia. Heroines named Amerinde and heroes named Cleonice. We've all read them."

"Think about it, guys," Gerry barreled on. "You won't even need enough time for someone to compose new music. Oh, your composer will have to add the high notes and low notes and chords and such, but I can give you enough pre-cooked melodies to carry it off, since this thing won't have a performance run."

He pulled out his harmonica.

"First scene. The Birth of the Scion. Daddy, Mommy, and attendants admire the new prince. All you'll need is a cradle and a spotlight. Someone sings, *Sleep my child and peace attend thee, all through the night; guardian angels God will send thee, all through the night* and everybody dances around the cradle. Somebody can translate it into French.

"And then he's a toddler. Here's the tune. *Bimbo, Bimbo, when you're gonna grow? Everybody loves the little baby Bimb-bi-o.* "He bit his lip. Don't use the word 'bimbo.' Some of the professional actors are bound to have little kids who are used to being around the theater and won't freeze on stage."

Benserade nodded. "One of Béjart's boys will do. The little one–Louis, I think his name is."

"Then the scion turns into a teenager and all his wonderful, extraordinary, excessive talents and abilities start to shine. From what I hear, it's hard to go overboard on flattery in this day and age. Fawning on monarchs is right up there with getting a Ph.D. Piled High and Deep. *When you gotta' glow, you gotta' glow. So glow little glow worm, glow.*" Gerry cocked his head. "I'd think up some different lyrics for that, if I were you, and not call Gaston a worm by inference, but this would be the *tour*

97

de force for whoever dances the part of the Scion. You know, lyrics about how, as he grew up, his qualities began to shine so much that he practically glowed when people looked at him."

Bismarck ran a hand over his receding hairline.

"Then he goes on some kind of a quest where he meets a foreign princess who is the true love of his life. Everybody will be able to tell that she's a perfect match for him, because the music for her dance sounds pretty much the same and uses the same chords. *Three little maids who all unwary, come from a ladies' seminary.*

"Then everyone dances a few more dances, the Scion is received as king with overwhelming joy. You go back to the lullaby and as the young king and queen are crowned, with his mama dripping tears and pride in the background, you have God singing from the roof, *Go, my children, with my blessing, never alone. Waking, sleeping, I am with you; you are my own.*"

Gerry leaned back, exhausted from this long excursion into the field of derivative imagination. "And they go off the stage. Outdoors, you have a crew shoot fireworks off. You can't do fireworks inside the theater. It's too dangerous, which is a pity. Up-time, there was some night club where a couple of hundred people burned alive because it caught on fire when they shot off fireworks indoors. They'll distract the audience's ears from what you're doing, though."

"Fireworks distract eyes, too," Marc pointed out. "All the outside gawkers will be looking up, or at least most of them."

"Can you write this?" the duchess asked.

"Nope," Gerry said cheerfully. "I'm a one note wonder. One note at a time on the harmonica; one finger on the piano, for that matter. Plink, plank, plunk. I'm no musician. I can't do chords. I'm no playwright. I can't do dialogue. But I sure can borrow ideas from bad books. You'll have to get your people to take it and run with it."

The conversation degenerated into cacophony.

"Montdory can take the lead. No, he can direct. No, he . . ."

"Whatever you do, don't touch Montfleury with a ten-foot pole. Everyone knows how strong his ties to Richelieu were."

"Scriptwriter? Has Gaston forgiven Voiture yet?"

"DesBarreaux could do it," Benserade said, "but by all that's sacred, don't put his name in the program if he agrees. Much less Sanguin. Schelandre is Calvinist, which might be an advantage, but he's old enough that his scripts sound fusty, and in any case, he's out of town, campaigning. With all apologies to you soldiers," he nodded at Ruvigny and Bismarck, "wars are a nuisance as far as literature is concerned. Not for subject matter—they provide a lot of grist for the mill—but for trying to find time to write if a man is sitting in some uncomfortable tent with people likely to shoot at him any day."

Bismarck, being without literary ambitions, laughed.

Benserade barreled on. "Mairet's good, and he's willing to write happy endings instead of being focused on the prestige of writing tragedies, but he's hung up on classical unities, plus he was born in Besançon, which isn't politically correct right now. I say get Rotrou, even if he has been writing for the *Hôtel de Bourgogne*. It will get his name before the new king, and right now they need all the help they can get over there if the theater is going to survive the change in regime. He writes fast. Last year he told me he's already done more than thirty plays, and he's not thirty years old yet. Some of those are translations or adaptations, though."

Then there was the matter of casting, which caused another conversational jumble.

"Marguerite will be the princess, of course."

"But who is to dance the young king?"

"Well, Cinq-Mars, since he's Gaston's current candidate for Marguerite's hand. Seeing them on stage together will appease the king's advisers."

"If Cinq-Mars dances the prince, in the coronation scene you can even throw in a reference to the heroic death of the former king in battle, and that will apply to the *marquis'* father and take everyone's minds off what happened to Louis."

"With you, *Madame Duchesse*, center stage as the proud and happy dowager in the *finale*."

"I can get Soûlas to come and be an acting coach," Ruvigny said.

"Who?"

"That theater-mad ensign who ran off to join a troupe of actors. They'd hoped to go to England last year, but didn't make it because of the political troubles there, so he's somewhere down in the Marais district, looking for work. Who knows? If Montdory likes him when he sees him working on this, he may get a permanent slot."

"So you've taken care of the religion and politics of the playwrights. Does it make any difference if the professional actors you bring in are Catholics or Huguenots?" Bismarck asked.

"Not really." Benserade shook his head. "The Catholic church excommunicates actors just for being actors, and the Calvinists aren't thrilled with them either, so no one will expect them to be in good standing."

A couple of days later, Bismarck wandered into the mews loft that Gerry had taken to calling the *chop shop*. "The moon will be full on the sixteenth."

Raudegen looked up, raising an eyebrow.

"They've gotten to the point of setting a date for this extravaganza. That's what they've decided to call it. An *extravaganza*. As far as I'm concerned, they can call it anything they please, but do we want moonlight for this project, or don't we? Decide now."

"It would give decent illumination for several days before and after. Unless it's cloudy, of course. We could see better to drive by night if the moon was out. If we had bad luck and someone followed us, though, they could also see better. It's a toss-up."

"The fireworks will make a better show without moonlight," Ruvigny said.

"Understood. Let me go tell them to pick one of the dark of the moon weeks, either before or after the middle of the month."

One could not, of course, give a gala in honor of the king and queen unless they agreed to come. The duchess sent out feelers. Their Majesties agreed, but Gaston's people insisted on insinuating Tristan l'Hermite, a hanger-on with literary ambitions (thus far not realized, in the sense that none of his plays had been performed) into the planning. His presence had a stultifying effect on conversation.

Except for Benserade and Cinq-Mars, who flirted madly backstage during the rehearsals.

"Oh," Cinq-Mars said. "I adore skirts; they're so wonderfully swishy, don't you know, with all those petticoats. I hated it when I was taken out of my baby skirts and made to put on 'little man' breeches. They're *so* tight and uncomfortable. At home, I've always snitched my sister's clothes to lounge around in, whenever she would let me."

✳ ✳ ✳

Tancrède adored the harmonica.

Gerry was quite willing to share. "Just don't lose it," he warned.

"I won't. Thank you so much, sir."

Tancrède's future did not involve a career as a musical prodigy.

He did lose the harmonica.

"Keep looking kid," Gerry said, "but don't worry Susanna too much if you can't find it. I have a spare."

On his way out, he threw a different admonition at Susanna. "If you're the one who hid it, I don't blame you, but I do want it back."

She threw up her hands. "Not me."

✳ ✳ ✳

"I am so thankful," Bismarck said, "for my two left feet."

"My inability to carry a tune," Gerry added.

They had found a comfortable refuge in the chop shop.

Within certain parameters of comfortable, of course. The hay was softer than any chair in the most luxurious rooms in any château in France, but it did tend to prickle.

"Would you mind if I asked something?"

"Nah."

"Why don't you object to addressing the duchesses as 'Your Grace'? I've heard that the up-times believe that all men, well, ladies too, are created equal."

"I make myself not think of it as giving a title to a person. I'm giving the title to an office. Say, the spring we got transferred here, if our class had taken a field trip to Washington, DC, which we didn't, and I had gotten to meet President Clinton, which I never did . . . but if I had, I wouldn't have called him 'Bill.' I'd have called him 'Mr. President' and I should have. That's only polite. It was a matter of the office he held. In spite of Monica Lewinsky and all."

Bismarck enjoyed what Gerry could dredge up about Monica from his recollections. Which wasn't much.

"Hey," Gerry protested, "I was only a kid."

Ruvigny enjoyed it a lot. So did both of the duchesses when he had Gerry repeat it after supper that evening as they all stood around in the back rooms, free, for once, from the busy ears of l'Hermite.

While Gerry played the *raconteur*, Susanna was walking around and around Marguerite, looking at her. When he had finished, she turned toward Ruvigny. "There's no way on earth to disguise her as anything other than a noblewoman." She sighed and curtsied to the duchess. "Much less you, Your Grace!"

"Why not?" Marguerite snipped, in full objection and protest mode.

"Because . . ."

"Because," Gerry interrupted. "When people say that up-timers act like nobles, they aren't really thinking. They mean that we act different from them, and we pretty much don't kowtow to anybody just because he thinks he's better than we are. Or she. But we don't act like nobles. We don't have the mannerisms, what people call body language. We don't act subordinate, but we don't act entitled, either. Because we—make that most of us—don't think we're better than they are, either." He cocked his head. "I've got to be fair. Some up-timers do, of course—think they're better than someone else, that is. They did even back in West Virginia. There was a sizable bunch who thought they were a lot better than the hippie Stones. But you guys have the body language, and there's no time for us to teach you how to get rid of it."

"But," Marguerite persisted. "How can you tell?" She glared at Susanna, who gave an exasperated sigh. "I've been dressing ladies of the high nobility for eight years now. Gerry's right. I can tell, and so could anyone else who took a close look."

"Disguise the duchesses as lesser noblewomen," Bismarck suggested. "Someone like my mother or sisters. The lady of a country manor, somewhere out in wherever France's equivalent of rural Brandenburg is." He grinned. "A lady like that will think of herself as just as much entitled, in her own bit of the world, as a *duchesse de Rohan* is in France as a whole. But a country lady with her daughter and a small entourage won't attract much attention"

Susanna eyed Marguerite critically. "Yes," she said, nodding her head. "Yes, that might work."

"I will be her bodyguard," Raudegen said.

He intended to be the older duchess' bodyguard. He didn't trust her an inch. Given her well-known reluctance to leave Paris, she was being suspiciously compliant about this project, whereas Ruvigny and Bismarck were being much too gullible about her apparent change of mind. If necessary, he would physically remove the tied and gagged body of the duchess.

"You . . ." He pointed at Marc. "You are the assistant to the steward at her manor. The rest of you . . ." He pointed to the redheads. "You four are her staff. Upper servants—household servants. There's enough difference in your ages. Three brothers and a sister. This family is not fabulously wealthy—Susanna will be doubling as maid for the ladies and nanny for the child. Susanna and Gerry won't have any problems in their roles; you other two are their brothers in local militia. I've brought you along for extra muscle because of all the unrest. You've have been in the armies long enough to know how ordinary soldiers act. Now, what is your name?"

Gerry grinned. "Lapierre," of course. "Or Stein, since three of us are more at home in German than in French. Ruvigny's accent in German is execrable, but maybe he can keep his mouth shut."

"Why would a French country lady have servants named Stein?"

"Alsace. She's heading home."

Raudegen nodded. "That will do. She and her daughter are French-speaking upper class. The four of us are German-speaking peasants. Cavriani? Any preference?"

Marc shook his head. "Either one is fine."

"It's getting out of the theater that will be the trick," Ruvigny said. We're lucky that Cinq-Mars has that curly red hair and wears it *au naturel*. In that last scene, Gerry can substitute for him and get Marguerite away when they promenade out. We'll need to use plenty of spotlights, multi-colored and strobing around the stage, to distract people's eyes from noticing that the lead actor has changed.",

Raudegen frowned. "Who will distract Cinq-Mars from realizing that he's not onstage at the high point?"

"Benserade, of course," the duchess said.

"What if you end up needing more than fireworks?" Gerry asked Raudegen as they headed back to their rooms.

"I've been asking myself the same thing."

"Well, I don't have the famous Stone Boys' Box of Tricks with me, but I might be able to cobble some primitive stuff together. Down-time kitchens don't offer the chemical options that up-time kitchens did, and we don't want to draw attention to ourselves by buying any, or gunpowder, or stuff like that. If you can get them to order a few extra fireworks, though, and a couple dozen of those little earthenware storage containers . . ." Raudegen headed into the *Palais*.

A couple of days later, Gerry eyed a sputtering firepot with dissatisfaction. "They're smoke bombs that put out nauseating smells, basically, but they aren't working as well as I hoped they would."

"At least they seem to be reliable," Raudegen answered. "Finish up the rest of the supply." He walked away.

Gerry kept standing there. He wrinkled up his forehead. *They need more zip. The fuses are way too slow, for one thing,* he thought. *Before I finish them up, I'm going to talk to Susanna and see if there's something up in the dressmakers' stash that would burn faster if I unraveled the fabric and twisted it into fuses.*

July turned inexorably into August. The letters that Rohan sent to Paris turned just as inexorably from demanding and requiring to threatening the most dire of consequences if Something Wasn't Done and Soon.

"We can't hurry this," Raudegen wrote back patiently. "Trust my professional judgment, please. This is an instance in which haste would make waste."

Virginia DeMarce

CHAPTER 12

I n Magdeburg, Veronica Dreeson, still called *Grandma Richter* by half
of the people who knew her, threw the daily paper down on the
breakfast table of Jeff and Gretchen's comfortable home. "How
ridiculous can newspapers make themselves? The Ottomans are
besieging Linz, the king of France has been assassinated and that
ridiculous Gaston is on the throne, Cardinal Richelieu has disappeared,
not that I'm mourning him, archduchesses—well, an archduchess and an
archduke—are either dead or more likely in some Ottoman dungeon in
Vienna, there's chaos in Poland, and what is being covered by the USE
newspapers? The possible fate of a cat in Paris!"

She glared. "Richelieu's Siamese cat, on top of everything else. Just
because it came from Grantville!"

Thea, her first husband's niece, said, in her most conciliating tone of
voice, "Now, Auntie."

"Don't 'Auntie' me!"

Thea's husband Nicholas, who had obligingly transferred from the
West Virginia County administration to the USE bureaucracy when the
family in its collective wisdom decided that *Grandma needs someone younger
to keep an eye on her now that Jeff and Gretchen are never home*, cleared his throat.
"That's the kind of story that increases circulation. Personal interest. It's
easier for a lot of people to think about something small, something of
the size they can understand, than the big picture. Which, right now, is
complicated to the point of being tortuous. They can understand the
plight of a lost cat. I don't think anyone, not even the most competent

spymasters on the continent, can understand what Gaston may be up to or predict what he might do next."

Grandma refused to be distracted. "It was bad enough during the Saxon uprising, when they whipped up that ridiculous letter-writing campaign to demand that General Torstensson should not attack the doors of the Castle Church in Wittenberg where Luther put up the Ninety-Five Theses. Why on earth would the general have chosen to attack a set of church doors in the first place?"

"It was symbolic. The doors, I mean, were symbolic for probably every Lutheran in the USE and beyond." Moser frowned. "Probably the name, also. Before we moved I was talking to one of the teachers in Grantville. Avery, that was his name. Isaiah Avery. It's symbolic for the up-timers, too. Before he was born, but not much before because his parents remembered it, a man named Martin Luther King, Jr., had nailed a list of demands about 'civil rights' to the doors of the city hall in a city named Chicago, which is the place that Dr. Nichols came from. A lot of up-timers have trouble telling the difference between Martin Luther and Martin Luther King, Jr. So they got upset about the doors. 'Emotionally invested,' Avery said. He had studied something called *psychology* at the university. Up-time, that was not the study of the soul, but of the mind." He pushed his chair back. I have to get to work."

Grandma, from the perspective of a woman who had spent several involuntary years as a camp follower in the bedraggled train of a mercenary regiment, picked up the paper again, looked at the headline, and snorted. "A cat."

CHAPTER 13

On performance night, as if to spite everyone's nerves, things went well. Rotrou had indeed written the script in such a way that in the last scene, the "young king and queen" did not dance, but had the remainder of the cast dance around them. Nymphs floated around in billowing, if salaciously knee-length, chiffon skirts. Muses in classical draperies struck attitudes. The Scion's crown was so immense that it shadowed his face nicely. God sang and the leads processed off the stage with great dignity.

The dignity held until they were well in the wings. Then Gerry took a firm grip on Marguerite's wrist and scampered as fast as he could move in order to get her safely outside in the course of the after-performance confusion.

Marc and Susanna were already on their way out of town with the first carriage. It also transported Tancrède and most of the supplies for the trip. They planned to wait at a predetermined location for the second carriage to catch up.

Bismarck, reins in his hands, waited at the stage door at the back of the theater until the older duchess came out.

Raudegen and Ruvigny would follow on horseback as soon as they were reasonably certain that there had been no slip 'twixt the cup and the lip.

The fireworks were a success.

The royal party exited from their boxes, there being too many to fit in a single box.

There was a lot going on outside the theater. The crowd went oooh! and the crowd went aaah! at every detail of the dresses and hair styles.

Cinq-Mars saw the Rohan ladies leaving, the only person to notice, but why should he care? Once the choreographer told him he wouldn't be needed in the last scene, he had made his own plans to take advantage of the after-performance confusion. He slipped into a dressing room and formally accepted an offer of employment at the *Théâtre du Marais*. He would act under a pseudonym like all the others, of course, but he had a vision. Someday he would become a tremendous success, adored by all of the *literati* of France, a power to be reckoned with. He would become the pet of all the salons. He would make and break careers. Until then, he and Isaac were going out for a late supper, and he would never again have to listen to his mother rant and rave at him about his behavior.

Outside the theater, "We have a problem," Ruvigny said.

Raudegen grunted.

Four Royal Guards had been paying attention to what they were supposed to instead of the distractions that had been laid out for them. They were trotting down the street, positioned to keep the carriage Bismarck was driving in sight.

"Good men," Raudegen said. "They have enough sense not to try to stop it until they've figured out the size of the opposition. I hope they get commendations. But for right now, let's spook their horses."

Ruvigny had been more in demand by the Rohan ladies, which meant that Raudegen had the experience with the little smoke-and-sparks-spitting firepots. Gerry called them oversized sparklers.

"A half dozen should be enough." He hefted down one of the saddlebags and reached inside his buffcoat for a flint—the new kind with the little fuel reservoir and small roller.

Ruvigny led their own mounts around a corner, since a man's own horse was as subject to spooking as anyone else's.

Raudegen lit the first fuse and went to toss the ersatz Molotov cocktail down the street toward the riders.

"What? Oh boarpiss! Shit on this fucking fuse!"

The first firepot went off while he still held it, throwing sparks in all directions before the clay cracked, split, and spilled the spitting gunpowder out on his hand. He had lined up the other five neatly on the ground next to him. The closest caught a spark from the first. That fuse also ran much too fast and hot. The pot exploded, throwing potsherds rather than just cracking, and ignited the rest. He fell to the ground, nauseous with pain.

"They didn't work as reliably as I had hoped," he groaned, once Ruvigny had pulled him up, shouldered him around the corner, and boosted him onto his horse.

Ruvigny walked around the horse's head to the other side. "How's the bleeding?"

Raudegen glanced down. "It's mostly cauterized, I think."

"You're lucky you throw overhand. If that first pot had been on a level with your head, you might have lost your eyes instead of your hair. Use this hand to hold the cloth against the cuts on your scalp above your ear unless the burns are so bad that you can't stand the touch. Otherwise, try to balance in the stirrups. I'll put him on a lead rein."

Raudegen grimaced. "They worked, though. Those guards are riding some thoroughly spooked horses, if they've even managed to keep their seats. City slicker horses with no battle experience."

They couldn't move rapidly, but the carriage Bismarck drove was proceeding through the moonless gloom with even less speed. When they caught up, Ruvigny transferred Raudegen into it. Gerry winced, straightened the mangled fingers as well as he could, and improvised a splint.

"That's all I can do here. My med kit's in the duffel. Marc and Susanna have it."

It was still dark when they caught up with the other carriage. The new splint reached from beyond the tip of Raudegen's middle finger to above his wrist. Gerry sprinkled the mess with a powder from his duffel bag and wrapped it in a clean bandage. "That's the best I can manage until we get some daylight and I can see what I'm doing. Even these new-model lanterns with the mantles flicker."

Ruvigny looked at the splint and bandages critically. "That hand will never grasp a sword, or anything else, again, despite the best care that our angel of mercy can provide you."

Raudegen also looked at the splint and bandages. "There goes my career."

"Nah," Gerry said, tying the final knot. "Don't go all 'if it weren't for bad luck, I'd have no luck at all' on me. You're already too high up the totem pole. The grand duke will just kick you up higher. He'll probably assign you to Erlach for planning and logistics, with your own private secretary to write down what you think for you."

He lifted a beaker to Raudegen's lips. "Now drink this. It's not like you're some ordinary person, like a tailor, who actually needs to use his hands to earn a living. It's not like you're a clockmaker or a lens grinder. Or a blacksmith, for that matter. No matter how well it heals, though, that hand will ache in bad weather and be a constant nuisance. You'll remember tonight every day for the rest of your life." He put away the med kit, shuddered, and then shuddered again.

"I can't help it," he said to Bismarck a couple of hours later. He still had his arms clutched across his chest, shaking and shivering as if it were February rather than August. "Ever since Rome, when I shot Marius after he shot at the pope, I can't help it. I did fix Raudegen's hand before I lost it, but I can't help it. My gun was at Marius' throat and it went off. The blood sprayed out of him, all over everyone. It almost took his head off. I'm sorry guys, but it was my fault, too. I changed the fuses after Raudegen tested them the last time, trying to get more bang for my buck. I know you're soldiers; you've seen worse, but I can't help it. Marius' head sort of exploded and now Raudegen's hand blew off and it's my fault again because I didn't tell him that I changed the fuses. Nurses and doctors see worse all the time, I know. I'm a disgrace to Lothlorien Pharmaceuticals. I'm okay with vaccinations, but when I have to look at the insides of someone's body, I can't help it, and it's all my fault again. He's just lying there on the carriage bench because I gave him some opium; he's just lying there."

It was not the most opportune moment for someone else to join the party. Candale was fortunate that neither Ruvigny nor Bismarck shot him when they were alerted by Marc's sudden sharp *Pssst!* from the lead carriage.

"The duchess invited me," didn't go far as a rationale with anyone other than the duchess.

"See, I am already dressed in the guise of her husband, an Alsatian country gentleman," didn't go much farther.

"With all due respect, *Monsieur le comte*, Ruvigny said, "You are just what we don't need."

"It's my fault," Gerry moaned. "If I hadn't blown up Raudegen's hand, we would be two hours ahead of him by now."

Candale turned his horse and looked into the carriage that was now occupied by two duchesses and one comatose colonel.

"Shouldn't you be going back to your regiment?" Marguerite asked him. "I'm sure it misses you."

"If you people wake up this child or disturb Colonel Raudegen," Susanna hissed through the window of the first carriage, "it will not matter because all of you will find yourselves dead before morning."

Bismarck took Gerry up on the driver's seat as they headed out of the suburbs through what was left of the night.

"What were you chanting?" Susanna asked him when they stopped for a rest. "It sounded like you were chanting while you drove."

"I was reminding Gerry. 'The just shall live by faith. Jesus Christ, our God and Lord, died for our sins and was raised again for our justification.' He needs to remember that now and always."

"Do you believe it?" Marguerite asked. "Actually believe it?"

"I do." Bismarck bowed his head. "In joy and happiness, in suffering and sadness, help me at all times, Christ the salvation of my life."

On the Road Again . . . and Again . . . and Again

To avoid Candale, who usually paced his horse next to the duchess' carriage, Marguerite decided to ride with Susanna.

"Have you read the Bible?" she asked.

"Mostly only the parts in my missal."

"People are supposed to read it for themselves. *Grand-mère* Rohan read a great deal of it to me when I was a child, and of course the preachers read it in the temple when we went to church, which wasn't often because the Edict of Nantes prohibits Protestant churches within five leagues of Paris, so it takes a whole day to go and come back even when the weather is good. You haven't missed much, though. It's a disappointing kind of book."

"What?"

"Oh, it's true. It's supposed to be the story of God's chosen people, but they were horrible, smiting one another all the time. The sons of Adam must have married their own sisters, because no one else was alive, and Abraham certainly did, for it says so. There was the man who cut his concubine in twelve pieces and distributed them to the Twelve Tribes. They were supposed to be God's people, but they were not one bit better than we are, and some of them were worse. Even Henri IV only had a dozen or so mistresses besides his wives and less than two dozen bastards that we know of. David and Solomon had lots more wives than two, and at the same time instead of divorcing the first one, plus all those concubines. If the preachers want to denounce libertines, then they ought to denounce those. Don't you think?"

Susannah was about to reply, but Tancrède woke up.

"Are we there yet? Tell M. von Bismarck to stop the carriage, please; I gotta go. I'm hungry; when's lunch? These turnips are nasty. I'm a *boy*. I don't care if you're older; you're nothing but a *girl*. I don't *want* to sit still. Read me a story. Can I ride in the carriage with the lady who used to visit me at the LeBons? Why can't I go visit the LeBons; they were always nice to me. Will you read me another story, please? I'm hungry; when are we going to stop for supper? I liked the first story better. Read it again, pleeease! I gotta go. I don't *want* to behave myself. If you had brought books with short words, I could read my own stories. Are we there yet? I gotta go right now."

Closer acquaintance reinforced Marguerite's already ingrained hostility toward Tancrède.

"There are four of us," Bismarck said to her while Susanna followed the boy to his chosen spot behind a tree. "Four boys born within a space of six years. With my sisters, eight of us born within twelve years. I believe that we may owe our lady mother an apology for existing."

"It's a farce," Marguerite proclaimed. "In a just world, Candale's old valet would not have been surnamed LeBon. LeMal would make a lot more sense for this one."

Tancrède, by fate and fostering surnamed LeBon, showed up in time to regard her with a defiant pout. "I don't like you. I want to ride with the other lady."

Marc put an end to the impasse by picking the boy up and plopping him in front of Candale, muttering, "I understand that you're responsible for his existence, so you deal with him for a while and give Susanna a break."

"*Merci, M. de Candale*, for letting me ride your horse. Am I going to get to ride a horse the rest of the way? I like Susanna better than I like Marguerite. I want my *own* pony to ride. I wanted a pony before, but the LeBons always said that there is no room for a pony in Paris. Do you live in Paris? No? You're in the army? Do you have armor? Do you have a sword? Do you have a pistol? Can I shoot it? Hey, look at those cows. I gotta go. Honest, M. de Candale, I gotta go right now. If you don't let me go right now I won't be able to hold it."

Candale did his best to ignore the child, but the boy wiggled. He squiggled, wriggled, and upon occasion lunged toward something that caught his eyes. Two hours later, he started to cry.

"His legs hurt," Bismarck said. "Marc, you can't put a child who has never ridden on a horse and expect him to stay there all day." He picked the boy off, motioned for the coachman to halt, followed him into the bushes for yet another 'gotta go,' and returned him to Susanna.

"Do you always pay him so little mind as on this trip?" he asked when he pulled his horse up next to Candale's again.

"There's no way under the law that I can make him my heir and I have no intention of raising false expectations by making a fuss over him. It's not as if I'm a king who can furnish his *légitimés* with titles and estates the way Henri IV did for Vendôme and the others. Or even as much as Maurice of Nassau did for his illegitimate brood. I've provided him with foster parents since he was born. I've paid LeBon and his wife. If the duchess wants to send him to Saumur when he gets a few years older, I'll pay his school fees. Not," he added, "that she can't afford to pay them herself.

"If my father ever dies and I succeed to the title, maybe I can do a bit more, a commission or something, but that will depend on the fates. My father may be immortal. The odds are against it, but he will manage it if any human can, or at least achieve a personal return to the era of Methuselah."

Several days later, Tancrède squirmed his way up from the floor of the carriage and stuck his head out the window. "Well, if we aren't there yet, when will we be there?"

"It's about two hundred and fifty miles," Susanna said. "We have been on the road for eleven days. I think it will take at least another week. We will be in the County of Burgundy, though, before we come to Besançon. We will follow the Doubs River, more or less, until we reach Grand Duke Bernhard's capital city. It is a very twisty river."

"May I go fishing when we come to the river? I love to fish."

"Perhaps you can go fishing once we get to Besançon. I don't think there will be time until then."

"I want to fish *now*!"

"There isn't any river *now*," she pointed out.

"What worries me most," Marguerite said, "is that we are driving along–well, the men are riding along–without any opposition. We haven't been pursued, as far as any of them can tell and all of them except Marc and Gerry are accustomed to military campaigning and knowing who is chasing you and finding the people you are chasing. Marc has been asking questions at every inn and stable. Even when we came through Auxerre, there was no more than the normal in the way of checkpoints. We haven't even had to use the elaborate fiction about being a household from Alsace."

Susanna nodded. "Why does this worry you?"

"Because, I think, there must be problems in Paris that make even the disappearance of the Rohan heiress and her mother unworthy of immediate royal attention. Under the circumstances it is good to be insignificant, but I can't imagine what is causing it. The only reason I can think of that the king would not have sent people to find us is that—really, I can't think of any at all. I don't have any idea what may be causing it. How can I even guess, when I am riding and riding and riding in this carriage with no news at all?"

Marguerite was not alone.

"I haven't heard a single word about the court," the duchess told Candale. "Not a single word since we left Paris. I didn't even manage to buy a measly, out-of-date, provincial newspaper when we came through Auxerre. Raudegen, curse him, says it would not fit with my *persona*. You could get one for me. Even the most countrified of country gentlemen might occasionally buy a newspaper. It's maddening. I know in my heart that Soubise is ruining everything. The next time I do hear something, it will probably be that Soubise has lost what minuscule remnants of royal favor that I had managed to retrieve for the family."

Candale ducked his head toward the window. "Have you seen those new *kaleidoscopes* that are coming out of Augsburg?" he asked. "Fascinating. When I was in Nancy, I attended a lecture on how they are made. Mirrors, and a few little specks of colored glass. Every design is made with the same pieces, but it changes every time you turn the tube, which amounts to an object lesson on how the court functions. The pieces remain the same, but from one turn to another the picture alters a great deal. The Rohan piece will still be in the little compartment, no matter where it falls at each turn, and another turn will always come." He smiled. "Also, I think you underestimate your brother-in-law and *Mademoiselle* Anne. It's possible that a lot of royal interest is currently directed toward the old Rohan holdings in Brittany."

*　*　*

The conditions in eastern France had not changed significantly since Ruvigny and Bismarck had observed them on their first trip to Paris the previous October. The villages were still half-depopulated from plague that passed through the region in the summer of 1635. The road was better than it had been in January, if one considered dust better than half-frozen mud, but it was not better because anyone had been doing maintenance on it. Trade, Marc reported after a few chats with local shop owners, was down.

Innkeepers warned of wandering bands of ex-mercenaries, most of them men who left Lorraine after the grand duke and the king in the Low Countries started to make a real effort to restore order there. They weren't huge bands of bandits, the townsmen emphasized, but rather small groups, six to a dozen men, enough to steal some livestock or fall upon a farm wagon, but even a small village was safe enough from them if the inhabitants were determined and well-armed, which most of them were, since after this many years of war almost every peasant had managed to steal some kind of a musket or take a long-barrel from a former soldier who lay passed out drunk. Never call it theft. The French were law-abiding people. However, the Lord assured his children that He would provide, and if he chose to provide by making soldiers careless with their weapons, who were they to question His will?

"I don't recall," one innkeeper who doubled as a village *maire* commented to Marc, "that I've seen a single probate settlement in this district in the past five to ten years in which the deceased did not have a gun included in his inventory." He looked the party over. "Three women and a child, but also six men, all mounted. Don't worry about them. They won't even think of coming near you."

The ambushers, when they came, were neither ex-mercenaries nor bandits. The ambush did not take place in a dramatic vale with overhanging cliffs, nor in the face of an oncoming storm. The landscape did not feature abandoned medieval ruins; neither were they lured into it by a piteous cry for help. As Marc would say later, it wasn't an ambush that would furnish anyone with a good after-dinner story. It took place in the middle of the morning, in full sunlight, on the edge of one of the half-depopulated villages. No riders on thundering mounts drove down upon them. In point of fact, they had halted, dismounted, or climbed out to stretch their legs, and were wandering around the vicinity of the well for one simple reason.

"I have to go," came the shrill cry.

"If you ask me," Bismarck commented to Gerry, "he's figured out that having to go is a way of getting out and running around for a bit."

"Well, can you blame him? It's not natural for a boy to be cooped up like this. Dad let us run around and scream all we wanted to."

"Even if he is crying 'wolf' on occasion," Marc added, "nobody else has volunteered to run the risk after that interesting episode suffered by M. de Candale the second time the boy rode with him for a while."

"Again! How many times this morning does that make?" Marguerite asked.

"The bright side," Susanna said, "is that at least he doesn't wet the bed."

"Anybody else who needs to go, go now," Raudegen ordered, an implacable tone in his mild baritone voice. He looked at Ruvigny. "I can't believe I said that."

As a point of fact Tancrède was behind a hedge, going.

The attackers took out Candale and Ruvigny first. They were standing next to one another and got bashed on their heads by villagers wielding a couple of pieces of window frame. They didn't get bashed tremendously hard, nothing like a cavalryman with a saber could have done in battle, but it was enough to knock them down and daze them temporarily.

119

Raudegen turned and, in spite of the practice he had been doing at every opportunity, reached for his sword with his injured hand. Another attacker swept a bladeless scythe handle at his knees.

Bismarck scrambled up, pushed the two duchesses into one of the carriages, and stood at the door, his weapon out.

Marc, at the well where he had been lowering the bucket to get water for the horses, pulled the bucket up, pivoted, and threw the water on someone's head; then ran to grab the reins of the horses on the front carriage, thinking in a disorganized way that if the riding horses spooked, they'd be able to chase them down, but a runaway team could destroy the carriages before anyone managed to catch them. Susanna came around from where she was standing in the bushes to keep an eye on Tancrède and grabbed the reins of the horses harnessed to the carriage that the duchess usually used. It was a neat trick, since she had to keep holding onto Tancrède with her other hand.

Gerry, still in the coppice where he had retreated for his turn at taking care of private business, pulled his harmonica out of his shirt pocket and made it wail. *Ghost Riders in the Sky* produced a sound effect that bore no resemblance to the plinky little flute-like separate notes he had played to provide the melodies for the extravaganza, even when the instrument was in the hands of an utterly incompetent musician. He hoped that none of the attackers headed in his direction. He still had his pants down.

Tancrède pulled his wrist out of Susanna's grasp and ran toward Marc at the well. She was about to start after him, horses or no horses, when an appalling shriek arose from behind its low mortared wall, resembling the sound of a soul in torment, the drawing of fingernails over a slate board magnified by a thousand, or, perhaps, an untutored six-year-old blowing into a harmonica with all the power of his breath.

With two sets of shrieks coming at them, Ruvigny picked himself up to join the fray. Candale immobilized the boy that Marc had drenched with water, and Marc stuffed his harmonica into his jerkin in order to demonstrate the usefulness of a small but practical dagger. With

Raudegen now having a businesslike sword in his functional hand, the attackers hesitated and faltered.

Three middle-aged women, a boy who might have been coming into his teens, two old men, one of them very old indeed, and a scrawny dog.

"We need the horses," one of the women explained. "We saw you here. It's not that we expected anyone to stop at our well this morning. It's not as if we had time to plan. We saw you, grabbed whatever we could find, and ran out."

"What do you want horses for? Not to ride, certainly."

"To sell," one of the old men said. "To trade," the other quavered. "To eat," the strongest of the women answered.

There weren't any other men. Between the war and the plague, they were gone. Because they were gone, most of the harvest had not been brought in last fall. Because the survivors were starving, they butchered the last ox so that the rest of them might survive the winter, but that meant that this spring they had not been able to plow, but only dug the kitchen gardens with spades, so there would be no grain, not that they had any seed to plant if they had an ox to plow with, because the previous fall's harvest had rotted in the fields, as they had already told milords. The cows had been bred last year; two of the calves had survived, but the only bull calf had died, so there was no prospect of having them bred again even if they waited two or three years, which they had hoped to be able to do. They had no money to pay stud fees to the village three miles over, which still had a bull.

"Yes, we knew we might have to kill you to get the horses," the strongest woman said. "But what more right do you have to be alive than we do? How is it different for you to be dead than for the six of us and the children younger than Jean over there to be dead? If we don't do something, we will all be dead by winter. Eight of you; thirteen of us counting the other children. We could survive for a year, live well for a year, on what you are taking with you on a drive down this road from some place we have never been to some place we will never go."

"You have fine animals," the oldest man added. "Just one of your horses sold in Auxerre would bring the money for a blacksmith to put blades back on our tools, with some left over. The foragers stripped off all the metal. I know how to bargain. I don't walk well, but Jean here could put me on the most docile one and lead us to Auxerre. The price of that one horse would buy us metal for the blacksmith and a donkey to bring me home. Then we would have a donkey."

"Why don't you leave?" Gerry asked.

"What would we do?" The second man snorted. "We are serfs, yes, and tied to the land, but that means that this land is also tied to us and we have the right to farm it. If we leave, we won't have a right to farm anywhere else. All we know how to do is farm."

"We ought to have done something for them," Gerry insisted that evening. "There was a man who fell among thieves . . ."

He leaned back against the wall. This inn was surprisingly good for eastern France–clean and tidy, if not spacious. The proprietor, a German from the Palatinate, had managed to get out, with some of his money, enough to buy another inn, ahead of the Imperials back in 1622. He kept chickens and rabbits to feed his guests, a couple of goats for milk, and his wife cultivated a good-sized garden. The village was strong enough to keep random marauders away. Recent events, the death of the king and the troubles, he said, he had caused him to question his decision to settle in France, but in the end no man could defy the will of God. If he was destined to die a pauper, then he was destined to die a pauper. At the moment, he delivered a second round of beer to the table.

"We didn't punish them. Beyond that, what can a person do?" Raudegen lifted his good hand, counting off on his fingers. "If we left a horse with those people, we would be short a horse and perhaps that would cause us to fail in our charge. If we left a horse in that village, there would still be other villages, behind these hills." He gestured to the left side of the road they had come in on. ". . . and behind those." He gestured to the right. "Villages where the people are living in equal misery. You can't help them all. You can't even find them all."

His logic was, in its own way, inexorable.

"I'm wondering about that *maire*," Gerry continued. "The one who told us that all the estate inventories that he recalled included guns. How many inventories do you think he's seen, this past year, with the plague and stuff? When it comes to defending their homes, dead men can't shoot guns, even if they owned one when they were alive."

"In the matter of weapons," Susanna gave Tancrède a nudge. "Now, before you have to go up to bed."

"I'm sorry, Gerry." Tancrède clasped his hands behind his back and dropped his head. "I told you a lie. I didn't lose the harmonica you loaned me. I just didn't want to give it back." He looked up. "That's stealing, isn't it? But I took good care of it. I hid it so that nobody else could find it." He looked down again. "But I almost did lose it, because when Susanna and Marc came to take me away from Paris, I *barely* had time to get it and stick it inside my breeches."

"You're a hero, kid," Gerry said, his voice rough. "Thank you for being polite and apologizing. That's the right thing to do when you've made a mistake. Keep the harmonica with my compliments. You may need to save the day again some other time."

It was the duchess who took the boy up to put him to bed. She often did, if an inn was decent.

Gerry watched them go. "We've turned into a team, I think," he mused. "We ought to start calling ourselves something. Teams always do in RPGs and comics, or most of the time, at least. I don't suppose that *Teenage Mutant Ninja Turtles* would do."

"What's an RPG?"

"What are those, whatever you called them?"

"One up," Bismarck said with glee. "I've seen a comic. It's like a whole bunch of broadsides bound together."

"Turtles?"

"Hey, Dad was opposed to bourgeois culture, but we went to public school. He didn't try to homeschool us or anything. I know about as much about Raphael and Donatello and Michelangelo and Leonardo as anyone else. Not to mention Splinter. I loved Splinter. He sort of reminded me of Dad."

"Those," Marguerite said, "are famous artists. Not Splinter, whoever he is, but the rest. Italian painters whose canvases cost a lot if you want to buy one from a dealer. Not turtles. I have at least that much education."

"The turtles were named for famous artists. They're still turtles. Mutant ninja turtles."

This required about an hour of discussion. At the end, Gerry was still of the opinion that the name would not do. He looked around the table. "We could call ourselves the Carrot Tops, after Corporal Carrot, but I'm the only one who's carrotty. The rest of you have more decent shades of red heads."

"What do carrots have to do with red hair?" Susanna asked. "Carrots are white, or sometimes purple."

"Up-time, carrots were orange. Mutations along the way, maybe."

"What's a mutation?"

"Remember what I told you about the turtles?" Gerry scratched his head. "There was some Sherlock Holmes story that Dad read to us. He likes the writings of A. Conan Doyle and his philosophy of reading out loud was that it had to be something that he enjoyed reading, too. The *Red Headed League*. That's it. We can borrow that. Doyle won't mind; he was dead even up-time. Maybe we can make Corporal Carrot our mascot."

"Should we make Cinq-Mars an honorary member?" Marc asked with a grin.

"Why on earth?"

"Well, you said that he did assist us, if only by lounging around backstage and not alerting anyone that Gerry was making off with Marguerite and that the duchess was heading for the hills."

Gerry was idly twirling his pocketknife around. Suddenly he said, "It's not relevant to anything, but, Marguerite, when you try to practice English with me, why do you have a Scottish accent? There are a whole lot of Scots in Grantville and I recognize it."

"Oh. *Tante* Anne's English tutor was a Scotsman. He came over to study at Saumur. He was pretty interesting, but went back home to become a preacher. Maybe Papa will find me another one if nothing else interesting happens all next winter."

Paris
August 1636

When King Gaston and his advisers became aware that the two Rohan duchesses had not returned home after the extravaganza, Soubise and Mademoiselle Anne were left scrambling and scurrying to soothe the government and drop misleading hints about Brittany.

Upon receiving formal notification from the authorities that they could only assume that some unfortunate event had happened during the confusion after the extravaganza, even though no body had been found, Cinq-Mars' older brother, the marquis d'Effiat, heaved a private sigh of relief behind his public display of grief. The boy's tendencies were embarrassing and could not have been disguised forever. It's one thing to have your brother beheaded for conspiring against the monarch, as happened according to the up-time encyclopedias. That could be considered one of the normal hazards of belonging to the French nobility. To have him survive and perhaps later be burned at the stake for sodomy if the *dévot* party expanded its influence in the court would have caused unpleasant difficulties for his relatives. There was no guarantee that even rank and wealth could have protected him if he became flamboyant enough. He did not push the authorities to pursue the matter.

Virginia DeMarce

CHAPTER 14

August 1636
Still on the blasted road in Eastern France

"Since this whole project is about who Marguerite going to marry or not marry," Gerry said the next evening, "we ought to take stock. What's the status of the rest of us? Maybe we could do one of those mass marriages some-day, all lined up one after the other, like the Moonies."

"Moonies?"

Gerry had more explaining to do. "There was this preacher from Korea. I saw pictures in the papers. He'd arrange marriages between men and women who followed his cult and then marry them off to each other, hundreds at a time, all the guys in suits and the women in fluffy white dresses."

"Where was Korea; in America?"

"I thought up-timers were supposed to marry for love!"

"Mass polygamy?"

Gerry rapped on the table for attention. "No, guys. Korea's somewhere south of China. Was then; still is, I suppose. No polygamy; one husband to one wife, but he married hundreds of couples in the same ceremony. And yeah, generally speaking, at least in the US of A, people were expected to marry for love, but we weren't all clones of each other."

"What's a clone?"

"I'm pretty sure that German doesn't have a word for it. Nor French. Nor the folks over the channel in England in this day and age, for that matter. It's like this . . ."

By the time he finished with that, it was time for the adults go go up to bed.

The next night after supper, he persisted. "Start with Ruvigny. Henri, what are your preferences in a bride? Prerequisites?"

"A dowry. I think 150,000 livres would be nice, but what do I have to offer in exchange?"

"There is sure to be some banker somewhere," the duchess said. "Some *noblesse de cloche*, who would regard friendly ties to the *Maison de Béthune* as a quite sufficient compensation for a penniless son-in-law."

"*Noblesse de cloche?*" Gerry wrinkled his forehead. "Bell nobility? I've never heard of that. In Rudolstadt, at the Latin school, they instructed us about the difference between *noblesse d'épée* and *noblesse de robe.*"

"It's not a legal term like the others," Marguerite said. "It's what you call slang. Wealthy townsmen, rich urbanites, social-climbing *bourgeois*. Men who live within hearing range of the bells in the steeples of city churches."

"Do your best," Ruvigny assured the duchess. "Given the right girl with the right dowry, I'm prepared to go into matrimony with good intentions and live in amicable fidelity for the next forty-plus years."

"Er! Okay. What about you, August?"

"God-fearing," Bismarck answered. "Ah, nice and plump, if I can take my choice. Ideally with a equally nice dowry."

"Define *nice* in comparison to Henri's *nice.*"

"Where I come from, it's a trousseau and usually about four thousand to five thousand Thaler, to be paid in installments, but you have to calculate in the reality that dowries and dowers are hardly ever paid in full. You can use the promissory notes as security for loans, though, even if they haven't been paid out. When collection time comes, the lender has to deal with your father-in-law, because a betrothal contract constitutes a legal obligation. Four to five thousand is plenty if you're farming in the Altmark. It wouldn't go far to support the lifestyle of a colonel, if I ever get that rank. But it looks like I'll still be a captain when I die or retire, whichever comes first, so the question is moot. I can't afford a wife."

"Candale?"

"Not until Épernon dies. I can't afford to remarry on my own funds and he's too tight to fund another try after the fiasco with the duchess of Halewijn. That cost him a bundle and we didn't get anything out of it in the end, neither a higher title nor heirs." He turned to Raudegen. "Anything to contribute?"

"I had a wife, once. She died a long time ago, in Bayreuth, before I joined the army. The baby was stillborn. My mother arranged it, but everything was all right. Our families were friends and we were friends. There wasn't any money involved because all of us were refugees from Lower Austria. We were peasants before we left. There wasn't any money around. Ferdinand II confiscated everything when he drove the Protestants out." He shrugged. "I'm not likely to marry again."

Not even Gerry had the nerve to ask anything on the order of *what was her name?*

Raudegen's expression did not invite further questions. He stood up and disappeared in the direction of the stairs.

After a short period of silence, Marc opened his mouth. "I don't suppose you have to speculate much about my marriage." He winked at Susanna. "I give it five years, more or less. But what about you, Gerry? You started it all."

Gerry winked back at him, grinning at Bismarck. "God-fearing is good, but since I'll probably marry a pastor's daughter, it's not likely to be a problem."

"Why a pastor's daughter?"

"Because most of the girls I'll meet will be the daughters of pastors. It's propinquity. It's hard to marry someone you haven't met." He looked at Marguerite and cleared his throat. "Unless you're a member of a royal

129

family or such. Or a Moonie. Plump isn't bad, but I think 'willing to put up with me' would top anything else. I don't have to worry about it yet, because it will be at least fifteen years before I can go looking for a wife–longer, if I keep getting yanked out of school to do this, that, and the other for Dad and Ron."

"Let's set up a wager," Ruvigny said. "Each of us makes up a list of the order in which we think we'll wed and throws some money in the pot. We'll invest it. Marc can take care of that or get Cavriani to do it. Then when the last of us ties the knot, or dies unmarried, we'll open the envelope that we deposited with the money, compare the lists, and the winner who was closest to right will collect the pot."

"Great idea," Bismarck said. "As long as it's cash that we get from the investment. A part of the widow's dower assigned to my mother, all specified in the marriage contract, consisted of annual allotments of *Wispel* of rye. Nineteen *Wispel* of rye every year. By the time the last of us marries, that would be a lot of rye piled up."

"What's a *Wispel?*"

"Um." Bismarck ran his hand through his hair. "About 24 American bushels, I think."

"What on earth did she do with it?"

"She had it ground into flour and we ate it. Brandenburg is really strong on rye bread. Rye bread, cabbage soup, and pork sausage. That's a meal that breeds up real men."

Every French person in the room shuddered.

The next morning, at breakfast, Marguerite asked. "Henri, do you ever think about Jericho?"

"What?" The sudden question, popping up out of nowhere, disconcerted Ruvigny a bit.

"Jericho. It was one of the stories that *Grand-mère Rohan* used to read me from the Bible. When the Chosen People marched around the walls for seven days and they fell down. Then Joshua's men killed everyone in the city except the harlot who helped them and her family. You know it, don't you?"

"I know it."

"Have you ever stopped to think about La Rochelle? And Magdeburg? The sieges and the sacks? It was the Catholics who were outside the walls. It was the Huguenots and the Lutherans who got massacred. Could God be trying to give us a hint about something? That we're on the *wrong side*, maybe? Is that why God let Louis's armies defeat Papa and Uncle Soubise and send them into exile?"

"Trust me, little seed pearl. If God talked to Tilly or Richelieu, nobody heard him." *This is way above my pay grade.* "Ah, who else have you talked to about this concern?"

"Nobody. Nobody ever listens to me. Hardly anybody else ever listens to me at all, and I couldn't ask Susanna because she's Catholic. And she doesn't know any more about her religion than I do about mine. As far as I can tell from things she's said, not discussing theology but talking about how she lives, for her it's mostly habits and actions; smells, sounds and colors. Habits of going to mass on certain days, actions like the incense censers going down the aisle and smells like the incense burning in it; sounds like the bells they ring with the incense; colors in the stained glass windows and the idolatrous statues of the saints. And, also for her, because she loves fabrics so, the brocades and tapestries, the embroideries and laces, on the paraments and vestments. She's used to it, and when she goes to church it's like she is pulling a warmed blanket around her on a cold day and cuddling in. Calvinist churches aren't cuddly."

"They aren't supposed to be cuddly, little daisy. They are designed to be spare, to focus our minds on God's Word as expounded from the pulpit."

"I'm not sure that Susanna even connects what Richelieu and Tilly did with what she feels when she goes to mass."

More of the group came into the breakfast room, turning the conversation into generalities.

"We have to leave tonight," the duchess said to Candale while the rest of the travelers stretched their legs at mid-morning. "I've deferred to your preferences this far, but we're getting too close to Burgundy. Once we pass the border, it will be far harder for us to slip away, and getting

131

back out through the grand duke's border posts without being stopped would be chancy. In any case, the escort I arranged before we left Paris will be waiting for us on this side."

"Assuming that they have arrived in a timely fashion, which isn't a safe assumption given the road conditions I've observed."

"Be reasonable, *mon ami*. They are men on horseback; they won't have had to concern themselves with the various other delays this party experienced. They've probably been waiting for several days, spending my money on wine."

"Are you still sure of this?"

"I am sure of this. There will be nothing for me to accomplish in Besançon. I have no connections in the grand duke's picayune little court, the Archduchess is Catholic and Italian to boot, and Rohan will keep me sidelined from his concerns. I belong in France, where I intend to see that Soubise does not garner any glory that may still be available for our cause and that we collect every ounce of advantage that we can from the new king's political uncertainties. Even though we have *still* heard no news, there are bound to be political uncertainties. Even without fresh news, I can be certain that there are political uncertainties because the world hasn't come to an end yet." She took a deep breath. "We evaluate, and we throw Rohan's influence behind the party that appears most likely to triumph. I belong in France, and so do my children."

"On the basis of candid observation thus far," Candale said, "it is not easy to travel with children. It will particularly not be easy to take the boy *sans* Susanna. Having him will slow us down immensely—delay us as much going as he has delayed us coming. He can't ride—the plan was that all of us would ride once we rendezvoused. If you bring him, your escort will have to find a carriage again. Marguerite will not come voluntarily: I'm more than sure of that. In any case, if you take her, willing or not, Rohan will never stop his pursuit. Do you want Raudegen, Ruvigny, and Bismarck on our tails all the way?"

"Tancrède, then. Please Candale? Just let me bring Tancrède."

They all woke up no more than an hour after the last of them had gone to bed, to the banshee wail of a six-year-old blowing on a harmonica as loudly as he could. Susanna jumped out of bed and dashed toward the cot in the corner of the chamber where he was sleeping. Or, rather, had been sleeping. Bleary-eyed, she tried to make out shapes in the darkness. The harmonica howled again. She scurried faster, grasped an arm that was much too long to belong to a child, and bit the attached hand. Hard. A soprano scream joined the shrillness of the harmonica as the hand's owner tried to shake her off.

Tancrède untangled his legs from the sheet and started kicking.

Susanna got an arm around his waist. "Don't kick me. Kick him. Kick her. Kick the other person."

Marguerite woke up in the adjoining room she was sharing with her mother and, still half-asleep, managed to light a lantern. The men poured out of the rooms across the hall, at first trying to break through the inside bar to the room where Susanna was, until Marguerite yelled that the door to her room was unbarred and open, so they could enter through that. Three of them headed that way, but by the time they arrived, the intruder was gone through the window and Susanna remained in possession of the prize.

A few minutes later, the duchess wandered in, clutching together a long, loose cloak thrown over her nightclothes. "What's all the excitement? I had to go to the necessary."

"Are you sure," Marguerite hissed, "that you didn't find it 'necessary' to pay a visit to M. de Candale's room?"

Susanna unbarred the second door. Candale, who had been standing outside it, came in. "No, she did not. Nor do I think she appreciates your impertinence."

"What happened, anyway?" Marc asked.

"I wasn't asleep," Tancrède said. "But I'm not supposed to get up and wander around at night, so I didn't. Not this time. Sometimes I do, when I'm at home with the LeBons and know my way around, but I don't know my way around any of these new places. I was lying there, playing with my harmonica. I sleep with it under my pillow. Somebody

133

opened up the window. I thought it might be an interesting monster, so I waited. But it was a person and the person tried to pick me up, so I blew and blew and blew and blew and . . ."

"All right," Bismarck said. "We believe you. You blew."

"I tried to make out some trail," Raudegen said, "but whoever it was headed back toward the outbuildings. It's dark, and there's too much of a mess of footprints in the loose dust behind the inn. The best thing to do is for the rest of you to go back to bed. Ruvigny, you stand guard on the ladies' doors inside. I'll take the outside."

"Let me take the outside watch," Candale said, "since I have two hands available. If Susanna's teeth did their work the way she describes, you and he would be evenly matched if he dares to come back, but I will have the advantage."

In the morning he was gone, and so was the duchess.

"I could have told you if you asked me," Tancrède said. "But you didn't. I knew it was the lady who visited me sometimes who tried to take me out of my bed. She smelled like she always does."

Bismarck predicted the worst possible vocational outcome for all of them if they turned up in Besançon without the duchess. Raudegen, although on this particular venture he was not responsible to Rohan for getting the duchesses to the duke but rather, along with Marc, for getting Susanna to someplace she would be safe, was not at all inclined to let them go. Bismarck reiterated that Rohan would not like it. In his opinion, it could be a career-ruining event for Ruvigny—well, for him, too—to turn up without the older duchess.

"Not," Marguerite said, "if you bring me. Maybe only career-discouraging or at worst career-transferring. Henri can always go to *Grand-père* Sully and find another patron. And you work for the grand duke, not for Papa. Well, so does Henri, for that matter. Papa just borrowed you. I doubt that the grand duke will place so much importance on all of this."

Raudegen pointed to Gerry. "What did you tell me the night of the extravaganza? 'If it weren't for bad luck, I'd have no luck at all?' Bismarck seems to be adopting it as his motto."

"Theme song, actually." Gerry played a few notes. "Gloom, Doom, and Agony on Me."

"Up-time must have been a strange world," Marguerite said. "A world in which people turned deep, dark, depression and excessive misery into a joke."

"Some didn't," Gerry said. "They ended up doing stuff like committing suicide. If Magda and Pastor Kastenmayer, he's the Lutheran pastor in Grantville, hadn't talked to me, there was a point when I might have done something stupid like that myself after we came home from Rome. A person has to keep going. It helps to laugh about it if you can. When you can. Sometimes it all drops down on your head at once, but the rest of the time, you might as well make jokes."

"*Melancholia*," Ruvigny said. "The ancients knew about it."

"More practically," Raudegen said, "if we aren't going to retrieve the duchess, we might as well sell one of the carriages here and those two horses as well. We don't need them without her and it never hurts to have some additional resources. Especially since she took most of the money, but I suppose we can't honestly complain about that, since she provided it in the first place. At least Candale was decent enough to only take his own horse."

"Rohan didn't send money to get them out?" Susanna asked.

"Not enough to last Ruvigny and Bismarck in both directions. He expected his wife to pay her own way to join him. She has more money than he does. As for Marc and me, it's been an expensive trip. We cashed in the last bank draft from Madame Cavriani before we left Brussels."

"Keep the smaller carriage," Marc advised. "As we get up closer to the Jura, the roads aren't meant for vehicles at all. We may end up selling everything but the horses in a couple of days, to someone who's headed out in the other direction."

135

The grand duke had more guards than usual on the Burgundy side of the border where the road crossed toward Dôle. The king also had more guards than usual stationed on the French side. That wasn't surprising, considering the amount of traffic that the conclave in Besançon had generated throughout the summer–unsurprising, but unfortunate and inconvenient.

Raudegen dismounted, handing his reins to Gerry, and talked to them. He called up Marc, who also dismounted, handed his reins to Gerry, and talked to them. Raudegen produced paper. Marc produced more paper. The guards shuffled paper.

Susanna, looking as nursemaidly as she could, stepped down from the carriage, lifted Tancrède from the steps, shot the guards an apologetic smile, and said, "He has to go."

Gerry trotted after the two of them, leading the horses.

"Hey you," one of the guards yelled. "Come back here." He was speaking French, but his gestures indicated what he meant in any known human language.

Gerry answered. "I'm going that way." He pointed. "I'll be in plain sight. I'm supposed to keep an eye on the kid." His voice was sulky, his German accent was provincial, and his facial expression indicated that although his body was moving, his mind had never fully caught up with it.

Just a dumb ol' country boy, that's me. He'd seen the role played up-time. He'd seen it played down-time. One of his classmates in Rudolstadt had been a genius of a mimic. He could probably do it in his sleep. He watched Susanna lead Tancrède back and then ambled over to the guard who had yelled, still leading the horses. "What'ya want?" It was bad *Hochdeutsch* in a dialect that couldn't be understood ten miles from the speaker's home village, but it was definitely some variety of down-time German. It was also amiable, cheerful, and unthreatening.

"Go back, stupid." The guard shoved him.

Tancrède started to screech, in French, of course, "Why are we stopped here? I want to go home. I'm tired. I want to go *hoooome!*" What he wanted was to go back to the LeBons in Paris, but there was no reason to mention that to the border guards. Let them assume that "home" was someplace in Burgundy.

One of the senior guards looked up in annoyance and shuffled more paper. Marc walked back, stuck his head through the door, and talked to Marguerite, with much waving of hands. "Marguerite," Tancrède screeched, "I want to go home!"

None of the alerts that the guards had received from Paris said anything about a child and they were supposed to be watching for an older woman and a young one, not two young ones. The alerts mentioned two army officers, but said nothing about four red-headed siblings from Alsace. They didn't even adumbrate the *personas* of a bodyguard and assistant steward, though, naturally, no sensible man would have sent a young woman he cared for anywhere without such precautions. After more shuffling, the lieutenant handed the papers back to Raudegen and motioned them through.

Bismarck flicked the reins in a disinterested manner, stuck his legs out straight as far as they would go, and slouched his shoulders, about as far away from the image of a smart city coachman as a driver could be unless he was in charge of a donkey cart. Raudegen and Marc climbed back on their horses. Gerry climbed back up to ride postilion. Ruvigny prayed that the two extra horses would be taken for spares. It wasn't as if they were highly bred chargers. In accordance with the party's original fairy tale, they were utility horses, the kind that could be used for pulling something light or a servant could use if he needed to keep pace with his betters. Only Raudegen and Marc rode halfway decent mounts, and they were no prizes.

Ruvigny rode ahead and Marc next to the carriage, with Raudegen bringing up the rear. Ruvigny was well into the space that separated the two sets of posts when Bismarck brought the carriage up to pass through. One of the indolent-looking guards gazed lazily into the window, stopped looking lazy at all, and cried out, "Stop them! I've seen that girl in Paris. She's the one we're looking for." He leaped to grab the collar of the lead horse.

Ruvigny started to turn back, but was blocked by another of the French guards. Bismarck jumped off the bench and onto the shoulders of the soldier who was gripping the collar. Marc, from the other side, leaped off his horse and onto the bench, to take charge of the reins. Gerry, like a monkey, climbed up the back, across the roof, and came down on another soldier who was heading toward the collar of the other horse. Raudegen yelled, "Go!" and Marc went, right toward the Burgundian border post. Not very rapidly, though, since each horse had a Frenchman on his collar, each Frenchman had a limpet on his back, trying to pull him off the collar and in the opposite direction, and the spare horses had no idea what was going on and were inclined to dig their feet in and refuse to move at all. The speed of Marc's brave steeds was more comparable to that of two snails than to that of the legendary Pegasus as they dragged their burden along toward the border of the Grand Duchy of Burgundy, inch by reluctant inch.

Two of the soldiers grabbed guns from the guardhouse. Old guns. Functional, but not the modern design. The new ones went to Turenne's army, not to undistinguished infantry companies in regions of the country where nobody expected anything to happen right now. Of course, the officers kept their men drilled. Something might happen here someday, if not in the immediately foreseeable future, and the French military establishment was in a constant budget crisis. Wherefore, they had to go through the whole, by current standards stupendously, excruciatingly, slow, routine of getting them ready to shoot. Which they did as they had been trained to do. They might be on the far edge of what was happening, but their officers knew that could always change and some day they might be, on short notice, *in medias res*. There was no such thing as a stable front in seventeenth-century warfare. Armies moved around.

They aimed at the carriage. One shot grazed the flank of one of the spare horses, who reared and broke his lead, but not before slowing the progress of the carriage even more. The other man might well have made his shot except that Bismark, taking advantage of the delay caused by the slow fuse, dropped off the soldier he had been pulling down and ran toward the muzzle of the gun.

Raudegen's horse didn't like any of this noise and confusion at all. Raudegen had wrapped the reins around the wrist of his incompletely healed hand, but that didn't give him much control, and he'd had very little time to practice using his sword with the 'wrong' hand since they left Paris. The horse refused to come around, much less move in the direction of loud noises. Raudegen threw the sword.

It didn't hit the shooter. No reasonable man could have expected it to, under the circumstances. It did flash by the side of his head, into his peripheral vision, the light reflecting off its blade, close enough that he closed his eyes and flinched a few seconds before he was ready to pull the trigger.

The shot would have hit right where Marguerite was sitting. If she had still been sitting there, that was. She was on the floor with Tancrède. Susanna was on top of them.

It did hit Bismarck, but, thanks to the flinch, not quite in the chest.

Marc got the carriage onto Burgundian soil. Gerry dropped off the back of the second soldier, who had been hanging onto a horse collar, landing on his rear end with a thump. The soldier dropped off in turn, managed a better landing, and ran back toward French soil before the Burgundian border guards could catch him.

The rest of the escape party, being no fools, did not remain to conduct a brave and valiant rear-guard action. They scrambled after the carriage as fast as they could, Raudegen dragging Bismarck, with his good hand, by way of a firm grasp on the other's collar. He left the sword behind. It was an ordinary sword, not some fabled blade long sung by bards in legend. He could buy another one.

* * *

"You're an idiot, you know," Ruvigny said bracingly, while Gerry patched Bismarck up. "Normal people don't run straight at guns. At least

139

not when they're on foot. We're all a little strange, I suppose, in that we've chosen a profession that causes us to run right out to get shot at, but we're supposed to do it on horses, while we're wearing armor. The infantry on foot don't normally charge guns. At most, they stand there and take it, hoping that one of the balls doesn't have their number."

Gerry, although he was stoically continuing to swab the wound out, was going from pale to greenish. Ruvigny turned to him. "How did you do it? Tricking that soldier into thinking you were a down-time peasant when you're an up-timer."

Gerry fought down his gag reflex. "Think about it. I was twelve when the Ring of Fire hit. I've lived nearly a third of my life down-time. I've been going to school with either a majority of down-timers in Grantville and now at the university in Jena or to a school where *everybody* else was a down-timer when I was at the Latin School in Rudolstadt."

He rearranged the tools he was using to probe at Bismarck's shoulder. "This is going to take a surgeon, you know, once we find one."

After that bit of drama, the rest of the trip to Besançon was just a matter of moving forward.

CHAPTER 15

August–September1636
Besançon

Rohan was not happy, but he was pragmatic. "Has she resumed her liaison with Candale, then?"

"I wouldn't put it past her," Marguerite said.

"I saw no sign of it while we were in Paris last summer." Ruvigny shook his head. "He was rarely around. On the way here, he shared a room with the other men every night."

"It's probably political, then, but that's neither here nor there." Rohan looked at Raudegen. "I'll have a letter ready by morning. With Bernhard's approval, if he will agree to continue to second you to me for a span of time, you will be on your way back to Soubise shortly thereafter. He needs to know I'm aware that she is out there, somewhere, spinning her intrigues."

"You have probably been receiving more information here, through the radio connection to the USE, Your Grace, than we did the last two weeks we were in France. Do you have any sense where they might have gone?" Ruvigny asked. "We speculated, of course. Brittany? Back to Sully? To Brunswick to negotiate Candale's brother out of captivity?"

"Back to Paris to make Uncle Soubise's life miserable," Marguerite contributed. She paused. "Why don't you divorce her, Papa?"

"No." Rohan shook his head. "I won't say never, but not as long as your grandfather is alive. I respect and admire him more, perhaps, than you can believe. In my estimation, Sully is one of the greatest men of our age with perhaps the greatest of political visions."

* * *

"Do you believe, Henri?" Marguerite asked.

Ruvigny cocked his head a bit to the side. "Believe what?"

"The teachings of John Calvin. The tenets of the faith. What the theologians write and the preachers say?"

"How come you ask?"

"Because Susanna believes, I think. Bismarck believes. Gerry believes, in his odd way. I'm pretty sure that Uncle Soubise does believe; at least he did as a young man. The court considered him something of a zealot for the Reformed faith and he got into several confrontations. Papa can talk about theology in learned ways, but I don't think he has a belief that informs his life. Nor *Maman*, or at least only that God's favor has not fallen upon her and she is predestined to damnation, so she might as well do as she pleases on the way there. Do you believe?"

"Sometimes . . . sometimes I think that we–Rohan, Sully, Coligny, Bouillon, Trémouille, the great Protestant houses and their clients–have been placed in France to defend the faith of those who do believe." He paused. "I am prepared to expend my life's blood defending the right of Huguenot believers to follow their convictions, without forced conversions, without expulsions, without confiscations. Is that belief? Make of it what you will."

* * *

"I hadn't given it enough thought," Rohan said to Marguerite. "Here you are, without your mother, and your presence is disrupting my bachelor household. You must have a mature woman as your companion, since your mother did not come. How many ladies-in-waiting will you need? A personal maid. A chambermaid." He ticked items off a list as he muttered. "It's already September. There's not a lot of time left to bring suitable persons here."

"If I may speak, Your Grace?" Ruvigny was standing with his back to the wall. "You no longer have close personal ties with the major Huguenot families, and the constellations at court are changing every day. You can't be sure that any woman you bring from France won't be acting as an agent for Gaston. Or for the duchess, as far as that goes."

"Then what do you recommend? Marguerite can't stay here without a proper establishment."

"Borrow someone from Archduchess Claudia."

"Most of her attendants are Catholic. She has accepted a few Protestants as a concession to the Grand Duke, but they are all Lutheran." Rohan chewed on his upper lip for a moment. "As for that, this girl who came with you . . . she's Catholic, isn't she?"

"But betrothed to Cavriani's son." Ruvigny steepled his fingers, briefly considering how much of a diplomatic career would consist of balancing the relationship among the down-time equivalent of 'lies, damn lies, and statistics'. "So it is possible that her Catholicism may be interpreted as a temporary or interim condition." *When pigs fly.* "We should certainly behave in such a way as not to discourage her from converting if or when the possibility should arrive. In addition to that . . ." *Ah*, he thought to himself. *What would we do without the subjunctive case?*

Rohan coughed politely. "I know Cavriani. I enjoy conversing with him. However, I'm never sure whether I'm on solid rock or shifting sand when I'm dealing with the man. Still . . . oh, well, yes. The girl can stay in Marguerite's household until Cavriani sends for her and Marc. That doesn't reduce the need for suitable Calvinist attendants."

* * *

Rohan did not fully understand why they were in his conference room. He hadn't summoned them; they had just filed in after his daughter. Why were all of them taking such an interest in her marriage? It wasn't as if, aside from Ruvigny, any of them were Huguenots. The up-time boy had even stuck his hand up in the air and replied, "Present," when he called the meeting to order.

"Understand, ladies and gentlemen. If a time comes when there are only two members of *la religion prétendue réformée,* as Henri IV chose to call our beliefs when he issued the Edict of Nantes, left standing, I will be one of them. That is the point from which all our discussions start. Now, first, as to the Catholic nonentity to whom the crown married Marguerite according to the up-time encyclopedias, impelled by Anne of Austria and Cardinal Mazarin: he was a terrible *mésalliance* to be forced on the ducal house of Rohan. He was a minor Poitevan nobleman, merely a *seigneur* with not even a title, of no special fortune. That is unacceptable and will not occur. Understood?"

They signaled that they understood, Ruvigny whispering to Gerry, under the general murmur, that *prétendu* was one of those 'false friend' words that foreigners had to regard with suspicion.

Nonetheless, I am having difficulties in locating matches of suitable rank among the Calvinists. Turenne would be the ideal candidate, but circumstances make such a match impossible. Rupert of the Palatinate is out of play; so are Amalie Elisabeth's brothers." He slammed one hand on the table, palm down, waving a list with the other. "Not one of these other possibilities is acceptable." He slammed his hand down flat on the table again. "I can't identify a single French nobleman of suitable rank who would place Rohan first. Not with any certainty. By now, my minimum requirement is a *Protestant* nonentity."

"Don't pick a dumb one," Gerry advised. "It's like breeding horses, if you don't mind my saying so, Your Grace. Look at every single one of the possibilities and ask yourself, 'Would I mind having a grandson exactly like this guy?' If your answer to yourself is, 'I'd rather have a pig,' then he's not the right choice, no matter how many political connections his family has."

"So," Bismarck said. "One requirement on the list is, *smart*. At least reasonably so."

"Smart, kind, and reliable," Gerry qualified. "You can vary the proportions but you need all three of those. At least, if you're honestly trying to make a decent marriage for her, Your Grace, and not just use her as a pawn in your political games."

Ruvigny looked at Rohan uneasily. People, at least most people, didn't say things like that to dukes. At least not more than once.

Rohan ignored the up-timer, going back to his original train of commentary as if the boy hadn't said anything. "She needs someone to be Rohan for her." He frowned down at the papers in front of him.

"I'm here, you know," Marguerite grouched at her father. "Sitting right here at the table."

Gerry, blithely indifferent to the peril in which he kept placing himself, ignored her and kept on talking to the duke. "Yeah, I can see that, Your Grace. Politically, I mean." He gestured toward Marguerite with his thumb. "For some important guy, she'll just be a territorial annexation, so to speak. Land and money walking on two feet, to add glory to him. The tail that some dog would be wagging. As an even better analogy, she'll be a commodity on the futures market and her husband will be speculating that she'll retain her value—survive childbirth and not have anything happen to cause the French crown to seize the Rohan estates."

"There's a story that Gerry told me and the young duchess," Bismarck whispered to Ruvigny. "About some emperor and some new clothes and a child who calls it the way he sees it."

Gerry was still full steam ahead. "But some unimportant guy doesn't have the clout you want." He leaned back. "Maybe there really isn't anybody suitable. Like there wasn't for Queen Elizabeth of England last century."

Bismarck shook his head. "She needs a husband. On that, I agree with the duke. Otherwise, she won't have the heirs she needs. That Rohan needs. The queen of England got it wrong. She'd have been better off to find some guy, even if he wasn't ideal, and have a half-dozen kids rather than let Mary of Scotland's son take the throne after her."

"I'm here, you know," Marguerite grouched at Bismarck. "Right here at the table."

Gerry glanced at her. "Yeah, I know you're here, but I wouldn't count on getting any of them, your father and his advisers, to listen to you. Face facts. It's not as if you have any say in the matter. Not even if you think you should or I think you should. You know all of us guys in the Red Headed League better than you'll have a chance to know the man you eventually marry before you have to stand up in the church to say, 'I do'."

He turned back toward Rohan. "But why does any guy you pick to marry her have to be Rohan for her at all?"

The duke popped his head up from studying the papers. "What do you mean?"

Before Gerry could answer, Bismarck gestured. "Why can't she be Rohan for herself? She has us, Your Grace, if Grand Duke Bernhard will accept our resignations in your favor. Give us a few years. Ruvigny for her Secretary of State, so to speak. Raudegen, when he gets back, as Chief of Security." He nodded at Marc. "Head of the intelligence service." At Susanna. "A *confidante* representing the voice of common sense, I suppose. I nominate me for her commander in chief." He started to nod at Gerry. "Uh, chaplain? You could always convert to Calvinism. I'll have to if I become her general, I suppose. It won't be that complicated. The Brandenburg Electors are Calvinist already; they didn't force their subjects to give up Lutheranism, but they'll be pleased enough if one of them does. She'll have our whole Red Headed League, with Raudegen and Marc as bonuses."

"Nope," Gerry preempted him. "I'm going to be a *Lutheran* pastor and as soon as this is over, I'm going back to Jena. *Finally!* Maybe I can be a consultant for you guys."

Marguerite looked at him. "Are you sure?"

"I am, Your Grace. I know who I am and I know what I am. Out at Lothlorien, where I grew up, we had lots of vinyl LPs and a lot of those were Pete. He sang it, 'Keep your eyes on the prize.' You have to hold on and keep an eye on where you're going. And there was Horton."

Nobody else in the room had the vaguest idea what either vinyl or an elpee might be. This wasn't Grantville. It wasn't even Magdeburg or Bamberg. Neither did they know who Pete might have been. Nor Horton.

"Horton?" Marguerite asked.

Rohan tried, though. "Horton. Frau Dunn's late husband, the one who was involved at Suhl. You know the up-time nurse that Grand Duke Bernhard brought here, don't you? She prefers that we not speak of him."

"Not the Suhl Incident Horton." Gerry shook his head. "The other Horton. 'I meant what I said and I said what I meant.' *That* Horton—the elephant who was faithful, one hundred percent."

Rohan finally broke the ensuing silence. "A fable perhaps, similar to those composed by Aesop?"

"I tell you," Gerry said. "We had a lot of books out at Lothlorien, but Dad bought them at yard sales and flea markets. They were pretty beat up, so we didn't give them to the State Library. They're still out at the dome. I'll have Ron send someone out to find Horton for you, when he hatches the egg and when he hears the who. 'A person's a person, no matter how small'."

Murmurs of translation fluttered around the table, along with the making of lists of topics to be investigated further.

Bismarck thought that even though Gerry had so casually refused the jocularly offered ducal chaplaincy, a prize which almost any cleric of any denomination would grasp with both hands, there might yet be, in the form of this scrawny, unprepossessing, boy, someone, who would give thought to providing a moral compass for a girl who certainly would need one. Still, the up-timer was, like himself, of the wrong confession. And also going back to Germany . . .

"*Are* you sure," he asked Gerry after the others left, "that your true desire is to serve God for pure love of him? Are you sure that you aren't trying to atone for what you see as your own unforgivable transgressions

147

by following this path, relying on works rather than faith and grace? Are you sure that you aren't following the same mistaken path that Luther took when he vowed to become a monk?"

* * *

During the last course of that evening's dinner, Marguerite leaned her chin on her hand. "Do any of you care what I think about it? Anybody? How can I be Rohan for myself if nobody listens to me?"

"I'm listening, little daisy. What do you think?"

She sat up straighter. "Don't indulge me with that soothing voice, Henri. Do even you *really* want to know what I think?"

"I do." That was Bismarck.

"Me too." That was Gerry.

Susanna and Marc waved from the other side of the table.

"Well then." She pushed back her chair and stood up. "If Papa won't divorce *Maman* and marry again to have more heirs, *I think* that he should make Uncle Soubise get married. He can put on 'crusty old bachelor' as what Gerry calls his public face as much as he wants to, but he's several years younger than Papa. He can't be much past fifty. If he had children, then it wouldn't all depend on me. And it shouldn't all depend on me, because I'm a girl."

"Girls can do things for themselves," Kamala Dunn began with the almost automatic up-timer's reaction. She started to say more.

Marguerite pressed her hands together. "I know that I'll have to marry the man Papa chooses . . . and . . . and get pregnant . . . whether I want to or not, because it's my duty under God. If my husband is kind, like Gerry said, then it shouldn't be so bad. But what if I die in childbirth, the first time? What if the baby dies with me? What will become of Rohan then?"

Nobody answered.

She reached up blindly, clasping the wall tapestry behind her in her left hand and squeezing it into pleats. "What if I'm like *Maman*? What if I

148

become pregnant time after time after time and watch the babies die? And die, and die, until my husband tires of it and says no more, so that I will know that God has cursed me because I have failed in the only reason women are on earth, to give male heirs to their husbands? And then she had Tancrède, after Papa said there would be no more childbearing, and he was a boy and was healthy and he lived and she thought it was a sign that God had forgiven her for being a daughter of Eve, for as the preachers say, the pains of childbed are God's retribution on us for her sin?"

Marguerite's voice rose higher and higher in a pathetic wail. "So *Maman* loves him and she at least tried to take him with her when she went her own way this time, but she left me behind. She didn't even *try* to keep me. She just left me behind."

Letting loose of the tapestry, she sank back down in her chair. "But I am a daughter of Eve, too, so my babies will die and die, and the preachers will tell me that I must humbly accept God's will. And then there will still be no more Rohan!"

She looked at them, almost desperately. "Do you know what it's like, to have your brothers and sisters die, and die, and die?"

Bismarck shook his head. "Our family has lost none."

"Nor ours," Gerry said. "Presuming that Frank and Giovanna are okay, that is. Wherever they are by now."

"Yes," Susanna said. "I'm from my father's second marriage, so I mostly didn't see it. But almost all the children of my father's first marriage have died, seven out of eight. I remember two of them besides Maria, who is still alive. My full brother and sister also died. I barely remember them at all. I was four when Ercole died and five when Lucretia's time came. It's my half-brothers Giuseppe and Gian Armando that I miss. I was eight when Seppi died and twelve when the smallpox took Mando."

Ruvigny bowed his head. "You know that only Maximilien and Cirné died. Max was an adult, already in the Royal Guards. The other four of us are fine."

Gerry thought of slipping out, but the radio room was at the top of the citadel. No reasonable person would climb up the path to the citadel in the dark if he didn't have to. He'd try tomorrow. Which he did, the first thing in the morning. Ron wasn't available, but he got a response from Missy.

"At *this* hour?"

"It's important. Honestly."

"Oh, all right. I'll get in touch with someone I know at the State Library, see what she can find, and have her get back to you."

He waited for an hour and a half for the response, climbed back down the path, and then wandered into the breakfast room.

"You know that Catholic nonentity your father keeps harping on, little duchess?"

Marguerite, who had been staring miserably at her griddle cakes, raised her head.

"He wasn't entirely useless. You had six kids. Four of them lived and had kids of their own. I don't know why the duke didn't think to mention it to you. He obviously has that same article about your family from the EB1911 that Missy just had one of her friends look up for me, or he wouldn't have known who your husband was."

Marguerite pursed her lips. Her eyes lit up with new interest. "Who *was* he?"

"Uh. I forgot to ask."

From: Gerry, in Besançon

To: Ron, in Nancye

Dude, a second thought. When you have someone at Lothlorien hunt for those Dr. Seuss books I asked you to send, can you have them dig out Yertle the Turtle, too? I'm pretty sure we packed it in the same crate. I'll give it to Ruvigny and Bismarck to think about. I'm not sure the rest of these guys are anywhere near ready for Yertle yet, much less Mack.

And if Pratchett's Guards! Guards! is in there, send it, too, please.

"Don't let *Maman* get custody of Tancrède," Marguerite warned her father. "She's an *intrigante*. She'll try to use him, somehow. Don't let Candale have him, either. That would be tantamount to letting *Maman* have him." She bit her lip. "Especially if you do die in two years, my lord father, which I most sincerely hope that you do not."

"What are you thinking?" Ruvigny pushed away from the wall.

"That she might use him to become regent of Rohan for a far longer time than she will be if I inherit. I'm almost of age."

Bismarck looked doubtful.

"She could, you know. Now that I am out from under her control, if she has Tancrède she can invent some fairy story about how he is a legitimate heir. She could peddle it to his advisers as how she and Papa hid him for fear of the evil machinations of Richelieu. She could create a tale that Papa feared that the cardinal would seize the infant heir and bring him up Catholic, thus depriving the Huguenots of their strongest pillar. Now, under the magnanimous generosity of a new monarch, there is no reason to fear. She can bring him out of the shadows into the protection of the royal sunlight. I could practically write it myself, and Benserade most certainly can write it. Heroic. Sentimental. Shocking. Touching. The Epic Poem of the Protective Mother and her Defenseless Son."

Marguerite flicked her finger. "With a Greek chorus of lawyers.

"If nothing else, Papa, if you are so sure in your heart that you will die soon, then when you write your will, don't just name me as your sole and universal heir. Put an explicit, unmistakable, unarguable statement into your will that you know the child exists, name him by name, state that he is a suppositious child, a bastard, and that in no way and under no circumstances should he be acknowledged as your heir."

"He should be safe from her right here," Rohan said. "Or safe from her ambitions, which amounts to the same thing."

"I won't have him here. There was a certain air of focused menace slithering around the room. Most of it was slithering out of Marguerite. "I won't have him in my household."

"It's my household," Rohan pointed out.

"I won't have him in any household where I am. Take him somewhere else."

"We can't send him back to LeBon in Paris," Ruvigny pointed out. "If Gaston's supporters get hold of him . . . That would cause more complications than even the improbable scenario that you are predicting, my panicked little puppet. I had planned to take him up to Leiden. Board him anonymously with a university professor who would bring him up to be a specialist in ancient linguistics or something," Ruvigny said. "It was an actual plan. It was a workable plan before everything went sour in France."

Marguerite glared. "I take it that you developed this plan before you actually met the little goblin."

"I do agree," Bismarck said, "that he doesn't come across as a prime candidate for a career in Babylonian linguistics or anything of the sort. I don't believe the sciences would be a prudent choice. I hate to think of what he could achieve in an alchemical laboratory."

Gerry cleared his throat. "We can take him." He waved his hand vaguely. "Marc and I. We're leaving anyway. We can take him with us."

"Why?" Rohan asked.

Gerry looked at Marc. There were limits to what you ought to say to a duke and he had reached his.

"He means," Marc said, "that we've got something that as far as we can tell is pretty much missing in the whole French upper class. We both have fathers, good ones, with experience in bringing up boys. Either one would take him—Dr. Stone or my dad."

"I think that Magda would *like* to have a kid," Gerry said. "It looks as if she's not going to have any of her own. But she's Lutheran, like me. If you want him brought up Calvinist . . ." His voice trailed off.

"I can take him to Geneva," Marc interrupted. "Um. I agree with August that he's not likely to turn into a pedant, but being a Cavriani is enough to keep even a kid as energetic as Tancrède is busy."

He thought, *enough to occupy even a boy as naturally ambitious as the child of a certain politically adaptable French count and that intriguante of a French duchess may to grow up to be.*

He didn't say it, though. Instead, he looked at the younger Marguerite. "Busy enough that you won't always have to be thinking of him as threat to your security just over there on the horizon—on the margin of everything else you have to think about."

Ruvigny nodded. "Busy, and well out of the way of anyone who might be considering how to use him as a pawn in some power play." He thought of the elder Marguerite. His voice firmed up. "Anyone at all."

"I should stay here," Susanna said. She and Marc were standing in a not-very-busy hallway, his arms around her waist and hers around his, their foreheads resting against each other. "Not go with you. Here as a dressmaker. Visiting Mama was a pretext, anyway. I should work for *la petite Marguerite.*"

"Why? I thought we had agreed with what Raudegen said, before France. That you would go to Geneva with me and have the pick of the world's Huguenots to choose among." Marc tried for a judicious, impartial, tone of voice. He wanted to take her with him. To Geneva. To wherever came next.

"Because I haven't learned enough," she answered. "Brussels was a Catholic court. It's as Catholic as Vienna was, at least when you're down in a dressmaker's workshop. When you're there, you know that the alliance with Fredrik Hendrik exists, but it's kind of abstract. You don't see it or experience it. I never went up to Amsterdam or Rotterdam or . . . Leiden, or . . . The Hague. Not to any of those northern cities. So I need to be where I'm working with Calvinists every day. To find out, you know, if I can stand living among Protestants. The way you found out in Naples whether you could stand living among Catholics." She wrinkled up her forehead.

"I'm not sure how much you will learn about living among 99.99% of the world's Calvinists by working for the little duchess," Marc said. "I don't think anyone would describe the Rohan family as typical of the breed. You could come to Geneva with me. It's full of Calvinists."

"All of the ladies in Geneva wear black dresses with white collars. Not one of them needs a court dressmaker."

"There is that problem. Calvinists come in different varieties. The court of Frederik Hendrik would not have been typical of Calvinists, either."

"So the little duchess is better than nothing. Even if the Rohans are not typical, I will meet their associates."

Marc lifted his head and nodded. The nod was affirmative. Reluctant, but affirmative.

"If Rohan agrees to having you in her household longer term, then all right. I'll be back."

He was thinking *no, no*, we've agreed to take Tancrède to Geneva and we'll be doing it *without Susanna*.

She was thinking, *serves them right* for volunteering to take that kid to Geneva with them and expecting me to babysit him the whole way without even asking in advance whether I'd be willing.

Since September was often the last month to offer decent weather—October fell into "if you were lucky" and November into "if you liked to gamble"—Marc and Gerry were off to the livery stable the next morning.

The rain kept pouring. It dripped off Marc's cape, down onto the hand by which he was holding Tancrède. The boy pulled away from his increasingly slippery grasp and dashed into a passageway to which the description *alley* would have assigned undue dignity. It had been swept, but the running water was scouring residual slime from deep between the cobblestones and dropping it into the occasional puddles that formed in low spots. Tancrède splashed through them, uncaring, in pursuit of a feral cat.

Gerry dashed after him, indifferent to the muck landing on his boots and the hem of his cloak.

Marc stayed where it was cleaner. *Mama will be thrilled to have another little boy to bring up*, he thought to himself. *Of course she will.* If he thought it often enough, perhaps he would convince himself.

That Papa would be thrilled went without saying. Ruvigny's "Anyone at all" shouldn't be interpreted as applying to Leopold Cavriani, and it would be a decade before the child would be old enough to do anything interesting. Who could predict what would be happening in the world by then?

SECTION III

September 1636-January 1637

CHAPTER 16

Paris
September 1636

"Can you believe the news?" Mademoiselle Anne tossed the latest report from one of their observers onto the table. "What am I supposed to say when I start my cycle of attendance upon the queen? That's Monday, which doesn't give us much time to develop a reasonable narrative."

Soubise rescued the report from the most immediate danger of sinking into the sauce for the fish fillets. "Of course I can believe the news. I can believe almost anything I hear about that infuriating little bitch." He snorted. "Anything derogatory. I'm not surprised that she absconded. She made it plain enough all along that she had no intention of rejoining Henri."

"It's not as if she can come back to Paris, though."

"I wouldn't put it past her." Soubise shook his head hard enough that his curls wobbled. "To come back with some touching fable about how she was forced to leave Paris against her will but at the first opportunity bravely, all alone, dared the dangers of the roads and joined an escort party she had arranged to be available for her in order to return, because perish the thought that the House of Rohan would ever be disloyal to the monarch."

"She'd be capable of that, I suppose." Mademoiselle Anne wrinkled her nose in disgust. "I expect that she *was* forced to leave Paris. I just don't know by whom. Those men of Bernhard's that Henri sent, I suppose, but I can't imagine how they managed it with all the guards that Gaston had in place." She sighed. "Where do you suppose she linked up with Candale again?"

"I'm sure they arranged some rendezvous well in advance, similar to the one she might have arranged with an escort party. Well, *did* arrange with an escort party, according to this." He picked up the report and shook it at his sister. "He'd been in Paris for weeks."

"Why wasn't he with his regiment?"

"Because she has involved him in one of her schemes. Again." Soubise gnawed on one end of his flourishing moustache. "At least, they're not at court yet."

"But where are they?"

"No idea. We'll find out." He stood up. "I'm going to send for Sandrart."

"Who?"

"The artist I worked with in Frankfurt am Main a couple of years ago. If he isn't already tied up with preexisting commissions. They're bound to be sneaking around from one prominent Huguenot family to another. Artists hear things. Sandrart can claim he's here for an educational tour or something. Maybe studying the work of the Le Nain brothers. The style that they have developed is different enough from anything the German artists have been doing to make a good reason. He can visit their studio here in Paris and then set out on a tour to look at paintings that they've already sold, ones that are scattered around the countryside.

"Before I set out on this last trip to England, Henri told me not to bring him on my staff again. I'll pay him out of my own pocket, since I have the revenues from the estates that *Maman* left me coming in again now that Gaston revoked the exile. If our brother complains, I'll present it as being more a one-time commission than a permanent hire."

Sandrart replied by letter that the Le Nain brothers themselves were in Magdeburg for a major competition, or would be soon if he could believe the latest *Calendar of the Arts*. It seemed as if every artist on the continent was or soon would be in Magdeburg. However, as most of the works they had already completed were still in France, he would be more than happy to tour around and view them.

Besançon
September 1636

Marguerite and Susanna watched Ruvigny and Bismarck ride out, headed for the Rhine, a raft, and a task.

"I wish they weren't leaving," Marguerite pouted.

"You can't complain. Marc and Gerry left last week. It's going to be a dull winter."

"At least Papa didn't make the grand duke fire them because Mama ran away. He even asked to borrow Henri again. Why didn't Bernhard let him?"

"For the first, your father probably realized that your mother was beyond their control. As for the other, the grand duke needed them to do something else."

"How long does it take to go to the Low Countries and come back?"

"Not too long at this season, but there's no way to predict how long they will be in the Netherlands. If that is where they are going."

Laubach, Solms-Laubach
September 1636

Käthe found the newspapers unsettling. Almost everything in them contributed to her general restlessness. She put the latest edition down, dipped her fingers in a small bowl of water, and dried them on the linen towel. Only then did she pick up her embroidery.

An airship had lifted off in Copenhagen last week. She had not been there to see it. Amalie Elisabeth hadn't been there to see it, either, as far as she knew. But Amalie Elisabeth could have been there, if she had wanted to be there.

With the emperor's connivance, Gretchen Richter, a printer's daughter and former camp follower, had risen to astonishing heights in Saxony and Silesia. Gustavus' new secretary of state was a Jewess. The Anhalt-Dessau girls were making names for themselves; Eva was an author. Her own cousin Litsa had become a journalist.

Whereas she was . . . She put her embroidery aside and stood up. She didn't enjoy embroidery, but it kept her hands occupied with something useful, rather than picking at the upholstery. Or at her own skin. The devil found work for idle hands.

A sudden, sharp, very welcome, cramp pierced her abdomen. She was, with deepest thanks to divine providence, at least not pregnant again. Which, for the past couple of weeks, she had been afraid that she was. Albert Otto was enthusiastic about marital relations.

Geneva
Early October 1636

"A cat!" Potentiana Turettini, by marriage Mme. Cavriani, put the newspaper down. "Marc, why on earth are they making so much fuss about a cat?"

She was a woman inclined to accept life's vicissitudes phlegmatically. In her twenty-three years of marriage, her husband Leopold—a fine man, an excellent provider with a sly sense of humor, not a husband she could complain about—had actually been present in their mutual household for . . . she stopped and calculated . . . something less than six. There had been that stretch of time early in the war, between when he left in 1618 and did not reappear until a couple of months after the end of General Tilly's 1622 Rhineland campaign. She often had not even been certain where he was. That absence had resulted in a four-year age gap between her daughters Crescencia and Fabiana.

The children showed signs of taking after Leopold. Idelette had taken off at the age of eighteen to the astonishing Grantville, where at Leopold's wish, she was learning to be a businesswoman rather than a businessman's wife. Marc showed every indication of becoming as peripatetic as his father, but at the moment, for the first time in several years, he was here at her breakfast table.

With the third genuine up-timer she had ever met, a red-haired boy named Gerry Stone, whom she would never have expected to be the son of one of the wealthiest men in Europe. He reverted back and forth, almost at random, from acting like a ramshackle boy reaching the end of his apprenticeship years to acting like a solemn young theology student.

The first and second up-timers of her acquaintance were also theology students, possibly not typical of the Grantvillers. The first she met, some two years ago, Charles Vandine, had been a sturdy man in his fifties who had come to Geneva to seek ordination as a Presbyterian minister in the heartland of Calvinism. The dominies had granted it almost immediately after the assassination of Mayor Dreeson and Enoch Wiley, already a year and a half ago now, and he had returned to take up his duties at the church there. The other, who had come with Vandine, was also not a boy, but rather an earnest man in this thirties who now, aside from his height, could scarcely be told from any Scots student from the realm of John Knox, so strictly did he imitate his mentors.

But Marc was here this morning. It was inevitable that he would soon go again, but while he was here, she would be glad and rejoice in it.

He was here, not just with Stone, but also with a six-year-old boy whom he expected her to keep. "But *Maman*," Marc had said blithely, "you only had me, amid all these girls. I would have loved to have a little brother, but it turned out to be one more sister, every single time. It will be such fun for you."

She eyed Tancrède. She had listened the previous evening to Marc's entire convoluted tale of the saga of Tancrède Le Bon, comprising

Huguenot dukes, adulterous wives, scandalous lovers, outraged half-sisters, and . . .

"About that cat . . . ," Marc started to say.

"Stop that," Potentiana's youngest daughter and namesake screeched. Tia, now eight, grabbed for a piece of ham that the boy had snatched off her plate.

Tancrède waved it triumphantly over his head, gloating, "It's mine. I got it fair and square. Which cat? I like cats, at least most of them, but some of them bite if you pull their tails. Do you have a cat? I see three dogs; the white one with black spots is cute. Are they friendly?"

"There's plenty more ham on the plate. That piece was *mine*." Tia, with the advantage of two years and three inches, jumped out of her chair, took a two-handed grasp on Tancrède's wrist, and shook it. The greasy slice flew out of his fingers and landed on the floor, where the spotted dog promptly provided a final settlement for the argument.

"Hey, no fair. Why did you do that? Is there any more bread? I like white bread better than rye bread. Have you ever been to a flour mill? The flour coming down into the sacks looks sort of like a waterfall. My nanny took me to see a waterfall once, but it wasn't big. I fell in and she scolded me. I get scolded a lot."

"My *ham*," Tia wailed.

"As for the cat . . . ," Marc tried once more to get a word in.

"*Maman*," seventeen-year-old Crescencia protested. "Make them stop. You never let *us* act like that at the table."

Marc and Gerry looked at one another, recalled that they had an appointment, and made their excuses.

"Ideally," Gordon Partow said, "I'd like to stay in Geneva for a couple more years, get deeper into the theology, plus I should continue to keep an eye on the Vandines' two foster sons—they wanted to stay in the Latin school and they both have another year and a half. But I've also been thinking that I need to get back home. I'm an only child and farming's a hard life. Dad's not sixty yet, but Mom keeps adding postscripts to their letters to say that his back is starting to go out on him and his knees are getting bad. I've still got plenty of cousins in Grantville, though, so maybe, for a while longer . . .

"Vandine was ahead of me–not with the languages, of course. We both had to start from scratch on those. He came up to Jena to begin on them in 1632. I'd already started teaching English lessons there, freelance, the year before. I'd done temp work through an agency up-time, so freelancing right off the bat didn't frighten me the way it did some people. We both picked up the ones we really need, the Latin, Greek, and Hebrew, enough to barely get by here. Nobody expects us to hold a conversation in Greek or Hebrew; we only have to be able to make out the grammar and vocabulary in the Bible. Vandine was a deacon, though, before the Ring of Fire hit, and had done a lot more reading in churchy stuff.

"It was really hard for me to get back into the swing of studying. I just had a high school diploma, and it was close to twenty years old when the Ring of Fire hit. Vandine must have graduated not much later than 1970, but he'd kept taking classes every now and then–courses he took one at a time at the community college when he needed to learn something specific, but they were all in business management." Gordon stretched. "Since he's been back home, he's written that the business management stuff comes in as handy for running a church as it did for running an auto parts store in Fairmont."

He stood up and walked over to a small brazier filled with coals. There was a pot of water boiling on it and a contraption that could have come out of the laboratory of a mad alchemist on a small stand next to it. "Coffee? I've rigged up my own Drip-o-Lator(TM), as you can see. I had Grandpa Miller send me a description of how theirs works. It's one of the originals, from before World War II."

"Look," Gerry said. "I know your mom and dad. I see them every now and then when I'm in Grantville. Your mom misses you, but she's too proud and stubborn to break out in a chorus of–his voice rose–*Come home, come home, ye who are weary, come ho-o-o-ome.* Your dad's still on foot and able to work. You can always check in with Doc Adams by mail; see what he thinks about your dad's health, if you're worried. But you should be fine, and I think you ought to stay and finish. That way, when you go back, you'll be on an equal footing with the other Calvinist ministers. Mr. Vandine, well, Rev. Vandine now, has as much education as Rev. Wiley did, so the up-timers think he's fine as he is. The down-timers figure that he's an emergency appointment, so they cut him some slack, but it will be a lot better in the long run if you get your degree before you're ordained."

Marc, who was not acquainted with any of the people under discussion, kept his mouth shut except for saying, "Coffee, yeah, coffee. Thanks."

Gordon pulled three mugs off a small shelf nailed to the wall of his room, looked inside to judge how clean they might be, and set them down on the stand. "Sometimes, it's a relief to be able to talk to someone." The coffee-contraption sputtered, spraying drops of brown liquid on the newspaper that was already lying there.

"By the way," Gordon said, picking it up and waving it at them, "What's going on with this ridiculous cat thing? Has everybody back home gone nuts?"

Magdeburg
late October 1636

"It was gracious of you to receive me so promptly, My Lady." Marc bowed to the landgravine-regent of Hesse-Kassel and handed over a packet of correspondence that she passed on to her secretary. "I have been in France and Burgundy with Gerry Stone, whom I left in Jena for the winter semester. The packet includes a note for you from him."

"It is my pleasure," Amalie Elisabeth replied. "I have the greatest respect for your father. We have cooperated on several projects over the years. Also for the elder Mr. Stone." A round of protocol-induced pleasantries ensued until she thought of the time and got down to the point. "Do convey my respects to M. Cavriani when you next see him. Now, how may I assist you."

Marc resisted the temptation to twist the curl that was always falling down right in the middle of his forehead. He had been rigidly schooled by a tutor who believed it was bad manners for a gentleman to twitch, wiggle, purse his lips, rub his nose, puff out his cheeks, put his hands behind his back, or, well, pretty much anything, during a conversation with his elders and betters.

He explained about his almost-a-fiancée Susanna Allegretti and the circumstances which persuaded her to believe so firmly that she needed to see if she, as a Catholic, could live contentedly among Calvinists before she would marry him. "So I thought . . . Here is the letter from my father. If perhaps, My Lady, you could find her a position in your household for the next year or so, it would be the best possible choice. You will soon be out of deep mourning for the late landgrave; your attendants will be needing more in the way of court clothing, you have so many contacts among the highest and most influential ladies in the city."

The landgravine agreed that when the time came, she would make the appointment.

Marc took a deep breath. "I haven't mentioned the next idea to my father."

"Ye.e.e.e.s.s?" Amalie Elisabeth's older sons might be aged six and seven, but she had encountered a lot of young men over the years of her life.

"If you please . . . It's about the cat."

"Cat?"

"Richelieu's cat; the Siamese kitten that Rebecca Abrabanel took him from Grantville; the one all the newspapers have been talking about for a couple of months."

The langravine raised her eyebrows.

"Oh, the kitten!" Her ten-year-old daughter Charlotte jumped up from the floor, followed by six-year-old Philip. "*Everybody* knows about the kitten."

Amalie waved her hand. "Go to your lessons, now. The tutor is already in the schoolroom. Your sister and brother went the *first* time I told them." She turned back to Marc. "It's not that I don't know about the cat. It's inescapable. However, I do not understand how the cat is relevant to USE politics."

"Well, it's this way. Papa says that the cat is probably safe, but nobody in the USE seems to be convinced of that. Additionally, it's possible, given the current situation in France, that the cat is not safe."

The landgravine tilted her head to one side.

"I was thinking . . . Maybe if someone inconspicuous went into France to find the cat and rescue it, and it leaked that the person who funded the rescue expedition was the landgravine-regent of Hesse-Kassel . . . we can add in now, because her children are so tender-hearted and worried about it . . . it might well garner a lot of favorable publicity for you. Which would be favorable publicity for the Calvinist minority in the USE, incidentally. 'See, the landgravine went to the rescue of a Catholic cat. Surely in the interest of tolerance, others also can see beyond narrow sectarian limits.' That sort of thing. Or it might give you some leverage in the House of Lords, if some issue important to you came up."

He swallowed. "Of course, it would have to be kept under wraps until I actually find the cat. If I can find the cat."

CHAPTER 17

Grantville
early November 1636

After it occurred to Marc that he should familiarize himself with what a Siamese cat looked like, since he would be searching for one and the various etchings and engravings that accompanied the newspaper articles often bore a greater resemblance to mythical monsters, he headed to Grantville, kissed his sister Idelette's cheek, and requested pertinent data.

"Hazel Patton is the Siamese cat breeder," she said. "She's old. I can take you to see her."

Hazel might be over seventy, but she was lively. "You have no idea how much trouble it's been," she said. "As far as I know, there wasn't a single un-neutered purebred Siamese tom in this town. I've been breeding my mixed boy back with various white females that I've managed to beg and borrow, but it's unfortunately going to be a very narrow gene pool."

"Then where did Rebecca Abrabanel get the kitten she took to Cardinal Richelieu?" Idelette asked. "It was a kitten, and that was a year and a half after the Ring of Fire. Everyone says it was Siamese."

Hazel looked down at the animals rubbing around her ankles. "You know, that could have been one of Alberta O'Donnell's cats. Bertie didn't die until right at the end of 1633, but with both of her daughters passing away the year before and poor John long gone, nearly fifty years before the Ring of Fire happened, and being almost ninety herself–well, she wasn't in good shape there at the end. Probably, either Hank or Marsha took her cats–those are Maude's kids, you know. Poor Carrie never had any. Anyway, with Hank Jones so busy with the mines and backing up Mike Stearns in everything political, I don't think he'd have taken Bertie's cats home with him. But he probably knew about them and could have told Mike. Ask Marsha Jones. She's still working at the grocery store. Not that she's in good shape herself, what with Jeffie Garand dying in that epidemic over in the Rhineland last summer. Say what you will about Marsha, and a lot of folks do say that she's sort of feckless and aimless, she gets out of bed and does her job every day, and she loves her kids crazy much. Jeffie's death slammed her."

Idelette set up a meeting with Marsha Jones, at her house that evening, with her twelve-year-old daughter Miranda much involved. Miranda had been following the cat saga as reported by the newspapers with great anxiety.

"Yes, Ma had Pitty Pat and Pitty had three kittens that year. That was her last litter–she was getting old and died before Ma did. Pitty might have been purebred, but she wasn't pedigreed or anything. Pretty, though, and the kittens she had usually looked more like her than like ordinary cats. Or some of them looked sort of odd, like that orange tabby of Gladys Johnson's that has a Siamese nose, ears, and tail. Poor Gladys; she passed away last year, too, but not before her time. Liney Linder, that's her daughter, has the cat now. You might have heard of Liney's granddaughter Marla. She's gotten to be a famous singer. Anyway, there were three kittens in that litter and I gave my brother Hank the cutest one when he said that Mike Stearns' wife needed it for something important."

"Marsha, what did you do with the other kittens?" Hazel asked.

"Well, Miranda here kept one of them. A girl; I took her to the vet and had her fixed. One cat is enough in any house, if you ask me. I wasn't going to be trying to find homes for kittens the rest of my life the way Ma did. Let me think. Randi, honey, what did we do with Pitty's third kitten?"

"I gave him to Kara Washaw. I guess they took him to Magdeburg when they moved. Mrs. Washaw got it fixed, too. She said that no way was she going to live with the smell of tomcat pee in her house."

"Damn," Hazel exclaimed. " 'Had I but known,' like the heroines in all those old romance books were always saying. I sure could have used those kittens for breeding if I'd known you were getting rid of them."

After emphasizing the need for utmost secrecy ("I won't say a *single word*," Miranda promised) and being furnished with a couple magazine pictures of more or less typical Siamese cats and a precious polaroid photo of the late Bertie O'Donnell with a young Pitty Pat (Marc swore upon his honor to bring it back unharmed) for identification purposes, Marc kissed his sister on her other cheek and set off for Paris.

Paris
mid-November 1636

With everything that was going on in Poland and Austria, Soubise was fairly sure that France's problems were not currently high on Gustavus' list of concerns. Nor would France be at the top of the concerns of the emperor's prime minister. Nor those of his generals. Nor even those of his spies. Which was why Gaston was having so close to a free hand. True, the Netherlands, Lorraine, and Burgundy had their eyes fixed on what France's king was doing, but that was scarcely equivalent to having the Lion of the North looking directly over a man's shoulder. Things would probably change once Gustavus got a handle on things in the east. If he got a handle on things in the East. If the Ottomans would let him get a handle on things in the east.

Meanwhile, Burgundy equaled not only Bernhard but Rohan, who had let it be known that he was displeased by the—in his view excessive—overtures that Soubise and Anne had been making to King Gaston.

Soubise raised one eyebrow at his sister.

"We need to distract him," she said.

"How?"

"I have been casting around. Do you remember Robert Traill?"

"That Scotsman who tutored you in English?"

"Yes. His brother is now right here, in Paris, bear-leader for a young nobleman. Given Henri's fixation on finding a suitable Protestant match for his heiress and considering that the young man is Presbyterian . . . Oh, the young man is not a viable choice, really. He's from a miserably *nouveau* origin. However, if I arrange things so that he's right there under Henri's nose, demanding a maximum amount of attention . . ."

Soubise nodded. "It could buy us some time and space for negotiations with Gaston, both of which we need."

France
November 1636

Marc had plenty of time to think about the possibilities as he made his way across France. Here he was, four or five months after the presumed death of Richelieu, or at least since the cardinal's disappearance if one put any stock in the unlikeliest of the flying rumors. He didn't have the vaguest idea where to look for the cat. Was the cat in Paris, or in a suburb, or on an estate somewhere out in the country? Or, in the worst case, dead? Would one of the cardinal's servants have adopted the cat? Could the cat have been removed to the cardinal's country estate by one of his relatives? Or was the cat, even if it wasn't probable, in some kind of dire danger and needing to be rescued?

While his boring horse plodded along the road, he started his mental timeline with the summer. Richelieu had been in residence at the *Palais-Cardinal* last spring.

Presumably, so had the cat.

After the imbroglio in May, *Père* Joseph, who was rumored to have been named as cardinal *in pectore* by the pope, had taken charge of the residence.

Presumably, the cat had still been there unless someone had taken him away.

It was now fairly reliably known that in August, Marie de' Medici, King Gaston's mother, had thrown *Père*-Joseph-who-was-maybe-also-Cardinal-Leclerc-du-Tremblay in prison and moved into the *Palais* herself.

Presumably, the cat had not been sent to the prison with the cardinal.

It was said that the queen mother was not particularly fond of cats. Because of that and given her conflicts with Richelieu . . .

Presumably, it was unlikely that she had kept his cat.

Sometime after those events, again according to the rumor mill, she and Gaston had quarreled bitterly . . . but that kind of thinking led into an endless loop.

Not a presumption. There were no specific rumors that anyone else had adopted or removed the cat. So—start at the *Palais-Cardinal* which the queen mother had renamed as the *Palais-Royal*.

*   *   *

Sandrart's art tour went well until the country house at which he encountered the duchess and Candale. Looking down from the musicians' gallery, he saw them, right there in the main salon, talking to Madame de Boileau. It had to be them. Not news that they had visited this château a few days previously. Not someone remarking that they were expected to arrive in a couple more days' time. No, they were here. It was impossible to mistake the head full of corkscrew ringlets that was such a mark of the duchesse de Rohan's appearance. His fingers itched for a paintbrush. *Could the great Albrecht Dürer himself have done justice to that hair?*

171

He started to back away slowly from the railing of gallery, reaching behind him to part the curtain that closed it off from the servants' passageway. As he moved to step through, his heel caught the hem. In the high-ceilinged room, the sound echoed. He thought, off-topic, that he acoustics must be terrible; the instrumentalists who attempted to perform from the gallery would receive his commiseration. It must be like trying to paint with fireworks flashing all over the studio.

Madame de Boileau and her guests looked up. Of course. With a mischievous smile, Candale beckoned him to come down. Sandrart complied at a deliberate pace, allowing himself some time to think. The only ameliorating aspect of the situation was that Candale's amusement appeared to be genuine.

After that harried encounter, he reported to Soubise that the objects of his scrutiny were well aware that he was an agent who had been sent to watch them. Not to mention that the duchess had made advances to him.

"She would not have been genuinely trying to seduce you," Soubise assured him with a shrug. "She must have been teasing that evening because they caught you in the middle of your supposedly discreet observation of their activities. My sister-in-law, as appalling as her morals may be, selects her lovers only from the highest levels of the French aristocracy."

"As to that," Sandrart replied, "she and Candale are sharing a chamber, making no effort to disguise it."

Soubise shrugged again.

Laubach, Solms-Laubach
November 1636

Someone had poisoned the grand hetman of Lithuania this month.

What had she accomplished? Käthe crossed her arms over her chest. "Nothing anywhere near that dramatic," she could assure anyone who might ask.

She picked up the newspaper again and turned the page to the fine arts section. Opera, ballet, mural competitions. Everything was happening in Magdeburg, it seemed. Amalie Elisabeth, because of her political obligations, had not observed the obligatory year of mourning strictly in any case. Now she was out of mourning. She could take advantage of any of those.

I wish I was in Magdeburg, she thought. *Magdeburg, where they have, or so I have read, efficient heating systems. I wish I wasn't in this freezing cold, far from modern, horseshoe-shaped, wretched, fortified castle where the 'new' wing is a hundred years old and the drafts coming from under the doors dance with the drafts that rattle the windows.*

She shivered and ordered a footman to check whether or not there was plenty of firewood on hand for the hearths in the nursery and, if not, to have someone haul more upstairs. Turning to her desk, she started a letter to her oldest sister, the unmarried Charlotte Louise.

I was delighted to receive your letter; it seemed as if it had been a long time since I heard from you. It would be so wonderful if we could arrange a visit, but with winter coming on I know it would be too difficult. Our brothers hardly ever write me; I haven't heard from any of them for three months. Philipp Moritz has his own household and concerns now. The other two lack that excuse, but of course they are men and have more important things to do than write to their sister.

Especially, she thought, *they are too busy to write to a sister who is marooned out on the fringes of the political world, with no political connections to bring them advancement in their careers. One who did not manage to poison the hetman of Lithuania this month.*

173

Paris
November 1636

On a day blessed with bright sunshine and a temperature not too far below freezing, Marc sat on a low stone wall bordering the gardens (unfinished) at the rear of the now-*Palais-Royal* (also unfinished) and thought about the nature of the universe, or at least the immediately adjacent small part of it. The building was still, to a considerable extent, a construction site. The front facade, the major ceremonial rooms behind it, and the rooms Richelieu had used as his personal residence were complete.

Back here, though, it was a work in progress: both skilled artisans and common laborers all over the place, carts and wagons of supplies constantly coming in and going out, the gardens-to-be blocked out but unfinished, with gardeners and other workmen with tools and small wheelbarrows there, too. All of which meant that it was not going to be much of a challenge to infiltrate the place. He continued to sit on the wall, goggling his eyes like a tourist, swinging his feet and absently-minded chewing on a baguette he bought from a street vendor.

The boy who shortly thereafter, baguette in hand, sat down next to him was probably coming to the end of his apprenticeship—maybe even a very young journeyman.

After all the *bonjour* bits, it came down to, "I'm Denis Lemercier."

"You have the luck to be working on this building?"

"Ah, *oui*. It's a great deal. I'm a stonemason aiming to become an architect in the long run. I'm one of those Lemerciers, which is how I got this chance. It's Jacques who is the architect for the whole thing. It's been in process since I was a kid, a big coup for our whole family, which is huge. Jacques is a some-kind-of-a cousin to my father. Close enough that we can call him kin, but not close enough that we visit one another's families unless it's something big, like a funeral."

"Do you have a lot of problems with vermin? I know that construction sites always attract them, and since there are so many food carts . . ."

"And the gardens!" Lemercier rolled his eyes to the sky. "But at least, the place has cats, too." He waved cheerfully as he went back to work.

Marc watched lazily for a while longer and then wandered idly off, to cast touristy glances at some other of Paris' famous attractions. In his room that evening, he pulled off his boots and sat down to once more take a careful look at the pictures and photo he had brought along from Grantville.

In only a couple of hours, at mid-day, watching the gardens behind the *Palais-Royal*, he had seen at least a half-dozen cats that looked suspiciously Siamese-ish. He pulled a piece of paper and pencil out of one of his saddle bags, propped his feet up on the table, and began to calculate. Given that the kitten was a male . . . given that such a kitten might well be mature and capable of procreation within six months of its arrival . . . given that it was likely that to some extent Richelieu had deliberately bred it . . . given that there was no indication that the cat had been regularly confined and prevented from promiscuous unions with random females . . . then in the course of three years, during which its descendants would themselves have produced several probably-inbred generations, whether by the cardinal's deliberate choice or by random mating . . . it might be quite possible that there weren't just a half-dozen suspiciously Siamese-ish cats around the *Palais-Royal*. There could be hundreds. Even thousands.

Calvinist doctrine, unlike Catholic, maintained that the age of direct divine intervention was over. It wasn't going to be a problem to get a cat, but he could use Susanna's approach to prayer right now. Unless someone had really taken special charge of the Grantville-born feline, it would be a modern miracle if he got the right cat.

The next day he went back to the gardens. With fish. When a half-grown kitten crept near enough to him, he dropped a bit of it. The kitten was a perfectly ordinary tabby in its coloration, but a person had to start somewhere.

Denis plopped down next to him on the wall. "You're crazy to feed them. You'll never get rid of them, and after you finish your business here and go back to where you came from, they'll be hassling other people for food for days and days before they give up."

Marc repeated the process for several days, by which time he had collected quite a crowd of adoring feline fans, a few of which showed points. He also felt confident enough that he showed one of the magazine photos to Denis.

"Yeah, some of them do sort of look like that. I've seen the USE papers, too. People bring them into France, even if the king *has* made a proclamation against it." He pointed at one of the half-grown kittens with the hand that was not holding his baguette up in the air, out of the way of over-interested feline observers. "Over in the right wing, on the other side, there are more cats like that. Most of them with white fur, a little dirty-looking, sort of gray-blue dirt, like sculptor's clay. Mostly dark gray on the noses and paws, but not all." He waved his other hand at a sleek mature tom. "Like him. Now, that is a cat of a different color. Like chocolate."

Marc was not going to be able to leave on the horse he came in on. It wasn't trained to harness and he was going to need . . . cages for cats. Something to feed cats. If he didn't want to be driving an intolerable cart across France, something to use for kitty litter. If the cats were not to freeze to death, as no inn would possibly agree to take them, he would need a covered cart.

He confided these needs to Denis, giving his intentions as mercenary: inspired by the newspaper furor, which apparently meant that the up-timers considered these cats valuable and everyone knew that up-timers were all rich, he was here to catch as many as possible of the prettiest ferals and take them to the fabled Grantville to sell.

Denis came on board. He was a journeyman, after all. It would certainly broaden his horizons if he went and studied the architecture and building techniques of the town from the future. Which he could fund, at least in part, he stated with enthusiasm, by helping in the cat project and sharing in its anticipated proceeds.

On balance, Marc thought, Denis' help would be worth it. Plus, if he took enough cats—maybe, with two of them to drive, got a freight wagon instead of a cart—they could sell the extras to the benefit of Denis' budget.

Everything went pretty smoothly until they got overconfident. In the evening dusk, a few days later, one of Marie de' Medici's servants spotted them in the back garden holding up a polaroid photo to compare it to a hissing, spitting, cat that they had trapped under a loosely woven basket. They made a hurried emergency departure from the *Palais* grounds, managing, because of considerable recent practice in the maneuver, to tip the basket up, fling the lid on, and take the cat as they went.

As they ran off toward the wagon yard where they had the rest of their loot stockpiled, a shrewd tom with a dark nose and tail, dark paws, and light body, who had evaded being seen each time the evil beings who were trapping his clowder appeared at the *Palais*, watched them go from his sanctuary under a pile of lumber. A traumatic encounter earlier in the fall, in the form of several hostile servants chasing him away from his favorite perch in his favorite room in the *Palais*, waving brooms and dusters, one of them even hitting him in the side, had thoroughly spooked him about unfamiliar humans.

Virginia DeMarce

CHAPTER 18

Besançon
November 1636

At the time Marguerite arrived, Rohan's quarters had been too cramped for his suddenly-increased household, given that they consisted of two rooms in the former *Hôtel Jouffroy*, which over time had become the Inn of the Green Lion, one of which had provided sleeping quarters for him and his long-time confidential secretary, Benjamin Priolo, a clergyman's son from Saint-Jean-d'Angély, one of the French cities where the Rohans held governorships. The other had served as parlor, library, office, and general all-purpose room. He used to eat out. He had been fond of his view, though, which included the old Roman bridge across the river that gave access to the city proper.

Two rooms would not do once he had a daughter in residence, for a daughter involved a chaperone, a couple of ladies in waiting, a couple of maids at a minimum, a kitchen, a cook . . . His mind had boggled, so he had called a real estate agent and they were now occupying half of the *Hôtel de Buyer* in the main part of the town, at an utterly exorbitant rent. But it was, at least, a modern house, built during the previous century in the Italian style, far less drafty than the older medieval ones. Moreover, he had a private study to which he could retreat when the level of female chatter became unendurable. He left Priolo in his old rooms in the Green Lion and used those as his office when he was on the grand duke's business. Early morning walks were beneficial to an aging man's health, after all, and he found the thought that the up-time encyclopedias said that he would be dead in two more years rather discouraging, even if Bernhard did keep repeating that he had, after all, been killed in a battle that there would be no need to fight in this version of God's creation.

Security, he thought. The followers of Ducos would not, perhaps, be indifferent to the chance to attack him, and by extension attack him through his household members. He added six footmen to the household staff, two to be on duty at all times. As Bernhard did not require him to make a stylish appearance in court society, he did not hire matched sets of well-built young men, but rather unmatched sets of recently retired non-coms. He hoped that what they lacked in elegance, they would compensate for in vigilance.

Marguerite's arrival was not the only cause for the restructuring of his household, though. "I," he had announced one day at dinner, "have decided to write a treatise on up-time assumptions and attitudes." In the comparative peace of his new study/library, he had been thinking about this for several weeks. Being far too busy a man to go visit Grantville and study his subjects *in situ*, he asked the grand duke for some of the up-timers already in Besançon to supplement his reading.

Using Marguerite's arrival as a rationale (and at the mischief-making suggestion of Gerry Stone by way of Ruvigny), the grand duke had generously complied by transferring those up-timers he had by now determined were least useful for his purposes—namely Madame Calagna and a couple of youthful females, the nearly grown daughters of Mesdames Calagna and Dunn—keeping the specialists in medicine and the mechanical arts for himself.

Carey Calagna had never anticipated that when the *duc de* Rohan's marriageable daughter made it out of France and out of the grasp of the new King Gaston's matrimonial machinations, that she would be transferred to the status of combination English and up-time government tutor and senior chaperone for said daughter and also consultant to the duke. It was temporary, Bernhard promised, until

Rohan's sister arrived to serve as the female head of his no-longer-bachelor household.

Bernhard, born a duke of Saxe-Weimar and now by conquest and self-aggrandizement the Grand Duke of the Free County of Burgundy, had hired her to explain to his bureaucrats how up-time government worked. She wasn't entirely sure that the grand duke's representatives understood precisely where her unfinished college major in business administration and prior employment as Grantville's probate court clerk after the Ring of Fire had placed her in the overall hierarchy of "up-time experts" when they went through on their recruiting trip, but she and Kamala had packed up and moved to Burgundy. Kamala had been more successful with her medical and public health duties than Carey with her instructional ones. Only a few of the grand duke's staff had either the time or inclination to listen to her.

By a happy chance, those least useful to the grand duke would be the most useful to Rohan. As Marguerite had explained to Carey, by appointing to his daughter's household up-timers who were, if not Calvinist, at least not Catholic like Susanna Allegretti, the duke could, for the time being, manage to equally offend all the families of French Huguenot nobility who thought that such appointments should go to their wives and daughters, but not offend any of them particularly, and thus not exacerbate rivalries among his potential supporters should *something happen*. Most of the French Huguenot community would not care that the up-timers now resident in the ducal household, unlike Priolo, could help elucidate the deeper meaning contained in the collected works of Dr. Seuss.

Something, Carey suspected, was the revocation of the ducal exile. She personally thought, just based on reading the newspapers, that *something might happen* when hell froze over, but so far no one had asked her opinion on that matter.

The two Dr. Seuss books that Gerry Stone had asked Ron to send for Marguerite had arrived. She read about the adventures of Horton the Elephant, with assistance from her new up-time ladies-in-waiting, Shae Horton and Dominique Bell, with mild interest. *Yertle the Turtle* now reposed in the study of Henri *duc de* Rohan, who read and re-read it with utter fascination and deep concentration. Then he confiscated the other two books for his own use and hired a researcher in the SoTF State Library to find out more about Seuss and his works. The researcher ate well for several weeks; the expanded Rohan household somewhat less so. The money had to come from somewhere.

". . . so since he also holds the rank of *prince étranger* because of his descent from the ruling house of Brittany before it was incorporated into the territories of the French crown, Papa is not only entitled to be formally addressed as "Your Highness" rather than "Your Grace" although the up-timers in general do not appear to have learned this, but he also has the right to wear a hat in the presence of the king at receptions for newly appointed ambassadors from other countries. Thus, he is of precisely equal rank to the older brother of General Turenne. Turenne is a cadet of the house of La Tour d'Auvergne. Turenne's brother is still in fact as well as in law the independent ruler of Sedan, although not for long, if that usurper *Monsieur* Gaston has his way. Papa also has a hereditary claim to Bouillon in the Spanish Netherlands. I believe that Papa, when he was young, truly wished to carve out an independent principality such as Sedan for himself, as the grand duke has done here in Burgundy. For a while, before King Louis was born, Papa was the nearest heir to Navarre. It would have been nice for the house of Rohan to acquire Navarre." Marguerite ended her lengthy disquisition on the finer points of court protocol as they applied to the *ducs de* Rohan in a rush of words followed by a regretful sigh.

Carey's mind wandered. She had not expected to learn as much as she taught, if not more than she taught. Or, since she had vaguely expected that she would learn a lot of new stuff, she hadn't expected it to include a practical survival guide for the courtiers who surrounded the kings of France. It was just weird that her daughter Dominique, only five or so years younger than the perpetually chattering Marguerite, *duchesse de* Rohan, was now a lady-in-waiting for said *duchesse*, along with Kamala's daughter Shae Horton. That was temporary, also, until Marguerite's aunt could sift through the competing claims and desires of various prominent Huguenot families.

Carey winced, forcing herself not to give a frazzled pull at her straight brown Dutch boy bob. She and Kamala Dunn cut one another's hair these days, and the kids' hair too, with a little home barber kit that she wouldn't sell for a fortune. Well, maybe, if they didn't get electricity in Besançon in the next few years and she was faced with paying college tuition, she would sell the clippers out of it for a fortune . . . though the kit as a whole in its original box would be worth much more to a collector than an individual piece and maybe she could wear a braid . . .

When Carey resurfaced from her internal monologue, Marguerite had finished with court protocol, but she was still talking, having moved on to the ever-fascinating (at least to a lot of people, both up-time and down-time, but not to her current audience) discipline of genealogy. "Our senior line of Rohan descends from René I de Rohan, who died in 1552 and held the titles of *vicomte de* Rohan, *prince de* Léon, *comte de* Porhoët, *seigneur de* Beauvoir and de La Garnache. In his day, the feudal holdings in Brittany were still important. Even Papa was born at Blain."

The rattle of French continued non-stop until Marguerite yawned. "I have to go to bed. The idea that I should become Rohan for myself frightened Papa so much that now he expects that I will come to him for two hours every morning, right after he rises and before breakfast, to receive lessons on being Rohan. Which is not much like it seemed to be when I lived in Paris with *Maman*. Since Papa rises three hours before dawn, I suppose I can only be grateful that there is hardly any social life in Besançon."

It was temporary. Both Grand Duke Bernhard and the duc de Rohan had assured Carey of that, and she hung onto the word as to a lifeline in a tempest. Toward the end of November, Rohan's spinster sister, Marguerite's *Tante* Anne, would arrive to become the female head of her brother's expanded, no-longer-bachelor, household.

Well, errr. She was supposed to arrive. What actually arrived was a letter. It appeared, according to Marguerite's report, that Uncle Soubise also requested Mademoiselle Anne's services, and she opted to stay inside the borders of France and help him hold the Rohan banner high.

"In fact," Marguerite told Dominique and Shae, "*Tante* Anne rather ranted about Papa's imprudence in having taken me to Burgundy, because while my personal safety is one consideration, she says that if the family is to maintain its standing and influence at the court, its members have to *be* at the court, whichever court it may be, and the family needs to decide which direction they will throw their support in the matter of Gaston's troubles. That's pretty much what *Maman* said, too, the last time she wrote."

That might be the only subject upon which the two sisters-in-law agreed.

"Then *Tante* Anne asked a dozen questions. Has Papa been in contact with the king in the Low Countries? Does he know where Anne of Austria and her son are? Has he heard what Mazarin was currently up to and . . . ? Well, also," Marguerite said, "she wrote something unflattering about *Maman* and Candale and whatever they are up to. Papa did not read that part to me, but I will find out, I assure you. Then she finished by saying that Papa should rely on his brother and sister and it was much more important for them both to be in Paris than for her to come here."

Rohan said to Carey that his sister was legendarily stubborn–this referencing her willingness to accept imprisonment after the defeat of the Huguenots at La Rochelle rather than be included in the amnesty and her several years of captivity, along with their equally stubborn mother, at the *Château de Niort* in the aftermath. Under the circumstances, he requested that Carey and her daughter, along with Shae Horton, remain in his household for longer than the original appointment.

Carey agreed. It had dawned on her that refusing the "requests" of dukes, unless one had an extraordinarily good reason indeed, simply was not done. In theory, *demander* was supposed to translate into English as "ask," but she was developing doubts that it was as much of a "false friend" word as it was reputed to be by the grammar textbooks. Certainly not when one was living this far from Grantville and being paid by a down-timer. Requests and demands tended to skip down Shakespeare's primrose path arm in arm with one another.

Kamala agreed to keep Ashlyn, who was almost the same age as Kamala's Shaun, along with little Joe, who had been born after the Ring of Fire, in what had been (and, she hoped, would again be) their joint apartment as long as Carey kept paying her half of the rent and three-fourths of the wages of their full-time babysitter.

"I think you would have liked *Tante* Anne if she had come," Marguerite said. "Just like *Grand-mère* Rohan was, she is highly educated and knows several languages, including Latin, of course. Less Greek, but even while she was in prison after La Rochelle, she found some wandering Scotsman to tutor her and used the time to learn English. She is still strong and healthy, even though during the last weeks of the siege of La Rochelle the inhabitants were reduced to living on four ounces of bread per day, or less, or worse, and many people there got sick and died. She is talented and brave, a patroness of Mademoiselle Schurman in Utrecht. She writes poetry, too, although in my estimation it far from being the best poetry in the world. In fact, it is not very good. But some of it is interesting, especially the poems she did for her sister, *Tante* Henriette, who died about a dozen years ago, back when she was in love with the duchess of Mantua-Nevers."

"With the duke?" Carey asked cautiously, still a bit uncertain of rapidly spoken French.

"Oh, no. With the duchess," Marguerite answered with good cheer. "It is called Sapphic love. *Tante* Henriette was quite heartbroken when the duchess died."

"I, ah, see."

"When we go back to Paris, because we surely will, because *Tante* Anne is right that I cannot stay in exile permanently if Rohan is to maintain its position in France, I will take you and Shae and Dominique. Then you can come with me to the salons, because I like *femmes savantes* much better than *Maman* does, and meet many interesting intellectual ladies."

185

That evening, Carey commented to Kamala Dunn that she was less than enthralled by any such prospect. "I signed up for Burgundy," she said, "not Paris."

"Ask Marcie Abruzzo and Matt Trelli," was Kamala's answer. "I think they've learned that when you work for Grand Duke Bernhard and Archduchess Claudia, you go where you're sent. It's along the same lines as the up-time proverb that if the army wanted you to have a wife, it would have issued you one. It's probably pretty much the same when you're working for Rohan. They say 'jump' and your only question is 'which way?' There's really no distinction between being a soldier and being a civilian employee as far as the seventeenth century is concerned."

Paris
November 1636

"Of course, they know that I have someone watching them," Soubise said. "It was pretty clever of them to figure out so quickly that it was Sandrart and let him know it. Just as we know that Bernhard and Henri have someone watching us. They didn't lend us Colonel Raudegen's assistance simply out of the goodness of their hearts. There are probably others."

"Then find out who they are," Mademoiselle Anne replied.

Soubise propped up his other foot. His sister was not only stubborn. She was impatient.

CHAPTER 19

Besançon
December 1636

"Henri is married!" Marguerite looked at her father with shock. "Married to a daughter of the king of Denmark! I'm surprised, but that's just . . ."

Shae Horton supplied the necessary word. "Awesome!"

"I can't believe it," Marguerite repeated.

"Surely you knew that he would marry someday," Rohan answered.

"Yes. But he kept saying that he needed a girl with the right dowry, but he didn't have anything to offer her. So I supposed that it wouldn't happen for a long time."

"He had something to offer Christian. A face-saving escape from a difficult political dilemma. The dowry was included." Rohan handed the newspaper from Amsterdam across the table.

Dominique Bell let out a surprised whistle. "I should say so. I wonder who leaked the amount."

"Honestly, Marguerite, I'm surprised you didn't have a crush on Ruvigny yourself," Dominique said later that morning.

"Crush?"

"Oh, umm. That you didn't think you were in love with him. Since, you know, he was really the only young guy you actually knew and all that sort of thing."

"Oh, then, I did have a crush, for years and years. He had been wounded when he came to Venice. I was 12 years old. I thought it was romantic. I thought about him with hearts and flowers in my head, dreamed about him as my hero, and wrote, 'Mme. de Ruvigny' in the margins of my *cahiers* when I was studying languages."

"What made you stop? Or have you stopped?"

"Yes, I stopped."

"Did you, umm, find out that there was something wrong about him—something that made him unsuitable to be a hero?" Shae asked.

Marguerite shook her head. "He's brave. He has good sense and honor; he is upright and prudent. I stopped dreaming that dream the day I became old enough to realize that even if by some improbable constellation of the stars, my father gave permission for me to marry him and the royal court concurred, I would never be a 'Mme. de Ruvigny.' Anyone who married me would have to become Rohan. I'm pretty sure that he wanted a wife who could be, will be, 'Mme. de Ruvigny' for him. In many ways, he is conservative." She smiled slyly. "Not that a Danish king's daughter is likely to become a domestic little Mme. de Ruvigny, any more than I was. Does somebody else here have a crush on someone, perhaps?"

"Not me!" Dominique disclaimed in a hurry, pointing a finger at Shae. "Her!"

"I don't mean do you have one on Ruvigny. On someone else?" Marguerite asked. "Bismarck, maybe?"

"Oh, no, no," Dominique said. "I want to be a doctor. Since I'm too old for school now, I follow Kamala Dunn around when I'm not being your lady-in-waiting and learn as much as I can from her, and the Padua doctors when they will let me. But to become a real physician, I'll have to go back to Grantville, to work some of the time at the Leahy Medical Center while I do the course at the University of Jena, and I'm not sure that I'd have a warm welcome there. Or even a neutral one."

"It sounds to me," Marguerite proclaimed, "as if Grantville is a very narrow-minded, *petit bourgeois*, kind of town." She drew a deep breath and looked at Shae. "Who do you have a crush on? Is it a down-timer?"

"None of your business, really. But why?"

"Because, if any man is going to make a successful career, he needs a wife with a dowry, and I can hear your mother now. 'A dowry? They expect me to bribe some guy to marry my daughter? If he doesn't value her for herself, he can simply go to hell!' "

Shae winced. "Yeah, I can hear her now, too." She rested her chin on the heel of her hand, her face gloomy. "I can see that. To tell the truth, though, even if Mom didn't freak out at the word 'dowry,' she'd never be able to come up with one. A lot of people think that all up-timers are rich, but we aren't. The grand duke pays her a really good salary, but . . ." She started to count on her fingers. "There's housing, food, saving for our education. All that adds up. With Dad executed for treason, there's no way I'll ever qualify for a scholarship in Grantville, any more than Dominique will."

Shae turned around, pointing a finger. "You're nearly eighteen now and unless Carey can come up with the money to send you to Magdeburg, you're in a bind."

Dominique nodded.

Shae lifted another finger. "My brother Shaun will be ready for high school in a few years—then maybe some university, if he starts taking his school work more seriously. It'll have to be some university other than Jena, which is too tightly tied to Grantville now . . ."

"Stop!" Marguerite waved a hand in front of Shae's face. "Tell me, why are the Grantvillers so upset about Suhl and your dad? Or Dominique's father and that money he embezzled? There probably isn't a noble family in France that doesn't have at least one member who has been beheaded for treason, or imprisoned for malfeasance, at one time or another. That's a normal part of participating in politics. Some other member of the lineage will come into the king's favor at the next turn of events. So explain!"

Shae couldn't even think where to start.

Dominique managed a save. "The grand duke hired my mom to explain American government to his staff," she said. "I think you ought to ask her, since the duke works for the grand duke, and you're the duke's daughter, and she's temporarily your chaperone. Maybe you should ask her about Bill and Monica and impeachment, too, since we're even younger than Gerry Stone and remember even less about it than he did."

Marguerite nodded solemnly. "Yes, I should make a special appointment with Carey, just for this. I honestly do not understand this 'impeachment' at all. Especially not for having sex. It's not as if it was your president who was wearing the blue dress and the beret. People take lovers all the time and she, this *Monique*, wasn't even from an important family of the opposition party."

Dominique grinned. "I'll put it on your calendar. And I want to listen in, to see how Mom gets through this one."

"Me too," Shae said.

Carey heaved a deep sigh. Explaining Monica Lewinsky to a seventeenth-century French noblewoman, aged nineteen, was easy compared to explaining Dr. Seuss to a seventeenth century French nobleman, aged fifty-nine. He had titled his book-in-the-making *Les Futuriens*, with a subtitle of *A treatise on these people from the future (ces gens du futur) and how their ideas and philosophy of life may be expected to influence our times.*

CHAPTER 20

Besançon
December 1636

R ohan waved a letter. "It looks as if this household is about to
have uninvited guests."
        "Can they just show up and move in?" Carey asked.
"Without an invitation."
        "The letter is from my sister Anne in Paris. It appears that she has
invited them on my behalf. Her former English tutor, a man named
Robert Traill, is now a most formidable Scots Presbyterian clergyman, a
grim Geneva minister. At the time, he had already graduated from St.
Andrews and was in France to study at our academy in Saumur. Her
tutor's brother is also employed as a tutor and is currently shepherding a
young Ulster nobleman around Europe on his grand tour. It's not his
first enterprise, since he's already been around the continent a couple of
times, once with a son of Lord Brook and again with a son of Lord
Carlisle. This boy is a couple of years older than he should be for such an
experience: the original intent was that he should come in 1633, but he is
an only son and his father delayed his departure because of the troubles
with the League of Ostend. They're basically on their way home now, but
the tutor wants to get his charge out of France, so they will detour in our
direction and finish their trip through the western USE."
        He glanced at the letter again, threw it down, and screamed "*Non!*"

Carey said nothing.

"The father, the Scotsman, is one of those who defrauded Con MacNiall O'Neill of most of his lands thirty years ago. This is not an accident. The tutor and this . . ." he looked at the letter again, ". . . this Hamilton have been lurking in Paris, waiting until the conclave was over and Owen Roe O'Neill and his associates were well out of Besançon. Anne, also, never does anything without some motive, some reason. I need to know more about these people."

He picked up his newest toy. He had read about 'ringing for' a servant or secretary, but one of the up-time mechanical artists had told him that the cost of installing such a system in what was, after all, a rented house would be more expensive than it was worth. As he was frowning, his daughter's young dressmaker had asked, "Why don't you get a cow bell?" So he had. No one could hear it from more than a room away. Then Ron Stone had sent, from Grantville, a genuine long-handled nineteenth century brass school bell. The din that arose when he shook it brought a footman into the room at a rapid trot.

Rohan tossed the letter to him, though he was still talking to Carey. "My sister says they are coming so that this young Hamilton can obtain an understanding of what Grand Duke Bernhard is organizing here in Burgundy and a comprehension of the issues in regard to Lorraine. I don't believe it for a minute." He turned to the servant. "Take this to Priolo at the Green Lion and tell him to find out what is going on, as fast as you can. What is on their minds? What is on my sister Anne's mind?"

The man backed out, holding the letter as if it might catch on fire at any moment.

＊　＊　＊

"So," Rohan said, "these *juvenalia*, Madame Calagna. What do you think of them?"

Carey raised her eyebrows. "No Latin here, Your Grace. No Latin at all. Well, maybe a few words, but they all have to do with probate law."

"Ah. Well, my Latin is also minimal. I have Priolo check my manuscripts over before I send them to be published–sometimes he even takes the ideas I talk about and puts them into writing for me. One thing that Bernhard and I have in common is that we are woefully undereducated by the standards set by the rest of our families. I never attended a *collège* any more than he completed a university degree. "*Juvenalia*–books designed for young children learning to read. I have concluded that they can be useful for understanding the up-time cultural *milieu* and the up-timers' *mentalité*. Or, sometimes, *juvenalia* may be an author's early works, written when he himself was a youth."

"English words do that too," she said. "Jump around and change their meanings on a person."

* * *

Grand Duke Bernhard announced a public dedication ceremony for the new central heating and intercom systems in the garrison's barracks and mess hall. Carey thought that it could have been postponed until . . . um . . . somewhat better weather. Everyone invited, at least everyone who accepted, which for a grand ducal invitation was almost everyone invited, was arriving by climbing up to the Citadelle on foot. Grand Duke Bernhard refused to allow his horses to be taken out unnecessarily in this *minor storm*, which certainly said something about how the ghastly stuff falling from the sky today related to the rest of the winter yet to come. So as the grand duke was walking, they were all walking. Once they got to the top, it was like being on a windswept mesa. In the Arctic Circle. The only thing missing was a hungry polar bear.

The speeches didn't keep them long. Within two hours, everything, including the remarkably terse and concise remarks by a few town officials (the grand duke tried to be nice to the city fathers, given that he had stolen their status as an imperial city right out from under them) and the refreshments, was over. The grand duke had said that it had *better* be over on time, because he didn't want anyone falling and putting himself out of commission by breaking a limb on the way back down to the town and the *Quartier Battant*. Carey drew a relieved breath when she spotted the outline of the Church of St. John the Baptist ahead. It was getting dark fast, but once they reached the church, the worst of the downward slope would be behind them and the path would turn into a street—a narrow street, but at least paved.

"Watch yourselves," the footman in front called as they walked around the little bend where the path skirted the steps into the church. "As soon as you get to the paving, this sleet has frozen hard and you'll be trying to walk on ice." Then he called again, "Wait a minute, everybody. Stop now." Past the church, toward the archbishop's residence, there was a small cart overturned, blocking the center of the street, with two donkeys standing on the right side, tethered to one of the cart wheels, and no driver in sight.

They flailed and slipped, trying to stop. Shae fell, her arms extended. A man came running out of the archbishop's winter-dead gardens, slipped when his feet hit the pavers, and tripped over her arms. The footman fell on top of the man who had fallen on Shae. A second man, holding something that glinted in the bit of light coming from the partially open doors of St. John's, followed the first. Dominique, still standing on the rougher path above the paving stones, yelled, "Ride 'em, cowboy!" swung her tote bag by its long handle, and let it fly at the second man. He dodged back a little, slipped, and fell.

The footman at the rear of the party managed to stay on his feet long enough to come forward six feet and deliberately sit on the second attacker.

Carey shook her head. "What's going on?"

Marguerite blinked. "I don't have the slightest idea."

The watch apprehended the two men. The only injury was to Shae's arm, badly broken in three places, but the attackers hadn't done that. It happened when she fell.

"But why?" Marguerite asked the next morning. It was closer to noon, actually.

"Grand Duke Bernhard's people are questioning them," Rohan answered. "It appears that they are supporters of Ducos, the man who led the assassination attempt on Urban VIII–the one in Rome that the Stone boys and their associates averted. They do not appear to have had any contact with Ducos himself for nearly eighteen months so can't provide us with any good intelligence as to where he may be. So far, it is not clear whether the attack was aimed at any specific one among you, or at all of you, or had any determinable purpose at all. They certainly did not take into account that there isn't a single one of you who has so much as seen a pope."

"I suppose it's some comfort that the supervillain doesn't have his eye on us," Dominique said. "That it was just a couple of loose screws."

After they explained loose screws to the duke, he said that they were dangerous, whether in machines or in human organizations. All of them were to take extra care. He hired two more footmen.

CHAPTER 21

Besancon
December 1636

"This Hamilton's father began life as nothing but a schoolmaster," Priolo reported, "the son of a Presbyterian minister, who in turn was the illegitimate son of some minor 'laird' as the Scots name their untitled nobility, but still nothing but a schoolmaster who went to Ireland fortune-hunting and opened an academy in Dublin, thereafter becoming associated with the founding of Trinity College. A cunning fellow, by all reports, but still just a schoolmaster. Then, in the service of King James of Scotland as he weaseled his way onto the English throne, the father became first *Sir* James Hamilton when he was fifty, after he had acquired a lot of Irish land by more than dubious means, and then, some dozen or so years past, Viscount Clanboye. Thus, the young man coming is the heir to a title of nobility. A new title, a minor title, an Irish title, but still a title. All this comes, of course, from my recent brief and hurried visits among the Scots officers in the service of Grand Duke Bernhard, and is hearsay. Or gossip.

"Still, the father holds a lot of land in County Down, acquired by defrauding Con MacNiall O'Neill, one of the most powerful of the native Irish chiefs, but still a lot of land, with his title confirmed by the English monarch when said King James of Scotland became King James of

England, and more granted to him by the same King James elsewhere in Ulster. Old man Hamilton is past seventy now but still alive and healthy. He divorced two childless wives before he took a third. She is Welsh and some thirty years younger than he is. Her father bought one of the baronetcies that King James put on the market for money; her brother now holds it. This boy is an only child, so one can only assume that Clanboye puts a lot of faith in the lady's virtue by believing that her son is his."

"Or was so anxious for an heir that *he* was willing to accept any son born in wedlock," Marguerite interrupted.

"Little cynic." Rohan smiled. His daughter rarely bypassed an opportunity to make a snide reference to her illegitimate maternal half-brother, Tancrède.

"I would say," Priolo commented, "that the precise relationships among the dates of the boy's conception, his father's second divorce, and his parents' marriage appear to have been somewhat obfuscated."

Rohan rapped his knuckles on the table. "This O'Neill your mentioned—what exact relation is he to Owen Roe O'Neill who was here in the summer?"

"Was, not is. Brother-in-law. They were also cousins in varying degrees, of course, but that is the closest connection. Con MacNiall O'Neill left two sons. When he died in 1619, they were children. King James took them as wards of chancery and had them brought up in England as Protestants. Thus far, neither of them has married."

"So the Hamiltons will be in feud with Owen Roe?"

"Yes, and with the Montgomerys as well, who did the first level of fraud against Con MacNiall, and then old man Hamilton pulled a favor from King James and got a third share of the whole of the Clanboye lands. Hugh Montgomery did the work of breaking O'Neill out of prison at Carrickfergus and then Hamilton cut himself in on the payoff."

✳ ✳ ✳

"As the second element, I believe . . ." Rohan paused for a sip of coffee. "When I first tasted this beverage, Madame Calagna, I thought it to be surely the most horrid substance that any person ever voluntarily took into his mouth. Yet, within the week, I tried it again. Then again, a couple of days following. Now I have a cup every morning, and sometimes, as now, once more in the evening. It is quite insidious, so enlivening for the mind, rather than the dullness that ensues from hot cider."

Carey nodded. She had no objection to drinking coffee at the duke's expense. It still cost quite a lot.

*　*　*

"He hulks," Shae said.

Dominique nodded.

The guests, Mr. Hamilton and his tutor Mr. Traill, had arrived.

"He's disgusting," Shae said, "and I'm not the only one who thinks so. Twenty years old, twenty pounds overweight, too much hair, and the expression on his face only manages to go from pout to sulk and then back again. For all the world, he looks exactly like some over-entitled WVU frat boy trolling through the evening in search of a girl who's stupid enough to swallow a doctored drink."

"Shae!"

"Mom's a nurse, and she's a realist. They may not have roofies down-time, but they'll probably come up with something else, so she's made sure I know all about what some guys do. All he does is complain."

"Well, I'll grant that," Dominique giggled. "First he gripes that he hasn't had any fun at all on his European tour, stuck with this tutor, meaning Mr. Traill, who was recommended to his father as 'a very learned, discreet, and religious master.' I'd love to go to Italy myself, but Hamilton said, 'We went to Florence and Rome, first, which involved a lot of art galleries and language lessons.' Then he griped, 'after that, he made me go to Geneva, of all the dull spots on earth that he could have found. We were there much longer than I had any wish to be, because Mr. Traill decided to qualify for his ordination and receive it there, in the home of Calvin himself. We have *duties of piety* at the beginning and end of each day. Once we got to France, I got to start my day, *after* prayers, mind you, at seven o'clock in the morning with two hours study of French or Latin grammar, then classes in dancing and fencing, then oral French, followed by an hour of translation, followed by logic and mathematics.'

"On he goes, blah, blah, blah."

"Dominique, you are a wicked mimic." Shae grinned.

"I tried, honestly. I said that surely Mr. Traill gave him some time for entertainment, and off he went again. 'Only if you think that literary salons are entertainment. Or, while we were in Geneva, sermons.' "

"Then what's he doing here?"

"Well, according to Susanna, who heard it from the cook, who heard it from one of the footmen, who heard it from Hamilton's manservant, while they were in France, he and Mr. Traill heard the gossip regarding a search for a husband for Marguerite. Given the troubles in England, Scotland, and by extension Ulster, Hamilton decided that it's probably not smart for him to put all of his eggs in the basket his father manipulated his way into, and that he, being definitely not only Protestant, but Presbyterian, and not quite a "nonentity," clearly qualifies as Marguerite's future husband. So they weaseled their way into getting the duke's sister to send them here. It looks like Marguerite has a suitor on her hands."

* * *

Hamilton did not like Shae and Dominique any more than they liked him. He was outright rude to Susanna.

Hamilton and Traill had not been in residence for a week when a package arrived from Marc Cavriani, "wherever he is at the moment,"

Susanna said. Her face was cheerful enough, but Dominique thought that the bright tone in her voice was more than a little forced.

The girls all started pulling off the wrapping paper right there in the entryway.

"Oooohhh!" Susanna screeched with delight. "It's a little nativity scene such as the Italians make. He must have ordered it all the way from Naples. Unless he's back in Naples, of course."

Traill's voice came from the door leading into the salon. "Destroy those idols at once."

"No!" Susanna screeched, hugging the box to her chest. "It's mine!"

Hamilton, following Traill into the entryway, reached out and snatched the box out of her hands. He was about to pull the little carvings out and smash them on the floor when Shae and Dominique each grabbed one of his wrists, Dominique with both hands and Shae more by poking her good arm through the crook of his elbow and tugging.

"Give me back my crèche!" Susanna's voice, echoed and amplified by the tile floors, resounded as far as the duke's second-floor study.

"Mom," Dominique screamed. "**Mommmm!**"

"Marguerite," Shae yelled. "Carey!"

The footman stationed by the front door looked on, not at all sure what his duties might be in a situation where dissension arose among his betters in the household in which he had recently taken service.

"Give her back the crèche," Rohan said as he came down the stairs, followed by Carey.

"There can be no toleration of idolatry," Traill screamed.

"There obviously is," Rohan pointed out. "In spite of the storms of destruction that our co-religionists visited upon stained glass windows, statues, and paintings in the previous century, large numbers of them survive. Artists create more day by day. I would think that you would have noticed this during your various tours of Italy. I see no real sign that God is busily striking them down."

"Not in a Reformed household, though," Hamilton said, trying to shake the girls off his arms. "In Ulster, we have been scrupulous about repressing the mistaken practices of the surviving natives."

"*This* Reformed household," Rohan said, "happens to be mine rather than yours, and the girl is my daughter's guest."

He beckoned the footman, who, with some relief at having an order he should clearly obey, took the box away from Hamilton and then looked around blankly, wondering what he should do with it. "Give it back to the girl."

Rohan waved in Susanna's direction. "Take it up to your bedroom and leave it there."

Susanna curtsied and backed out of the hallway as fast as she could.

Rohan looked at his uninvited Scottish guests. "Has either of you, perhaps, ever heard the name Leopold Cavriani'?"

* * *

"It's hard to focus on serious scholarship in the middle of all this domestic turmoil," Rohan said. "However, in regard to the third major section of *Les Futuriens*, I believe I will subdivide it into several subsections. The first will be headed: Underlying Moral and Ethical Presuppositions. I will begin with this subsidiary story about Gertrude McFuzz and the repudiation of worldly vanity."

"It was scarcely universally accepted up-time any more than it is down-time," Carey commented. "This can be documented by the amount of time that girls spent in shopping malls. Susanna . . ." She paused. The duke had a lot going on. "Do you remember who Susanna is?"

"The little Italian Catholic girl whose nativity scene caused such a fuss."

"Yes. Well, her reaction, when she read the book, was hostile to the whole underlying premise. Of course, she is a court dressmaker. After objecting to the moral of the story, she requested permission to draw copies of some of Gertrude's more fantastic feathers, which she planned to send to M. Cavriani for forwarding to the silk weavers of Lyon, thinking that they might make lovely designs for brocades."

Rohan cleared his throat. "I have recently paid some of Marguerite's bills for various feminine fashions. My household was much more economical when I lived in two rooms and her mother paid her bills. Conclusion: the moralists of the up-time had no more success with this premise than did the Hebrew prophets, the philosophers of classical antiquity, or those of our own modern day, although this unblemished record of failure did not keep them from trying."

* * *

"My Lord Duke," James Traill began. His voice was quivering with barely restrained outrage. "My young master . . ." He gestured at Hamilton. ". . . has observed that you permit your daughter's dressmaker to leave this house on the Lord's Day in order to attend the blasphemous Catholic mass. It is bad enough that the Grand Duke has not closed all of the Catholic churches in this city but rather permits them to continue to be used for this unacceptable purpose. It is worse that he allows his wife to have a Catholic confessor and to maintain a private chapel in their residence itself. But he is a Lutheran, and therefore, what could a person expect in the way of zealousness?

"However, it is worse that you, a professor of the true Reformed faith, do not require this young woman to attend the Lord's Day observances in your own household in order that she may hear scriptural sermons and be informed of her errors." His general squawks of outrage continued for quite some time.

"If we want *la religion pretendue réformée* to be tolerated in France," Rohan commented, "which for my part I most certainly do, I think it behooves us to extend some toleration to the practices of others."

"Certainly not!" Hamilton exclaimed. "It is one thing for us to require that errorists tolerate truth, but quite another for those of us who hold to the truth to tolerate error. Let me tell you a little about the superstitions of the native Irish peasants with whom my father has to deal." Which he did.

"I assure you that the lands of this Irish Catholic chieftain that my father claimed—for that matter, also the ones that Hugh Montgomery obtained and the ones that Con O'Neill kept—lands in Upper Clandeboye, more around The Great Ardes and around Castle Reagh, were entirely desolate and gone to waste."

"I don't suppose," Rohan asked, "that their condition might have in any way have been the result of the English wars against the Irish during the years preceding your father's settlement? *Non?*"

"Well," Hamilton answered, "the Irish had resisted all the prior efforts at Protestant settlement, so the condition of the land was their own fault. Queen Elizabeth's agents had to put down the resistance, obviously. The region was almost without population. Therefore, it was only right for the king to confirm grants to men such as my father who were willing to bring in Protestants from Scotland, settle them, and once more assure a flow of rents to the landlords and taxes to the royal treasury.

"In fact," he barreled on, "I believe that it would be only fair to say that the successful efforts of my father and some other Ulster entrepreneurs served as the pattern that encouraged King James to authorize the plantation of Jamestown in Virginia and other ventures in the Americas. Therefore," he beamed at the up-timers, "your nation and your very existence were? are? will be? actually the result my father's enterprising nature. Part of what Mr. Traill has made me study is the nature of the "Scotch-Irish" settlements in West Virginia. *My* opinion is that all of you owe due gratitude to the Hamiltons."

"A little bit full of himself, maybe?" Shae asked later that day.

Dominique didn't answer directly. "What I would like to know is why he has been spying on Susanna closely enough to know that she goes to mass. Isn't he supposed to be listening one of Mr. Traill's properly Calvinist discourses on Sunday mornings?"

"He's probably trying to trap her and rape her," Shae said. "That's what villains always do in novels. They ravish the maidservants."

"I don't think so," Susanna said. "Young Master Hamilton is following me around, but I believe that he is looking for my nativity scene, so that he can destroy it. He did force his way into the bedroom where I sleep, but I wasn't there. Neither was my crèche. I hid it better than that."

Virginia DeMarce

CHAPTER 22

Grantville
late 1636

"Good lord," Hazel Patton said. Idelette Cavriani's brother had actually gotten the cat. Or, to be more precise, he had gotten a wide selection of more or less Siamese-looking cats of French origin, several of them being uncut toms that she estimated to be three or four years old. With assorted females. And kittens.

She called Marsha Jones in as a consultant. Marsha took the polaroid photo back, looked at the eligible contestants presented for her review, and said, "Well, their markings do change as they mature and Saucy was just a kitten, still almost white when Becky took him. He only had pale outlines where the points would develop. I'm not real sure. . ., but that one there looks the most like Pitty Pat. Let's go with him."

Hazel officially declared "him" to be "The Cat." That is, the official, genuine, article. The same kitten who left with Rebecca Abrabanel.

Marc got on the train to Magdeburg with the Official Siamese Cat in his cage and two of the prettiest kittens in smaller cages, radioed ahead so that Amalie Elisabeth would be prepared, and basked in the satisfaction of a job well done.

Marsha Jones firmly told Miranda that, no, she could not have another kitten. "In a few years, you'll be going off to school or getting married and then where would I be? Stuck with your cats, that's where!"

Denis handed over to Hazel Patton the male whose appearance she declared to be second most close to breed standard and therefore to be best utilized in her rebreeding program, as a token of thanks.

He then set out to sell cats, buoyed up by excellent marketing advice provided by Idelette Cavriani. Once he countered her wary, "I suppose you're Catholic," with a bright, "Oh, no, our branch of the family is Huguenot," she threw herself unstintingly into Project Lemercier. By January, he was able to afford a semester's tuition at the technical college.

Magdeburg
early December 1636

There was a triumphant reception committee waiting for the train when it pulled in, including many ladies of high rank. The landgravine-regent of Hesse-Kassel formally received The Cat on behalf of Secretary of State Abrabanel and the USE government. Marc gave one kitten to a representative of Princess Kristina and the second, in heartfelt gratitude for their timely intervention in the October interview, to Charlotte and Philipp.

The newspapers went wild.

But, somehow, none of them ever mentioned Marc. As far as the public knew, The Cat had been delivered by an anonymous courier who had already left town before any reporter lined up an interview.

* * *

"The cat caper appears to have been a considerable success," Leopold commented. "Although you might possibly have seen fit to mention it to me in advance."

"There wasn't anything else going on right then," Marc countered. "It was something to do."

"That involved going into Gaston's France?" Leopold turned around again, continuing to pace the anteroom in the Magdeburg town house of Landgravine-Regent Amalie Elisabeth of Hesse-Kassel.

"Well, yes." Marc didn't say *obviously*, even though he thought it was fairly obvious, given that he had been and returned. "It wasn't as if I needed to be conspicuous about it. No talking to important politicians. No getting in contact with courtiers. I didn't even check in with Soubise."

Leopold tilted his head to the side, one eyebrow raised.

"No, I didn't. Not even with Raudegen. Nothing that would have drawn any attention to me on the part of Gaston's surveillance operatives."

"I'll grant you that . . ." Leopold started to say.

The door opened. "The landgravine will see you now," her secretary said.

After all the demands of *politesse* had been satisfied, Amalie Elisabeth gestured. "Do sit down, please, both of you. This may take some time."

Both men responded with half-bows and each took a chair. "You have summoned us because . . . Leopold began.

"I have heard that you received news from France, by a somewhat circuitous route, that might be of concern to the USE administration. As the Crown Loyalists are still not entirely within the emperor's confidence, much less that of the Fourth of July Party, I am hoping . . ."

"I am not certain, My Lady. This came to us from Colonel Raudegen, who at the instance of Henri de Rohan is currently in the household of the duke's brother Soubise and his sister, Mademoiselle Anne, in Paris. Rohan, of course, has borrowed Raudegen from Grand Duke Bernhard, so in a sense he monitors French developments, specifically Huguenot developments, for both of his superiors. The household is watched by Gaston's men, of course. Raudegen sent the information encrypted, by way of my sister-in-law in Brussels, disguised as a portion of an ordinary banking transaction . . ."

By the time the landgravine and his father finished being discreet with one another, Marc realized that, as a consequence of the success of his illicit escapade, he was about to be off to Brussels to see Aunt Alis, which would most likely be followed by off to France to check in with Raudegen, both of which errands were on an urgent schedule, which signified that he wouldn't be going back to Besançon to see his almost-a-fiancée any time soon now, which meant that it would be some time before he could bring her to Magdeburg and install her in the landgravine's household, even though Amalie Elisabeth had committed herself to make that happen at some future date. One that seemed to get vaguer and vaguer as the months went by. Which meant that the possibility of his actually marrying Susanna was floating off toward some foggy and undetermined future day. Again.

As soon as he and his father got back to their rooms, he scribbled a hurried note, addressed to his love in care of the duc de Rohan's household in Besançon, and stamped it. That would have to do.

Upon hearing his son's quite intentionally deep and melodramatic sigh of despair, which he was not about to take seriously for even one minute, Leopold looked at him. "No, it's not easy for the girl," he said. "It's never been easy for your mother, either."

"What?" Marc was a bit disoriented by the sudden new topic.

"That you are perpetually on your way to somewhere else. That I, all my life, have been perpetually on my way somewhere else. That I have hopped about all over the European continent, from pillar to post, from long before the Ring of Fire occurred and with no cessation since it happened."

"I suppose that it always seemed normal to me."

Leopold looked out the window. "My intention has always been to ensure, so far as I could, that in any given year, there would be some polity willing to serve as a refuge and sanctuary for those of my co-religionists who were in that same year being expelled from some other principality. If Gaston revokes the Edict of Nantes . . . There's no guarantee that he will; we don't have anyone sufficiently deep inside his close circle of advisors to know what he may or may not be planning, which is frustrating. But he's well aware that it was revoked in that other future."

He turned around. "Right now, in regard to the Huguenots in France, I believe that Hesse-Kassel is the best option. There are overtures from Ansbach, even from Solms-Laubach, but Hesse-Kassel is preferable. For one thing, it's much closer to France than Ansbach and far larger than Laubach. It's not just that the landgravine is herself Calvinist, but that she is anxious to promote economic development in the principality for the benefit of her son. The principality has instituted a form of primogeniture, so young Wilhelm will become the sole ruler in due time. Also for her other children, of course, but she is mainly anxious that Hesse will, in the coming years, maintain a position of influence within the USE. It's natural. Claudia de' Medici is seeking the same for Tyrol. The USE brings benefits, but unification also brings implied threats to the quasi-independence of the component parts of the realm, so it is only prudent of them to be alert.

"As for how her anxiety for Hesse may benefit us . . . Yes, the USE has a policy of toleration, but it really is not applied equally in all the component states and provinces. The northern Netherlands might provide refuge, but Frederik Hendrik has to balance thoughts of how many potential refugees, additional Calvinists and foreign ones at that, he could receive without upsetting Fernando. The current English regime is not favorable to those who might logically, and in practice would, ally with the Puritan faction. Poland is hopeless; Bohemia unpromising. The balance among the Swiss cantons is precarious and they have the immediate challenge of integrating the Swabian cities. Hesse, by contrast, is fairly close and apparently willing . . . though Ansbach would do in a crisis situation."

Leopold turned around and leaned on the back of a chair. "So for the time being, do the landgravine's bidding. Do Rohan's bidding. Passing inconveniences for us and our family are minor, insignificant, compared to the catastrophes that might occur and which I dearly hope to avert. If you get discouraged, think back to how useful the information that you brought back from Naples was when it came to our assessing

211

Spanish intentions. And hope that if Gaston fails, if a new Louis XIV ascends the French throne, that in another fifty years you will not still be crisscrossing the map of Europe looking for places that will accept Calvinist refugees."

CHAPTER 23

Besançon
December 1636

"Thank you, Bernhard." Rohan watched the grand duke pace around the room, his hands clasped behind his back. "I know that it wasn't convenient for you to send replacements to Lorraine or for the men I'll need to come back here in this weather, for that matter. I only wish that Ruvigny and Bismarck were available to me again."

Bernhard leaned against a window frame. "I have other tasks for those two once they report in. If the weather holds, their party will be here in a few days. You needn't bother to thank me for the loan of Henry Gage and Lion Gardiner. It was simply fortuitous that I managed to catch them before someone decided to send them back to observe what is happening in Austria. I think your concerns about Ducos' people are perfectly justified. He seems to have an astonishing number of followers."

"There are a lot of Huguenots in France." Rohan pursed his lips. "Several million of them." He twisted his mouth wryly. "We can't expect them all to be rational, particularly since many have lost family members, homes, employment, property, and the occasional body part to the policies of the crown since the death of Henri IV. If I had to guess,

Ducos is drawing his few hundred from a pool of possibly a quarter of a million physically capable adult men. Along with an occasional woman."

"So if they see a chance for what appears to be retaliation, they will take it."

"That's pretty much the case. Especially when they have found a leader who, no matter how undesirable we find his tactics to be, appears to have a great ability to attract and influence others. *Charisma*, Madame Calagna calls it."

"She knows Greek?" Bernhard turned around. "Nobody told me that."

"No, she just knows the word. Up-time English apparently had an eclectic approach to vocabulary."

Bernhard's secretary stuck his head through the door.

Rohan picked up his stack of red-tape-tied bundles for another day of paper-pushing.

* * *

At the *Hôtel de Buyer*, Marguerite dashed down the staircase into the hallway screaming, "Henri, nobody told me you were arriving today," and threw herself into Ruvigny's arms.

"You will note," August von Bismarck said to Ruvigny's astonished young wife, "that he braced himself firmly in anticipation of this event, one leg extended and slightly bent and the other held to the rear to provide support and balance. A perfect fencing stance. Experience has demonstrated that since the young duchess reached her full growth, although she is still quite small, she has enough weight to overbalance a man standing with his feet together, especially when she moves rapidly and then leaps."

The expression on the face of Ruvigny's Danish Sophia indicated that she was far from sure what to make of this. Whatever it might be, it was nothing good. She didn't like it.

Hamilton, following Marguerite down the stairs, protested volubly that he didn't like it.

Shae spotted the pout on his face and gave Dominique a perfectly demonic grin. This could be fun.

✳ ✳ ✳

"You young people entertain yourselves in the dining room, since it has a fire going," Rohan said that evening. "Play cards or something. Don't destroy the furniture. I have reached a stage in my study of *Les Futuriens* that requires more consultation with Madame Calagna. Traill, stay and observe, but do not interfere unless there is danger to the furniture."

Traill sputtered at being treated as an upper servant, but there wasn't anything he could do about it. He might now be an ordained Presbyterian minister, but in reality, as a tutor, he *was* an upper servant. His obligation was to Lord Clanboye rather than to Rohan, but as he was a guest . . . .

Not even Hamilton and Traill could permanently distract the duke from his determination to understand the up-time mind. "Is this *Marvin K. Mooney, Will You Please Go Now?* really part of the *juvenalia*? The language is simple, but . . ."

Carey frowned. "There was something political about it; I honestly can't remember." She made a note on her list for the Grantville researcher.

"Now we reach *The Cat in the Hat.* I will analyze it together with the sequel, *The Cat in the Hat Comes Back.* There is far more substance here."

"If you say so," Carey answered.

Virginia DeMarce

CHAPTER 24

Besançon
December 1636

Christmas came to Besançon. Or, as far as the great majority of the people who were Catholic and the modest minority of the population who were Lutheran were concerned, Advent came. Aside from the ever-mounding piles of baked goods in the marketplace, they wouldn't get around to Christmas until late on December 24.

Susanna did not have high hopes of being asked to make holiday clothing for the household. "Not the way that Carey and Kamala think about clothes," she sighed. "Much less the way that the techies' wives think about clothes!" She shuddered at the recollection of Michaela Stavros' preferred garb, which leaned heavily in the direction of well-worn cargo pants and even more well-worn plaid flannel shirts. Lisa Lund's current taste, in half-deference to her down-time husband, ran to rather full gaucho pants at a mid-calf length and fitted jackets.

From the perspective of Traill and Hamilton, Christmas might as well have been Armageddon. Traill would probably have preferred Armageddon.

Both men objected to the keeping of Christmas altogether, partly on the grounds that it was a pagan holiday adopted by the Catholic church and partly, in Traill's case, because he interpreted the second commandment to forbid all religious festivals other than the Lord's Day.

Not to mention the connected train of argumentation which held that, 'every day is the Lord's,' which he took to prohibit singling out any day in particular other than the Sabbath, as commanded in Scripture.

"Your Grace," he admonished Rohan. "In this city, which for all intents and purposes is so full of Catholics that it might as well be pagan, you, as the leading Huguenot, must be particularly strict. Because the grand duke is Lutheran and his spouse Catholic, the city, during the coming season, will be subjected to many non-scriptural celebrations. Incense. Pageants. Moreover . . ."

"Hah!" Shae whispered to Dominique. "He missed candles."

"That's because everybody uses candles all the year around, down-time. They're not Christmasy," Dominique whispered back.

"Moreover" covered quite a bit of territory. Traill objected to the traditional church calendar observed by Catholics, Lutherans, and the Church of England. He objected to liturgies. He objected to "man-made hymns" rather than psalms, and he was being assaulted by them every time he stepped outside of Rohan's door. He objected, in fact, to all worship practices not specifically commanded by Scripture, "man-made hymns" being only one of them. He digressed into the Scots' quarrel with English episcopacy (and, for that matter, in the few moments when he had leisure to think about it, with Swedish episcopacy, Danish episcopacy, and the occasional German Lutheran episcopacy), not to mention Lutheran *Damenstifte*, which he described as barely disguised nunneries, and abbeys that had not been destroyed but turned into schools whose students were daily subject to the idolatrous stone carvings on their walls.

Rohan pointed out that Charles I permitted foreign embassies from Catholic countries to maintain chapels in London. Traill's view was that simply because one Protestant monarch followed grossly erroneous policies, it did not follow that others should make the same mistake. Indeed, he complained, that Grand Duke Bernhard was not only permitting his wife's private worship, as Charles I had done for Henrietta Maria, but was generally tolerating Catholicism in Burgundy, although, he said, he must admit, being a fair-minded man himself, that it did not appear that Bernhard was doing so with any great degree of enthusiasm.

At this point, Hamilton disagreed sharply and made his own pro-royalist, even pro-Cork-administration, position crystal clear, showing that when it came to matters of political principle, he was as willing to quarrel with his tutor as with everyone else.

"The principle," Shae said behind her hand, "being 'what's in it for me?' I presume."

Marguerite shushed her.

Traill reiterated his imprudent statements in regard to Grand Duke Bernhard's allowing Claudia de' Medici to have an in-house chapel and confessor. Rohan advised him strongly that if he said such things where Bernhard's men could hear him, he would be expeditiously expelled from the Rohan household.

Traill countered with indignation, being of the opinion that Rohan was in no position to consider himself immune to criticism, considering that he had not only permitted Shae to remain at the archbishop's palace for several days following her accident, but had also permitted the other women in his household, including his own daughter, to call upon her there.

Somehow, Traill was by no means mollified when Rohan pointed out that Grand Duke Bernhard was also tolerating Calvinism, as demonstrated by his own presence on the grand duke's staff and Traill and Hamilton's own freedom to worship with the Scots soldiers on the Grand Duke's staff who had founded a church in the *Quartier Battant*.

"Papa," Marguerite asked in pursuit of a less controversial topic, "how is your treatise on *Les Futuriens* coming? What will it have to say about the views of the up-timers concerning religion?"

"As far as Dr. Seuss is concerned, it will have little to say about religion in the up-time world. I may have to reserve a more detailed study of that topic until I have other sources. Only one of Seuss' books deals with religion and it displays minimal concern with doctrine, indeed manages to discuss Christmas without a single mention of our Savior, and gives general approval of gift exchanges and feasting, with maximal concern for other people. Madame Calagna assures me, however, that the costume created by the Grinch is a veiled reference to the custom in the Low Countries of seeing Saint Nicholas of Myra as the patron of gift giving."

At this point, Shae and Dominique chanted in unison several rhymed sentiments about the non-commercial nature of the holiday when properly observed, and the proper size of charitable hearts, including those of fabled creatures such as this 'Grinch.'

Rohan stared at them, once more confirmed in his growing conviction of the incredible significance of Seuss for comprehending the up-timers, as the two girls, backing up to the beginning, managed, without the slightest review, to render most of *The Grinch Who Stole Christmas* with far fewer errors than most down-time adolescents made when called upon to recite their catechisms, whether said catechisms were of the Calvinist, Lutheran, or Catholic persuasion.

There was one point on which the Grinch and James Traill were in utter concord. No matter what they did, the disgusting holiday known as Christmas, or rather, here in Burgundy, *Noël*, came every blasted year, and there didn't seem to be any way to get rid of it.

Traill was rather more prepared than the Grinch to dispute the undesirability of this recurring phenomenon. In place of a dog named Max, he had a degree in theology from the University of Leiden in the Northern Low Countries, as they were now called, and an ordination from Geneva.

"Calvin himself," he proclaimed, "in his own day, disapproved of the celebration of Christmas because its observation had been corrupted by Roman Catholicism."

"He did not, however, forbid it as a violation of the second commandment," Rohan countered. "Geneva in Calvin's day originally observed the four great feast days, or festivals of Christ, that did not always fall on a Sunday, including Christmas. He accepted this practice. That the Scots now find this to be insufficient . . ."

Traill countered with a discourse on the regulative principle of worship, with a relatively brief digression into the acceptability of special days of thanksgiving as modeled upon the Old Testament festival of *Purim.*

"For various values of *relatively brief,*" Shae whispered to Marguerite.

Rohan retaliated with the prescriptions of the *Confessio Belgica* of 1561 that had been produced to regulate Reformed practice in the Low Countries, the Heidelberg Catechism that came out of the Palatinate in 1563, commissioned by Elector Frederick III and written primarily by Zacharias Ursinus and Caspar Olevianus, and Bullinger's Second Helvetic Confession, which expressed the position of the Swiss Reformed.

Rohan pointed out with some satisfaction that while the Heidelberg Catechism explained the second command as requiring that a Christian should, "especially on the Sabbath diligently frequent the church of God," it did not prescribe that such a Christian was to attend church "exclusively on the Sabbath." Nodding his head decisively, Rohan concluded, "For, as Bullinger said in the Second Helvetic Confession of 1566, how can we, if we profess the Christian faith, not take note of Christ's passion as well as of his resurrection? How can a Christian ignore his ascension?"

Traill objected that the church does not have liberty to introduce into worship any element of worship besides those commanded by Scripture, which gave no place to the four great feasts as a part of congregational worship. Referring to the Heidelberg Catechism in his own turn, he insisted that God requires in the second commandment that believers should not worship Him "in any other way than He has commanded in His Word." He reiterated the Scots interpretation that anything not specifically commanded was excluded.

"The Scots may choose to take exception to Bullinger's formulation," Rohan replied, "but no Reformed tradition on the continent does so. As long as Christmas is celebrated without superstition, that is, which Bullinger specified: 'Moreover, if in Christian liberty the churches religiously celebrate the memory of the Lord's nativity, circumcision, passion, resurrection, and the ascension into heaven, and the sending of the Holy Spirit upon the disciples, we approve of it highly.' The crucial words are 'religiously celebrate.'

"I will grant you that many of the English mid-winter traditions to which you object appear to be of pagan origin, but they certainly have little to do with the observation of *Noël* in our French temples. Moreover," Rohan drew in a deep breath, "when we come to the Church Order of the Synod of Dordt, adopted less than twenty years ago, it not only permits, but rather requires that the Reformed churches 'shall observe in addition to the Sunday also Christmas . . .' and it specifies precisely that such observance 'shall be a public worship service on December 25 during which the minister shall preach on some aspect of the birth of Christ, usually and preferably the history as told in the Gospels, and the congregation *shall* praise god with appropriate psalms in congregational singing.' Which you," he pointed at Traill, "*may* do for us or we will find a Reformed minister who *will.*"

"I believe," Rohan commented to Carey the morning after this marathon disputation, "that Mr. James Traill may have a famous future as a controversialist. If I had my preferences, however, I would *prefer* that he develop his reputation in some location other than my residence."

She smiled. "Overall, Your Grace, I would say that you held your own."

* * *

"Marguerite, my dear," the duke said at breakfast.

"Yes, Papa."

"You have complained upon occasion that nobody really listens to you."

She looked down at her plate. "I may have. Upon occasion." Then she grinned. "Rare occasions."

"It may ameliorate your distress to learn that in one matter, I have listened to what you say during our morning sessions, heeded it, and taken action."

"How? What?"

"Today, I will send a letter to your *Tante* Anne and Uncle Soubise. They are still in Paris, although things are disrupted there. It authorizes Anne to begin the process of searching for a suitable bride for your uncle, thus, should they find one and she prove fertile, removing some of the burden of Rohan from your shoulders."

She jumped out of her chair and curtsied.

"This will take time," he admonished.

"From what I've heard," Shae said after breakfast, "Your aunt oughtn't take too much time looking for a bride for Soubise. Your uncle isn't exactly a spring chicken."

"Is Colonel Raudegen still with him?" Bismarck asked.

Marguerite nodded. "The grand duke has given permission for him to stay with Uncle Soubise indefinitely. Or, at least, until things calm down a lot."

Dominique bit her lip. "The newspapers don't seem to be hyping *calm* when it comes to France."

Ruvigny leaned back. "Have you . . . "

"What?"

"Well, have you heard any news in regard to what your mother and M. de Candale are doing?"

Marguerite shook her head.

"I can ask Marc if he's heard anything," Susanna offered. "The next time I write. My letters have to go through Geneva, so it isn't fast, but I think . . ." She paused. "Well, I don't know for sure, but I *think*, from a reference he made in the last letter that came, that Marc is somewhere in France right now."

"How?" Ruvigny was suddenly on the alert.

"He said something about talking to M. d'Espinay de Saint-Luc. Of course, I don't know where *he* is either, but I would think it's likely that he's in France."

"And he would probably know what *Maman* is doing," Marguerite said. "If I remember all the gossip right, he was the lover she left for M. de Candale, the first time around, before we went to Venice and Tancrède was born."

CHAPTER 25

Besançon
December 1636

"**U**p," Bismarck said. "Out of bed. You were supposed to meet us in the *Quartier Battant* this morning for sword-fighting practice. You didn't show up. Again! We've had to walk all the way up here to get you."

James Hamilton rolled over and groaned. "Up? Lord of Hosts! I am NOT going to get up today. Well, not this early."

"Quit with the blasphemy! It is NOT early. There are only two more hours until breakfast," Ruvigny said. "You just drank too much beer last night. Again. If you would cut down on it, you could get rid of some of that extra weight that slows you down."

Bismark raised his eyebrows. "Up and at 'em?"

Ruvigny nodded, grinning at the Gerry Stone quote. Bismarck grabbed Hamilton's shoulders, Ruvigny grabbed his feet, and they swung him onto the uncarpeted floor with a thunk.

"Arrrgh! I'll complain to my tutor. He'll complain to my father."

"No, he won't," Traill said. "I'm standing right here in the doorway. After your third sequential refusal to attend your fencing lessons, combined with your sixth sequential refusal to rise for morning devotions, I'm the person who asked them to start hauling you off to the barracks in the morning. May I remind you about taking the Lord's name in vain?"

"You may not," Hamilton grumped. "At least not with my permission, as if that's going to stop you." He sat up on the floor and glowered at his tutor. "I'm too old to have a self-righteous prig of a bear-leader supervising everything I do."

"If you acted your age, your father would be less apt to think you need one," Bismarck countered. "At least until you get back to Ireland, you have him and can't get rid of him. He's authorized to exercise discipline over you, so you might as well stop complaining and," he took a mighty heave at the back of Hamilton's shoulders, "get up, get dressed, get yourself out of this house and out of the hair of everybody else in it, and head for the *Quartier Battant* with us."

"Every minute you don't move is a minute of breakfast you'll miss, because we don't intend to cut your drill short," Ruvigny said.

"And I, for one, get cranky when I'm hungry," Bismarck added. "You don't want to fence with me when I'm cranky."

*　*　*

The two young officers in Dutch uniform leaned against the wall of the room, watching the grand duke's men and their assorted guests practice swordsmanship.

"It's so nice to have friends," one said to the other in their adopted language, after he had glanced around to make sure that no one was paying any attention to them at all.

"True. Good intelligence, confirmed two ways, independently. From young Cavriani in Paris to General Turenne's brother, to the *Stadhouder*, to us, giving us several weeks' warning that he was coming here. Enough time for us to get leave. From the archbishop's housekeeper, to the archbishop, to our uncle, to the *Stadhouder* to us, that he had arrived and exactly where he would be staying for several weeks. I do love radio. As soon as I get a little money ahead, I'm getting a better receiver."

"You spend all your money, ahead or not, on that 'techie stuff.' "

They watched a little longer.

"He certainly is a fatty pudding," the first one commented.

"For his age. He wouldn't be in bad condition for someone thirty years older."

"What next?"

"Being brought up in England as wards in chancery wasn't a total loss." The second man reached for his cape. "There are occasions when it's handy to be certified young Protestant Englishmen in Frederik Hendrik's service. Let's figure out how to get ourselves introduced to some up-timers. I understand they tend to be happy to meet other people who speak English and there can't be many in Besançon."

✳ ✳ ✳

Dinner, or, at least, the largest meal of the day, occurred about two o'clock in the afternoon.

"I hate French food," Hamilton said, glowering at his plate. "I didn't like Italian food, either. I want to go home."

"Nobody's stopping him except himself," Shae muttered to Ruvigny.

"And Traill," he answered.

The Danish Sophia, after her husband translated the comments, giggled.

This entire exchange was, luckily, buried under the rest of the conversation, which today centered around *The 500 Hats of Bartholomew McCubbin*. This, according to Rohan, indicated that the up-timers taught the value of tradition to their children, the hat in question having belonged to Bartholomew's father and grandfather before him. "It is also visually fascinating because of the mirror view of the same landscape from king's palace on the hill down to the humble peasant's cottage, and from the humble peasant's cottage up to the palace on the hill."

"Wait! Wait a minute," Ruvigny said, looking up from his plate and waving his fork. He turned toward Bismarck. "Remember what Gerry

Stone said to us, back in Paris last summer, about why up-timers have the stereotypes they do about the nobility? Some book with a picture of a castle on a hill containing a lord who was oppressing the peasants in a village at the bottom?"

Bismarck nodded. "Wait until after we eat. Gerry sent me a copy of that fourth-grade social studies textbook he was talking about then." He asked one of the footmen to go down to the *Quartier Battant* and get the book from his storage and returned to the important task of eating enough mutton to see him through the rest of the day.

"In Denmark," Sophia said, "Our castles are not on hilltops. There aren't any hilltops."

Rohan returned to the deeper meaning of the five hundred hats. By the time he finished, nearly a half-hour later, the footman was back with Gerry Stone's book. Carey, Dominique, and Shae agreed that, yeah, all of them had used a textbook with a picture sort of like that when they were in grade school.

"How old were you?" Rohan wanted to know.

"Umm. Nine or ten? About that?"

And now, Rohan said, "we find the set of beliefs reinforced by Dr. Seuss." He started a verbal dissection of literary tropes and memes. The rest of the group focused on dissecting apple tarts.

*　*　*

"Delighted to meet you," Lisa Lund said, shaking hands. The Christmas market on the town side of the Roman bridge was crammed with people. She nodded toward a man standing a few feet away, next to a table on which toys were displayed. "My husband, Tom. He's from the Palatinate. The bunch trailing him are my two kids and his younger brother and two younger sisters. This one here," she pointed to the denim carrier on her back, "is ours. We met in Grantville. He has another brother who's working in Grantville as a butcher and another sister who stayed there, too. She's running the sales counter in Burckhard's shop."

The first of the two officers in Dutch uniform blinked, a bit startled by this torrent of information and pulled his hand back a little bit too quickly for what he had been told was appropriate if one was being courteous to an up-timer.

The other stepped up, offering his own hand. "Constantine here. You can call me Con. That excessively earnest, serious, and overly-conscientious young man next to me is my older brother Dan. Your husband works for Grand Duke Bernhard?"

The woman shook her head. "Nope. He's a butcher, too, like his brother. The grand duke made the guild let him open a shop because if he couldn't, I wouldn't come to Besançon. I'm the one who works for the grand duke. Mechanical support. I'm one of the bunch who put in the intercom system up on the Citadelle and stuff like that. You're in uniform, so I'll take a guess that you've already been up to see it."

Con grinned and then grinned more broadly. "You know about radios?"

"I'm no specialist, though I can put the pieces together. You'll want to talk to my first husband's sister and her husband. They're working here in town, too. And her husband's brother; his wife's local. They do phones more than radio, but they all love to talk shop."

"I have died and gone to heaven. You are all of the up-timers who work for the grand duke? One extended family?"

"Oh, no. There are Kamala and Carey and their kids. Are you guys here on vacation? If so, hang around with us for a few days and you'll meet them. Tom's a Calvinist and there's a Scots preacher staying at the duke of Rohan's house where Carey's working now, so we've been going there to hear sermons because he preaches in English that we can understand. I was only starting to learn German when we moved over here and my French is still pretty much at the level of 'how much does that head of cabbage cost?' Your English is great, by the way. I'm in awe. Let me give you our address. Send us a note and let us know when you have some free time." She handed him a slip of paper, gave a glance, noticed that her husband was moving on, and darted after him.

"My goodness," Dan said.

"If we were Presbyterian," Con answered, "we might be forgiven for suspecting that the success of our enterprise is foreordained. Predestined even."

"Don't mock the will of God. The best laid plans . . ."

* * *

"It's sort of a pity," Ruvigny said as they hiked their way across the Roman bridge to the *Quartier Battant*, "that the duke got to read this before we did. Gerry sent it to us; not to him."

"He was here, Henri. The book arrived here. We were not here."

"August, do you have to be so constantly phlegmatic?"

"Maybe it's my temperament. I've never bothered to have my humors analyzed. Seemed a waste of money. Why get excited about things you can't do anything about?"

"All right, then, August, what does *Yertle the Turtle* tell us about the up-timers? The duke is bound to ask what we think."

"I'm not sure about that. I do think it's delightful, given the USE's recent problems with Bavaria, that the discontented little turtle at the bottom of the stack is named Mack. Surely that should be Max? It must derive from Maximilian."

"It certainly seems intended to ingrain revolutionary ideas in them from their earliest years."

"They're a bloodthirsty bunch. Their President Jefferson, the one who wrote the 'Declaration of Independence,' wrote in a letter that, 'The tree of liberty must be refreshed from time to time with the blood of patriots and tyrants. It is its natural manure.' "

"Have you been reading about revolutions? Is that what you've had your head in? All that reading you were doing while we were in the Netherlands and Denmark this fall?"

"It was something that my family's possible descendant, the Prussian chancellor in their nineteenth century, wrote. I came across it by accident. It was something to the effect that if change is inevitable, it is better to make a revolution yourself than suffer through one that others make. So I wrote to the researcher I used before and asked him to send me some things about revolutions. Trust me, the French Revolution is enough to make a man's blood freeze in his body, and not just in the middle of winter."

*　*　*

On the day before Christmas, Hamilton made a formal offer for Marguerite's hand, detailing to the duke, at considerable length, the many advantages of the match as he saw them.

Rohan, as politely as possible, reminded the young Ulsterman that he was not yet of age according to either French or English law, and thus was not authorized to make contracts. Without question, Rohan pointed out, in a matter of such significance as marriage, he needed to consult his father and obtain his consent.

Hamilton expressed his belief that his father did not entirely grasp the immense dimension of the changes that were impending in Europe.

Rohan stated his conviction that the possibility of disruptions to the established state of things made it even more imperative for a young man to take into account the wise advice of his elders. He offered that if, after Hamilton had returned home, he should receive a renewed overture from the proper source, namely from the hand of *vicomte* Clanboye, he would give it due consideration.

"Papa," Marguerite said when he relayed the information to her. "You wouldn't!"

"I said that I would give it due consideration. If I should receive any such proffer, I will give it precisely the amount of consideration that I consider it to be worth."

"Well, that's a relief."

The years during which France's Huguenots had lived in a state of persecution had resulted in quite a few compromises with the Calvinist principle that church services should be public and take place in a properly dedicated house of worship. It had become, if not common, at least tolerated, for noble households to maintain chapels and chaplains if they so desired. Rohan had never so desired. The little Scots Presbyterian church in the *Quartier Battant* wasn't a properly dedicated house of worship yet. It had once been a hat shop and shared its walls with two still operating retail stores. Nor did it have a regular minister. Nor did the majority of its members believe in celebrating Christmas. Its door would be locked today.

Still, Rohan bowed to the theory of public worship. As long as he had an ordained minister as his guest, he placed notices of the times of the sermons to be delivered by Mr. Traill on his front door and opened that door to all who wished to hear them. At six o'clock the next morning, Thomas Wedekind and Lisa Lund, family and two guests in tow, appeared at the door of the *Hôtel de Buyer* to hear Mr. Traill's sermon, along with a couple of dozen other resident and visiting Huguenots. Given the size of the foyer, it was standing room only. Given that the foyer was unheated, it was standing on cold feet. That was, however, quite normal in Calvinist churches in the winter, so no one complained (a few whining children excepted).

Introductions and socializing were minimal. As soon as the sermon ended, the duke thanked everyone for coming and left for work, taking Ruvigny and Bismark with him. He didn't really have to. The grand duke, being Lutheran, had given the day off to everyone who was not absolutely needed for garrison duty and maintaining his residence. It was more a sop to Mr. Traill's feelings. He even intended to eat in the general officers' mess, to demonstrate that he was not sponsoring anything that might superficially resemble a holiday meal.

"Ugh," Shae said. "Oatmeal, and not even brown sugar to go on it."

"Marvelous," Hamilton said. "Oatmeal." He was serious. His head still ached and his stomach really wasn't ready for anything more demanding than porridge in the way of sustenance. After evening prayers with Traill the previous night, he had slipped out for more than a few beers.

CHAPTER 26

Besancon
December 1636

As soon as breakfast was over, the girls stormed Carey with a wish to go out for a walk on the ground that there was *absolutely nothing to do*. She couldn't think of any real reason why they shouldn't. It was cold, though, and she had no intention of going out if she didn't absolutely have to. After standing through Traill's sermon, she had every intention of retreating upstairs to the duke's study with its nice little Franklin stove and putting her feet on a couple of hot bricks.

Still . . . three girls, four if Susanna got back from mass in time, and two sturdy footmen. People in the streets.

"Sure," she said.

They got their coats.

Traill and Hamilton went upstairs.

About an hour later, Susanna ran into the study, her hands full of chips and scraps. "I just got back and I found it like this. They smashed it," she wailed. "My nativity scene from Marc. They smashed it."

Upon investigation, Mr. Traill proved to be in the room he shared with Hamilton, reading. He protested that he had not in any way damaged the girl's blasphemous idols, popish though they were.

Carey was inclined to believe him.

Hamilton was nowhere in the house.

"I'm going to look for him." Susanna put on her cloak and was out of the house before Carey could say, "Take one of the footmen with you." In any case, Susanna wasn't usually accompanied by a footman when she ran errands in town by herself.

After about fifteen minutes, Susanna saw Shae and Dominique, with one of the footmen, headed toward the upper town. "We thought we'd watch a mass at St. John the Baptist," Shae explained. "Just to see if they're as naughty as Mr. Traill says. They weren't up-time. We had joint Girl Scouts meetings at St. Mary's in Grantville every now and then and nothing interesting ever happened at them. Except that the church had stained glass windows, which he thinks are abominations before the Lord."

"Good grief," Susanna said. "You could come to mass with me any time you're interested."

"It's not exactly the same if we're allowed to," Dominique said.

Susanna looked around. "Where's Marguerite?"

"She didn't think she should come with us. Sneaking into a mass—if she did that and somebody found out, it could get the duke into real political trouble with his supporters. She stayed down by the Latin School. We'll pick her up again on the way back."

"But she's not there," Susanna said. "I just came by. She wasn't there, nor her footman either."

"She can't have gone far."

Susanna threw up her hands and shrieked. "Ducos. Do you remember? Guys with knives! Look at your arm, Shae! It's still in a cast! Do you mean to tell me that you let the little duchess wander off by herself? Are you insane? Are you fools? You're ladies-in-waiting! That means that you're supposed to stay with her absolutely all the time! Now where in this godforsaken pit of vipers is she?"

This tirade aroused the footman from his contemplation of the sky. "We'd better go look," he said. "Now, young ladies, there's no need to panic, but we'd better go look." They started back down toward the main part of town.

They found her in front of the Convent of the Poor Clares, waving her hands at the footman who had stayed with her. Not a single assassin was in sight. Hamilton was sitting on the bottom step, holding his head in his hands, with one of the young men who had come to the morning sermon with Lisa Lund's family standing over him. The other young man was standing further out in the street, obviously keeping an eye out for them. He waved them down.

Susanna pulled away from the rest of the group and ran for the *Quartier Battant*, to bring Ruvigny and Bismarck to contribute what they could to the general confusion.

Everybody started to talk at once, which didn't help much.

"He was pressing unwanted attentions upon her," the footman said.

"He was actually trying to persuade me to marry him now rather than waiting for his father to write to Papa," Marguerite screeched.

"Good grief!" Shae exclaimed. "As if! Whatever gave him the idea that you would even think about marrying him?"

"Marriage without consent of the parents is an old Scottish tradition, I've heard," the man who had been standing in the street said. "Elope, have a blacksmith marry you over his anvil, and leave the families to deal with it, whether they want to or not."

"But Marguerite doesn't *want* to elope with him," Dominique said. "And anyway, even if it's a Scottish tradition, you can't do that in Burgundy. Or in France. Or in the USE. Scotland is a long way away from here and, anyway, he's Irish."

"I am *not* Irish." Hamilton recovered enough to lift his head and make that point. "I'm a Scottish Ulsterman. I will *never* be Irish."

"That's one thing you certainly have right." The man who had been in the street looked down at Hamilton. "I'm Con, by the way. That's my brother Dan over there, the one who isn't talking. He's a little shy about meeting new people. As for what you say, Mistress . . ." He nodded at Dominique, who hastily said, "Bell. Dominique Bell."

"Neither are such marriages fully legal in the Low Countries, Austria, the Italian states, or the Spanish Empire, to the best of my knowledge. Nor under the English law that governs Ulster, although the validity of clandestine marriages is still a matter of some controversy, particularly when one or both of the contracting parties is under the legal age of consent. The young duchess was expressing her opposition to the entire concept quite loudly. We heard the argument and came to the rescue, but were scarcely needed, as you can see from the condition of the young man's head."

"How did she do that?"

The question was reasonable, since Hamilton was probably double Marguerite's weight.

"Jumped off the fourth step up and knocked him over by landing hard against his shoulders," Con said. "We saw the whole thing. He wasn't expecting it and gave his skull a pretty good knock against that stone lion. Her footman kicked him to keep him down, but he dragged himself part way up anyhow. He must have a pretty hard head."

"Not for beer," Shae commented. "He's a sloppy drunk."

"Not a drunk," Hamilton growled. "I stick to beer. I don't like wine, nasty stuff, and Traill says that I can't have whisky."

Susanna came dashing back, Ruvigny and Bismarck in tow.

"Hi, Henri," Shae said. "Hamilton insulted Marguerite. Don't you have to have a duel with him now?"

"Don't be stupid," Marguerite said. "Henri has outgrown dueling."

Ruvigny frowned at Shae. "I don't have any intention of fighting a duel with him. I've fenced with him quite a lot in practice and he isn't good enough go through with a formal French duel to first blood. He has no finesse but he does have a lot of brute strength; no speed, but a pretty long reach. If we fought, it would be altogether too likely that one of us might kill the other because of his sheer incompetence."

"But he insulted her."

"I did *not* insult her," Hamilton said to Shae. "She is the Rohan heiress. Thus, I respect her, and I want to *marry* her. Even if I had to carry her all the way to Scotland to find someone willing to perform the wedding, I would not so much have touched her on the way. After all," he concluded, pleased with his own logic, "my future wife must be a virgin on her wedding night, and for me to violate her person before our marriage would make that impossible. I just wanted to make sure that there would *be* a wedding night."

The rest of them stared at him, each in his or her own way enraptured by this feat of logic.

"Maybe he didn't insult the duchess," Susanna said in a low, menacing, voice, "but he *did* smash the nativity scene that Marc gave me. I found it when I got back to the house after mass. I left the scraps with Madame Calagna. Mr. Traill says that he didn't do it, so there's no one else who might have."

"I don't just admit that," Hamilton said. "I take pride in my action, which follows in the footsteps of the great Presbyterian iconoclasts of the last century who were inspired by the sermons of John Knox."

Everyone else stood there silently for a minute.

"You know," Con said to Hamilton. "What you really need is a few whiskies." He looked at Ruvigny and Bismarck. "Things will obviously be unpleasant in the duke's household if you return there with him right now."

"Oh, yes," Marguerite said. "Please, don't anybody say a word about all of this to Papa or Madame Calagna. Papa will never let me set foot out of the house again."

"Also," Dominique added, "Shae and I will get in a lot of trouble for not being proper ladies-in-waiting and leaving you alone, and that will make trouble for Mom because she's in charge of us, and she's the one who said we could take a walk, and the duke might complain to the grand duke, and then he might decide that it's too much trouble to have up-timers on his payroll and Lisa and everyone could lose their jobs."

One of the footmen started to open his mouth.

"Don't," Dominique said. "Whatever you're thinking, don't say it. You would be in trouble, too."

"Did anyone see you knock Hamilton over?" Bismarck asked Marguerite.

"Nobody was close. Except us, that is. Nobody else. There haven't been many people out and about this morning. None close enough to hear that we were arguing. All the Catholics and Lutherans are probably at church or at home having Christmas dinner or something."

Ruvigny frowned. "All right," he said. "Those of you who were out for a walk, go home like nothing unusual happened. August and I go back to work, giving a most virtuous impression of two men who are completely unaware that anything unusual has happened. These two . . ." He nodded at the other men. ". . . will take Hamilton down to the *Quartier Battant* and give him a few shots of whisky. Tomorrow will be another day and we can figure out what to tell Rohan about all of this then."

CHAPTER 27

Besançon
December 1636–January 1637

By first dark, after his fourth shot of whisky, Hamilton was snoring, his head on the table.

"I can see why his tutor doesn't let him have it," Con commented. "Shall we load him up and be on our way?"

Dan nodded. They shouldered him between them, two friends walking another who had imbibed a bit too much in the way of holiday spirits to his bed. They were shortly joined by a half dozen other County Down men who had come on this little expedition with them, flopped Hamilton over a saddled horse, and left town. They wouldn't get far that evening, but the day after Christmas would be a great day for riding, since most of the rest of that part of the world that might come after them would also be recovering from more than a bit too much in the way of holiday spirits.

The next morning, Traill reported that Hamilton's bed was empty.

Rohan sent footmen out to find him. They returned, their hands also empty.

Ruvigny and Bismarck went to find Con and Dan, who somehow had never, they now realized, given their surname or the location of their lodgings. They also returned empty.

"The lying rascals," Ruvigny said.

"They agreed to take him for a couple of whiskies," Bismarck said. "I don't recall that there was a single word to the effect that they would bring him back. So perhaps 'lying' is not the correct term."

They eventually located the lodgings. The bill was paid up, so the landlord hadn't taken any particular interest in his renters' departure.

When the grand duke sent soldiers out on the hunt, they looked for a party of three, two of them Dutch officers who spoke English well and one a Scotsman, not a party of nine wild geese making their way back toward winter quarters, all the while chatting merrily in Gaelic. For, as one of the grizzled old non-coms now serving as a footman for Rohan said to another, "Well, the girl told me not to say whatever I was thinking. If they don't want to hear me say that for my part, I think those boys were Irish, then they won't hear it."

James Traill's reaction was serious apprehension about Clanboye's reaction to fact that he had misplaced his valuable charge. Bismarck advised him to write a letter to Ulster and then, given that he was probably correct in feeling deep concern about the consequences that would ensue if he returned to Ireland, inquire whether or not the church the Scots soldiers had founded in the *Quartier Battant* would be interested in having a full-time minister.

*　*　*

"It's too late to be having second thoughts," Con Oge O'Neill–Constantine, or Con the Younger–said.

His older brother Daniel frowned. "How long will he stay tractable? The boys did sort of put the fear of God in him, but still . . ."

"Make sure he doesn't get his hands on any money. Traill took care of all the practicalities for all of the Grand Tour, if I understand what he said. He has no idea how to survive on his own."

"What will Uncle Owen think of this? For that matter, what will the *Stadhouder* think of this?"

"You might as well ask what the king and queen will think of it? Or Archduchess Clara Isabella Eugenia? We knew from the start that this little enterprise would be one of those situations where it's a lot better to ask forgiveness than permission."

"Well, what are we going to do with him once we get him back to the Low Countries? We could send a really flowery letter to Clanboye. I suppose."

Con shook his head. "I've come to admire the terseness of radio style. Forget the flowers and flourishes. How about: 'You have our lands. We have your heir. Shall we talk?' "

Paris
December 1636–January 1637

Henry Gage and Lion Gardiner got into town as Rohan's observers, delegated to monitor what his brother and sister were up to beyond what Raudegen could observe from inside the household.

They soon encountered Sandrart, who was monitoring what the duchess and Candale were up to and had come back to the city for a few days for consultations with said siblings of the duke.

"What are they all up to, for that matter?" Gardiner asked. "Not just the specific Huguenots we're being employed to watch. What is the court doing? What is Turenne doing? Is anyone doing anything about Queen Anne's baby? What's the latest rumor that Richelieu may have survived the assassination? Who is doing what to whom or with whom in general?"

"It might be more efficient," Sandrart answered, "if we pooled our information and only sorted out what needs to go into the different reports to different bosses once we've collected it all."

Gage laughed.

But it wasn't such a bad idea.

SECTION IV

February 1637-July 1637

Virginia DeMarce

CHAPTER 28

Laubach
February 1637

"It's too slick to ride this morning," Käthe protested. "Too slick for a hunt up in the hills. Why don't you put it off. Take a rifle and walk."

"I want to take advantage of this bright weather. Conditions won't improve until spring and spring's been coming late these last few years. Today's frost will go off as soon as the sun gets a little higher."

"No, the cold is too sharp; there will still be slick spots in the shade."

"Glänzer is sure-footed, even on the narrow trails."

"He a horse, not an acrobat." She didn't care for her husband's showy gelding. But she bit her lip. Anything else that she might say would just make him more determined to go out.

The gamekeepers came back late that afternoon with the news that they had to shoot the horse.

And with Albert Otto's body on an improvised stretcher.

She had been fully prepared for a broken leg.

Not for a broken neck.

At least the lawyers had insisted that he draw up a will.

She sent one of the footmen for the minister, another for the steward, and started to reckon up mentally how many letters of notification she would be expected to write in her own hand and how many she could leave to Albert Otto's secretary.

Besançon
February 1637

"Why did the grand duke have to send them off again?" Marguerite pouted. "They had scarcely gotten back."

Carey Calagna sighed. "You friends are employed by the grand duke. They go where he sends them. In this instance, to Savoy."

She thought that Ruvigny's Danish "king's daughter" had not been sorry to see her new husband removed from the immediate orbit of *la petite Marguerite*, who was more than slightly possessive about her old friend. Much in the way a sister might be possessive when an older brother who had spoiled her all his life decided to marry, but still possessive. Noticeably possessive. There had been some tension during the holidays. Mild, but real. By the time the Savoy expedition returned in the spring, Marguerite would have adjusted. She hoped.

Paris
February 1637

"She has never liked her sister-in-law," Raudegen said. "At present . . ."

He and Marc were talking in a tavern. Not a low tavern. Not a dive, filled with suspicious characters. Nobody was skulking around. It was a quite nice, middle-class, tavern in one of the suburbs of Paris, with most of the tables taken by quite nice middle-class people who were entirely preoccupied with their own business and discussing the price of construction bricks, their sister's most recent miscarriage, how long it was going to take the bishop to assign a new priest to the parish of Ste. Barbe, or boring the rest of the diners with repetitions of what a clever thing little Mimi said the day before.

For surreptitious discussions, it was ideal. Nobody for at least a quarter-mile in all directions cared in the least about what someone else might be talking about, whereas the things the residents did talk about on a daily basis were so utterly tedious and repetitious that even Gaston's most dedicated snoops, having acquired much more information than they ever wanted about baby Marie's teething agonies, the cheap *hors d'oeuvres* served after Madame Clisson's funeral, or the low quality of service being provided by Jeanson's Hinges now that young Pierre had taken the business over from the old man, had long since given up in despair and gone to exercise surveillance in low dives along the docks of the Seine where there was more hope of detecting villainous spies.

As long as Marc and Raudegen stuck with pronouns, using 'she' in place of 'Mademoiselle Anne de Rohan' for example, there was no way to distinguish the subject of their conversation from any of the other conversations rattling along at the surrounding tables. So Raudegen paused a moment and then repeated, "She has never liked her sister-in-law at all." Within a space of fifteen minutes, he managed to convey that the duc de Rohan's rather lamentable wife, who had been openly keeping company with the *comte* de Candale for the past several months, was most recently spotted at the rural château of her father, the very wealthy Maximilien de Béthune, duc de Sully, and, moreover, was believed to be pregnant by Candale. To be pregnant by Candale again, given the son she already had.

All of which Raudegen said in such a way that he could well have been talking about the reprehensibly-behaved sister of a local wax chandler or textile merchant.

Marc occasionally interjected a suitably shocked, but mild, exclamation, as if he were a youthful nephew being introduced to the local scandals.

249

There was nothing mild about the things that Anne de Rohan was saying about her older brother's wife. Even 'furious' scarcely applied. "At least, there is no possible way that she can assert that this coming bastard is a legitimate Rohan heir." Mademoiselle Anne was, in her early fifties, still a vigorous woman who retained all the stubbornness that had led her to insist on being imprisoned with her mother after the end of the siege of La Rochelle several years earlier.

"There is only one blessing I can see," she said to Soubise, "namely, that Henri has sent a letter authorizing me to begin the process of searching for a suitable bride for you. I don't have the slightest idea what finally moved him to agree to your marrying; he's always wanted to see *Maman*'s estates fall back to his own heirs after your death rather than let you establish a permanent cadet line of the family. I remember how grudging he was about accepting her will. He can't have already heard about that woman's pregnancy when he wrote: I hadn't heard it myself before Christmas. I know the genealogies of every Huguenot family of appropriate lineage in France and I will begin at once, but there's a sickening shortage of eligible unmarried and potentially fertile women among them. I may be reduced to praying for the untimely death of someone's current husband."

✳ ✳ ✳

Raudegen informed Marc as to every wealthy Huguenot household he knew that the duchess and Candale had visited on their peregrinations of the past few months and how each of them had responded to her constant fund-raising efforts. "If only," he said, gritting his teeth, "she and Candale had not peeled away before we got to Besançon from Paris last fall, but had continued to accompany the rest of the group the way she was *supposed* to, it might be possible to produce some coloration that she was temporarily reconciled to Rohan and the child is legitimate. As things stand, it is generally known to everyone interested in the matter that she never showed up in Besançon at all."

Raudegen clearly still took their failure to deliver the package containing *one recalcitrant duchess in early middle age* to its prescribed address as a serious dereliction of his duty and an insult to both his honor and his competence, even though Ruvigny and Bismarck were the ones who had actually been sent to do the job.

"You know," Marc said mildly. "There's no way the little seed pearl would ever have stood for that."

Besançon
March 1637

In early March, Marc wandered unheralded back into Besançon from wherever he had been. He refused to either confirm or deny that it was France, but delivered a large packet of correspondence from Soubise, from Mademoiselle Anne, from Raudegen.

He was glad that he wouldn't have to be in the room to see the duke's face when he read what they had to say.

He hoped fleetingly that the Creator was as merciful as Gerry Stone believed Him to be, rather than more along the lines advocated in Geneva. If so, perhaps *la petite Marguerite* would not learn the latest disillusioning stories about her mother. Not that she harbored many illusions, but these might impinge not only on her emotions as a daughter but also on her status as the Rohan heiress. If Raudegen's suspicions in regard to what Soubise and Anne were planning panned out . . . Things could get dicey.

He only managed a few hours with the object of his affections, given everything else people were wanting him to do. He spent quite a bit of time meeting with the grand duke. He did finally have time to tell her that he and his father had found a perfect placement for her in the USE, in the household of Amalie Elisabeth, regent of Hesse-Kassel, Calvinist.

"She is politically influential and has many friends," he said with enthusiasm. "Her surviving girls are a bit young yet, but within a few years, when you should be at the height of your abilities as a designer, they will be coming into society. In Magdeburg, you will have access to all the latest up-time fashion influences. And the landgravine is willing for me to use her household as a place to stay when I have errands in the USE, so we'll see each other more. Part of the time you will have to follow her to Kassel, of course, but much of the year she is in Magdeburg, and Papa will try to persuade her to make you a permanent part of the establishment she maintains in the national capital."

"What's going to happen," Susanna asked, suddenly off-topic, "given all the rumors, if Cardinal Richelieu gets resurrected, goes back to the *Palais-Cardinal*, and the Real Cat suddenly comes running out from under a bush and welcomes him home? Considering the cat who was in all the newspapers."

Marc cocked his head to one side. "I hope that the newspapers will have forgotten all about the cat in such an eventuality. At least, Denis and I bought back quite a few sort-of-Siamese cats and, with all the publicity, he made a good profit on selling the extras. Everything could be sort of smudged, if necessary, the way that artists do with charcoal drawings. Or, sometimes, Gerry calls it *airbrushed*. Fuzzed. Fogged. Sufficient unto the day is the evil thereof. I think you can pray Psalm 32:7 on my behalf for a while, because I suspect I'll need it."

Carrying even larger packets of confidential correspondence, he kissed her several times and went back to France, shrouded in paternal admonitions not to do anything to bring himself to the attention of Gaston's men or cause them to sharpen their focus when they looked in his direction. He called upon Soubise only to discover that Raudegen was in Brussels.

* * *

The weather stayed horrible. The girls mostly stayed indoors, Marguerite busy with lessons from her father, Shae busy with the materials she needed to prepare for her correspondence course final exams to get a degree from Calvert High School in Grantville in June, and Dominique because her mother told her so.

"It would have been nice," Susanna said, "if Marc had asked me if I wanted to be in the landgravine's household. He treats me like a package that needs to be delivered: pick it up here and drop it off there. I guess I should go, though, since his father has taken so much trouble over it."

The follow-up letter from Leopold Cavriani contained detailed information, and indicated that someone would be in Besançon, probably in early May, to act as Susanna's escort.

The girls debated quite a bit as to whether the coming escort might be Colonel Raudegen, but as they had no data whatsoever on which to base their discussions, even that topic of conversation petered out, and they went back to enduring a spring that promised to be as dreary as the winter.

Virginia DeMarce

CHAPTER 29

Besançon
April 1637

The repercussions of Hamilton's disappearance seriously ate into the time Rohan had available to focus on the deeper meaning of the works of Dr. Seuss. "I do sort of wonder who those young men were and what they've done with Hamilton," Carey said, as she worked her way through the latest completed section of *Les Futuriens*. The duke's reflections on *Green Eggs and Ham* included notes on xenophobia when it came to foodstuffs, tied to reflections on the experiences of young gentlemen on the Grand Tour.

"I doubt he's come to any harm," he answered. "As we continued to investigate, we found that one of them introduced himself to Madame Lund with his full given name as Constantine. And they were Dutch. We know that the Cavrianis are closely allied with the Huygens family, so the name may indicate that these two young men are in some way related to Constantijn Huygens. The grand duke's intelligence analysts have therefore concluded that the whole matter had something to do with English politics, since Hamilton's abductors also spoke English well and the Huygens have not only mercantile but also diplomatic ties in London."

* * *

Gerry Stone, who for once had managed to get in two fairly uninterrupted semesters of study at Jena, wandered into town late in the month to once more try doing his familial duty by representing the "face of Lothlorien" during Grand Duke Bernhard's deeply desired smallpox vaccination campaign—this time along with Sophia's brother, the teenaged Danish not-a-prince, Waldemar. He also brought frisbees or, to be accurate, one up-time plastic frisbee imprinted with an advertising slogan for the grand duke's museum and numerous new down-time made frisbees, shaped of boiled leather and then covered with lacquer to keep damp from seeping in and changing the shape, for his friends to play with. His popularity soared.

* * *

The single longest portion of *Les Futuriens* focused on Dr. Seuss' two most serious philosophical works, which were obviously *Horton Hatches the Egg* ("at least it's obvious according to the duke," Carey said to Kamala over lunch one day) and *Horton Hears a Who*, which brought, at least from Rohan's perspective, a much matured and more sophisticated expression of the thoughts that Seuss had first presented in the much earlier *500 Hats of Bartholomew McCubbin*. The egg required extensive consideration, not only of the importance of keeping one's word faithfully, as spoken by the elephant, and irresponsible parenthood as demonstrated by Mayzie, but also of the sequence of Roman "good emperors" from Nerva through Marcus Aurelius and the concept of adoption as a means for monarchical systems to ensure competent successors. Rohan deliberated for some time about the tactfulness of bringing it up, but did finally add a paragraph in regard to the selection by Gustavus Adolphus of Prince Ulrik of Denmark as, for all practical purposes, his adoptive successor as well as prospective son-in-law.

Carey listened and nodded her head.

Shae and Dominique finished reading the semi-final draft of the *Futuriens* treatise. "What do you think?" Kamala asked. "Since both of you are both veterans of 'Dr. Seuss childhoods'?"

"Honestly?" Shae answered. "None of this would have ever occurred to me."

"Often," Carey commented, "an outside perspective can be useful. Maybe it should have occurred to us what we were really teaching you when we read these books out loud."

"I think," Dominique said, "that we should keep on reading Dr. Seuss to the little guys."

Laubach, Solms–Laubach
April 1637

Käthe had never before considered the possibility that there might be some merit to the Catholic practice of confession. Even Lutherans went to confession, for that matter. Whatever the theology of the matter, confession at least meant that if you desperately wanted to talk about something, there was somebody who had to listen to you. A confessor was a captive audience, so to speak. Someone to whom you could speak; to whom, even, you were supposed to speak. Someone who wasn't allowed to tell anyone else what you said.

Someone she didn't have. The minister at the church was not a man who invited confidences. She certainly couldn't say anything to Albert Otto's sisters or aunts. Her companion and ladies in waiting were all from lesser noble families of the region, dependent upon one or another of the branches of the Solms family, and certainly could not be depended upon not to spread gossip. She wasn't the type to make a confidante of her maid or dressmaker.

The seal of the confessional that made it impossible, or at least contrary to the rules, for the confessor to gossip about what he heard had been a truly brilliant idea upon someone's part.

She could talk to one of her sisters, she supposed, if one of them were here. Charlotte Louise might even listen. What she would probably get from Amalie Elisabeth would be something along the lines of, "Pull yourself together and don't be so morbid."

In any case, they weren't here, no letter was safe from being opened and read in the ordinary postal system, and if she asked for a secure courier, the children's guardians, all of them brothers-in-law of Albert Otto, would want to know why. She would have to justify the expense. They would tell their wives and then all of her sisters-in-law, to whom she certainly couldn't talk about it, would also want to know.

What should she have done? Was it her fault? Should she have tried harder, that horrible morning in February, to persuade him not to ride out? Had she, in her heart, stopped urging him because she was sure he would become more defiant? Or had she stopped urging him because she was so tired, tired, tired of eternally, everlastingly, trying to coax him into doing the sensible thing, whatever the sensible thing might be on a given day or in a given set of circumstances? Had she been derelict in her duty as a wife?

Was it her fault?

There was no one she could ask.

CHAPTER 30

Besançon
May 1637

The beginning of May brought a huge sack of mail with all sorts of news. Mademoiselle Anne wrote that she had found a suitable chaperone for Marguerite.

"A Madame de la Rochefaton," Rohan said. "The family is from Poitou, old Protestant nobility. That makes her a good choice, in the sense that no other family will take too much offense at the appointment. She is a childless widow; her husband, who was from a cadet branch, served under my command in the 1622 campaign. Anne has also chosen three girls as ladies-in-waiting: de Brémond, d'Albin, and des Brisay—all suitable families but not of sufficient importance to threaten the status of anyone else. Anne says that they should arrive within a month."

Marguerite looked . . . hostile to the prospect.

"Kamala Dunn has made some decisions also," Carey said. "Shae's going to the University of Prague."

"I don't want her to leave," Marguerite said.

"If I may say so, it's not something that you can control. She's been doing a favor for you; not you one for her."

Rohan motioned his daughter to silence with his head and motioned Carey to continue with the hand that wasn't holding a coffee cup.

"It will work out. Kamala's also sending Shaun to her parents in Grantville. She won't need a nanny at all anymore."

"You will stay with me, though, won't you?"" Marguerite asked. "And Dominique."

Carey shook her head. "Dominique's going to Magdeburg. I've cobbled together the first year's tuition by selling my up-time barber kit to some really rich collector named Fugger whose agent was willing to pay through the nose. She'll board with the Washaws. Between the Imperial College of Science, Engineering, and Technology and the up-timer-designed new hospital there, she can get her medical degree without having to run the gauntlet in Grantville. It won't be as prestigious as Grantville/Jena, but the stress reduction will be worth it."

"But . . ."

"She was doing you a favor, too, Marguerite. Just as Shae was. It was temporary that they were here. Temporary."

"You could stay, though."

Carey shook her head. "Ashlyn's old enough that she would be okay as a latchkey kid, but Joe's just turning four, so I still need full time childcare. I'm keeping Ashlyn here. I'm not ready to send her off to a boarding school, though I'll have to, I guess, in two or three years. If I can find the money. For now, she's doing fine in the day school for girls. So I'm going to have to find an apartment and a babysitter once your new chaperone arrives. It would be a real imposition if I asked Kamala to continue to share and keep having my kids underfoot once she's an empty-nester."

"Bring your children here," Rohan suggested. "I'm going to have to rent the other half of this house in any case, with more people coming. My absentee wife managed in the course of her peregrinations through the French countryside, before she settled in with her father a couple of months ago, to run down and collect a lot of the back rents and dues owing to us from the estates in Brittany and forwarded a bank draft, so I can manage the expansion—just barely, but I can manage it."

"Won't Madame de Rochefaton resent that?"

"You aren't here as my household's chatelaine. You work for the grand duke. You are correct that your chaperonage of Marguerite was described as a temporary measure from the beginning. We will simply make that clear to Madame de Rochefaton that you are a special tutor in English and up-time matters. I will locate your family's apartment in such a way that she cannot imagine that you are in any way her subordinate. What is your term? 'Gover?' "

"Gofer," Carey corrected absentmindedly. "To go for something or someone. A runner of miscellaneous errands."

He patted her hand. "See how impossible it would be for me to remain *au courant* in regard to the modern, post-Ring of Fire, world without my resident expert on all things up-time. So that is settled.

"Now as for the rest of what Anne has been doing, so far, she has been unsuccessful in finding a bride for my brother. She complains that there is a real shortage of marriageable daughters among Huguenot families of ducal and princely rank. She is almost hoping, I believe, that some suitable lady will soon be widowed in an untimely fashion."

"Maybe she should cast her net wider. Too much inbreeding isn't a good thing. You could tell her to look in the Netherlands, or think about some young noblewomen of less than 'ducal and princely rank.' Up-time we used to tell each other, 'get your priorities straight.' Do you want him to get married for prestige or do you want him to get married to have kids and have a lot of little Rohan toddlers to bounce on his knees?"

"Soubise toddlers," the duke said, looking at his daughter. "Marguerite is the heiress of Rohan."

*   *   *

Carey had no intention of precipitating a crisis with her suggestion, but by that casual remark, she achieved it unwittingly. If anything in this whole process had seriously interested her, it would have been the idea that they might dump a bit of their preoccupation with rank—not only look beyond the high nobility of the Huguenot community in France to

261

consider someone from the Netherlands, perhaps, but, even more, that they might even consider a young woman of less than 'ducal and princely' rank.

Rohan, however, passed on the suggestion in his next letter to Anne with the stipulation that, of course, the suitable young woman must be Calvinist and of appropriate rank, but as head of the family, he would not require that she be French in order for the match to obtain his approval. If he himself had contemplated the possibility of Eva of Anhalt-Dessau's brother for Marguerite, then someone from the Low Countries or the German Calvinist high nobility for Soubise was worth considering.

* * *

Later that month, Ruvigny with his Danish Sophia, Matt Trelli and Marcie Abruzzo, Bismarck, and a former cardinal of Lorraine trailed into Burgundy from Savoy, several weeks later than they had been expected, foiled in their return plans by lingering cold weather and excessive snow cover.

He found Rohan maintaining his daily routine as one of Grand Duke Bernhard's loyal cadre of administrators and continuing to stalk the deep inner meaning of the works of Dr. Seuss as he completed the manuscript revisions.

Ruvigny suspected that the duke's calm was only on the surface. Henri de Rohan could do a good public face. Amiable he might be, and restrained in his exhibitions of bad temper, but that also was 'earned behavior' as Gerry Stone would say. Below the surface was the inborn assurance of someone who knew most thoroughly who he was. Not the king; not an independent ruler like Bernhard; not in essence a feudal subordinate in France; just the embodiment of being Rohan.

There was enough going on that if Rohan's public face ever wavered, he would have reasonable excuses. They had already seen *la petite Marguerite's* young up-time ladies-in-waiting out into the world, and Carey Calagna was preparing to bow out of her role as chaperone for

Marguerite, though not, it appeared, to the considerable resentment of Benjamin Priolo, out of Rohan's household. The secretary had come to regard the up-time woman as a potential obstacle to his ambitions should *something happen* and the duke return to France.

La petite Marguerite was seriously unhappy with the prospect of an unknown *Mme.* de Rochefaton arriving from France as an 'appropriate' chaperone (her *Tante* Anne's word, *Tante* having chosen the lady) and the selected young, equally unfamiliar, noble Huguenot ladies-in-waiting who were looming upon her horizon, also chosen by *Tante.*

Carey Calagna, ably seconded by Kamala Dunn, kept pointing out that there was no way that Dominique and Shae could have stayed, that the ambivalent and ambiguous status of Susanna Allegretti in the household was only possible as long as it was both small and not particularly socially active, so she, too, would go as soon as someone appeared to escort her to the USE capital city, and that, ultimately, the little daisy of a Rohanette should grow up and get over it.

Marguerite's freedom of movement was greatly curtailed by having no ladies-in-waiting to accompany her. She complained at supper one evening that if the Huguenot ladies were unavoidable, she at least wanted to get married to someone, anyone at all, before they arrived, because as a matron she could give orders to her *companion* rather than being under her *chaperone*'s supervision.

Rohan just looked at her, a tired, tense, stressed, expression on his face.

Paris
May 1637

Anne de Rohan was calculating some odds. She had not found a satisfactory wife for Soubise yet, but her mind was already circling around the possibility that if she did, and if Soubise should beget a son, they might have Henri's *alleged* daughter Marguerite declared illegitimate. It might have to wait until after her older brother's death, but according to the up-time encyclopedias, that would happen next year—albeit in a battle that was unlikely to be fought in this timeline. Still, a fair number of people were nonetheless rather fatalistically expecting that he would drop dead on schedule. From what she had heard, he was among them.

Just in case, she notified Mme. de Rochefaton and the three highly appropriate potential ladies-in-waiting to delay their departure for Burgundy until certain circumstances clarified themselves.

And that was not the only possibility. The ploy with Hamilton had been fairly successful. Perhaps she could once again insert herself into the matter of Marguerite's marriage prospects. She picked up her pen.

Laubach, Solms-Laubach
May 1637

Käthe looked at her hands. She had bitten her fingernails into the quick. Again. While she was asleep, she supposed, even though she wore gloves to bed at night, trying to prevent it. Maybe if she strapped the gloves on, somehow, so she couldn't pull them off during those restless, half-asleep, hours before dawn . . .

Surely the apothecary would have some kind of salve. Also, something bitter to paint on the tips of her fingers, to shock her aware whenever she started to gnaw on them like some little rodent, some vermin.

Besançon
June 1637

At the beginning of June, the grand duke, his wife, and most of their entourage trailed off in the direction of Nancy and the major "What is Gaston going to do and what can we do about it?" conference that had been called by the duchess of Lorraine, and her consort, leaving Rohan once more behind to watch the domestic situation and ensure that all papers were pushed in the direction they needed to go.

Where Rohan stayed, his daughter stayed also. "What has happened to Mme. de Rochefaton and those girls?" Marguerite asked at supper one evening. "Shouldn't they have arrived by now?"

Rohan thought about it. They should have arrived by now. He wrote a memo directing Priolo to double-check.

*   *   *

Marguerite emitted a truly impressive squeal.   "Susanna, look!"
"What?"
"*Tante* Anne has found out who I married in the other world. She says he is nice and pleasant. Handsome and an excellent dancer. So not at all resembling Horrid Hamilton. Since he successfully begat children upon my body in that other world, she wrote him and asked whether he would be interested in converting to Calvinism, marrying me, and duly providing those children in this one. He replied and didn't precisely refuse. She's enclosed a letter from him to me, and suggests that I answer it."

Susanna winced. "I suggest . . . in fact, although it is not my place to do so, I absolutely insist . . . that you take this to your father right now."

"No, I won't. He won't let me answer. He insists absolutely that I have to have a Protestant husband. Just because this man is Catholic now, it doesn't signify that he always will be. According to *Tante*, he didn't precisely say that he would never convert. I'm going to answer it."

Susanna recognized that defiant expression.   She grabbed the letter with both hands, opened her mouth, and shrieked **Caaarrreeeeeyyy**.

*   *   *

"This last book is very different from the others," Rohan said.
"It's the same illustration style, but it wasn't aimed at kids."

The duke smiled. "Cicero also wrote on old age. *De Senectute*. Since the beginning of time, I suppose, men have given thought to becoming 'the creature that walks on three legs.' But I would not have thought of *You're Only Old Once* as a title."

"It's a joke," Carey said. "It's a lot more common for people to say that 'you're only young once.' The idea is that you should make the most of it, whatever it is, while you have the chance."

"That may be a commendable idea," Rohan said. "Related to *carpe diem*, I presume. I am afraid, though, that after all this effort I am more inclined to embrace another of Seuss' maxims: 'They say I'm old-fashioned, and live in the past, but I sometimes think progress progresses too fast!' What do you say?"

"He wasn't the first person to say that. And you're not that old, either."

The peace of Rohan's study was pierced by a shrill, clarion-volume, voice. They dropped everything and ran.

There were no deaths or serious injuries—just two girls, one of them holding a packet of papers.

"Look!" Susanna shook the letter. "Look, look. Look at this!"

"See Jane run," Carey muttered.

The other three looked at her blankly.

"Okay, bad sense of humor. What's the matter, Susanna honey?"

"It's what Marguerite's aunt is trying to get her to do." She swallowed. "Err, Your Grace, that is." She pushed the papers at Rohan as if they were burning her fingers.

He looked at them; then at the girls. "Come into my study," he ordered.

Marguerite turned. Susanna followed on tiptoe. Except when he was giving lessons to Marguerite, the duke didn't allow any of the younger residents of the *Hôtel de Buyer* to enter the Sacred Sanctuary of Seuss, as Gerry Stone had started to call it.

"What do you want to *do* about *Tante*'s latest ploy?" An hour had passed and as far as Marguerite could tell, they were no closer to a decision.

Her father frowned. "Perhaps I should let you reply to her and to this Chabot man as if you were going behind my back. That might elicit some information . . ."

Susanna prudently refrained from mentioning that Marguerite had been prepared to do that without permission, but Carey guessed as much.

Virginia DeMarce

CHAPTER 31

Paris
May 1637

"The duchess and Candale haven't contacted Mirepoix, as far as I know." Joachim Sandrart dropped that into common pool of data that they had gathered over the previous two weeks. He added nothing in regard to his speculations about why this might be or whether they might yet still do so. One agreed principle of this cooperative venture was that they would share only information. "Just the facts, Ma'am," he had said, quoting an up-timer acquaintance. Sharing interpretation of the facts might skirt perilously close, on occasion, to betraying confidences received from their employers.

"Neither has Mademoiselle Anne," Gardiner said. "Not as far as I can tell."

He also carefully refrained from stating his speculations. Nonetheless, now each of them was in a considerably better position because . . .

The first wife of Mirepoix had been the younger daughter of Sully and consequently a sister of the *duchesse de* Rohan. She had also served Anne of Austria as an honorary lady in waiting. However, after the bitter separation between Mirepoix and Louise (who had her problems--Sully had offered a huge dowry to get her married off at all) and Mirepoix' subsequent rapid remarriage after her death . . . No one was certain which of the developing Rohan factions he would throw his support to. If neither had even bothered to send out feelers, then the answer might be neither—something they could speculate upon independently and include in their respective reports to their respective employers.

Gage, who was an English recusant Catholic, added some facts concerning some gossip which was based upon some rumors pertaining to Richelieu, Tremblay, and the king's reliance, or possible lack of reliance, upon the *Dévots*, and whether this would lead to harsher restrictions upon the Huguenots, no matter which internal faction they might opt for.

They parted with all three of them feeling considerable satisfaction with the new system.

*   *   *

That was about the time that Marc managed to run Raudegen down for an urgent conversation.

"Soubise hasn't been talking to me much lately," Raudegen said. "If this has been coming up toward a boil, that's not surprising, since his brother and Bernhard put me in his household and I'm quite sure he doesn't want them to find out. I'll ask around among some of the servants. Meanwhile, if you could make a run up to Brussels with a few things I'd like your Aunt Alis to bring to the attention of Huygens personally when she has the opportunity . . . "

"He's already been through Brussels on his way to Lorraine," Marc said. "I saw it in yesterday's paper. You must have missed it because you spent the whole day on horseback."

"Oh," Raudegen said. "Shit. Well, I'll send a letter to Mme. Cavriani. How do you feel about joining Bernhard in Lorraine by way of Besançon?"

Besançon
June 1637

Since Susanna was still there, Marc felt that "by way of Besançon" was a fine idea. He didn't get there before the Burgundian delegation left for Lorraine and Rohan told him to stay put rather than follow it, so lacking other instructions, he stayed for a few days, bunking with Waldemar and Gerry Stone at the otherwise-unoccupied Ruvigny apartment, Henri and Sophia being in Nancy with Bernhard.

After months of nearly non-stop running, during which he had occasionally dropped in, left a packet of diplomatic correspondence, kissed his dearly beloved almost-fiancée a couple of times, and dropped out again, he finally got clued in by Gerry that it was high time that he sat down and actually listened to her for a couple of hours.

"I like all the people here," Susanna said to Gerry. "Most of them, anyway. I've learned a lot since our expedition from Brussels brought me here. I've learned about French court life in Paris from Marguerite, even though I've never experienced it. I've learned about how the up-time was from Dominique and Shae, even though I'll never be there. Knowing those things may do me a lot of good as time goes by, if I'm ever in France or Grantville; I realize that."

She pulled one foot up under her skirts and turned around on the bench to face Marc.

"I don't like that I'm not working; that I'm really living on your father's charity. It's not as if any woman in Burgundy, the way things are now, actually needs a court seamstress. Not even Marguerite. Or could afford the kind of work I do, even if she wanted it. Not even Grand Duchess Claudia, who has a couple of seamstresses of her own in any case, who make the things she does need. Mama worked for one of her Italian ladies-in-waiting, of course, when we were still in Tyrol. Those were magnificent clothes. But Mama rarely did anything for the Grand Duchess herself. They certainly weren't so close that Claudia would have brought Mama to Burgundy as part of her own staff."

At which point Carey wandered through the room and sent her off to do something for Marguerite.

It took Marc a couple more days, but he finally managed some time and an alcove.

"Tell me your troubles." He pulled her onto his lap and kissed her again. "All your troubles."

"I've not been asked to make many clothes for anyone in the duke of Rohan's household. There are . . . well . . . budget issues and Marguerite had to leave all that lovely fabric and trimming we bought in Paris behind when we escaped. The up-time women that Grand Duke Bernhard has hired wear clothes that are incredibly plain. None of them have that 'you can only make a public appearance in it once' mentality. Shae says that there were women like that in the up-time world, but none of them ever lived in Grantville, and even a *grande dame* like Mrs. Simpson won't have much of it. She'll be more along the lines of 'you buy something that's high quality and then you wear it and wear it and wear it again' than going the flashy route. Shae says that Mrs. Simpson's style is *classic*. Did you know that the up-timers even classified the ways that women chose to dress?"

"Um," Marc answered. "No. Nobody ever mentioned that to me."

"Well, they did. Almost like library catalogs. I can tell you all about it some other time."

Marc hoped, deeply hoped, that *some other time* equated to *some far distant day.*

"And even if I had made any connections into the household of the grand duchess, she's had two babies since she and Bernhard got married and wasn't inclined to spend much on clothes she couldn't wear for more than a few months, even if they were having fancy court functions, which mostly they don't, because Bernhard doesn't have any extra money and the regents in Tyrol have put her on a strict allowance. She hardly has any ladies-in-waiting at all because there aren't many Lutherans who want to come from the USE and there aren't many Catholics who want to come from Tyrol, and there isn't room in their house down in the *Quartier*

Battant for many attendants, even if they did want to come. It's not like Bernhard has a proper palace."

"No elaborate court functions; two babies in three years, no ladies-in-waiting, no fancy clothes," Marc summed up. "Not to mention that you haven't met her. Got it."

"Plus, all the wealthy merchants are trying to pretend that they don't have any money so the grand duke can't collect it in taxes, so they aren't letting their wives buy expensive clothes either. I made some things for Sophia, both before they went to Savoy and since they got back, but that won't last. Now that Ruvigny has enough money to support an ambassadorial lifestyle, he'll be getting some more prestigious diplomatic appointment to a court somewhere else and they'll be moving away." Susanna jumped up off his lap. "I've got to get ready for taking Marguerite to her latest tutor. World geography, this time."

✳ ✳ ✳

"She has a point," Gerry said that evening after dinner. "Even the wives of Bernhard's high army and civilian officers haven't been in a position to buy expensive or extravagant clothes, because the grand duke was barely managing to pay them, given his viewpoint that the enlisted ranks should also get their share of whatever payroll is available. Erlach's wife, who might have set some kind of a dressing-up mark for the rest of them, is also his cousin, and stayed in Switzerland to manage their properties. Now that Bernhard has money again, and his officers *are* getting paid, they're cautious about spending it because there's no telling how long the good times will last. The whole Burgundian luxury goods market is in a slump and likely to stay there for a while.

"Also," he added, "As far as the whole 'learning to live among Calvinists' project is concerned, Rohan's ménage here is about as far from typical as anyone could get. You would have been ahead to send her up to Frederik Hendrik's court, the way she wanted you to do in the first place." He closed his mouth and then opened it again. "If you asked me, I'd say that you were at least a little bit inconsiderate and more than a little bit selfish to haul her along with you when you picked her up in Brussels. She hasn't even gotten to so much as see the inside of a normal Reformed church–just the duke's little open-to-the-public-on-the-Sabbath foyer in his house and the little Scots thing down by the river where Traill has planted himself until the whole fiasco with Hamilton has sort of slipped people's minds."

"Has anyone spotted Hamilton?" Marc asked.

"There have been a lot of supposed sightings. According to Ron, probably the most reliable one was in Antwerp."

"Antwerp? Antwerp!"

"Wild geese. Supposedly, he was with a couple of their officers in a *salle*. They were trying to improve his swordsmanship."

"Oh. Irish politics. I don't believe for a minute that Hamilton's in Antwerp. No way would Fernando and Frederik Hendrik put up with that."

* * *

Marc and Susanna finally managed to find another bit of time to talk. "You know that there is a place for you with Amalie Elizabeth, the landgravine-regent of Hesse-Kassel. She's Calvinist."

"I am tired," Susanna said, "genuinely, meaningfully, tired, of being picked up like one of your packages of diplomatic correspondence and moved around from one spot on the map to another according to your whims."

Marc hadn't thought about it like that. "I've told you that in the landgravine's household, you will get to work for what my father calls 'the pick of the world's Calvinists.' Or at least of the USE's Calvinists. The only possible better situation for you would be in The Hague."

"Then why didn't you let me go to The Hague in the first place?"

Marc decided to duck that issue. "Even though she moves her household back and forth between Hesse and Magdeburg, the landgravine spends most of her time in the USE capital rather than Kassel. She has daughters who are growing into adolescence. She had equally prominent friends who have daughters. That should be enough to satisfy the aspirations of even the most ambitious young fashion designer or court dressmaker. There will be young people in Kassel also. Aren't the Stones involved in making the Hessian university into the best?"

"That's in Marburg," Susanna snapped. "Not Kassel. Even if it were in Kassel, the young people at the university will be students. Pretty much by definition, students don't have money to spend. Oh, a few have well-to-do parents but most of them don't."

Susanna paused. "And as for the landgravine's daughter, 'growing into adolescence' is stretching things a bit. Amalie, the oldest, is eleven. Charlotte, the one you gave the kitten to—remember the girl? remember the kitten?—is ten. Little Elisabeth was born after the Ring of Fire. She can't be more than three or four."

"Maybe," Marc said, "you can adopt a long-term economic perspective."

"You," Susanna answered, "have to be the most exasperating man ever born on earth."

"My father and I already made the arrangements with the landgravine last fall. Before the cat caper and all that. I told you so then. She's already agreed to appoint you as a member of her household. I'm going to be using it as the base for my various comings and goings for a while. I've just been too busy to take you to her."

He didn't see Susanna for three entire days after that conversation.

All the other ladies of the Rohan household assured him that he was better off not seeing her until her temper had cooled down a bit.

Before he had a chance to talk to her, he got an emergency radio transmission from his father and headed off to The Hague, leaving a note behind.

"I do love him," Susanna said. "He can just be so desperately obtuse."

"You're contaminated," Carey answered. "By us. We up-timers have contaminated you."

"Plus," Kamala added, "you've grown up. How old were you when you met Marc? Eighteen? You're three years older now, and you haven't even spent much time together. That was the big problem with early marriages, up-time. A couple got married when they were kids. Then, after they had both finished growing up, one of them discovered that he, or maybe she, didn't much like the finished version of the other one. What do you really know about another? Are you in love with the real Marc Cavriani, or Marc-some-kind-of-a-romantic-idea-that-you've-built-up-in-your-mind?"

"I'm pretty sure," Susanna answered, "that I'm in love with Marc-whom-I-want-to-be-the-father-of-my-children."

"Have you talked about those children? About which church you're going to bring them up in? Since this Catholic/Calvinist split is so important to you?"

"Oh. I guess I assumed we'd do what everybody else does. Like the grand duke and grand duchess. Their boys will be Lutheran and the girls Catholic. So our daughters would be Catholic and our sons Calvinist."

"Hmm. I didn't know that, I guess." Kamala hummed,

Tea for two, and two for tea;
A boy for you, a girl for me.

"That's . . . strange," she continued. "How does the Catholic church deal with that arrangement? What will your confessor say? For that matter, will you be married by a priest or . . . Up-time, I know, the Catholic church insisted that it had to be a priest and the other person had to agree that all the kids would be Catholic. The old priest, Father O'Malley, the one before Father Mazzare, well, Cardinal Mazzare, was pretty fierce about that."

"What could they possibly do, though?" Susanna was bewildered. "If the families set the terms in the marriage contract, they're set. They could fuss, I guess. And it would be different in someplace like Spain, but that's

Spain. Or if someone like Ferdinand II was back as emperor in Austria, but he's dead. He didn't mess with marriage contract terms, though. He just expelled the Protestants and if they had Catholic husbands or wives who went with them, that was mostly their own problem."

Kamala fixed her with a firm gaze.

"Okay. So I haven't talked to Marc about it. About any of this."

"My advice is to take enough time in Magdeburg to think about it. My advice is that the time to talk about it, whatever "it" is, is definitely, totally definitely, before you marry the guy. Believe me, trust me, the voice of experience is speaking to you."

Just before the Lorraine delegation left, Grand Duke Bernhard had written to Colonel Raudegen and directed him, when feasible, to resume his escort duties for one Susanna Allegretti, this time to Magdeburg. "When you get there, stay put for a while," Bernhard directed. "I've heard a few rumors. Just stay there for a few weeks. I'll get in touch by radio from Nancy if there's anything else   I frantically need you   for"

CHAPTER 32

Paris
May 1637

Mademoiselle Anne remained focused on her most important task. The widow of the marquis de Boësse proved recalcitrant. Undeterred, she persisted.

Rohan's letter arrived. She read it, read it again, then re-read it.

Yes, it said what it seemed to say. She was no longer limited to searching within the Huguenot aristocracy for a bride for Soubise. The woman must fit the requirements Rohan had stated in regard to rank and religion, of course, but . . .

The consent of the head of House Rohan to *any* suitable marriage she arranged was implied in that casually worded letter, she decided. No more consultation would be necessary. Who might be a suitable possibility within these wider parameters? Suitable from her own political perspective. Suitable on the basis of the advantages it would bring to Benjamin.

She could safely ignore Rohan's suggestion that she look to the Netherlands. Even if it was not Frederik Hendrik himself, he must have conspired with the king and queen's harboring of that pestilent shrew Anne of Austria, that devious Italian cardinal Mazarin, and the demon-possessed infant who would someday in the future revoke the

Edict of Nantes, exiling and destroying the Huguenot nobility of France. Along with the rest of the Huguenots of France, of course.

Unless they converted to Catholicism. Which, the up-time encyclopedia informed her, Turenne had done. She spared only one bitter thought for Turenne, his brother, and the entire ruling family of Sedan. Complicit with the king in the Netherlands. Who had been a cardinal himself not too long ago. What else could anyone have expected? And the infanta. Who had married an ex-cardinal. For a few minutes, her thoughts revolved around nests of Spanish vipers.

Then she went into a flurry of activity, largely focused on the past year's collection of obituary notices for members of the German Protestant *Hochadel*. And smiled.

The unfortunate Albert Otto, count of Solms-Laubach, had toppled off his horse while hunting in February, leaving a widow. She, the newly widowed Katharina Juliana, née Gräfin von Hanau-Münzenberg, was in almost all ways the ideal bride for a man of Soubise's age.

She was thirty-three, so young enough to bear more children but not so young as to make him look like a fool.

She had already borne three children, two of them boys, healthy and surviving, so she was proven fertile.

She was Calvinist.

No reasonable person could complain about her rank. Katharina Juliana was a half-niece of Frederik Hendrik, the "second gentleman" in the Low Countries. That would even cover the "Netherlands" suggestion in Rohan's letter, if a person looked at it from the correct perspective.

And, she was a sister of Amalie Elisabeth, landgravine-regent of Hesse-Kassel and governor of the USE Province of Hesse. There was a wheel into which Mademoiselle Anne would be quite content to throw a spoke.

If there were need for some indication that God himself looked with favor upon this, she was, like her better-known sister in Hesse-Kassel, as fully fluent in French as she was in German.

Mademoiselle Anne had never heard of the grinch, but if anyone who knew him had seen her at this moment, the smile would have been familiar.

Katharina Juliana had not completed her mourning year yet, but . . . an inquiry could not hurt.

Soubise couldn't go courting. Things were quiet at the moment, the king having more pressing concerns, but still the odds were high that if he left France, Gaston would not let him return.

Mademoiselle Anne pounced.

Laubach, Solms-Laubach
June 1637

Käthe picked up what was bound to be another, if rather belated, letter of condolence upon the death of Albert Otto. She pulled up her list. This would be number two hundred and seventy-two, and she was up to date with her responses. Not a lot for someone of Albert Otto's rank, but he had not been well-known outside of the immediate region. She reached for her letter opener.

Mademoiselle de Rohan? She was not even an acquaintance. Why would she . . . ?

This was not a letter of condolence. Mademoiselle de Rohan did not even pretend to be sorry that Albert Otto was dead. *Praise and thanks be to the Lord our God*, Käthe thought, *that Albert Otto's meddling secretary, who is now the meddling secretary serving my sons' guardians, didn't open this.* Much less my companion. Much, much less any of the lawyers who are scurrying around Laubach, arranging how the county is to be administered until Gustav Wilhelm and Karl Otto come of age. Which, considering that Tavi will turn five this week, is going to be a while. Sixteen years of 'while,' stuck in Laubach. Sixteen years of 'while' during which I, who am neither regent nor guardian, watch the others cosset and coddle and hover over the boys, sixteen years of 'while' during which I inexorably grow old.

Somewhat less cosseting, coddling, and hovering would probably be the lot of Albertine Elisabeth, who wasn't an heir.

When would the men who complained about the uselessness of daughters notice that it wasn't women who had made the laws that excluded daughters from inheritance? When would they realize that they placed themselves in this dilemma and therefore had only themselves to blame? But that was a useless line of thought. It was unlikely to cross their minds until Princess Kristina grew up and pointed it out to them, hopefully having inherited a lot of her father's ability to slash right through traditional legal tangles.

She looked down at the letter that she had wrinkled up in her hand. Albert Otto's will didn't give her much room for independent action—probably because it had been drawn up by lawyers, irritating bourgeois academics that they were, immediately after their marriage. Lawyers, like preachers and professors, had a reprehensible tendency to think that women were useless because they didn't have academic credentials.

Which women could have if those same lawyers and preachers and professors had not, with some very few exceptions, prohibited women from attending the universities that issued them. Universities like Marburg.

Until the up-timers came to shake them out of it.

Too late for her.

She unwrinkled the paper and smoothed the letter out.

She added a number for it to her list, wrote one polite reply, worded as if it had indeed been a conventional letter expressing sympathies, thoughts, and prayers, and placed it, as usual, upon the desk of the *meddling secretary* for sealing and posting.

Then she wrote another one, got up, and went to her chamber. Three years ago, Albert Otto had bought her a sheet of the new "stamps" as a curiosity. Not a stamp, as she knew the word, but a sheet of perforated paper, a kind of pre-paid postage. She kept it in a little frame. It was not likely that anybody, not even the maid who dusted them along with all her other trinkets and keepsakes, would notice if the bottom row went missing. Most people did not take as much notice of such little irregularities as she herself did.

She folded the second letter, wrote the address in a hand as little like her own as she could manage, sealed it with a bit of plain candle wax without her signet ring, affixed one of the stamps—then, in case foreign postage was more expensive, a second one—and put it in the middle of the pile of finished outgoing mail on the secretary's desk.

She might come to regret this.

But it was bloody unlikely.

Mademoiselle Anne appeared to be a quite interesting person. Also, decisive. Not one who spent her nights wearing gloves so she would not to chew her own fingers off while her mind spent its days in an unending circle dance of guilt and regret about *might-haves* and *should-haves* and *if-I-only-hads*. Although it was said that French Huguenot artisans produced the finest gloves in the world, the best-fitted, with the thinnest, most flexible kidskin leather.

Whatever else one might think about Gustavus Adolphus, his new postal system was efficient.

Mademoiselle Anne expressed her delight that Katharina Juliana was willing to consider the possibility. She didn't define the apparently innocuous possibility she was writing about. It could have been a ladies' literary circle as far as her words went, now that she had been warned about secretaries, companions, and lawyers who had no compunctions at all about opening other people's mail.

"I am persuaded," Käthe wrote in her reply, "that your suggestion is the best option." And there went another of the precious stamps. If she had to use another row of them, someone might notice that there was no longer a full sheet in the frame.

Three exchanges, and all but one stamp, later, it seemed to Mademoiselle Anne that it had not taken a great deal of persuasion. Basically, Katharina Juliana agreed to come to Paris on a "sight unseen" basis. Beyond that . . . well, the young woman was right. Neither the guardians of the Solms-Laubach children nor her natal House of Hanau-Münzenberg nor the emperor of the USE was likely to approve the rapid remarriage of a recent widow to a foreign nobleman. It wasn't as if Katharina Juliana could easily obtain a rapid reversion of her dowry . . . or purchase a suitable trousseau for a Rohan bride while she was still in mourning . . . or . . .

"You will have to arrange everything, *Mademoiselle*," Käthe wrote, "if you still want the match for your brother under these circumstances. But if you provide a carriage that will be in a specific location in Laubach on a specific date and at a specific time, with a suitable driver upon the bench and a suitable chaperone in it, she being in possession of papers that will make it possible for me to cross the borders, I swear to you upon my sacred honor that I will, without looking back, step my foot on the little ladder, enter it and come to France, bringing nothing but myself and the clothing that I am wearing that day."

A few days later, as her buttocks landed on the bench cushion with a little plop, she thought, *Nobody in my family is going to like this at all. I'm fairly sure, though, that they will finally remember that I exist.*

France
June 1637

Within two weeks of obtaining the bride's consent, the scant two weeks that Anne needed to send the carriage to collect the bride and wait for Katharina Juliana's trip to Paris to be completed, a triumphant Anne sent out formal announcements of the *duc de* Soubise's betrothal.

Magdeburg
June 1637

"No!" the landgravine-regent of Hesse-Kassel shrieked when she saw the betrothal announcement that her secretary had opened and placed neatly in the pile of incoming correspondence to the left of her desk. "No, no, no, how could she? How could Käthe do this? What is it going to do to *every* plan I have been working on for *years*?"

Yes, Katharina Juliana was a perfect bride for Soubise in almost all ways.

The way in which she was *not* a perfect bride for him, at least in the opinion of Amalie Elizabeth, was that the potential complications of this match for the internal politics of the USE were massive.

Especially now that Soubise and Anne de Rohan had publicly swung their support to Gaston. Whereas Grand Duke Bernhard, and with him Henri de Rohan, had made clear that they had every intention of backing Anne of Austria and the infant Louis XIV.

✳ ✳ ✳

"She didn't tell our brothers, either," the landgravine lamented. "At least she left the children in Laubach, or whoever Albert Otto named as their guardians would be totally freaked out! Who *did* he name? Friedrich of Baden-Durlach, I suppose, though he is usually in Basel with that up-timer woman, General Jackson's wife, who is ambassador there. And a couple of his other brothers-in-law, I suppose. Oh, dear Lord, she's just like Uncle Albrecht."

Uncle Albrecht, the recently deceased head of the cadet line of the counts of Hanau-Münzenberg had been in a major struggle with the senior line (hers) over inheritance rights for years.

"Greedy! That's the only possible explanation for why she's done this. Sheer greed and ambition, with Albert Otto only four months dead! The next time I have a chance to talk to that Litsa . . ." Litsa, the reprehensible Uncle Albrecht's daughter and a burgeoning journalist, had the byline on the story in the Magdeburg paper.

"If there's anything which I frantically need you for" arrived via radio from Bernhard, who was still in Nancy. It was waiting in Magdeburg when Raudegen arrived. The instant he and Marc dropped Susanna off at the landgravine's townhouse, they headed for France.

The landgravine was still busy, plotting to contain the damage that her sister's marriage to Soubise would do to the Crown Royalists.

Effectively, she took five minutes to welcome Susanna formally and then tucked her into a corner.

Besancon
June 1637

Henri de Rohan had his secretary pull the file copy of the letter he had sent to Anne, re-read it, and concluded that he had no one but himself to blame. There were occasions when vague was *not* your friend. There were reasons why you asked a lawyer to review a contract before you signed it. There were occasions when sloppy syntax came back to bite you in the nose.

Nancy, Lorraine
June 1637

Grand Duke Bernhard guffawed. It had probably been years since anything had made him laugh like this, probably not since the ex-Cardinal de Lorraine had eloped with his cousin Claude, dispensing himself from his ecclesiastical vows in the process. It was a welcome relief from the tedium of Nicole, Aldringen, and fretting about Gaston.

CHAPTER 33

Paris
July 1637

Soubise looked at the bride chosen by Anne. "You realize, young lady, that you are committing yourself to marriage to a grouchy old man?"

Käthe gripped her hands together firmly but raised her chin a little. "It should be a refreshing change from marriage to a petulant child."

The groom chuckled. "You'll do."

The wedding ensued promptly at the nearest functioning Huguenot temple. Which was five leagues from Paris. Before King Gaston even knew that Katharina Juliana was in the country and most certainly before he had any opportunity to forbid the ceremony.

Soubise warned his new wife that there would probably be unfavorable repercussions.

"I expect to receive quite a lot of correspondence from my own family."

He decided to minimize the immediate impact of potential repercussions as much as possible by honeymooning at an undisclosed location in the countryside.

Very undisclosed, "Where are we?" Käthe asked when they descended from the carriage.

"La Garnache. It's one of Anne's estates that has come down from aunt to niece, from aunt to niece again; she owns it independent of the duke or myself."

She craned her neck upwards. "It appears to be well-fortified."

"It is."

She thought a minute. "Didn't the king order all your family's fortifications destroyed? Back . . . well, before La Rochelle. Then again after La Rochelle?"

"Back when we were in active revolt against the crown?"

She nodded.

"He did. The royal army took it in 1621 and, the next year, Louis ordered this, as well as Beauvoir sur Mer, up the coast—that's also Anne's—destroyed. It's far easier to issue a royal order, though, than to get it carried out. That requires men and equipment. Procuring men and equipment requires money in the royal budget. In 1631, upon the advice of Richelieu, he ordered it razed again. The authorities made some efforts, but the government's attention has moved to other crises, and many officials are slow to consider women to be as dangerous as men. In the past year, with everything that has been happening, Anne considered it a prudent investment to make some repairs."

In Paris, Mademoiselle Anne didn't wait for the honeymoon to be over, neither to extend hints of possible *quid pro quo* favors that the Soubise faction might offer to the court nor . . .

La petite Marguerite might be fully persuaded that she was the legitimate daughter and heiress of Rohan. Her aunt (and, for that matter, her uncle) was by no means so certain that Henri's wife had not taken any lovers until after the birth of her surviving daughter. Who was in Burgundy rather than here in France where she might have gathered her own partisans and sought to influence the mood at the royal court. How convenient of Henri to have summoned the girl away.

How extraordinarily annoying that the duchess was still running around France, intriguing on her husband's behalf.

With her current lover.

Need they wait?

Before the abbreviated honeymoon was indeed over, Anne sent out delicate feelers to King Gaston. Mere wisps. Bare cobwebs of suggestions. Would he perchance be interested in declaring the *purported Rohan heiress* illegitimate and ineligible to inherit in return for Soubise's throwing as much of the Rohan support as he could garner from among the Huguenot community to the king? Who could predict what might ensue from such sighing breaths of tentative rumor?

It was still all indefinite, of course, but even in the worst case, the half-whispered query would serve as an excellent distraction. A flaky monarch who was focused on the legitimacy of *la petite Marguerite* would probably not be concentrating upon whether it would be feasible for him to invalidate Soubise's marriage.

Mademoiselle Anne, who had often found confidential informants useful, also used a couple of them to put into the French newspapers everything that any gossip had ever said about who was where when in the weeks that would have surrounded the conception of Henri de Rohan's *purported* heiress Marguerite. Most of the extrapolations that opinion columnists derived from the statistics fell into the category of salacious.

As it happened, King Gaston chose to accept the *fait accompli* and recognize Soubise's marriage. The refusal of his brother Louis, under Richelieu's influence, to recognize his own marriage to the queen for so many years had been . . . far more than annoying to him.

Besançon
July 1637

When the newspapers reached Besançon, the little Rohanette daisy, for the first time, came to doubt her previously unshakable conviction of her own legitimacy.

"You must marry, soon." When Henri de Rohan used that voice, it meant that he would not budge. "Not merely soon. Now. No more nonsense. No more delays."

"Nobody will have me, now," Marguerite retorted. "Not that I had lines and lines of acceptable suitors even before *Tante* did this. Not genuine ones. Even Eva's brother preferred his morganatic Johanna to me. And now, *Tante* and Uncle Soubise are in France, snuggling up to King Gaston and controlling what little money the family has left. You're dead broke, we're dead broke, except for what the grand duke pays you. I'm dead in the water. No dowry."

"Not," Rohan said, "entirely. I've been prudent enough to put some things aside, investing modestly through the grand duke's bankers in the Low Countries and to some extent through the up-timers' exchange. And I remember who it was who first suggested that I teach you to be Rohan for yourself. Even if he does not, as things eventuate, become Rohan for you, he is someone who will, I am confident, always provide you with staunch support."

"Who?" Marguerite demanded. "Who?" She absolutely could not recall who made that suggestion, but it certainly had not been a Huguenot nobleman. And surely, surely, was not Gerry Stone!

"Patience, child. I really must ask him, first." Rohan fingered his goatee. "In the meantime . . ." He smiled. "Would you like to become involved, in a small way at least, in gathering intelligence?"

"Oh, yes, yes, yes. How?" She wriggled in her chair.

"Let us compose a letter to M. de Chabot, to see what he has to say in the light of your aunt's latest gambit. If he still presents himself as a serious suitor in his reply, it is possible that this is some feint, however hurtful to your feelings, and she has let him know that. If he shows signs of backing off, however . . . she may be serious."

"It wouldn't be news if he backs off," Marguerite said. "Every suitor I've ever had has backed off." She paused. "Except Horrid Hamilton, of course. I hope that's not an omen."

Her father reminded her that omens were a pagan superstition associated with the practice of astrology and thus to be eschewed by all good Christians, most especially those who adhered to Reformed faith.

When Chabot's answer arrived, she thought it was delightful. He admitted that Mademoiselle de Rohan had subtly advised him that

Marguerite might not be as advantageous a match as had originally been presented to him, but he also stated that he had, in the course of their correspondence, found her to be of such a lively mind and bright spirit that he would like to continue their association in spite of that.

"Isn't that sweet of him?" Marguerite asked.

Rohan found it deeply disturbing.

∗ ∗ ∗

Rohan leaned his arms on the balcony, watching a group of young people in the courtyard.

"Aren't they a bit old to be playing with beanbags?" Carey asked.

"There's no tennis court–the grand duke really ought to build one. They prefer the 'frisbees' that Gerry brought, but they sail too far, and the leather is too firm for them to be safe to use in a small courtyard surrounded by windows. Still, there is nothing wrong with keeping a bit of childhood in one's later life, I suppose, as Dr. Seuss reminds us. Beanbags are at least, for the most part, harmless."

Marguerite, too short to have much hope of intercepting a beanbag thrown overhand from one person to another in mid-flight, ducked under someone's arm and snatched a bag just as it was about to arrive in his hand, tossing it into another boy's face.

"I often thought," Rohan said musingly, "until these last few years, I often thought, no matter what other marriage projects arose, that eventually, unless the crown interfered and prohibited it, I would marry her to one of her distant Rohan cousins from a cadet line of the family and continue Rohan in that manner. The Guémené line would have been best. It is a pity that Pierre had no sons, for they would have been of approximately the right age. Hercule's son Louis, from his first marriage, married when Marguerite was barely two years old, but his surviving sons are about fifteen years younger than my daughter. Hercule's sons from his second marriage are also much too young."

He sighed. "Until this year, I had seen little of her since she was a small child. We were rarely in the same household. The military life is not conducive to what Madame Dunn refers to as 'involved fatherhood.' Yet, now that I have come to know her, I have grown to like her. Perhaps the members of their 'Red Headed League' are correct. Perhaps she can become Rohan for herself." He sighed even more deeply.

Carey pursed her lips. "These newspaper reports . . . your sister . . ."

Rohan continued watching the beanbag game.

"However that may be," he finally commented, "it is possible that it is not the worst of fates if I do indeed have a small elephantbird, which no one can ever know, whatever Anne may hint. I will continue to teach Marguerite to be Rohan for herself."

"Tancrède?"

"He is most certainly not my son. There is no way that I will allow him to supersede her rights."

After a few minutes, he continued. "With the troubles in France, which will certainly bring renewed unrest to Lorraine, I anticipate that my service to Grand Duke Bernhard will involve me in battles again, possibly as soon as this autumn and very probably by next spring, even if none of them will be precisely the same battle in which I was killed in your universe." He grimaced. "Every battle or skirmish carries its own risks. I may well die 'on schedule' and Marguerite still needs a husband: a Protestant husband."

Paris
July 1637

The meeting was unsatisfactory, because there weren't many solid facts to be obtained. None of them had much to contribute.

Sandrart finally said, "The duchess is furious with Mademoiselle Anne. Enraged. I can't find out much more than that. Since her current pregnancy has advanced to the point that she cannot conveniently travel any longer and has moved in with her father, there's not a lot to observe.

I only know that she is infuriated by way of reports from Sully's servants."

"Is Candale with her?"

That was a factual question. Sandrart could answer it, but not with a simple affirmative or negative. "He hasn't returned to his regiment. He is not moving around the countryside any longer, as far as I have been able to determine."

Gage and Gardiner took that as a sufficient answer.

Finally Gage contributed, "There have been some interesting theological discussions pertaining to . . ."

Gardiner shook his head. "Relevant facts, please. Not random facts."

"Do *you* have any?"

"Everyone's waiting for the other shoe to drop. Hoping it will be someone else's shoe."

Then Sully died.

Virginia DeMarce

CHAPTER 34

A village near Villebon
July 1637

The mill was located on a creek, of course. That was a prerequisite for a mill. So it had a bit of distance from the other houses in the village. The attached house was sturdily constructed and of fair size, which was just as well. As he entered into his sixtieth year, Thierry Durand was in the happy position of having several adult children, most of them male, three still living at home and working with him at the mill.

He also had a wife.

Fifteen years earlier, a group of young men, guests of Sully's oldest son, thoroughly intoxicated, riding drunkenly from the *château* toward the village, had stopped to harass a girl who was walking along the side of the road carrying two pails of milk. Not a young woman nor even a girl past puberty. A child, one old enough to carry two pails, but a child. She attracted their attention because Madeleine was not quite right in the way she looked, the way she moved her arms and legs. An easy object of mockery and derision.

It might have stopped at that except that Babette, his wife, had run out and started scolding at them to leave her daughter alone.

Waving a towel, her apron blowing in the stiff wind.

Horses are prey animals. Most do not react well to unexpected movement in the periphery of their vision field. These were not war horses, trained to steadiness in the confusion of a battlefield. They were riding horses: expensive ones, but prone to customary equine panic attacks. One of them reared and jumped, catching her on the shoulder with a hoof as he came down. The blow threw her aside. She landed hard, hitting her head against a corner of one of the massive stone slabs that made up the steps from the road into the mill house. And unseating his rider, who made an embarrassing, rump-first, landing in the dust.

Two of the young men, indignant that an ordinary woman had dared to rebuke them, dismounted and, rather than attempting to help Babette, spilled the milk in Madeleine's pails over her, while the others, including the unseated rider, watched, hooting and laughing. Then they remounted and rode on.

Nothing was ever done to them. They were of high rank, friends of the duke's oldest son. The one whose horse injured Babette *was* the duke's oldest son, who went by the title of *marquis de* Rosny. And they went away—to Paris, perhaps; to serve in the king's armies in the Low Countries, perhaps; maybe to go adventuring in far colonies. The miller and his sons did not know.

Babette mostly recovered, at least in body, but sometimes, ever since, she did not recognize who her husband and children were; she could not do much work, nothing that required close attention, because her mind forgot itself every half-drop of the hourglass or so, and she didn't remember what she had been doing before. Sometimes she wandered away, with no idea of where she was going, or why. Prior to the attack she had been a healthy, competent, helpmeet to her husband; ever since, she had become a burden whose constant care had to be borne by the rest of the family. Along with Madeleine who was, still, and always would be, not quite right, which made it more than twice as hard for the rest of them, since they also lost the care that Babette had provided for her.

It was a constant, grating, reminder of what happened, because of their mother's continuing condition . . .

"How can we forget?" Jean had asked his father over and over. "How many days, when it looks like we've just shrugged our shoulders and gone on with our lives, a bunch of stupid dullard peasants who accept that whatever fine gentlemen choose to do to us is inevitable, are we thinking about it? It's under our skins, like a festering boil. Why *should* we forget what they did to her and go on with our lives as if it doesn't really matter? As if she doesn't really matter? As if we don't really matter?"

Then Sully died.

"Do you suppose he'll come here for the old duke's funeral?" Claude asked at supper. "Who? The man whose horse clipped her?"

"Yes, Rosny."

"There's no way to tell until we see him arrive. Or don't," their father answered.

"Or the men who started it—who treated our Madeleine like she was a freak?" Jean said. "Brothers are supposed to protect their sisters. Remember Dinah. In the Bible. What her brothers Simeon and Levi did after Schechem raped her."

"Madeleine is fine," Renaud snapped. "Or as fine as she ever is going to be. Nobody raped her. She's forgotten about that day and the milk, just as she has forgotten the day before it and the day that followed. We're supposed to forgive our enemies. Jacob blessed Judah instead of Simeon and Levi."

"We don't even know who those two were," Thierry said. "We wouldn't recognize them if we saw them. Nor is it likely that even if the old duke's son comes for the funeral, every man who was with him on a certain day fifteen years ago will come again."

Jean bit down viciously on a slice of hard bread and chewed. "Not fucking likely that I'm going to forgive my enemies. Madeleine may not be any worse off than she would have been if they'd ignored her. I don't like to agree, but I'll grant you that. Except that she lost her mother, for all practical purposes. *Maman* isn't fine and never has been since it happened. It's like . . . like he knocked the soul out of her body. The corporal part is still here, but there's nothing inside it. Like the Bible says when it is written, 'the letter kills but the spirit gives life.' There's no spirit that gives her life. There hasn't been, all these years since . . ."

"If he does come, could we even get near him?" Claude asked. "It's not likely that we'll be able to weaken every man in the funeral procession by persuading them to all get circumcised the night before they bury Sully."

Jean talked to the rest of the family. Pierre so vociferously refused to have anything to do with a *revanche* that they quarreled. His twin Paul threatened to go to the *mairie* if Jean so much as mentioned the idea again. So he didn't mention it again. To them.

He ended up with about a dozen: three of his brothers, counting Renaud and Claude; five nephews ranging from the mid-teens to early twenties; a few cousins. Plus a couple dozen more from the village proper, friends of his nephews, older apprentices and young journeymen, who were enthusiastic about the chance to provide some kind of a distraction. Most of those didn't want to be involved in any actual attack, though. They had, as one of them said, lives still to be lived in a world where pestilence and war made mortal life uncertain in the best of times.

Thierry tried to talk his sons out of it on the grounds that it wouldn't work. "It's not as if you can go out and buy a bunch of weapons all of a sudden," he said. "Someone would notice."

"We have knives." Jean was nothing if not pig-headed. "We have daggers."

"So will they. Plus swords. Probably guns."

Renaud shook his head. "There will be ladies. I don't think they'll be so stupid as to shoot guns at us when they might hit their own ladies. They might not mind harming women like *Maman* and Madeleine, but heaven forbid that they would endanger fine ladies. Unless they're drunk, that is, and they shouldn't be drunk right after they've spent three or four hours listening to a funeral sermon. At least, not most of them. I suppose that some will bring flasks."

Claude asked, "Are you willing to accept that if we do what is needed to bring the man down, we're likely to end up dead too?"

Jean thought for a minute. "*Oui.* For that, I am willing to be dead."

He thought for another minute. "Last summer, when the duchesses escaped from Paris . . . Achille at the tavern had a newspaper . . . The reports said something about pots that made smoke . . . And one of them told how the things were made . . . We have knives and daggers. We have pickling crocks, too, and a couple of days until the funeral . . . That's what the boys from the village can do. Throw those."

"I read those reports, too," Claude objected. "Where are we supposed to get fireworks to put inside them?"

"We don't have fireworks," Jean retorted, "but we have flour." He looked around the mill. "Lots and lots of flour."

There might have been one miller's son somewhere in France who had never, ever, while he was growing up, made a bit of flour explode. Probably not two, though.

"I think we ought to focus on pots that just make smoke," Renard said. "At least, if what you want to do is kill him and not burn us up. I'll see if I can find out how they make those. How big does the pot need to be? If they're too big to fit under a tunic, it won't work."

"What are you going to use for fuses?" Claude asked. "How are you going to light them in a hurry with a lot of other people around? You've got to think, Jean. Think. We'll all have to be down at the road, mixed up with everyone else who comes to see the procession. What's the best time to make a move? Who's supposed to be doing what? How will we know when to start? It's all very well that you're willing to die, but while you're dying, we've got to get one of us close enough to kill the marquis or else it's going to be a big waste of time and money."

Paris
July 1637

Sully had died.

Maximilien de Béthune, *duc de* Sully, Rohan's father-in-law, had always been Rohan's major sentimental obstacle when it came to suggestions that had been dropped over the course of many years that he might want to consider the merits of divorce. The old man was close to eighty, but his death was rumored on the gossip circuit to have been caused by apoplexy at the thought of the possible impact of Soubise's marriage, combined with his daughter's current scandal, on the prospects of his granddaughter Marguerite. According to the encyclopedias, he had lasted for another four years up-time.

Sully's sons would not constitute a sentimental obstacle to a divorce.

If Rohan remarried and had more children . . . Neither Mademoiselle Anne nor Soubise was in the least pleased by the prospect of a Rohan divorce.

Divorces took time, of course, even among Calvinists. There were church courts to be satisfied. And the king could refuse to recognize a divorce's validity, should he be so inclined, even if the church granted it. Lawyers could drag it out so long that all of the principle parties died before there as so much as a hearing.

King Gaston refused permission for Rohan to attend the funeral. Not that it would have been safe for Rohan to attend, but it was a matter of principle for him to send a request.

Villebon
July 1637

Raudegen attended the funeral as a member of the household of the *duc de* Soubise. Looking around, he shuddered inwardly. Funerals were always nightmares from a security perspective: the procession on foot, strung out sometimes for a half mile or more, and no way to control who came to join the hundreds, sometimes thousands, of spectators along the sides of the street or road.

Marc attended the funeral as an inconspicuous member of the general public, standing among many other equally inconspicuous members of the general public in the immense crowd that gathered outside of the temple. His hair stood on end when he saw a certain couple approach the entry, even though the woman was heavily veiled. There was something about deep mourning. Not that half of the noblewomen in France didn't wear mourning on a regular basis, given the prevalence of death by war and pestilence. Not so much by famine—not for the nobility. In the ranks of society that died from famine, the survivors could rarely afford formal mourning clothes.

Few women, though, whether in mourning or not, appeared in public when they were so startlingly pregnant.

Raudegen had a much better view.

Soubise and his sister hadn't been able to prevent François de Béthune, usually known by his title of d'Orval, from inviting *la duchesse* de Rohan to attend her father's funeral. The two of them were Sully's only surviving children from his second marriage to Rachel de Cochefilet and, what was more pertinent, she had been living with her father for the past months.

D'Orval briefly considered not inviting Soubise and Anne, but his wife persuaded him that protocol wouldn't let him get away with it.

The king decided not to attend a service at a Huguenot temple. Sometimes life bestowed small blessings on a harried heir.

Before the service even got under way, Anne, dragging Soubise by the elbow, stepped forward, confronted the couple, and announced, "We are representing the House of Rohan."

"You!" In spite of the veil, the word was clearly spat out. "You are a traitor to the House of Rohan. I am representing the duke."

Katharina Juliana stepped sideways and took refuge behind a large man wearing a Geneva gown.

"You should be ashamed to appear in public. So advanced in your pregnancy; at your age; carrying a bastard. *Another one!*" Anne raised her hand.

Soubise, his elbow now free, stepped back behind the Geneva gown as well. This was neither the place nor the time . . .

Candale stepped forward, stopping the slap aimed at his companion's face.

"Oh yes, so charming," Anne spat. "Here with your lover. The father of your bastard. To represent your husband. It's not just that you have been regularly unfaithful to your husband; you haven't even been faithful to your lover. Yes, you've been with Candale at intervals, but you

301

certainly entertained yourself with others between those intervals. Which I do not have to say, because everyone at the court has always known it. You are a disgrace to the faith to which you claim to belong."

"Mademoiselle," Candale said in a moderating voice. "Perhaps . . . not here . . . not now."

"You're a fine one to speak." Anne managed to enunciate the word *convert* as an epithet. "Adulterer and not even a faithful adulterer."

"I may not have been faithful to her, as you mean it," Candale said, "perhaps it is not in me to be faithful to a woman that way. However, I have been loyal to her since the first day that we met. Just as she may not have been *faithful* to your brother, as you use the word, but she has been unswervingly *loyal* to him throughout the vicissitudes of their married life. Which, if I may say so Mademoiselle Anne, at present you are not."

It took quite some time for the assorted clergy to regain control over the ceremony.

Somewhat over an hour into the sermon, as the speaker paused to draw a deep breath, Candale stepped out of the cluster of mourners. This caused nothing more than a murmur. No one expected every member of a congregation to be able to resist calls of nature during services that frequently lasted for three or four hours. Sliding toward a side door, Candale passed by the location where Raudegen was standing, twitching the cuff of his coat.

"We feel," he said, as they paused outside the building, "some remorse that the existence of Tancrède plus this current pregnancy might be used and it looks like they will be used to cast doubt on little Marguerite's position. I, ah, thought you would be here. Sully had gathered some material; we have collected more these past few months. If you could make sure that it gets back to Rohan?"

As Marc had not been a prominent attendee at the funeral, all anyone else might have noticed, if anyone had been paying attention, was that an apparently bored young onlooker brushed by the two men. Candale returned to the service. Raudegen slipped the package to Marc and resumed his position near Soubise. Such was life in the vicinity of *a certain sneaky French count and that conniving French duchess*—he had thought that about them once before and didn't perceive any reason that he should change his mind now.

As Marc drifted away from the crowd, no one paid any particular attention to his departure. He was on his way to Besançon before the sermon was over.

The sneaky count, the conniving duchess, Soubise with his new wife on one arm and Mademoiselle Anne on the other, with Colonel Raudegen walking some distance to the side of them, far enough that he was clearly making no claim to be part of the noble entourage but close enough to intervene at need, followed d'Orval and the remainder of the late duke's immediate family in the elaborate procession back to Sully's estate, where the staff had spent the funeral hours laying out a lavish spread of buffet food.

D'Orval had taken charge. His older half-brother, the new *duc de* Sully, albeit the holder of such grandiose designations as peer of France, marshal of the armies, and governor of the Bastille, was stumbling drunk. As usual. If there was ever a case of a man who survived life upon the unearned privilege granted by his status at birth . . .

Raudegen looked around. He would have been happier if there were a fence, even a flimsy temporary fence, between the crowd of people who had come to pay their respects at a distance and the guests of more exalted rank. He would have been infinitely happier if the buffet had been set up in the courtyard of the massive brick pile with its towers and turrets rather than on the lawn, but nobody had asked his advice.

There weren't many bodyguards around the guests, either; most of those present had remained in the vicinity of the bier. Perhaps they were relying on the sheer dimensions of the nearly thirty acres of landscaping as a protection: the 'lawn' at Villebon would have counted as a large park most places. But, as his mother had often said, "it is what it is."

He snacked on salty things, avoiding those with cream sauce or custard, advising Soubise, his wife, and Mademoiselle Anne to do the same. His acquaintance with Madame Dunn had made him conscious of the most common causes of food poisoning.

Food poisoning was a constant hazard. So was poison, of course. Snipers. Bulls that escaped their pens. The monstrous reptiles that illustrated the pages of exploration narratives written by those who visited the New World. But food poisoning, caused by the invisible germs that Madame Dunn harped on so incessantly, was just as deadly and more easily avoided.

CHAPTER 35

France
July 1637

As the buffet tables emptied, the immediate male relatives of the late duke began to gather themselves into proper order to follow the bier to the cemetery, the less exalted guests starting to form up behind them. It was not customary for women to attend interments, so the ladies of the ducal family began to stroll slowly toward the narrow gate that provided entrance to the château, the female guests drifting gradually after them, protocol so engrained in women of the aristocracy that they automatically sorted themselves into the correct order of precedence.

Raudegen, in position alongside and a little behind Soubise, spotted movement among the spectators by the roadside. A couple of dozen men who had been standing among the crowd of onlookers were rushing the funeral party, throwing grenades.

Not many grenades. It looked like each man was carrying only one of them; at most, two.

Not even grenades, Raudegen thought as he backed up and positioned himself between the attackers and Katharina Juliana. Smoke pots. Cheap, amateur, smoke pots like the ones Gerry Stone had cobbled together from small storage crocks and a few fireworks at the extravaganza in Paris. Smoke pots like the one that had taken away the use of his hand. Smoke pots for which many newspapers had published the simple formula. Unless one accidentally made a direct hit against someone's face or unprotected limb, they wouldn't do significant damage. But . . . oh, how he hated matches. Shitty up-time matches that made it so easy for almost anyone to light a fuse in no time and with hardly any preparation. That was one innovation that he could happily have done without.

The danger would come . . . He looked around, spotted Soubise, who was still moving toward his assigned place in the funeral procession, and grabbed his arm, dragging him back toward where the ladies were standing. There! While most of the men who were running out of the crowd toward the château were throwing pots, a few others, perhaps a dozen, were drawing knives and daggers.

Not swords. These men, to judge by their clothing, did not belong to the social classes that were permitted by the sumptuary laws to carry swords. Nor did they look as if they had the money for anything on the order of a sword cane or purpose-made hollowed-out walking stick. Lacking those, a decent-sized sword was an awkward thing to disguise.

Soubise jerked away from him, drew his own sword, and attacked the attackers. A person tended to forget that behind his carefully cultivated façade of an aging, grumpy, man, there was a competent military officer who, back in the day, had trained under Maurice of Nassau in the Netherlands and commanded armies in the field.

Raudegen turned back to the ladies, hustled Mademoiselle Anne, the duchess, and Katharina Juliana to the buffet tables, overturned one, and pushed them behind it before he paused to check on the overall situation again, blinking his stinging eyes. The smoke pots made it hard to see—hard to breathe, for that matter—but at least they were neutral. Once thrown, they disadvantaged the attackers as much as the targets.

Candale and d'Orval were back to back, both fighting and perfectly competent to take care of themselves. Soubise was sensibly coming up on one of the attackers from the rear. Mirepoix, who had a lot of gall to have shown up, given the bitterness that accompanied his separation from the duchess' late sister Louise, though they had to invite him, of course, was . . . Raudegen glanced toward the edge of the lawn . . . circling around, trying to keep the trunk of a much too small tree between himself and a man with a long knife while shielding his ex-mother-in-law. With a rough, "Stay put, all of you," to the three ladies, Raudegen headed that way at a run.

Several of d'Orval's retainers came dashing out of the manor house. Armed, but armed with guns, which were useless unless they didn't mind taking the risk of hitting as many friends as foes. They appeared to realize as much, but . . . no, no, no. One dropped his gun on a buffet table in order to pick up a heavy tureen to use as a weapon, making it available to any of the attackers who might see it. Raudegen, aware that his skills with the left hand were far from first rate, simply slashed as hard as he could at the side of one knee of the man who was chasing Mirepoix around the tree, then tripped him and pushed Sully's widow toward the overturned table. Then he dashed for the dropped gun.

Too slowly. One of the attackers would get there before he could.

But not before Mademoiselle Anne could. She snatched the pistol up by the barrel and with an ululation that she must have learned from her once-upon-a-time Scottish tutor, bashed her opponent in the temple with the grip. Then, sinking back behind the overturned table, she said, "I've wanted to hit someone back ever since La Rochelle" and vomited all over her sisters-in-law.

Occasional sounds of 'clink' and 'plink' came through the black soot that floated in the air. Many of the attendees at the funeral, probably most of them, well aware of the history of Huguenots in France, were wearing chain mail between their underwear and their outer garments. After all, given the current unstable political condition of the country, if a marriage had provided the opportunity for the St. Bartholomew's Day massacre, it was not impossible that the funeral of Sully might become the site of a modern equivalent.

The hacking and coughing caused by the smoke took away, he thought, from the romanticized fictional depictions of duels shown in stage combat, where it often seemed that the participants might as well be dancing a ballet choreographed by Benserade. But given that probably ninety percent of the male guests had, at some point in their lives, served as army officers, and also that they were much better armed than their assailants, not to mention that there were probably ten times as many of them . . . it was not an equal fight.

* * *

Jean had been put out of commission by the man he was trying to push past to get to Rosny. Claude had lost hold of his knife. It wouldn't be long before he was down, but he had the brute strength of someone who had hefted sacks of grain, day in and day out, since he reached his adult height and he had also wrapped his arms in strips cut from a leather apron. Ignoring the probable eventual outcome, he stood there with a stubborn two-handed grip, holding the sword arm of his shorter opponent up in the air. Renaud, after his own knife went 'clink' on someone's chain mail and flew away into the grass, grabbed the Venetian stiletto that Claude's opponent had in his left hand, turned, and went directly after Rosny.

The grip was small and fiddly. He clenched his fist around it. The triangular stiletto proved to be an admirably functional device. He had enough time to admire its effectiveness in penetrating chain mail before his own death.

Most of the larger group of attackers vanished into the smoke and crowd. Once they had thrown the smoking pots, there was no way to distinguish them from any innocent bystander—and almost all the innocent bystanders in the sizeable crowd were also moving away from the fight. Rapidly, in every possible direction. They weren't hemmed in.

* * *

Raudegen took another look around, as well as he could. There was very little breeze, so the smoke was not clearing.

The marquis of Rosny, Sully's older son, who appeared to be the focus of the attack, was down, but he was a debauched drunkard. If he was dead, no one would miss him. He had been *duc de* Sully for all of five days, and his son was of age.

He moved back toward the buffet tables, checking on the ladies in Soubise's party. They were his responsibility; not pursuit of the escaping attackers. That was d'Orval's problem.

* * *

In the end, Raudegen reported back to Bernhard and Rohan, the best one could say was that it had been equal opportunity chaos. D'Orval's staff apprehended only those few who had entered the lawn proper and were too badly wounded to run away and blend in. Or who were dead.

"Candale recommended to d'Orval that he request my assistance which, with permission from M. de Soubise, I was glad to render. The first thing that came to everyone's mind, of course, was 'Ducos.' However, there was no shouting of slogans. The attackers did not in any way discriminate between known partisans of King Gaston and known partisans of Anne of Austria. They made no distinction between Catholics, not that there were many in attendance, and Huguenots. The attackers moved aggressively, it appears upon my speaking to those who were in the densest of the smoke and participated in the fighting, mainly for the purpose of pushing past those guests who, being in their way, resisted their advance. The target, from the beginning, was Rosny. It was not an absurdly unequal attack of a dozen poorly armed and trained villagers against ten times their number who were better armed and trained. It was an absurdly unequal attack of a dozen poorly armed and trained villagers against one specific nobleman. The rest of the guests were, for them, only the chorus in a play.

"The up-time matches proved to be stolen from a Catholic church located some seven leagues from the château. A parishioner who visited

Lyon brought them back as a gift for the priest, to be used for lighting votive candles. The priest bragged about them quite a bit, so everyone in the neighborhood knew that they would be in the sacristy.

"There were surprisingly few dead on the scene. Seven men: five of the attackers and two guests, including Rosny. Also, one of the men who was holding the team that drew the bier, but that was probably unintentional. The minister who preached the funeral sermon is among the more seriously wounded of the surviving casualties but will probably recover.

"Mademoiselle Anne states that she has wanted to hit someone hard ever since her experiences in and after La Rochelle, but had not realized quite how a man's head would sound when she hit it. The new *duchesse de* Soubise was disconcerted by the attack but did not panic. She appeared to be more distressed by the disorderly nature of the event than by its violence. The *duchesse de* Rohan has been of great assistance to her brother d'Orval in managing all the things that had to be done in the aftermath."

He paused, re-reading the letter to be certain that he had covered all essential points.

"The duchess has not yet been brought to bed of her child.

"The three living attackers who were captured have been hanged. Every one of the men taken into custody was local to Sully's estate or from one of the nearby villages. It was, as I determined at the request of d'Orval as described above, a matter of a personal grudge, arising from a long-ago situation in which no justice was done."

He looked at the chicken-scratchy handwriting that was all he could manage now that he was what Gerry Stone called "a lefty." Stone's guilty conscience about the injury had not prevented him from producing, as time went on, a plethora of bad multi-lingual puns incorporating such concepts as *sinister* and *gauche*.

He added a postscript. "I had M. de Soubise point out the lack of prior justice to Rosny's son, the new *duc de* Sully. He is barely of age and at first was inclined to level the whole village from which the known attackers came, plow the ground, and strew it with salt, on the model of the Romans' treatment of Carthage. Or, at the least, pressure the magistrates to execute the entire families of the captured and dead assailants, including an old woman who does not have use of all of her mental faculties and her backward daughter. I did not perceive those measures to be a reasonable application of force, much less a necessary one, in this instance.

"You may want to ask Bismarck what he has learned about the French Revolution that took place in the up-timers' world. I do not think it would be desirable to live through some equivalent of that in ours, if it can be averted."

His next letter, to Madame Cavriani in Brussels, expanded somewhat more on that train of thought and suggested that a closer acquaintance with the political theorist Scaglia and the 'soft landing' concepts he had advanced in *Political Methods and the Laws of Nations* might benefit the Cavriani firm. "Not," he concluded, "that my hopes are high."

Virginia DeMarce

CHAPTER 36

Besançon
July 1637

When the grand ducal delegation straggled back from Lorraine, Rohan put the marriage project to the Chosen One.

"I am not," August von Bismarck protested, "of the *Hochadel.* I am not only of the lower nobility; I'm minor even among the echelons of the lower nobility. No way am I qualified."

"You're as qualified as the man she married in that other world, as far as rank is concerned," Rohan answered, "with the advantage of being Protestant. You will be more reliable than any possible French Huguenot candidate I can think of at the moment. In light of the abduction attempt that Hamilton made last winter, in the light of Gaston's intriguing for a Catholic match, in light of Marguerite's correspondence with that Chabot, however carefully Madame Calagna and I have supervised it, and with the current . . . activities . . . of my sister and brother, I very much doubt the wisdom of delaying her marriage any longer."

Bismarck took an involuntary step backwards.

Rohan waved the other man in the room forward. "Ruvigny, tell him to just do it."

Ruvigny swallowed. "I am sorry my lord duke, but no. I will not tell him that. My family are your clients, but his are not. His oath is to Grand Duke Bernhard and he should not consent without the grand duke's approval, nor should he enter into such an agreement without notifying and consulting with his older brother and his mother. If it is to be done, it should be done properly. Not in a fit of pique."

"Not to mention," Bismarck added, "that you maybe might want to check whether or not your inspiration is all right with Marguerite."

Bernhard approved. More accurately, in his capacity as the prospective groom's military superior, he granted his permission. He wasn't enamored with the idea, but he allowed Bismarck, an officer in his employ, to enter into the match, presuming that all other interested parties gave their approval. Shaking his head all the way.

By way of an elaborate, step-by-small-step, radio relay from Burgundy to somewhere north of Magdeburg, Bismarck's mother and brothers also approved. More accurately, they agreed. It wasn't as if Brandenburg, in its current state of affairs with the elector's having decamped to Poland two years earlier, or the family estates, in their current condition, would offer August any better option.

La petite Marguerite approved.

"Or at least," Carey said to Kamala over lunch, "she took it with a sentiment best described as deep relief. I sure wouldn't call it wild enthusiasm."

"You can't blame her for that," Kamala answered. "He's not a great match the way down-timers look at it, but at least she knows him. And likes him well enough. Plus, he's turned out to be a pretty competent guy. She could have done a lot worse, if you ask me. Which nobody did."

"Relief," Carey said again. "Compounded with mild regret that she will have to end her amusing correspondence with Chabot."

Bernhard gifted Rohan with his best public relations man, Johann Michael Moscherosch, to put a desirable spin on the transaction. It came out as, "If the Iron Chancellor famed among the up-timers could do that for Germany, what can this man, his ancestor, be expected to do for Huguenot France?"

"I'm not at all sure," August protested, "that he was my descendant. I have several brothers. Not to mention distant cousins and the like."

"Never let details get in the way of a good narrative," Moscherosch retorted.

Bernhard tugged a bit on a couple of favors two prominent European men owed him.

This resulted in the groom's transformation into a baron in the king of Denmark's Duchy of Holstein. Minor baron. Baron of a successful dairy farm with a well-built house that any prosperous peasant farmer would be proud to own. But titled.

Also into a minor landholder in Frederik Hendrik's Dutch province of Overijssel. Minor, but he would hold the land in his own name rather than as one shareholder in a family corporation, which was the case with the Brandenburg estates.

Traill oversaw his rapid conversion to *la foi prétendue réformée*. At that news, the Calvinist electress of Brandenburg, in the name of her minor son and omitting any reference to her absent spouse, lifting high the banner of her own credentials as a sister of the late Winter King and granddaughter of William the Silent, tossed a celebratory and substantial bank draft into the pot.

Nicely substantial from the perspective of the new groom, who, being disinclined to go into debt, had been wondering just how he was going to acquire anything as basic as an appropriate suit for the wedding out of his captain's pay. Not substantial enough (the electress hoped) to cause anyone in the USE administration to wonder just where, given the situation in Brandenburg, she got the money.

Claudia de' Medici gave her husband a nudge and Bernhard promoted the groom to colonel (at large, for the time being, to fill a role similar to Raudegen's, since Bernhard didn't happen to have a spare regiment, but with a promise that if and when the next one became available, the young man could have it–as long as he promised to pay attention to subordinates with actual field command experience).

"Glorified aide-de-camp," Bismarck commented to Ruvigny, "but it's more than I ever expected to achieve. Plus, the pay is higher."

Ruvigny shrugged. "It's what you've been doing already."

The groom was now a trifle more eligible than one Henri de Chabot had been in another world.

Not to mention Protestant.

Bismarck reflected a little wistfully on the calm, plump, blue eyed, fair haired, God-fearing, dream bride who had occasionally floated through his head since he reached puberty. He dismissed her into the aethers and focused on what he would be called upon to do to defend the French interests of a far more real, tiny, fierce, constantly chattering, ballet-mad, brunette with a head of unruly curls.

It was likely that life as Rohan's son-in-law would involve not only army service, but more. He started a mental list of everything that St. Paul had included as among the necessary parts of the armor of righteousness according to Ephesians 6:11. His duty was clear. "Put on the full armor of God, so that you can take your stand against the devil's schemes."

EPILOGUE

Grantville
July 1637

Leopold Cavriani and Gary Lambert made their way to their usual spot.

"The varnish is holding up well," Cavriani said after they had ordered, rubbing the polish on the table with one forefinger. "A person scarcely notices more years of wear."

"Extra heavy-duty polyurethane marine spar varnish. Absolutely waterproof. Cal and Lauren got a special on it a year or so before the Ring of Fire hit and put three coats on all the tables." Gary shook his head. "We won't be seeing anything like it for a long time."

They ate lamb with baked potatoes in silence. Eventually, "I enjoyed the business with the cat," Gary said. "As a spectator, of course."

"Marc could have gotten into difficulties, going into France like that."

Mulling over the French situation took some time.

Leopold was inclined to despair at the imperviousness of even the best of the up-timers when it came to understanding politics. "Everything that has been going on among the Huguenots this spring does not necessarily signify a lasting estrangement between Rohan and Soubise." He twirled the wine glass he was holding. "In the final analysis, they are brothers. Not only that, but brothers who have been close to one another for several decades of life. This tactic has served European noble

317

families well for at least half a millennium. Some version of it has served families well since remotest antiquity. By having a prominent member on each side of any significant civil war between claimants to the throne, then no matter who comes out on top, the family estates don't escheat to the crown as a result of accusations of treason. They are transferred within the family, from one branch to another."

Gary simply shook his head.

AFTERWORD

Jack Alden Clarke, *Huguenot Warrior: The Life and Times of Henri de Rohan, 1579-1638* (The Hague: Martinus Nijhoff, 1966) is adequate as a biography, but certainly not brilliant. It has almost nothing to say on Rohan's private life–it doesn't even mention that Rohan had a daughter Marguerite, much less that she was his sole heiress. Pierre and Solange Deyon, *Henri de Rohan: Huguenot de plume et d'épée, 1579-1638* (Perrin, 2000) contains a more up-to-date bibliography than Clarke's work.

In some ways, the short sketch published by Charles Augustin Saint-Beuve in 1904 is more illuminating than Clarke, if a bit hagiographical and still less than forthcoming about Rohan's marriage (C. A. Sainte-Beuve, *Portraits of the Seventeenth Century, Historic and Literary*, New York and London: G. P. Putnam's Sons, The Knickerbocker Press, 1904). Auguste Laugel, *Henry de Rohan*, published in 1889, as customary with nineteenth-century biographical works, is stuffed with facts, but the author was a popularizer and, as he stated in the subtitle, only interested in "son rôle politique et militaire."

More useful for social history is Jonathan Dewald's online paper, "Rohan's World: A Political Culture in Seventeenth-Century France," which provides the reader with a rapid introduction to Rohan's political ambitions, religious views, associates, reading habits, and hobbies. There is further information about the family's economic status and internal relationships in Dewald's, *Status, Power, and Identity in Early Modern France: The Rohan Family, 1550–1715* (University Park, PA: Pennsylvania State University Press, 2015).

In regard to the "pen" rather than the "sword" aspect of Rohan's career, several of his works on then-current events, political theory, and military tactics have been translated into English; many of them, in both French and in English translation, are now readily available either as e-books or by way of print-on-demand versions. Aficionados of seventeenth century warfare may enjoy *The Duke of Rohan's Manual: Or, a Guide for All Degrees of Officers, from a Subaltern to a Captain-General. Containing the Whole Art of War, . . . to . . . . . . Translated by a Gentleman in the Army* (Gale Ecco, Print Editions, 2018).

Academic scholarship thus far has not done well by Benjamin de Soubise or by the ladies of the House of Rohan. For the mother of Rohan and Soubise, who had already died in 1631, there is Nicole Vray, *Catherine de Parthenay duchesse de Rohan: Protestante insoumise* (Perrin, 1998), which contains some useful references to her daughter Anne de Rohan. A limited amount of Mademoiselle Anne's correspondence has been in print since the nineteenth century as *Lettres de Catherine de Parthenay, dame de Rohan-Soubise, et de ses deux filles Henriette et Anne, à Charlotte-Brabantine de Nassau, duchesse de la Trémoïlle* (L. Clouzot, 1874) and is currently available via google.books.

Most comments on the Rohan women that appear in general historical works are still dependent upon Gédéon Tallemant, seigneur des Réaux, *Historiettes* (Paris Société du Mercure de France: 4th ed., 1906). There are a lot of other editions of the *Historiettes*, but no English translations as far as I know. In our world, rather than in the 1632-verse, Tallemant's younger sister Marie married Henri de Ruvigny (see below) in 1647, which is one of the reasons he knew so much gossip about the *Mesdames de Rohan.*

The only biography of Tancrède was originally published over two hundred and fifty years ago (1767). It is short and partisan. The author, Henri Griffet, took the position that the boy was definitely the legitimate son of the duke and duchess, eliding over all evidence to the contrary, and making the younger Marguerite the villain of the episode. The *Histoire de Tancrède de Rohan* has been digitized on google books and is also available in a paper print-on-demand version. There is also a fairly extensive and well-illustrated Spanish-language discussion of Tancrede online: http://retratosdelahistoria.blogspot.com/2011/11/tancrede-de-rohan-el-hijo-de-nadie.html

To the best of my knowledge, the documents in the case are not available in published form. Griffet included only a few in a brief appendix to his pamphlet.

✻   ✻   ✻

Some things in the material environment of this story, 1635-1637, are not precisely as they were in our historical time line for those years. For readers trying to orient themselves to the geography of Paris, I have the *duchesse de* Rohan and *la petite Marguerite* residing at what is now called the *Hôtel de Sully* in the Marais neighborhood, near what was then the *Place Royale* and is now the *Place des Vosges*. Part of a development project commissioned by the late Henri IV, this was a luxurious, modern, town house (https://en.wikipedia.org/wiki/Hôtel_de_Sully), constructed between 1624 and 1630. In our history, Sully, father and grandfather of the two Marguerites, purchased it, newly finished and furnished, in 1634. The change I have made is to leave him resident in the country still as of 1635, so he has made it available to his daughter. The reason for this is that although Rohan did have a quite nice city residence nearby, on the *Place Royale* itself, which had been built between 1605 and 1612, as the first of Henry IV's urban renewal projects (https://www.pinterest.com/pin/551057704388052716/),. Rohan's townhouse contained multi-room apartments for his wife and daughter and ten or so extra bedrooms, but it simply was not quite large enough for some of the activities depicted in the book, such as a ballet rehearsal in the ballroom.

✻   ✻   ✻

There is very little available in English for the other continental historical figures who pay a significant role in *The Trouble with Huguenots*. For August von Bismarck, see pages 85-97 in Georg Schmidt, *Das*

Geschlecht von Bismarck (Berlin, Verlag von Eduard Trewendt: 1908). It was, perhaps, ironic that in this case, Moscherosch got the descent right. As no detailed genealogy of the House of Bismarck had come through the Ring of Fire with Grantville, however, no one in the new timeline would ever know it.

In brief summary, after his father's death, once he had outgrown private tutors, his oldest brother Ludolf studied at Helmstedt and so did his younger brother Georg Friedrich, so August may have spent a couple of years there also; about 1628, he went with his older brother Ludolf to the Netherlands for two years of military training; about 1631 he entered the Swedish army and remained in several different regiments until 1652. In the early to mid 1630s, he was serving in the 'Weimarians'–the troops of Bernhard of Saxe-Weimar and subsequently in Erlach's regiment in French employ.

His autobiography covering twenty-one years of service in the Thirty Years War, included by Schmidt, is direct and terse, but unfortunately rendered into nineteenth century standardized Hochdeutsch, so the reader can't get an impression of how he expressed himself. It is not introspective, but in the style of: I served under X; we marched here; we fought there; I didn't get promoted; they captured the horses and my servant so I had to go to Basel on foot; I transferred, but again without advancement; I got sick and recovered; I was wounded and recovered. It was a lot of pain, trouble, exhaustion, and bad luck as far as advancement went. I experienced a lot of strange and wonderful things; sometimes it went well and sometimes badly. Of all the men in the first company in which I served, only two of us are still alive. "In joy and happiness, in suffering and sadness, help me at all times, Christ the salvation of my life."

The most comprehensive biography of Henri de Ruvigny, written in 1892, unfortunately does not have much to say about his life prior to the accession of Louis XIV. It's available as an on-demand reprint: A. de Galtier de Laroque, *Le Marquis de Ruvigny, député général des églises réformées auprès du roi, et les protestants à la cour de Louis XIV, 1643-1685* (Plon-Nourrit: 1892). A biography of his oldest son has a short (i.e. 26

pages) biography of the father: David Carnegie A. Agnew, *Henri de Ruvigny, Earl of Galway. A Filial Memoir, with a Prefatory Life of his father, le Marquis de Ruvigny* (Edinburgh: William Paterson, 1864). For his later life, as representative of the Huguenots at the court of Louis XIV, see Solange Deyon, *Du loyalisme au refus: Les protestants français et leur député général entre la Fronde et la Révocation* (Publications de l'Université de Lille III, 1976).

One of the better discussions of Cinq-Mars is online as "Conspiration et mort de Cinq-Mars": http://www.herodote.net/12_septembre_1642-evenement-16420912.ph p.

✳ ✳ ✳

There is apparently no published biography of Katharina Juliana of Hanau-Münzenberg, by marriage countess of Solms-Laubach, nor has any of her correspondence, if it survives, been published in book form (I have not attempted to track her down through every possible article in the last two centuries of German local history periodicals). She is not even mentioned in Tryntje Helfferich, *The Iron Princess: Amalia Elisabeth and the Thirty Years War* (Cambridge, MA: Harvard University Press, 2013), a recent biography of her politically more prominent sister, Amalie Elisabeth, the landgravine-regent of Hesse-Kassel and a superb example of history written according to Leopold von Ranke's principle of *wie es eigentlich gewesen* (although her husband rates a succinct description as "brother-in-law"). If she did not, in fact, suffer from obsessive-compulsive personality disorder, I apologize to her, but the historical outcome of her disastrous second marriage in 1642 to Moritz Christian von Wied-Runkel, which produced only one daughter, born in 1645, makes it at least a plausible diagnosis.

Readers interested in how emotional conditions were perceived at a time when "psychology" meant the study of the soul and neither "sadness" nor "happiness" signified quite what those words mean to twenty-first century readers can start with a convenient textbook, Susan Broomhall, ed., *Early Modern Emotions: An Introduction* (Routledge, 2016).

There is no complete edition of Amalie Elisabeth's letters, although Edwin Bettenhäuser, ed. *Familienbriefe der Landgräfin Amalie Elisabeth von Hessen-Kassel und ihrer Kinder* (Marburg: Veröffentlichungen der Historischen Kommission für Hessen, 1994) is useful. A few of her letters appear with English translations in Nadine Akerman, ed., *The Correspondence of Elizabeth Stuart, Queen of Bohemia, Volume II 1632-1642* (Oxford University Press, 2011). For general the nature of correspondence among women in the families of the German upper nobility of the time, I have utilized Susan Broomhall and Jacqueline Van Gent, *Gender, Power and Identity in the Early Modern House of Orange-Nassau* (Routledge, 2016). Although the senior Orange-Nassau line of the family became *Stadhouder* in the Netherlands, the wider Nassau line was German. The same two authors have published three other books that are similarly useful.

✳ ✳ ✳

For the "Scotch-Irish" Hamilton family, information is available as follows:

http://www.hamiltonmontgomery1606.com/Summary.asp

James Hamilton & Hugh Montgomery: The Founding Fathers Of The Ulster-Scots

http://en.wikipedia.org/wiki/James_Hamilton,_1st_Viscount_Clan eboye;)

http://en.wikipedia.org/wiki/James_Hamilton,_

http://www.bbc.co.uk/arts/yourpaintings/paintings/james-hamilto n-161716181659-1st-earl-of-clanbrassil-and-2nd-vis

✳ ✳ ✳

For Hamilton's hapless tutor, see "The Covenanting Traills":
http://www.electricscotland.com/webclans/stoz/traills3.htm

Made in the USA
Monee, IL
02 January 2021